'Mistakes made about people's faces are due to an eclipse of the real image by some hallucination to which it gives rise.'

Charles Baudelaire, *Intimate Journals*

'The past, I saw, is a formality, merely a dimmer present, for everything we are is at every moment alive in us.'

Arthur Miller, *Timebends*

'A man who gives a good account of himself is probably lying, since any life when viewed from the inside is simply a series of defeats.'

George Orwell, *Benefit of Clergy: Some notes on Salvador Dali*

First Published in 2021 by Echo Books

Echo Books is an imprint of Superscript Publishing Pty Ltd, ABN 76 644 812 395

Registered Office: Suite 401, 140 Bourke St, Melbourne, VIC, 3000

www.echobooks.com.au

Copyright ©A J Fielding, August 1996 (unpublished)

Creator: Fielding, Anthony Author

Title: Winter of Innocence.

ISBN: ISBN: 978-0-6488546-9-2 (soft cover)

 A catalogue record for this book is available from the National Library of Australia

Book layout and design by Peter Gamble, Canberra

Set in Garamond Premier Pro Display, 12/17 and Winsome regular.

Cover image courtesy of the National Archives of Australia. NAA: A1200, L38208,– *Darlinghurst Road, Kings Cross, Sydney, at night. 1961.*

WINTER OF INNOCENCE

ANTHONY FIELDING

echo
BOOKS

About the Author

Anthony Fielding emigrated to Australia from the UK in 1951. He was educated in the UK, Australia, Canada and the United States. He taught in high schools and universities for thirty-three years. As an academic he authored and co-authored a dozen books and published over seventy research papers and reports.

In 1989 he turned to full-time fiction writing. His short fiction is published in a range of anthologies, including *Picador New Writing 4* (1997). He won the 2012 Walter Stone Award for Life Writing for his work *Not Always, Just Sometimes—Part I of the Memoirs of a Reluctant Exile with Fictions*. Two novels received awards in national literary competitions for an unpublished manuscript. *Winter of Innocence* was commended in the 1996 FAW (Vic), The Jim Hamilton Award, and *A Fool's Spark* was a Finalist in the 2007 WARM Fiction Writer of the Year Award. He is married to Margaret and has three daughters, eight grandchildren and one great grandchild. Anthony lives and writes in the Blue Mountains of NSW.

For Margaret and Gail

1

Naturally Harry O'Brien would have laughed off the suggestion he was in search of perfect love. Anyhow, he and his mates would never have used the word 'love'. Love was a serious taboo word. Okay, so it was alright to tell women you loved them. That was fine. Part of the game. Said in private of course. To soften up the opposition, so to speak. Then you had sex—a good 'root', as Harry and his mates put it in the nineteen sixties—then you fell asleep or, if you'd been extra lucky, went home to your wife.

In 1965 Harry was twenty-two, healthy apart from his left knee, which was permanently weakened from a football injury, and at the height of his physical beauty. He had spare cash in his pocket, a steady job, and a devoted wife at home. And he had his mates, one of whom was Mackenzie. Now there are mates and there are mates. So far as Harry was concerned Mackenzie belonged to the second variety. Which is to say that though few could stand the fat man, you put up with him. This didn't mean you treated him better than he deserved; it meant you more or less gave him a fair go; within limits of course; it meant that even though he was a cranky old bastard you let him hang out with the group, drink with the blokes up the club, come out on stag outings, which were always monumental piss-ups anyhow, so it didn't really matter who turned up, provided they brought grog and weren't sheilas.

Born and raised in working class Sydney, Harry loved rugby league football. The game was in his blood. He didn't play himself, not after he wrecked his knee as a sixteen-year-old front row forward. But he followed his old club, the Balmain Tigers, until he moved to Arncliffe. In time his loyalties changed. He began to support the St George Dragons. The shift was made easier when his best mate, Gordie Sloan, and a few other of the Rozelle mates joined the new club with him. St George had been unbeatable champions for year after year. It seemed almost routine that they would win the New South Wales Premiership each year. They did so eleven times in a row.

When the Dragons won their tenth consecutive Grand Final in 1965, Harry's mates organised a celebration to match the importance of the event.

'Why don't we go up the coast?' Mackenzie suggested.

'How d'you mean?' asked Harry.

'Rent a cruiser. Sail up to Broken Bay.'

'Be a treat,' said Mackenzie's young brother, Gerry.

'You reckon?' said Harry.

'Yeah, get stuck into the grog,' grinned Gerry.

Harry hesitated.

'You ain't frightened of water, are you, Harry?' said Mackenzie throwing his smirk around the table.

'What's that supposed to mean?' growled Harry.

They were drinking in the Member's Bar at St George Leagues Club a few miles south of the Sydney GPO.

'Well?' repeated Harry.

Mackenzie's smirk broadened. Already, at twenty-two, his waist slopped over his hips.

'Everyone knows you don't go swimmin' any more, mate.'

This time the word 'mate' really grated.

'That's my business.'

'You used to swim a lot, down Drummoyne, when you was a kid.'

'Yeah, mate, when I was a kid.'

'With that young sheila, right, what was her name?'

'Judy,' said Harry softly.

'Yeah, that's right,' Mackenzie blundered on, 'yeah, Judy. Nice lookin' sheila. The one what was lookin' after you and your dad, right?'

'Yeah, that's right.'

Mackenzie sniffed.

'I reckon she'd have had to have been up the duff.'

'She wasn't up the duff,' said Harry.

'Then why'd she take off, then?'

'She was abducted.'

'The cops never proved it, but,' said Gerry.

'She'd never have gone any other way,' muttered Harry who'd been touching thirteen at the time.

'I reckon she was up the duff,' persisted Mackenzie.

Harry was breathing heavily.

'She was fuckin' abducted, Mac,' he said.

'Yeah, yeah, okay,' leered Mackenzie, 'Anyhow, you'd 'a bin' too young to dip the ol' wick, then, wouldn't yer, Harry?'

Harry's lips tightened. He was working very hard to prevent his fist from smashing into Mackenzie's face.

Across the table Gordie Sloan lifted his eyes.

'Drop it, Mac,' he said.

Mackenzie threw Gordie an injured look.

'Mac!' warned Gordie.

'Christ! what's the big fuckin' deal, anyhow?' said Mackenzie, glaring towards Harry.

Harry sighed. Suddenly he realised how little Mackenzie really knew about his relationship with Judy Connell. Nobody knew. Not even Gordie knew that much. Why should they? Harry had never spoken about it. Only his dad, Flan O'Brien, had once suspected he had a thing for Judy. In any case, even at sixteen, her age when she turned up to replace Mrs Reilly, Judy seemed like a grown-up woman to boys still bug-eyed over their first successful wank. Harry glanced at Mackenzie. The smirk was almost gone. Everyone around the table was twelve schooners drunk. One or two, like Mackenzie, were on the verge of becoming maudlin. Time to call it a day. Oh, they'd all be able to walk upright out of the club. That was obligatory. The fresh air outside would pose a bit of a problem. Nev Harris, Mackenzie's offsider, might have to throw up in the carpark. That was customary. And there'd be the usual argument about who would ride with Mackenzie in his dad's clapped out Vanguard. 'Okay, Mac,' he said. 'You want to spend a weekend on the fuckin' ocean, that's what we'll fuckin' well do.' He couldn't tell them he'd sworn never to go swimming again before Judy came back. He was sure she would come back. Harry believed this with great firmness. His belief acted as a kind of mental talisman.

There were six of them: Harry, Gordie Sloan, Mackenzie and his brother Gerry, Nev Harris, and Bill Vause who worked in Gordie's father's Newtown furniture store.

They hired a motor cruiser from Rushcutters Bay. Richie, a man from the boat hire, went with them as skipper.

Naturally they spent all Friday night drinking, first at the club, later in Bill Vause's bachelor flat. None of the married men went home to their wives. Gordie phoned Jenny. Harry asked Gordie to get a message to Joanie who was staying with Jenny, explaining what they were up to. There was some complaint from Jen, none at all from Joanie who still believed Harry was a sinless hero. By eight-o-clock on Saturday morning only Gordie was capable of sensible behaviour. As usual he'd organised everything. Later, when they were in the open sea and there was a cool wind cutting across the cruiser's stern, it was Gordie who threw blankets over his snoozing mates.

It rained most of Saturday. Not that the weather mattered. The six young men—Harry and Mackenzie were the eldest at twenty-two, Gerry the youngest at nineteen—merely carried on boozing after they came round. By late Saturday afternoon, they were mostly stupefied again. By the time the cruiser arrived in Broken Bay they were all awake, drinking beer and eating warmed-up meat pies. Then, more booze, more drunken arguments, more stupefaction. Generally speaking, the damage to the boat remained small.

Harry possesses only a handful of fleeting, disconnected and mostly unpleasant images of the journey. He does not remember the details, only the general outline of his fight with Mackenzie aboard ship in the Broken Bay anchorage. He does remember the stink of vomit, and the way it steamed like fresh scrambled eggs when he threw up on Mackenzie's balding scalp in the early hours of Sunday morning. He doesn't remember falling into the bay though he remembers being dragged back on board by Gordie and Richie. He has a hazy memory of Richie later in the evening throwing buckets of sea water over Mackenzie who the boat skipper thought wasn't breathing right, and of Mackenzie's terror-stricken face when he came round and mistook his mates for a gang of cutthroats. He remembers some of the more colourful snatches of Mackenzie's response to the sudden disruption of his nightmare—'Hey, what the fuck!... Fuckin' morons! Fuckin' fuck off...!' He remembers the blue water hissing past the boat as it sailed up the coast. He remembers watching empty beer bottles being whisked astern as they hit the water. He remembers the spread of white caps on the sea and a couple of stray gulls screeching in the boat's wake. He remembers the ocean swell and the heaving of his stomach. He remembers being glad that his best mate Gordie Sloan was on the boat with him.

2

Harry remembers as he sits alone in his Bondi Junction flat. The boat trip had been twenty-one years ago. He's forty-three years old now. Funny, he muses, that a bloke'd suddenly remember taking that trip up the coast. He looks around him. Curiously he can almost believe he's back on board the motor cruiser. He imagines he can feel the swaying of the deck under his feet. With great cunning he deduces it's because he's very drunk. For a while he sits still. He's a big man, and he fills the chair with his bigness. He can feel the pressure of the chair on his hips. He uncrosses his legs. The left knee stops aching. He stares into the gloom in front of him. Then he opens another stubby.

He drinks. Soon he's engaged in drunken conversation with himself. Tonight, he is both self-critical and self-justifying. His feelings about himself fluctuate wildly. Despite bursts of aggressive self-confidence, his dominant mood is one of despair. He cannot hide this from himself. It is as though he cannot escape from the terror that has built up inside him which, despite his attempts to blot out awareness of it with alcohol, he fears will soon overwhelm him.

'I've always been willing to learn,' he says.

'Find out about myself.'

'Jesus! who's more interesting than yourself?'

His eyes gleam with passion.

'Hey, listen to me,' he says loudly to the floor. 'I need to find out who I am—what the fuck it's all about...'

'Yeah, find out what it's all about?'

And he had tried. He told himself he had tried.

'Like my gambling.'

He'd certainly learned a great deal about the art of gambling, the art of losing money.

'Okay, so I fuckin' gamble.'

He empties his current stubby, opens a fresh one.

'Yeah, so fuckin' what?'

He blinks a few times, but his vision does not improve.

'Anyhow, life's a fuckin' gamble, isn't it?'

Yet he'd had his opportunities.

'Yeah, 'course I have.'

And plenty of them.

'Yeah, plenty.'

He adopts a knowing expression.

'Mainly from women, come to think of it.'

Harry had learned a lot about himself from women.

Women?

'Yeah, women. Great teachers, women. Always wantin' to teach yer somethin', women.' He giggles. 'Like fer instance how to have a good screw.'

Forgetting again, he leans over the side, frowns, the sea's not there, instead it's the carpet on his lounge room floor; 'What the fuck...' He searches for Mackenzie's head, but like the sea, it's not there.

'Hey Mac! Tubs! Fuckin' fat arse Freddie. Hey! Shit-fer-brains, where's yer fuckin' head?'

Not here, wherever he is, in this room, by himself—is he?

Women?

'What's that about women?'

Harry's women.

Harry's life seems to be all about women.

Good old Spanish Harry.

'Who the fuck's Spanish Harry?'

'Me?'

'What, me, Spanish? With a name like O'Brien!'

'Listen, matey! There aint no fuckin' Spanish in my family. Pure convict Mick, I am, and don't you fuckin' forget it!'

He giggles again, but cleverly recognises the danger sign.

'Listen! I'm not some snot-nosed kid, can't hold his fuckin' grog!'

Doreen.

Harry thinks of Doreen.

'Nice arse.'

'Great nipples.'

'She was in love with me, alright.'

(They always fell in love with Harry.)

'Finest nipples in Sydney.'

Something of a drama queen, though, the old Doreen.

'Yeah, acted like she was on the stage all the time.'

'Yeah, and all those posh books, and posh music.'

'Great sex, though.'

Harry's sadness spreads over his face. He wishes he could see Doreen now.

'Nah, never would have worked.'

'Couldn't talk to her about anything.'

'All them big words.'

For a few moments Harry tries to remember some of the big words. He screws up his face in concentration. His big frame squirms in the chair.

'Wonder where Judy is?' he says suddenly. 'Wonder where she got to, that night?' Tears form in his eyes. Suddenly he feels a profound self-pity. 'She'd no fuckin' right leaving me like that,' he whimpers, 'no fuckin' right at all.'

Harry suspects he's maudlin drunk.

'You're fuckin' soft as shit, O'Brien,' he tells himself mimicking Mackenzie's voice. He brushes the tears from his eyes. Then he glares at the empty stubby in his hand. With a swift motion he throws it against the wall. But it merely dents the plaster, drops and bounces unbroken across the floor. Harry smiles crookedly as he watches the stubby come to rest safely among all the other empties scattered around him. He opens another and continues drinking and thinking.

About his father again. Flan O'Brien. Great name, muses Harry. Flan, he says to himself, Flan. Then giggles out loud: 'Have to be fuckin' Irish, a name like that.' He often sees the image of Flan when he's drinking. It pokes around in the sludge of his drunken mind. A popular phrase of Flan's keeps recurring. 'Show me a fuckin' expert knows fuck all!' Yeah, bloody old Flan. His father.

Forget him. Forget the bastard.

Then Doreen again. Yeah, Doreen.

'Read good authors,' said Doreen. 'Better than psychology.'

'Yeah,' mutters Harry, 'read the old Shakespeare.' He smiles. He can see the sincerity on Doreen's face, hear her posh North Shore accent; 'Try this one, Harry, darling. Please do.' Harry still has the book Doreen gave him on the day they parted. He'd never read the book, he'd flicked through it once or twice, and he still remembers the photo of the bloke on the front cover; nifty sort of young bloke, wearing two-tone shoes and a smart old-fashioned suit with heavy pinstripes—newly dry-cleaned by the look of it, probably because he was having his photo taken—and one of those old time stiff white collars with the round edges so you could see the full knot in the tie; had to be some sort of ponce, though, a grown bloke holding a bloody great big brown teddy-bear under his arm—how could a bloke learn anything useful from a book like that? He wonders who the teddy-bear man was. Maybe he'd written that book, the teddy-bear man. Harry giggles, hears his own voice say 'teddy bear man.'

Then he's thinking about Gordie Sloan. Harry loves Gordie like a brother. A great mate, Gordie. Do anything for you.

'Good old Gordie,' says Harry still thinking of the teddy bear man. 'Good old gay Gordie.'

Harry drinks deeply.

'Okay, so what. Gordie's gay.'

He'd kept it a bloody good secret, though.

'Reckon they had no option in them days.'

And then Gordie had touched him that time, on the boat going up to Broken Bay. Harry remembers that. Suddenly. After all this time.

'Jesus!' Harry is still amazed by it. 'Jesus!'

What a weird feeling it had been, his best friend wanting to stroke his bum like he was a sheila!

'Bloody gay old Gordie.'

'And him married to sexy Jenny Phillips! Still married to her.'

'You wouldn't bloody read about it.'

Harry shakes his head. Carefully, which means very slowly, he places his empty stubby on the carpet square.

'Mind you, these days they reckon all of us are gay, to a point,' he says to the carpet. 'All a matter of degree. Some blokes are real gay, others just a little bit, and most of us somewhere in between.'

Harry ponders on this for a while.

'But strokin' a mate's bum,' he says. 'I mean, for Christ's sake!'

It had been early on the Sunday morning during the trip to Broken Bay, when he and Gordie were the only ones awake. Harry remembers Gordie offering him a cigarette and then himself holding a cupped match up close to Gordie's face and seeing Gordie's lips bunched up around the cigarette. They'd smoked in silence for a while. The rain had stopped and there was a sort of fresh salty smell of sea in the air. Then he'd felt Gordie's hand....

Harry swigs beer. For a while he draws on his memory of that incident with Gordie. Strange, he thinks, how his friendship with Gordie hadn't even faltered. Very strange. Vaguely he understood he loved Gordie. 'But only like a brother!' he asserts loudly to a fresh stubby.

It had been a different matter with his relatives.

'All bloody keen to teach me what they never knew themselves,' he mutters angrily. Including his mum and dad. Harry's face twists into a cynical sneer. No interest there. Deliberate interest, anyhow. Raelene, his mother, treated him like an unwanted lodger in their Rozelle house—when she was there, that was, which wasn't very bloody often. And Flan O'Brien. The old bastard would have strangled him at birth if the bugger thought he'd half a chance of getting away with it!

Suddenly Harry remembers Mackenzie's voice.

'Listen, mate, the only good rellies are dead ones.'

Bloody Mackenzie and his amateur philosophising.

Harry's lips curl down. A heavy gloom hangs over him. His head aches and he wonders if he's about to throw up. Instead he grabs an opened brandy bottle with his free hand, drinks deeply. At first he swoons, but then his head clears and his gorge retreats down his throat.

Mackenzie had said something eloquent. What was it?

Yeah, that's it.

'Fuck relatives before they fuck you!'

Harry giggles. 'Must have been in one of his better moods, the fuckin' old Mac.'

He remembers more. Yeah, it was after Mackenzie's father had had his stroke down at the Harold Park Trots, and Mackenzie had found out his father hadn't a penny in the bank, so there was no money for the funeral—'Fuckin' lovely, eh?'—and that Mackenzie Senior had left him the bill for the eight hundred bucks he still owed on the old Standard Vanguard, 'Fuckin' useless antique anyway.' Harry remembers the pained expression on Mackenzie's face. 'Eight hundred fuckin' dollars!' Mackenzie had said, 'the mongrel left me a bill for eight hundred fuckin' dollars!' And then, at the father's funeral. What had Mackenzie's uncle said while they were viewing the body: 'Still owes me five quid, the mongrel!' 'Five quid?' Mackenzie had replied, outraged: 'Five bloody quid. Jesus! Is that all! You were fuckin' lucky, weren't yer, mate?'

Harry laughs out loud. The sound echoes round the room. The echoes fade slowly. There is little furniture to swallow sound. The walls are bare paint. The carpet piece under his feet is just enough for the single chair. Empty bottles surround his feet. He stands up, in his socks, threads his way through the empties, not once does he trip, he arrives in clear space, goes into the kitchen, opens the fridge, carries an armload of cold stubbies back to the living room. He opens a bottle, drinks. The beer is ice cold. Gas hisses through his teeth as the chill of it hits his stomach. The effect revives him, revives his bitterness.

'They're all fuckin' dead now.' (He means his 'rellies'.)

'Who the fuck d'yer think, I mean?' he says angrily in his Mackenzie-like voice.

Harry first broods on then relishes the idea that his rellies now enjoy the perdition they'd always swore others deserved. And his father, Flan O'Brien, he was dead, and definitely down there, he giggles, 'Pissin' it up in hell with his old Zetland cronies.' And for all he knew his mother was dead, and Frank Mathews, the boyfriend she'd run off with to Surfers.

'Jeez! Frank Mathews!' The Bankstown butcher who'd raced off his mother. Who cares? Not me, he thinks, whipping the top off a new stubby, gulping beer, his mother running off with that Frank Mathews a fortnight after Flan stopped breathing in St Vincent's. He'd be surprised if the red-faced butcher was still kicking around twenty years later, but his mother, maybe she was still swanning about up the Gold Coast, one thing about Raelene, she looked after herself, watched what she ate, nothing with pork fat, had a thing about pork fat, strange bloody thing for a lapsed Catholic and a Palmer Street whore picked up during the war by sailor-boy Flan looking for relief after months at sea, two quid it cost to make Harry his father'd told him as he swigs angrily, thinks, 'Two fuckin' quid!' but she'd always looked smart, a smart looking sheila, his mum, bloody astute at business, too, making her fortune then clearing off with the butcher after Flan snuffed it and she didn't need the divorce any more, which Flan wouldn't give her because the silly bugger thought staying married would keep him in good with the Almighty.

Suddenly Harry feels very weird. It's not drunkenness. He doesn't feel drunk. The beer isn't making him drunk. He can drink beer until the cows come home. And so he fears this weirdness, struggles with it. He stands and hurries to the bathroom, 'Maybe if I take a pee,' he says, attending to his swollen bladder, 'yeah, the bathroom,' but not in the home of Col Maguire's worm farm, he reminds himself, not any more ('good old Col, love the old feller'), not here, he tries a giggle, 'those bloody earthworms in the bath, what a wriggling mass of shit, in the fuckin' bath, Jeez!' He opens his zipper, 'whoops, careful Charlie', pees in the toilet bowl, no more pissing out in the yard, no more blundering into old Annie's hydrangeas, he watches his stream, a strong healthy stream, pure and clear, a hell of a fine stream for a man of his age, a good sign, a good stream, he remembers, so said that doctor with the bottle of Black Label on his desk—yeah, no kidding—and them real shiny whiskey tumblers, real crystal they were, offered Harry a drink he did, not Harry's brew, though, whiskey, offered him a brandy instead—Hell! some doctor, eh?—and a ciggie, offered him a ciggie, yeah, that bloody doctor coughing like he had the whole fuckin' Warrumbungles down his neck. 'Would you say you have a good stream?' wheezed the doctor in his Doreen-like accent while polishing crystal with a yellow cloth; 'I reckon,' said Harry, 'never had no trouble pissin', if that's what you mean.' 'Fill that,' croaked the doctor behind the smoke cloud, handing Harry a middy glass. 'Fuckin' comedian, that doctor,' he laughs, remembering the incident, he'd given the quack good measure, 'Would've preferred a schooner,' he'd said, then feels his body shaking, leans his free hand on the wall, he feels sick but sober, holds down his vomit, he's sure he's sober, if only he can hold down his vomit, but he feels very strange, afraid, Afraid he can't make himself drunk, not even with twenty-three stubbies, he's counted them, he still feels sober, not the kind of sober he feels when he's drunk, this time he's sober inside his mind, cold graveside sober, even when he rises from the chair, observes his body reeling towards the bathroom, his feet scattering empties, he can tell he is sober—Christ! he knows if he's bloody sober or not!—he returns and drinks even faster, he bloats himself, his kidneys ache, he cannot make himself drunk; he resorts to brandy, drinks in anxious gulps. He *must* get drunk.

And now Harry's mind seems full of confusion. He cannot sort his tangled thoughts. They whirl like a tornado inside his head. Christ! Still married? Is he still married? 'What the fuck's goin' on?' Is he divorced? Jesus! His wife, queer? Joanie, a fuckin' lezzo? 'Christ!' He drinks. The brandy smacks the lining of his belly. He swoons. Suddenly a switch turns off inside him. His mind is blank. Why is he sitting here, in an empty room? He swoons again, vomit rises, he gags, swallows the vomit, his guts rumble, he feels churning down there, then stillness, a weird stillness inside him, an empty stillness, he feels hollow inside, as though his organs have suddenly vanished, he feels anxious about his internal organs, his eyes flicker, 'My fuckin' insides have gone!' he whimpers, imagines he sees steaming guts, glistening on the floor among the scattered bottles, among Joanie's magazines scattered around the room... Are they Joanie's magazines? Where's Joanie? Where's Keithy? Reaches a handout for Keithy, his son. O Christ! Keithy, I'm sorry, Keithy, I didn't mean it, Keithy...

He collapses into a stupor. He awakes an hour before dawn. His heart pounds. The movement seems chaotic, out of control. He snatches the brandy bottle. It's empty yet he tries to guzzle it dry. He sits back, angry, gasping. His knee begins to throb. He drives himself to get to his feet. He limps to the kitchen. He finds some dregs of brandy. The dregs help clear his head. He manages to wash himself, splash water over his head, even to comb his hair. Then he thinks of something. Shave. He'd better have a shave. There must be a good reason why he should shave. Clumsily he scrapes off whiskers. Dress. Get dressed. In good clothes. Better wear good clothes he tells himself. 'Joanie'll be real mad if I wear me' ol' clothes,' he mutters as he looks for his best shoes in the cupboard. Five minutes later he goes out and spends the day wandering Sydney's inner eastern suburbs.

It is a different sort of day. Harry knows this. At one level. At another he does not. He hovers between the two levels of awareness. Sometimes he hears voices. Sometimes all seems well. Otherwise he remains sealed off, shrunken inside himself, so that not even the thunder in the sky can penetrate his thoughts, or the rain, or the wind, or even the darkness which comes early on this winter's day.

He moves in this darkness. He travels as fast as his injured knee will let him. His broad shoulders camouflage the fat sitting thickly around his middle. He has a full head of hair, almost untouched by grey. He might have seemed younger than his forty-three years, except that tonight he is limping more heavily than usual and his head, wet and heavy like his clothes, droops low over his chest. He has walked a dozen miles. He'd really needed to walk, to immerse himself in movement; any kind of movement; the movement of himself, of people, of traffic. And he'd needed sounds, he'd hunted for sounds, shoes on wet pavement, tyres sizzling through the flash floods eddying about the Oxford Street drains. It is movement which restores him now, movement augmented by sound, as he heads in a westerly direction, towards Darlinghurst, leaving him with a mere dullness in the head, over the eyes, the memory rather than the substance of a headache, and the hazy understanding that this is only a lull in the battle, not an armistice.

3

A storm rages over North Sydney, its edge slamming sharply against Blue's Point and the Harbour bridge. Yet just a mile and a half to the south only an occasional stray thunderclap manages to struggle across the harbour and like a spent barrage fling itself weakly against the Paddington heights. Just off Oxford Street itself, not far from Centennial Park, there is only gentle drizzle. Drizzle suits Harry's mood; the light spray cools his face, blends with movement and sound, creates a synergy of calm inside of which he convinces himself that if there really is trouble, it is *out there*, has nothing to do with him.

'It's the rain,' he tells himself.

Heavy squalls have been pestering Sydney all day.

'Yep: it's the rain,' he repeats confidently.

He shuffles on. A siren wails somewhere to his right, towards King's Cross.

Harry cocks his ear.

'An ambulance, for sure.'

He pauses, listening for the Doppler change.

'Yep; on its way to St Vincent's.'

He wonders about its cargo.

'Probably some idiot who's run up the back of a tram.'

Tram? Harry frowns.

'Nah, couldn't be a tram. Last tram went off years ago; '60 or '61, it would have been; yeah, '61.'

He pushes on. The wailing vanishes inside the larger eddy of noise enclosing the city. Suddenly he feels cold. He thrusts his hands deep in his pockets. He wonders about the victim in the ambulance: a car driver; maybe some strung out kid who'd darted off the curb? Harry shivers. Suddenly, the noise of the siren shrills out, like a child's sudden scream, then is gone. He makes an effort to humour himself.

'Reckon the driver's playing silly buggers; yeah like the cops did sometimes. Yeah, hurrying back for a hot cuppa.'

He remembers that Gerry Mackenzie was a cop.

Or was it Bill?

Bill Vause?

Nah; Bill Vause died. Poor bastard copped some sort of bug in Vietnam.

Gerry?

'Yeah, 'course it's Gerry. Fuckin' Gerry'd do that—use his siren.'

Harry smiles, realises he isn't that cold after all. Wet, but not cold. Bloody wet. And it's good to be in the carpark. He knows the carpark well. It's one of the biggest open carparks on private land left in the Eastern Suburbs. So big that when Harry used to drive, he could always find a parking space; if you got in before six-o-clock, of course, especially on Friday and Saturday nights, just before the mob arrived.

Harry frowns. Mob? What mob? Why is he having trouble answering simple bloody questions? And why is he walking tonight? Why isn't he driving? The car's fine; still registered. Not much of a car, that's for sure. Getting old. Bit of rust here and there. But they ran forever, those old HJs. Great engines. Couldn't wear them out.

He forgot about the car.

Suddenly, he says: 'Thirty-three.'

Why had he said that?

'Thirty-three.'

His house number?

'Nah; not that.'

He'd never lived at a number thirty-three. His knee? What the hell did the number thirty-three have to do with his knee? Thirty-three. It's a simple number, popped up on the screen in his head. Maybe it's his age? For a long moment Harry struggles to answer this question. Is he really thirty-three years old? Christ! he couldn't really be thirty-three. Could he?

'Nah—'course not,' he decides.

How could he be thirty-three? How could he be that old?

'Don't be bloody stupid.'

He breathes deeply. It's good to be able to breathe. Yet the image of the number thirty-three persists. Then, as if it were a coin in his fingers, he turns the image around in his mind, examines it, searches for its edges, its hardness. The image holds, then begins to dissolve, becomes a strange frightening fluid abstraction in Harry's mind, seeps away like warm grease through his fingers. And Harry feels fear. Inside him something pummels his ribs. The feeling is so alien he takes time to work out it's his own heart. Quick, quick, he urges himself, think of something else. He thinks about his left knee. He looks down at his knee, tries to concentrate on the knee joint, on whether there is pain in there. He takes a deep breath.

'Ahh, ha!'

The pummelling eases. And he is breathing easily again. Now there is just his knee to think about.

'Bloody well don't give up on me now,' he says to the knee.

He pauses, adjusts the thick elastic bandage which, normally gripping the leg four inches above and below the joint, has slipped down out of place.

He sighs, 'Christ! that's better.' Then he says: 'Why am I limping?'

He hadn't always had to limp. Had he? He was certain there'd been a time when his knee had been fine. He hadn't limped then. Or worn a support. Christ Almighty! he could walk the city all day without having to limp. Couldn't he? Of course he bloody could.

'Taylor Square,' he says suddenly, 'Taylor Square.'

An image of Taylor Square is on the screen. It is dusk. Street and traffic lights are brightening the gloom that is fast becoming darkness.

Rain. Streets wet and glistening. Slippery. And traffic. Traffic thick and impatient. Yes, Taylor Square. The big intersection. Traffic coming up from the Harbour Bridge and Woolloomooloo. Up Bourke Street. Up Oxford Street from Hyde Park and Haymarket. Traffic heading south and south-east.

4

It happened in Taylor Square, at the crossing alongside the grounds of the Darlinghurst Court House. He'd missed his step at the curb and jarred his left knee. The sharp stab of pain he remembered. He remembered he'd cursed loudly. And the two young women, girls really, he remembered them. Well-dressed they'd been, in well-fitting casual clothes. Not street girls. Harry could tell they weren't street girls. And they shouldn't have been there by themselves. Shouldn't have been here at all. Just wasn't their scene. Asking for trouble. Yeah, asking for it, two pretty young things, out of place, out of their depth, here, at the Taylor Square intersection. They're crossing with him. Staying real close. He gets a whiff of them. Nice. They think he's friendly. Then he slips. The pain strikes. He's brought up short.

'Bastard!' he yells before he can stop himself. 'Fuckin' mongrel of a thing!'

Too late Harry realises he's scared them. They squeal. They grab each other's arms.

'Run,' they shriek, 'Run!'

'Hey,' shouts Harry, 'Hey, it's okay. It's not you. It's me. My fu—my stupid knee. Hey!'

But it's no good. They don't look back. Now they're on the low side of Oxford street. They run faster. A flurry of arms and legs. Long legs. And hips. Moving hips. Youthful hips heading towards Liverpool Street and Hyde Park. He's sorry he's scared them. Real young kids. Real young. Maybe fifteen or sixteen. Not much older than Keithy. Or younger? Keithy? Keithy? How old's Keithy? Sixteen? Seventeen? Maybe eighteen? Anyhow, about Keithy's age. It's all very fuzzy. As if the sludge in his brain is back again. His eyes lock onto the two girls. The sludge thins a little. Wonder why they're out? Maybe they live around here. He stares after them, cannot help enjoying the shapes of their hurrying backsides.

Then, as he's halfway across the road, the walk-sign already blinking red, there's a second, sharper jab of pain, sharp enough to draw another, more violent curse from his lips, force him to pause a second time. He freezes, hobbled by pain, his hands clutch the knee joint, his bent figure is caught in the headlights of waiting traffic. Tears of pain squeeze from his eyes. He grits his teeth, waits for the spasm to pass. Then the lights change, and he hasn't moved, and traffic is surging forward, noisily, and horns are hooting, and his heart is jumping around in his chest, and he's yelling STOP, YOU BASTARDS; STOP!' and mercifully one of the lead cars stops, creates an instant safety zone for him, he crouches there while the angry tide of traffic swirls around him. Then someone's calling out to him, a woman, in a high-pitched voice, above the traffic:

'Hey, I say. Yoo hoo, there. Yoo hoo... Don't move. Wait 'till the lights change.'

He stands still, all his weight on the good knee, he feels no surprise that it's a woman, funny bloody accent though, heard it before (Doreen? Nah, cut it out!): the lights change, and he's surrounded by stationary traffic.

'Get in,' it's the woman, shouting. 'Get in. I'll give you a lift.'

He squints at the car's windscreen. He makes out the figure of the woman.

'Get in,' she shouts again.

He hops to the passenger door.

'Get off the road, ya mug!' shouts a voice somewhere to his left and he gestures crudely in the voice's direction, but the door is already on the latch and he's soon inside the car—a BMW, he guesses, or a prestige Japanese model, noticing its luxury fittings and hearing the music which envelops him like there's a full live orchestra somehow packed into the back seat. (It's the sort of music Doreen would have liked.) He leans forward on his seat, massaging his knee.

'Thanks for stopping,' he says.

She lowers the music.

'Are you alright?'

There's a tell-tale breathiness in her voice.

'My knee. Jarred it on the curb. Froze up on me.'

'Maybe I should take you to a hospital?'

'Nah; thanks all the same. It's just an old football injury.'

'Oh, really, my ex-husband was a rugby player.'

They're on Flinders Street, in the right-hand turning lane, moving on the green light into Dowling Street, heading south. The woman slows the car, working it through traffic into the curb side lane. Harry glances towards her, cannot make out her features in the darkness, though he can tell she's solidly built.

'Should I drop you off, somewhere?'

She tries to sound casual.

'You going south?' asks Harry.

The woman takes a deep breath. He senses the heaving of her breasts; guesses she will say yes.

'I could do. Whereabouts do you want to go?'

'Arncliffe,' says Harry, mentioning the southern suburb some six miles from central Sydney.

'Oh—Oh, I see. Well, er—yes, yes, alright.'

She lets the car idle forward so that it keeps pace with the slow traffic stream. Outside, to Harry's left, the black emptiness of Moore Park glides past. He sees his reflection in the car window, a darkened face looking at him as he looks outwards, and the other face, the profile of the woman, shimmering and indistinct. As he watches he can hear the woman's short, rapid breaths, as though she's been running hard.

'I—I was wondering if you ought to have a hot drink, you know, something to steady you down.' She pauses, sighs heavily before continuing. 'There's a coffee lounge I know, near here.' She gives out a nervous, phlegmy laugh, a heavy smoker's laugh. She leans forward, turns down the volume on the hi-fi, gives Harry a whiff of hot, smoky breath. 'It's Italian. Really nice, and, well—you know, very discreet.'

'That a fact.'

'And they serve really first-class pasta.'

Harry smiles. He's in the mood for a bit of fun. Needs a bit of fun. And he could be hungry. And the woman's a regular Eve; tempting him with food; Italian food; a long time since he's tried Italian food; real Italian food; a bloody long time; he was just a kid and seeing Doreen out at Paddington; and having trouble getting spaghetti off his plate.

'I'm not real keen on spaghetti.'

'Oh, you don't have to have spaghetti. You can have pizza if you like. They do a very nice seafood pizza.'

'Sounds okay.'

'Fine,' breathes the woman.

They're at the Cleveland Street intersection. The traffic lights have just turned red, so the woman brings the car to a halt. Light from turning vehicles floods the interior of the cabin. The woman turns her head shyly, sneaks her first full look at Harry. Their eyes meet. Harry can see the woman's face clearly. She's about forty, he thinks, with tiny, anxious eyes, and puffy cheeks, and she wears thickly layered make-up which Harry guesses is her attempt at disguise, like her hair, which she had let down so that it flows in lush tresses over her face and shoulders, in a style totally unsuited to her round fat face, making the face seem distorted, compressed. Probably a wig, he thinks, feeling sorry for this rich woman with the beady eyes...

Beady eyes... Christ Almighty!

'Rosy.'

'What...'

'Rosy: is your name Rosy?'

He's sure it's Rosy, Flan's one-time live-in girlfriend. Older and well dressed, but still Rosy.

'I'm sorry,' mutters the woman. 'That's not my name.'

'Rosy!' cries out Harry in a strange, croaking voice. 'Rosy!'

The woman gawps at him.

'Listen, I told you; my name *isn't* Rosy.'

Now it's Harry who gawps.

'Christ, I thought you were fuckin' dead!'

'O my God, my God,' whimpers the Rosy look-alike.

'Where'd you fuckin' go,' insists Harry. 'That day, in the kitchen.'

The woman cowers away from him. She makes tiny, snivelling sounds, says:

'Oh, please, please...'

The voice is different. Posh, thinks Harry, like the car, like Doreen. Why'd Rosy be speaking with a voice like Doreen's?

Suddenly the woman lunges at Harry.

'Get out, get out,' she shrieks. 'Get out of my car, get out.'

She pushes, she's strong, Harry reels away, now the woman flails at him, he wards her off, thinks she really must be Rosy, begins to panic, starts wrestling with the door. 'Okay,' he yells, 'Okay, I'm goin'. I'm fuckin' goin''

Somehow the door opens, and Harry falls out onto the footpath, and he's free, and the car, door swinging shut, screeches forward, disappears, and he's on the wet pavement, on his hands and knees, crawling around, stupidly, as though he's drunk again, and gaping at traffic zooming by. He struggles to his feet, attempts to run, instead, can manage only a kind of galloping hop because of the fiery pain in his knee. He heads back down Dowling Street, towards Taylor Square.

'Rosy.' Wild-eyed he repeats the name as he runs, 'Rosy, bloody Rosy.' He remembers the face; close-up, the cheeks, the eyes, the beady eyes, beady eyes watching him. 'What the fuck!' And that lipstick. That hadn't changed. 'Fuckin' Rosy's purply-red lipstick. Fuck! But she's dead.' He killed her! 'What!' says Harry. 'Who'd I fuckin' kill? A killer? Me? Christ, no! Not me, Harry Martin O'Brien! Why'd I kill her? I never fuckin' killed no-one in my life.'

For a moment he pauses, leans on the low wall nearby. Despite the turmoil inside his head he has the clear idea that he's killed someone. 'Who'd I kill?' he asks again. 'Who'd I Kill?' Then he can't remember killing anyone. But Rosy. Could he have killed Rosy? But she was in the car, driving a fucking BMW, no, how could he have killed Rosy if she was driving a fucking BMW?

Then who? Then who? He hears the cry inside his head. For Christ's sake—Who!

Harry's memory crashes again and he pauses on the footpath, confused, looking about him. He wonders if he's drunk or been in an accident. He examines his clothes; they're wet; only wet. And his body. It's okay. Only his knee hurts. That's normal. He leans against the low wall bordering the park, watches traffic flowing by. He tilts his head back, allows rain to cool his face. Then he sets off, heading north, shuffling on his worn-out knee. He walks for half an hour.

5

Harry's in a carpark, moving fast, urging himself forward in the short, awkward strides he favours when his knee is playing up.

'Then get the bloody thing fixed?' Gordie Sloan had scolded him often enough. But something always held Harry back. He'd lived with that knee for a long time. It wasn't always troublesome. Even when it was the pain was often sweet, something he endured with a kind of satisfied pride.

'Got the bugger playing for Balmain,' he would boast, 'back in 1960.'

He shuffles on. Ahead he can see the glittering rectangle of light at the entrance to the big building. The light beckons: it stirs Harry's instincts, encourages the big man to break into a jog—a kind of lurching, levering half gallop.

'Thirty-three,' he mutters.

Then he says: 'Hope Thirty-three is free.'

He wonders why he's said this.

'Hope Thirty-three is free.'

Suddenly he needs to know the time. He has no idea why the time is so important. He squints at his watch. It is too dark to read the dial and he holds his arm high to catch light from the entrance ahead. Still he cannot make out the time. Then a car manoeuvres behind him as it searches for a parking space. He flings up his arm higher, catches the blaze of light from the car's headlamps.

Twenty-to-eight.

He feels puzzled. Should it have been twenty-to-eight? Or sooner? Or later? Does he have to be somewhere—by a certain time? He has no answers. He blinks rapidly, splashing rainwater from his eyes. He brushes the wet sleeve of his wind jacket across his forehead.

'Hope Thirty-three is free.'

He knows he's said the words, yet the words seem out there, beyond his face, they vanish into the darkness. And he's in a carpark. Why is he in a carpark; and out in the rain, wearing wet clothes? Where the hell has he been to get such wet clothes? He looks down at himself, sees his soggy trousers, his best pair. And his shoes, his four-year-old Florsheims, worn no more than a half dozen times since new. He remembers buying them from the pretty blonde chick in the Bondi Junction shoe shop.

Bondi Junction?

And why has he put on his best clothes? Jesus! he hasn't been out to Doreen's, has he? That's all over, isn't it? He can't remember if it's all over with Doreen. Maybe it's on again. Maybe they've patched things up. He can't remember. He can't even remember where Doreen lives. Surry Hills? Newtown? Bondi Junction? Arncliffe? No, not Arncliffe. He can eliminate Arncliffe. Turramurra? Why Turramurra? North Shore? With Derek. Who's Derek?

Maybe he'd been drunk. And wandering round Sydney, trying to sober up. He shakes his head like a fighter trying to recover from a heavy blow. He cannot remember. But Joanie would give him hell alright. Why would she do that? She never gives him hell. Does she? He can't remember the last time she'd given him hell.

'Hope Thirty-three is free.' There it is again.

Thirty-three. Three and three.

'Thirty-three,' he chants, 'thirty-three, thirty-three, thirty-three.'

He rolls the sounds around in his head, enjoying their mantric effect as his body flows forward below him, painlessly, separately, impelled towards the light, as the words curl upwards like incense, into his nostrils, soothingly, enter his brain.

'Machine Thirty-three,' he says suddenly. 'Machine Thirty-three. Yeah.'

He savours the words like he might be savouring fine liquor. Yeah, Machine Thirty-three; his machine; the one he always plays; his machine. He breathes deeply. The number thirty-three has become what it signifies—a link ten-cent poker machine, a five-barrel, five pay-line pokie with a worn coin slot. He visualises the coin slot, imagines he touches it, feels its hard metal cool and smooth against his fingertips, sees its inverted crescent shape with the front lip a touch lower and the brass showing through the nickel because of the wear. He lifts his head, sees raindrops glittering against a distant light, sees them become a stream of coins, pouring from his fingers into the slot, the credit meter tripping away at eye level, hope surging that one of the glittering seeds will strike, feels the pull against his stomach as his insides tighten with anticipation, the anticipation of the veteran pokie addict who knows he has a long stake, long enough for a serious game, a professional's game, long enough maybe to entice Lady Luck out of her fortress, a game which, because of its length, will guarantee a few big drops... maybe a biggie...maybe a really big biggie...Yeah, mate; the real top biggie... You bloody beeuwdie...!

6

Harry sighs happily. He feels much better, more focussed, ready. A good long session on Thirty-three; that's what he needs; a few schooners; a couple of minutes of conversation with his mates—just to be sociable, just to make sure he kept them on side—you never knew when you might need a small loan—a sheila to chat up, maybe more than chat up if things went well, which they probably would. Ah, yes, everything's beginning to settle down. He wonders what all the fuss had been about. He shrugs off a lingering doubt about the time. That was it; yeah, course it was; he'd let the time get away on him; easy to forget about the time when you're out walking, doing all that thinking. Taylor Square was at least a couple of miles, maybe more, from Bondi Junction.

Hang on! Bondi Junction? What the hell did Bondi Junction have to do with anything? He lived at Arncliffe, didn't he? And Taylor Square— Why was he thinking about Taylor Square? Or Centennial Park for that matter? Had he been walking in Centennial Park? He'd bloody well have remembered that! Surely he would. A bloody great park like that. Vaguely he remembered being in a park. Centennial Park? Why'd he been that far from home? Then there'd been this young kid. Not in the park. But there'd definitely been some incident. With this kid. He remembered the kid.

Fifteen or sixteen, he'd have been; maybe a bit less; wearing jeans with slit-holes in the knees and half the backside missing; ragged slit-holes, with shreds of fabric dangling from them; and a red shirt, torn at one shoulder so that pink flesh showed through; shirt tail flapping round the kid's backside; and a cap, a baseball player's cap, worn back to front, Yankee-style. Yeah; Harry remembers the kid; he'd had words with him; on Oxford Street; yeah, Oxford Street, near the Sacred Heart Church; the kid was stoned; he must have been stoned, pissing on the post box like that, urine splattering the pavement, angering passers-by, making them skip smartly to one side.

That was it. Now he remembered. The little bugger had splattered him. That's why Harry had tried to cuff him over the ear. The trouble was when the kid looked at him, he'd been reminded of Keithy, his son. He was nearly Keithy's age and build, tall and developing muscle, with a man's voice just showing through. And so, with his hand high ready to strike, he'd paused, because he'd suddenly felt very weird, as though he'd suddenly been trapped inside a dream, there on Oxford Street.

'Keithy!' he'd gasped.

'Take yer fuckin' hands off me, grandad!' the kid had screamed.

'Keithy, for God's sake! it's me, son; your dad,' he'd said

But the kid had just screamed some more.

'Fuckin' lunatic!'

And Harry had cried out, 'Keithy; Keithy,' and had had this overwhelming impulse to embrace his son, to hug him and squeeze him, to feel his warm young body close. And then people were staring at them, at *him*, this older man, this pervert, openly trying it on with a kid, an under-age kid, on the street; except that the kid had pulled free, and stared wide-eyed at him, as though he, Harry O'Brien, was a fucking pervert, and not the kid's father, as though the kid was suddenly terrified by the look on Harry's face, because he'd scampered away without another word, his shirt tail flapping redly, round a corner, disappeared suddenly, as though he'd never existed, and Harry was alone but holding the image of the kid's face in his mind, seeing the face transposing into and out of Keithy's face, seeing the questioning look in those eyes, the eyes in which the question became accusation, condemnation. Then Keithy's face dissolving into emptiness, into darkness, like in the movies, into the screen, behind the screen, gone, as though nothing had happened, and the tears streaming down Harry's face, and the expressions on the faces paused to stare at him were just like his tears—without any meaning at all.

Then he'd shambled on, passing through all the faces—he remembered the faces watching him.

'What you all fuckin' starin' at?'

As though someone else had shouted.

'You think I'm fuckin' mad, or somethin'!'

The faces dissolved. He was alone on the pavement.

Yeah, just some street kid, that's who he'd been, probably just snorted something, or dropped an upper or two. Yeah, thinks Harry, it wasn't Keithy; Keithy wouldn't have been out on the street; not his Keithy; nah, not a chance. Keithy was a good boy. Jesus! he was a football champion, his son. Wasn't he?

7

Harry knows something is wrong. He's having trouble with his memory. 'Fuckin' hell!' he thinks, why'd he be having trouble with his memory? Though he assures himself he's soberer than a Salvo on Sunday, he puts it down to all the beer he'd drunk, and all the brandy on top of the beer. Yet it is as though the loss of memory is happening to another Harry O'Brien, a younger Harry O'Brien. The older of him is just an observer of this younger version. The younger version is in the limelight; the older one in the shadows, watching; the younger one cocky and self-assured, as though mocking the wisdom of the older one. For the time being the older one holds his peace. He will find out first what the younger one is up to. Maybe then he'll step in, rescue the younger one, before things get out of hand. Harry feels reassured. He shrugs his shoulders, feels his old smile forming on his face, curling his handsome lips upwards the way the girls liked. 'Turns 'em on,' he reminds himself. Turns on the sheilas; those he wants to turn on. Everything's going to be alright. He thinks about his son, Keithy, and of all Keithy's triumphs. 'Good on yer, Keithy; good on yer, mate!'

He hurries faster in the car park. Ahead a bright light shines, beckons.

And then his left shoe finds a snag. He stumbles, twists his knee joint, hisses as the pain strikes. He only just manages to stay upright. Then a second stab of pain and Harry bites his lip, tastes the salty warmth of blood but cannot stifle the cry on his lips. And then his knee collapses and he crashes cursing against the side of a panel van at the instant its passengers, a couple, are getting out.

'Jesus, matey!' The man's voice is a shrill falsetto. 'For Christ's sake!'

Harry looks up through eyes watered with pain. The couple are just a blur in the shadows. Then there's more pain and he groans and leans his big frame heavily against the side of the van.

'I think he's had an accident,' says the woman.

'What's the problem, matey?' asks the man. He stares uncertainly at Harry through rain-spattered glasses.

Harry sniffs loudly.

'I've done my bloody knee in.'

'Knees can be a real mongrel.' says the man.

'D'you need any help, love?' the woman asks.

Harry struggles to focus his eyes.

'Nah, she'll be right, thanks.'

'We could get someone from the club to help you,' says the man.

Harry forgets his pain, has sudden visions of what his mates would do with a story like that. 'Christ! no!' He pulls himself upright. 'Listen, it'll be alright. I just need a couple of minutes.' The couple hesitates. 'Honest,' says Harry. 'It'll be fine.'

'You sure, love?' says the woman.

Inside himself Harry laughs insanely as he thinks: Hell! this sheila's got a sexy voice.

'Yeah,' he answers in his best deadpan voice, 'It's just my old football injury playing up.'

'Know what you mean,' says the man reaching his hand across his body until it cups his elbow. 'Got one myself, playing on the wing at school.'

'Got mine playing for Balmain,' says Harry.

'Yeah!' says the man.

'First grade,' lies Harry.

'Jeez! first grade, eh?'

'Tacklin' Norm Provan,' lies Harry again.

'Provan! Jeez; Norm Provan? Sticks Provan?'

'Yeah. Bloody hard man to stop, the old Sticks.'

'My very word,' says the man.

Harry pulls in a deep breath, massages his knee gently.

'You sure you'll be alright, love?' says the woman.

'Yeah. No worries,' says Harry. 'Go on. No need for all of us to get wet. I'll be alright. I'll just rest here for another minute.'

It is drizzling again as the couple hurry away. Harry's pain, subdued by the scale of his fantasy, has almost gone. For those few moments, when the man with the high-pitched voice had taken it for granted Harry was telling the truth, he was the footballer he'd always wanted to be. Now he closes his eyes. He's wearing Balmain colours. He's on the Leichhardt oval, Balmain's home ground. They're playing St George. The figure of Norm Provan, the great rugby league champion, steel-eyed, raw-boned, is charging towards him. And then Harry is colliding with the giant front-row forward, the sounds of contact between muscle and sinew sweet in his ears, and great joy in his breast as the St George hero crashes into the turf.

And the woman? Ah, well; a part of him is thinking about her, creating, recreating, her image in his mind. He attributes to the woman so much of the well-being he now enjoys. She's coaxed away his pain, caused his anxiety to fade. And so he now does what he's always done. He focuses his carnal attention on the woman. It had been difficult to see her clearly in the darkness, so he has little information about her other than her voice. He conjures up the memory of the woman's voice, dwells on its sensuous quality, allows the voice to speak to him again, to arouse him again. And strains to see her as she walks away, seeing she is much younger than the husband, that she is small-made, lovely, really lovely; even in the shadows, through the drizzling rain, Harry can tell she had great legs, and a really fabulous backside. Now she's entering the club, bathed in the glitter of light at the entrance, and Harry, good old stud-bull Harry, steps forward, barely limping at all.

8

Harry and his mates joined Mid-City Leagues Club after Harry's and Mackenzie's altercation at the Dragons'. They'd been expelled from the club. Older members still nostalgically refer to the no-holds-barred fight that had started in the pokie lounge between Harry and Mackenzie over some trivial matter or other—both combatants still argue about the cause and who started the fight—and had ended up in the club foyer with the two young men being bundled off the premises by a half dozen burly male staff. Later, they did attempt to re-join the club; naturally the executive committee ridiculed the idea. Mackenzie, whose father had once played second row for the Mid-City Reserves, managed to get them membership at Mid-City by promising to keep a close eye on the two of them during a twelve months probationary period. Harry grudgingly admitted that Mackenzie's dad was a 'good bloke' and always shouted him a couple of schooners when he was in the club. As a token of respect he later on donated a hundred dollars to the cost of Mackenzie senior's funeral.

Harry reaches the steps which lead up to the big double doors at the club entrance. He's so buoyed up he scales the steps two at a time. He strides onto the wide strip of porch tiled in the black and green club colours, catches the eye of the doorman and throws him an enormous grin.

'G'day, Reg.'

'G'day, Harry.'

Reg is burdened with an eye defect which he uses for much the same purposes as Harry sometimes uses his faulty knee. Tonight he aims his greeting at the space just to the left of Harry's head.

'Cow of a night, mate.'

'A real bugger, Reg.'

'Missus bearing up, is she?'

Harry breaks his stride, pauses. He's genuinely surprised by this glut of conversation from the normally tight-lipped Reg.

'The missus, Reg?'

'I suppose you've been up to St Vincent's, Harry?'

Harry frowns. 'No,' he says. 'No reason why I'd have been up there tonight.'

A rare flicker of surprise crosses Reg's features.

'Oh, then everything's alright, then?'

'Yeah, everything's fine, Reg.'

'Glad to hear it, Harry.'

Suddenly, Harry thinks he understands. He leans closer to Reg.

'You're talking about Charlie Robson's wife, right?' He smiles. 'She's home, Reg. Came home a week ago.'

And then Reg turns his eyes on Harry, and Harry feels the skin prickling on the back of his neck, for Reg, cock-eyed old Reg, is looking at him, his eyes for once peering into Harry's eyes.

'You sure you're feeling alright, Harry?'

But Harry turns away. Suddenly he needs to escape from Reg's eyes. Right now, the doorman, with whom he hasn't exchanged more than half a dozen words during the past year, is making him feel ill again, making him remember. 'Got to go,' he mutters. He takes a deep breath, wills himself to move away, to force himself towards the people in the foyer. 'See you later, Reg.' The doorman's voice follows him. 'Take care, Harry.' But the big doors are opening, urging him inside, already helping him correct his mood. Suddenly, he's in different light, cheerful light, among cheerful people. He breathes easily again, feels his spirits revive. He nods good-humouredly to an acquaintance, smiles wickedly at a young girl who, even as she saunters by on her boyfriend's arm, he's sure has thrown him an approving glance. (Women always do.) He moves on. Now he can hear the sounds of activity inside the club, drifting out into the foyer, familiar sounds. The last draw in the monster raffle is being announced. He hears the numbers being called. 'For the last of the meat trays, members and guests,' says club official Vincenzio's voice over the PA system, 'blue ticket, number 6937. The holder of blue ticket, number 6937, has two minutes to collect their prize.' Harry smiled. To hell with Reg and his silly bloody questions. The old bugger must be getting senile. St Vincent's? Must have been thinking of Charlie Robson's wife. She'd just had that big operation. Yeah, that must be it. Harry shrugs off thoughts of Reg. The doorman's behind him now, out of sight. Sure, he tells himself, his clothes are wet and he probably looks a bit messed up. He'll soon fix all that. Not a problem. The club's got bloody great facilities. First he'll get rid of his wet jacket, then sort himself out in the men's room. He reassures himself, 'Yeah, mate. That's what I'll bloody well do.' Then he'll enjoy his first schooner, yeah, he can taste it already that big beautiful glass of ice-cold old beer, and then, yeah, then his first lash at Thirty-three.

And the woman. He hasn't forgotten the woman. He notices her immediately. She's standing in the foyer with her husband, in the queue of visitors waiting to sign in. He appraises her quickly. He'd been right. She is good looking—extra good looking; nice mouth, small but nice, with a full upper lip, one of those plump upper lips, real sexy—he can't see her teeth but he knows all about them, he's invented sure knowledge about her teeth, the front ones, anyhow—and nice eyes, widely spaced eyes—sexy eyes, eyelashes mascara'd; hair very fair and, though she wears it piled on her head, he can tell it's thick and lush and he imagines it will spill around her shoulders in silken waves just like that sheila's in the TV ad; and still well under forty, he guesses; with good skin, good healthy skin without wrinkles or sun damage, just like his wife Joanie's skin; he dismisses thoughts of Joanie—no need for Joanie to be involved anymore; bloody nice hips, too, under that straight skirt, that black skirt; he imagines the hips, slender and soft, but firm, silky to the touch, sees them unclothed, and the buttocks and thighs, sees them all, firm and rounded; and the breasts? Harry can't see any evidence of the shape and size of the breasts, the woman's loose, burgundy-coloured top, high-necked and long-sleeved, forbids this; he simply conjures up a mental picture of breasts which match the perfection of his ex-girlfriend Tanya's; 'Yeah,' he says to himself, remembering, Tanya's beautiful boobs would be more than suitable for the purpose.

He moves past the woman, concealing his limp. His head's up and his eyes are flashing. He feels his old cocksure self again. He knows the woman is appraising him, knows she likes what she sees. It feels good, Harry's comfortable sense of certainty about realities which matter, his equally comforting ignorance of those which don't. To hell with all that stuff he'd been thinking about. Yeah, to hell with it—whatever it was. Couldn't have been that important, not if he can't even remember what it was—'yeah, forget it, mate'—the real point is that he's feeling youthful tonight. Youthful and vigorous. Very vigorous. Doreen used to say he was very vigorous. It was her word, vigorous. Doreen? Just one of his old girl friends. He'd had plenty. And he'd have plenty more. Yeah, Harry feels like he used to feel, years ago. 'Hey, not that many years ago!' 'Nah, not that many years ago.' Isn't he feeling like a young colt tonight? Bloody oath he is! Women, new women, older women, experienced women old and young, some of the young ones knew what it was all about—Tanya knew, she was young, sixteen, maybe seventeen, had those fabulous tits, made a young feller start quivering all over, made his balls ache so much they nearly fell off, yeah, Tanya—and women like the one here in the club foyer, standing next to that shrivelled up bloke of a husband squinting at the signing-in book through his thick glasses; yeah, women like that one did something for him, restored his vitality, put lead in his pencil, and some bloody pencil it is too! Hell! he feels like he's in his twenties again. He *is* in his twenties. He catches the woman's eye. He knows she's having exactly the same thoughts, the same feelings. He knows.

Harry opens the big swinging doors leading into the club proper, Members' Bar to the left, Mixed Lounge to the right, Long Bar in between, pauses briefly, then swaggers inside.

9

Inside the club proper it is pleasantly noisy and teeming with Friday night conviviality. And the air is warm, reeking of familiar smells, strong but friendly smells, of food, and people, and beer—of all those certainties Harry desperately needs this night, not least of which is the solid presence of his mates, especially their conversation, however brief, for its comfort of it to him, for its shy yet brutal character, its irreverence, which he understands, has made it a part of himself, the way he talks, noncommittal yet intimate, profoundly uncomplicated yet profoundly complex, which is the natural style of these men, Men like Mick who now rushes past Harry as he heads for the men's room.

'Hey, Harry, mate, how yer goin', y' ol' bugger?' Gives out a loud guffaw, cocks a bloodshot eye at Harry, 'whoops, can't stop, mate—see ya?'

Then, to Harry's right, 'Shit, Harry! you bin' out swimmin', have yer?' someone yells.

'What else, mate?'

A voice calls from a nearby table.

'G'day, Harry.'

'G'day, Norm.'

'Fell off the Mosman ferry, did yer?'

'Mosman ferry? Get real. Jumped overboard off the *QE2* on me way back from America,' grins Harry.

Laughter as he glances at his wet clothes, feels the cloth of his coat sleeve.

'Harry, hey, Harry,' calls someone else. It's Gordie Sloan, his usually pale, sun-damaged face now flushed with beer; his features made crooked by the tilt of his nose, broken when he'd had his one fight down at Leichhardt Stadium back in the fifties. Harry thinks he looks different tonight; his hair seems thinner, and his face, on Gordie's cheek bone there's a round scar, crimson, as big as a sixpence which seems new to Harry. And Gordie's eyes. Shit! His eyes. Staring at him.

'What' yer doing here, mate?' asks Gordie, as though surprised to see Harry.

Harry looks puzzled.

'What d'yer mean?' he asks, but his words are drowned out by calling voices.

'He's back for another lash at Thirty-three.'

'Hey, Harry, mate; heard the latest? Old Don says the club's *givin'* you Thirty-three fer Christmas.'

'Hey, Charlie, he already owns the bastard,' sings out a raucous voice Harry recognises as Mackenzie's.

'Yeah, twice over,' says Harry. 'Nowadays I just rent the bastard back to the club.'

'On the lease back, plan, right, Harry,' yells a voice.

'Yeah, right,' grins Harry, 'lease back.'

'Hey, O'Brien. Is it true you've given the pokies away!'

'Not fuckin' likely,' says Harry with conviction. 'Not while I've got my feeling.'

'Just like my old lady, last night,' squeaks Nev Harris trying to impress. Nev's a thin man with anxious, flickering eyes.

'Jeez! Harris: how'd you cope with the shock?' Mackenzie scoffs.

'Didn't have to, did yer, mate? Yer weren't home to notice,' says another voice.

'Nah; he was home alright; just too fuckin' pissed to get it up, right, Nev?' jeers Mackenzie who's now a beefy, sour-faced man with a paunch so huge and quivering he has to sit back from the table.

'Hey, Tubs,' scoffs Harry, using the nickname Mackenzie secretly detests, 'you still keeping the old lady happy these days?'

Mackenzie's face reddens, he seems about to explode, instead, he makes a tremendous effort to control himself.

'Never happier.'

'That a fact?'

'Fuckin' right, Harry.'

Harry smiles slyly at Mackenzie, aware of faces watching. His eyes flicker briefly over the fat man's pregnant belly.

'What d'you do with your gut, mate? Hang it up in the bathroom?'

It's a feeble, back-handed, slinging-off, drunken-style, attempt at humour and Harry is surprised at the response so early in the evening; even Mackenzie joins in the raucous laughter which breaks out around the table.

'Hey, Harry,' yells another voice above the noise.

'G'day, Les.'

Les is a fitness freak, at forty-three he still plays touch football.

'Feel like a game next week, mate? We got a spot in the team.'

Harry does not reply immediately. He's confused, unable to pin down the context of Les' question. Is Les serious? Game? What game? Les knows he doesn't play games these days. Not football games. An image flashes in front of his eyes. It's himself, as a youngster. He's running on wet turf at Leichhardt Oval, slipping, falling, the ball spilling out of his hands, knocked forward a few yards short of the try-line. He remembers the feel of wet grass, cool on his face. And the cracking noise inside his knee as he falls.

He stares blankly at Les.

'What game's that, mate?'

The buzz of chatter around the table falters; eyes turn guiltily towards Harry.

'Harry,' says Gordie, 'Listen; sit down and have a couple of beers with us, okay?' As Gordie speaks he fires a warning look around the table. Slowly, men's eyes look away. Slowly, conversation in small groups resumes. 'Come on, mate, sit down,' says Gordie again. Harry manages a grin. 'Got to check out Thirty-three,' he says. Gordie pushes himself up from the table, takes hold of Harry's jacket sleeve. He feels the dampness of the cloth and his frown deepens; in lowered, earnest tones, he says: 'Listen, mate. You know you can count on me, if there's anything you want me to do.' Harry feels the warmth of Gordie's breath, smells beer. He looks into Gordie's eyes. The eyes seem tired, dispirited. Again, he wonders why. 'Yeah, sure, Gordie,' he says. 'Just remember, then, old mate, okay?' says Gordie. 'Remember what?' 'Just let me know if you need any help.' 'Won't need any help with the biggie, mate,' says Harry. 'Yeah, right,' mutters Gordie. Then Harry points to the raw-looking scar on Gordie's face. 'Hey, and what the hell have you been doing to yourself?' Gordie's eye widens in surprise. 'That's where they burnt off the skin cancer, of course.' 'Yeah? when was that, then?' Gordie's voice falters. 'Why...er, last week, mate.' Harry shakes his head wonderingly, then strides away, not quite succeeding in concealing his limp. Out of Harry's earshot, the men are talking about him again.

'Reckon it'd take a nuclear war to drag O'Brien off the pokies.'

'You're not wrong, there, mate.'

'Listen,' says Gordie. 'The poor bastard's in big trouble.'

'So, what's new,' they reply.

10

Harry strides past the Long Bar, so-called because it is a very long, thin structure with two serving sides separated by a central wall. On both sides the wall is covered in mirrored tiles which create the illusion that the club, already huge, occupies twice its actual space. On one side of the Long Bar, trying to pretend it is still a misogynist sort of place, is the wide, haze-filled area of the Members' Bar furnished with high standing-tables and bar stools, and, at its far end, a bank of snooker tables among which nowadays the startling vision of a female backside pointing skywards sometimes appears as its unselfconscious owner prods skilfully at a difficult cue ball. On the other side—the greatest open space in the club—is the Mixed Lounge. Above its centre rises the vault of 'Don's Dome', so-called since it is the architectural brainchild of the Club President who, on his retirement trip to the old country, was given the idea as he stood dewy-eyed in the transept of St Paul's Cathedral in London enjoying the beatific vision granted to all true anglophiles. Beneath the dome lies the dance floor, a circle of polished hardwood parquetry surrounded by tables and padded bridge chairs. Above the dance floor presides a huge, imperfectly hung, chandelier—President Don, notwithstanding his Anglophilia, had also especially been taken by Versailles Palace which he visited on a side trip during his three day stop-over in Paris.

The Cafeteria occupies an elevated semi-circular platform overlooking the dance floor. Part of this platform is partitioned off by carved oriental screens behind which resides the *Flavours of Peking* Restaurant. Here is served 'Yum Cha Daily—All you can eat for $4.00', and a more expensive evening menu which offers the permanent (and popular) special deal of a 'Chinese Banquet at $12.50 per person (minimum of three persons).'

Directly behind the dance floor, to the right and rear of the Cafeteria is the Poker Machine Lounge (Pokie Lounge)—a label unable to disguise the fact that the 'Lounge' is merely a gambling pit. The Pokie lounge is surrounded and partly obscured by a three-quarter screen wall of tinted green glass. From other parts of the Mixed Lounge, and from certain vantage points in the Members' Bar, the poker machines (pokies) thus appear as ghostly, immobile presences, rectangular icons of worship, strange futuristic obelisks in metal and glass, standing in serried ranks, with the players, ghostly acolytes, ministering greedily to their needs.

Naturally only one poker machine dominates Harry's attention. Machine Thirty-three. Though he wishes it were otherwise, he cannot physically play Thirty-three twenty-four hours a day, and so he is very aware the odds favour that someone else will be on his machine when it drops the super biggie. But this is merely the rational argument, one Harry brushes aside now as he heads for the Pokie Lounge. Where pokies are concerned, Harry has scant interest in the voice of reason. He knows better. He knows that Thirty-three and himself have a secret deal, that they are partners, committed to one another, that as much as he knows he will never betray his faith in Thirty-three, Thirty-three will never betray that faith by paying the super-biggie to anyone but himself. It is entirely possible, indeed it has happened several times in recent months, that another machine will do the dirty on him. He understands this, accepts it with resignation; but not Thirty-three; sooner or later Thirty-three will drop him the super-biggie.

He passes by other machines, one dollar machines with five coin maximum bets, machines too rich for his pocket; then the banks of twenties; he likes the twenties, likes the feel of the large twenty cent coin in his fingers, it's reassuring weight, the solid sound it makes as it drops into the slot. But all this is academic compared to his driving need to play Thirty-three—as though there might be only one machine in the club, the others mere illusions, fake copies. It is Thirty-three Harry is after, and his anxiety grows as he turns a corner and sees the row of link ten cent machines numbered Thirty-one to Forty, and darts his eye up to the blazoned display above them, sees the bright numbers glittering on the electronic screen.

He reads: '$98,693.67', has his standard vision of five sevens neatly lined up in front of his eyes. He spins on his heel, his eyes flicking anxiously down to Machine Thirty-three. He breathes a huge sigh of relief, sees that it is free.

Then—Disaster! An elderly couple materialises out of thin air. And they're much closer to Thirty-three than he is. Even if he broke into his lopsided run he knows he wouldn't beat them to the machine. Defeated, he watches the wife punch the reserve button on Thirty-three. He's never seen the couple before. 'Not even fuckin' members,' he whinges under his breath, glaring at the couple. He's sure they're a couple of pros, on the club circuit, testing hunches, searching for machines on a roll, or on the verge, close anyhow to dropping the big one. He's sure they know something, that they've been tipped off that Harry's been thumping the shit out of Thirty-three, priming her up for the big drop.

He moves very close to them, pretending he's about to play Thirty-nine which is free. The couple are unaware of him; they crouch over Thirty-three, diminutive, in dark clothes, clothes which hang shapelessly on the old man, androgynously on the old woman.

The husband—he has one of those gummy, toothless mouths—is firing coins into Thirty-three's worn slot, the slot worn down by Harry's very own fingers. A true pro worries Harry as he watches the old man's skill at feeding in coins—a hundred and fifty of them—in a stream broken only when his palm empties and he pauses to refill it from the supply in his plastic cup. And the wife, a hard case he realises with a heavy heart, face like a dried fig, her expression meaner than a combat veteran's.

With the smooth action of experience, the wife begins punching the play button; the five-play one, of course, winces Harry. Soon, the stake is down to 97 coins. Despite giving the couple a few wins Thirty-three is being frugal, much more frugal than she'd be with Harry. But the couple are undaunted. Like seasoned troops, they press on, settle into their rhythm, the old boy watching gummily, the old girl pressing, Thirty-three spinning, both players peering, waiting, she clucking, he sucking, she pressing, both now cocooned emotionally inside the hot guts of the poker machine.

Yet already they're down to *thirty-three* coins. A good omen? Harry eyeballs the machine, sends his silent message: 'Go on, Thirty-three, screw the bastards!' He watches the barrels spin, eyes the credit meter. The old sheila sucks in her lips, angrily hammers the play button. Thirty-one coins. She thumps the play button, hard enough to interest Vincenzio, the attendant, who, resetting a nearby machine, flicks a casual but watchful eye over the old couple. The barrels lock in. Harry wills them all to be different. No win. Harry licks his lips. The old girl plays on. Three jacks. Then a string of losses. Only one coin left. 'Go,' Harry urges the couple silently. 'For Christ's sake, go!' Then the old girl reaches into her bag. The old boy is standing dead still, dead eyed. The wife rummages around, frowns, digs deeper, smiles, pulls coins out of some hidden recess. 'Must be out of paper money,' hopes the voice in Harry's mind. Four silver coins. Four tens. She hands the coins to hubby; he inserts them, she punches, the barrels spin,— Click... Click... Click... Click... Click.

Harry cannot believe it.

Four bells!

Two hundred and fifty fucking coins.

Twenty-five dollars.

A major fucking drop.

On their last five play.

The old boy actually shows signs of life; twice he shifts his weight from one foot to the other. The old girl has taken a pace backwards; she holds her hands clasped against her stomach while her elbows embrace her sides. She's smiling. (Of course she's bloody well smiling!) All Harry can do is hope and pray they will go; snatch their winnings and go.

Harry holds his breath. Yes, the old boy seems to have had enough. Yes, he's buttoning his coat, maybe getting ready for the wind and rain outside. Then, yes, he's edging away from Thirty-three! And the wife presses the pay button and Thirty-three begins vomiting coins.

Harry lunges forward.

'Hey, watch it, matey,' warns the old girl in a voice like working sandpaper.

'You finished, love?' he asks.

She turns her back to him, speaks to hubby. 'What d'you reckon, love; we finished, then?'

Hubby says nothing, merely sniffs. This seems enough for the woman, for she turns to Harry, nods her head, started scooping coins from the coin tray. Harry leans forward, presses the reserve button, makes Thirty-three his own. The woman clutches her filled coin cup, gestures with her head towards Thirty-three. 'A cow of a machine. Second time we've played it tonight. Taken eighty-five dollars off us.' She turns to hubby. 'Hasn't it, matey?' Hubby clears his throat in response. The woman smiles at hubby. 'Which one do you want to play next, my love?' she asks.

11

Harry makes his way back to Gordie's table. He's feeling nicely relaxed. Everything's sweet. Thirty-three is free. And he has this really good feeling. Maybe tonight will be the night? He forms a crooked grin around his lips. Yeah, that'd be Thirty-three's style—playing with him, making out she's a big tease, and then, maybe even as he's playing his very last game for the night, dropping the biggie, yeah, just like that, the clever little bitch, without any warning, a hundred thousand dollars. He grins as he removes his jacket and fits it across the back of the empty chair alongside Gordie.

'Look after this, will you, Gordie?'

Gordie's eyes flicker. Hesitantly he says:

'Harry, you, er—you staying on, then, mate?'

'Yeah, sure, Gordie. Why not?'

'Well—' Gordie stammers. 'What about Joanie?'

Harry looks surprised

'Joanie?'

'Yeah, mate, Joanie. She okay.?'

Harry shrugs his shoulders. Why is he being questioned about Joanie?

'As far as I know, she's fine.'

Gordy's eyes narrow.

'But—you'll be with her—tonight?'

Harry frowns. With Joanie? Tonight? What the hell's Gordie on about?

'No, not that I know of, mate,' he replies casually.

And then he is aware of silence around the table. His eyes rove across men's faces which seem strangely old, in bodies which seem strangely past their prime. For an instant he comes close to understanding what he is seeing, then, sensing danger, he rejects the understanding, yet feels compelled to remain standing there, confronting the silence, willing the silence into submission, daring these weirdly middle-aged men—men fingering their schooner glasses, hardly any of them smoking notes Harry uneasily, men with downcast eyes, unable to hide their discomfort—to break their silence.

Eventually one of them looks up at Harry. He seems embarrassed. He's trying to smile, but the expression comes out too crookedly, and his lips begin to tremble, so that when he speaks it's in a halting voice, like the voice of a child shyly addressing an adult stranger.

'So, the Missus is coping alright, is she, Harry?'

'Coping?'

'You know, she managing, an' all?'

Harry's lips tighten. Jesus, what kind of a question is this? Yet he does not explore the idea further. It is the men around the table who are acting queerly, not him, not Harry O'Brien.

'Yeah, sure, she's managing okay.'

The speaker's name is Cliff. Like Harry, he's a club regular. Cliff's jaw is dropped. He's gazing blankly at Harry. 'That's real good, Harry,' he mutters, then, just as he seems about to speak again, he hesitates and lowers his eyes and sits quite still, peering into his beer glass, and Harry has a strange sensation that space is forming around him, separating him, making it seem as though he's somehow become distanced from all of this, from his mates. He straightens up, vaguely aware, yet without knowing the reason why, that it is imperative he pull himself together. He glances at his watch. His three-minute reserve is almost up. He starts to move away.

'Harry,' Gordie calls to him.

Harry pauses, looks sidelong at his friend. Gordie really looks ill, tonight, he thinks, says:

'Jeez! you look like shit, Gordie.'

'I'm fine, Harry.'

'You got the flu, or something.'

'No—No, I'm okay. I-er, I—' Gordie's voice falters. He tries to smile, leans forward, takes Harry's arm. Again the warmth in Gordie's fingers.

'Hey, Harry—'

Gordy pauses again, clears his throat. His fingers stay holding Harry's arm.

'Go and win the biggie, okay?' he says hoarsely.

'No worries, Gordie.'

And then Harry hurries away. For an instant, just as Gordie had spoken, just as Gordie's warm fingers rested on his forearm, he'd felt like a small boy accused of wrongdoing, imagined the faces of Gordie and the others around the table were those of his accusers, as though he was on trial, yet as though the scenario wasn't real, was a dream, like... yes, like earlier today, at home, when he'd nodded off, passed out... Suddenly he needs a cigarette. He feels in his pockets, wonders why he has neither cigarettes nor matches. He glances at his watch, utters a muffled curse, hurries back to Thirty-three. Everything is safe. The reserve light is still on but at that instant it goes out. He presses the button again, makes sure the 'machine reserved' sign reappears, then he's off to the Long Bar. His eyes fall on at the barmaid, Trish. Nice looking sheila. In her mid-twenties, twenty-six or seven at the outside. Be a good bet estimates Harry, storing up the idea for the future.

He scans the shelves above the barmaid's head, frowns.

'You out of cigarettes, Trish?'

The barmaid looks at him quizzically. She's a small-made woman, with a compact figure, a nice smile, and a pretty face. Yeah, a good bet, Harry thinks again.

'Don't keep them here, anymore, Harry.'

'Since when?'

Trish thinks about it.

'Oh, since about last October, I reckon.'

'Yeah?'

'Try the machine,' she says, pointing.

Harry looks in the direction of Trish's finger. Against the wall he sees the cigarette machine.

'That one?'

'Yeah, that's the one, Harry.'

'You got matches?'

'Yeah, I can do you matches.'

Harry makes his purchase.

'In the machine, you reckon?' he says quietly as Trish hands him change.

Trish frowns again.

'Yeah, that's right, Harry,' she says as she's whisked away by the demands of other customers.

Harry punches coins into the vending machine. The price of cigarettes seems to have skyrocketed. He wonders when this happened. Bloody government, he decides vaguely. He pockets the cigarettes and hurries back to Thirty-three. The reserve light is still on, but he punches at it again.

Then he takes out his cigarette pack and house keys and drops both in Thirty-three's coin tray—no harm in a bit of extra insurance. He looks around to see if any other players are eyeing his machine. None are and he feels reassured. But you had to be bloody careful. Every club has its scavengers, watching, waiting to pounce on your machine when you run out of stake. Right now, though, Harry's safe. He has his machine. And there's a hundred and thirty beautiful bucks waiting in his pocket. Confidently he moves off, heading for the men's room.

12

He's in the men's room, surrounded by familiar sights, and coarse masculine smells, and frank friendly exchanges.

'How's it goin', old son?'

'Still rainin' like shit outside.'

Hurried emptying of bladders.

'Jesus, that's a fuckin' relief!'

Long sighs. Other noises. Farting. Belching. Men spitting. The men's room. Mid-evening. Harry's sense of well-being restored; his sense of self-possession returned, reinforced by his image in the mirror.

Harry's is a striking image. He is very good looking. He has what is regarded as an athletic figure. He possesses what women these days might call a cute little arse. Though now in his mid-forties, he excites women and gay men of all ages. Gordie Sloan has spent over thirty years secretly coveting Harry's body which he now understands will remain forever out of his reach.

An expert might classify Harry's features as Welsh, but they would be wrong. His dark complexion, his black hair and raked eyebrows, his deep brown eyes, have a different ancestry. Harry is vaguely aware of this ancestry, or of several of its more popular variations, for example, that his family arrived in Australia in the 1830's in the person of Rory O'Brien; of the lies spread by Rory's enemies after his death, that, instead of the brave fighter for Ireland's freedom that he claimed to be, he was merely a petty criminal, an obscure reprobate, a liar and a cheat, whose crimes though trivial were real, someone whose wanderings, after he'd manoeuvred his pardon, left no further evidence of his fate than a dozen sad-eyed urchins prowling the gutters of Surry Hills. Another, even less supportable theory devised by the third son of the fourth urchin—a man who leaned towards romantic scholarship and who became the father of the melancholic Dennis O'Brien, Harry's grandfather—supposed the truth lay elsewhere; that Rory was the most handsome O'Brien who had ever lived; a man, who, as this legend proclaimed, was descended from Irish Kings; a man of prodigious charm and vigour who, after gaining his ticket of leave, deflowered a hundred maidens between Sydney Cove and Parramatta, and who, with an uncharacteristic lapse into decorum—some (those with royal blood obviously still passionate in their veins) thought with an eye to history—had married several of them. One of these lucky wenches was Harry's great-grandmother, the famous beauty, Meg Donovan.

What Harry could never know—though there were times in his youth when he may have dreamed these things—for there was no written record of it, nor even the faintest whisper of family gossip surviving to expose this aspect of Harry's lineage, was that his exceptional good looks originated with the seduction of a more distant ancestor, one Mary Cathleen (maybe Mary Cathleen *O'Brien*, for the name O'Brien was common enough in the Sixteenth Century and, by the end of the Nineteenth, had become the sixth commonest name in Ireland), a local beauty who, fated to inhabit the remote shores of Dingle Bay in Southern Ireland, lost her virtue—indeed, abandoned it willingly—to a handsome rogue, a Spanish gunner, washed up from a foundered galleon, the *Santa Maria de la Rosa*, blown there by the freakish storm which followed the so-called defeat of the Armada. In the end the gods proved merciful, for, before Roderigo was finally cornered by a patrol of English soldiers, questioned, tortured, then deprived of his brains, he managed to plant his seed safely in Mary Cathleen, with whom he thus originated a new line of beautiful O'Brien men and women.

Of which Harry and his father, Flan O'Brien, were notable examples (Flan's father, the short-lived Denis, the most notable of all). All were tall, handsome Iberian-Irish replicas of Rory O'Brien, profligate and shiftless like Rory, as complicated and brooding as the maternal Donovan seed, as charming and sensitive as Roderigo, as troubled as old Meg O'Brien for whose career before marriage as a Sydney Rocks prostitute, though forgiven by her God, she could never forgive herself.

His hair is slicked back over his head, wet and shining, as rich and black and Spanish as his unknown ancestor's; he has smoothed out the collar of his Bond's tee-shirt so that it lies neatly around his neck and, with all three buttons unfastened, shows off the tufts of curly black hair on his chest; his arms are bare and muscled; his belly fat is more obvious now he's removed his jacket, but the width of his shoulders and his height offer still adequate compensation; he wears single-pleated Fletcher Jones trousers in lightweight wool blend (the combination of fine cloth and Harry's figure make these fit very well even though still damp), and quality black slip-ons which already are dry enough to display some sheen on the uppers. Harry applies a final touch; he bends down and brushes the quilted toe caps with a flick of his handkerchief.

He stands, takes a final look at himself in the mirror. He's just over six feet two, stands taller than this by a good half inch because of the depth of his hair. He glances confidently at his watch and, realising he needs to be back at the machine, strides away.

13

arry has pressed Thirty-three's reserve button for the third time. As well as his keys and cigarette pack, he's placed his handkerchief in the coin tray. Even if he exceeded his three minutes of reserve time, it would take an uncommonly determined 'pokie freak' to 'steal' Thirty-three. Now, he's standing at the Long Bar waiting for service.

'Schooner, Harry?' says Trish, grabbing a glass.

'Yes, love.'

Trish lifts her eyes, looks evenly at Harry as she flicks the serving tap open and shut, open and shut, over the glass.

'How're you, tonight?'

'Real good, Trish.'

The barmaid pours Harry's schooner and stands the foaming beer on the drain shelf. Harry watches as the collar settles. He admires Trish's skill in pouring an honest glass with minimum wastage. Yes, he tells himself, she has a real sexy mouth. As she punches up the cash register, Harry leers good-naturedly and asks:

'Any chance you could be free later tonight?'

Trish takes the ten-dollar note proffered by Harry, gives him change. Against her better nature, she says:

'Why; you got something in mind?'

Harry throws her his smile.

'Always got something in mind, love.'

Trish laughs, turns to pulling beer for her next customer.

'Shame I'm getting married in a fortnight.'

'What's that got to do with anything?' replies Harry casually.

14

Harry is waiting for poker machine change. Though already long, the queue at the change booth is lengthening rapidly with the arrival of the evening crowd. In the queue people are especially tight-lipped, thus conversation, what there is of it, is stilted, delivered staccato, impatiently, especially if the person at the head of the queue is thoughtlessly wasting valuable gambling time by engaging the kiosk attendant in conversation.

'Bugger of a day,' someone mutters.

'Yeah.'

A shifting of feet. A glance towards the change booth grill. A sigh.

'Biggie's due, I'd reckon.'

'Eh?'

'The biggie—reckon the biggie's due.'

'Huh, yeah, yeah.'

'Bill, have yer seen Bill?'

'Yeah, he's playin' snooker with his new girlfriend?'

A shaking of the head in disbelief.

'Yeah?'

'Yeah; she loves it, he reckons.'

'Bloody marvellous.'

A movement forward. The sound of paper money crackling between anxious fingers.

'Bulldogs for the Grand Final?'

'Yeah, I reckon.'

Harry shuffles with the queue, squeezed in behind a fat, stocky woman, short enough so that he can easily look down on her head, see the wispiness of her hair on the crown, the bald spot where white skin stretches over the skull and where, like miniature snowflakes, whiter flecks of dandruff lie visible.

Harry is always aware of women. He is always in the business of appraising women. He holds himself back as the woman moves forward. He sees she has a wobble so grotesque that he makes no connection between it and the finely tuned turn-you-on-instantly wobble possessed by the woman in the carpark. But he does wonder vaguely if the husband of this forty-odd year-old fat sheila has the passion to have sex with those gargantuan thighs. He wonders how a man would find his way through all that flab, for Harry has never had sex with women built like this one.

'Excuse me, mate.'

He turns. It is the man from the carpark. Harry towers over him, sees the thick lenses shining like sapphire crystal in the overhead light as he stands, face upturned, gaping rapt-like at the ex-Balmain first grader.

'Yeah,' replies Harry.

For a moment the man is speechless, overcome with the realisation he's engaged in conversation with a football star. He gapes more widely, but he does find his voice.

'How's your knee, mate? Feeling any better?'

Unlike back in the men's room, Harry's knee isn't feeling all that brilliant.

'Not a problem,' answers Harry.

'They can be a real bugger,' says the man with enthusiasm. 'Injuries, I mean.' He rubs his own injured elbow, turns it towards Harry so that Harry sees it is permanently twisted, taps it proudly. 'Fell on this back in 1949. Like I told you outside. Playin' on the wing at school.'

'That a fact,' says Harry.

'A-grade, of course,' says the man, then, smiling ruefully, adds, 'Might have had a chance at grade football, myself, if I hadn't buggered up the elbow.'

'Know what you mean,' replies Harry.

'Played many games, did you, mate?' The man's voice has changed. Now he speaks in the voice of a comrade.

Harry purses his lips, pretends deep thought.

'About fifteen or sixteen, I reckon.'

'Fifteen or sixteen, eh?' The man thinks about this for a while as the queue shuffles forward. 'I suppose you got real good compo?'

'Compo?'

'Yeah, you know. Compo. I always thought they gave you a real good deal on compo if you got a bad injury in the first grade.'

Harry must think quickly. He has no idea if injured first grade players get or don't get compensation.

'That! Oh, yeah; too right; yeah; they gave me really good compo.' He dreams up a figure he guesses will sound impressive but plausible.

'Ten thousand quid.'

'Jeez! ten thousand quid.'

'Oh, and they gave me life membership in the club—the Tigers, I mean.'

The man falls silent at last, overawed by Harry's story. At length, he holds out his hand.

'Andy Simpson,' he says huskily. 'It's a real honour to meet you, mate.'

Harry shakes the man's hand.

'Jack Irvine,' he says, deadpan.

Andy's eyes pop. 'Jeez! any relation to Ken Irvine?'

'Nah,' says Harry. 'My second cousin's married to a mate of Reg Gasnier's, though.'

'Jeez!'

Harry turns away. For a few more seconds his gratification survives then fades rapidly. He realises he'd felt strangely irritated by Andy's servile behaviour. He knows what he'd said was because of Andy's wife, because he'd already committed her face, her sexy backside, to memory. So he'd had to prove what a greatly superior man he was to this near blind, little weed of a bloke. It was one of the ways anyhow he used routinely to achieve self-justification. He switches his attention to the nearby machines. All are going full bore. He squints as he tries to read their credit meters. None seems to be showing big numbers. The highest he can make out is a hundred and eighty on a twenty-cent machine. 'Nothing,' he tells himself, 'just peanuts.' They're good omens though, these signs of gambling failure around him, they improve his own chances of success, someone has to do well, there's always someone who does well, really well, maybe even half a dozen lucky players on a busy night like this.

Then he's at the change booth. He catches a whiff of pungent body odour as the fat woman waddles her thighs away from him, shudders briefly, suddenly wonders why he should do this, he's as familiar as anyone in the club with the smells given off by fat women in this hot air. Sure he is. So what if she stinks? So bloody what?

'Yes, Harry?' asks the bored looking woman behind the grill. It's Shirl speaking to him, Shirl who everyone swears was born behind that grill.

'Twenty of tens, Shirl.'

He hands over the scarlet-hued note, watches Shirl lay it neatly on a pile of similar ones in her drawer. He can see other piles, fifties, and hundreds, has a mental picture of Vincenzio counting them out into his hand...one hundred, two hundred, three hundred... yeah—three, four, five thousand—

'Back on Thirty-three, Harry?' says the expressionless voice behind the grill.

'That's right, Shirl.'

Shirl sweeps back her hair. She's a woman of fifty, with hair the length more suitable to a twenty-year-old. But that's the only allowance Shirl makes for her other, hard-baked attributes. She keeps her distance does Shirl. Her voice, her manner will tell you that, and plainly.

Harry moves away, clutching his coin cup to his chest, keeping distance between himself and Waddling Thighs who's beginning her search for an unused machine.

Shirl turns her attention to Andy Simpson.

'Yes love.'

'Twenty-five of ones,' says Andy, asking for dollar coins, then, adds, 'that bloke, the big feller you just served; you called him Harry.'

Shirl sighs wearily. 'Everyone calls him Harry, love.'

Andy nods his head sagely.

'Yeah,' he says, 'yeah.' He looks up at Shirl, gives her a broad wink. 'Must be hard, being a celebrity. Reckon I'd change my name, too, if it was me.'

15

Harry quaffs his first schooner. The cold beer sizzles against his throat: he feels the familiar, friendly chill of its arrival in his stomach. For a few moments he cradles his glass, absorbing its coolness into his fingers, then places it down on the narrow shelf alongside Thirty-three. He glances at the players to his left and right, notes they are preoccupied in losing money. He allows himself a sly smile. The more the poor mugs lose, the more he will eventually win. Silently he sends them messages of encouragement, urges them to accelerate their pace, cram that money into the mouths of the pokies, make sure the super-biggie keeps growing towards the big magic six figure value Harry knows he's soon to win. For a few more moments he pauses. He tosses up whether he'll get another schooner before starting his game, realises his urge to play is stronger than his willingness to queue for service at the bar.

He gets down to business. He feeds coins into Thirty-three, pouring a long smooth stream of them from the conveyor belt formed by his upturned and extended palm and fingers into the familiar slot.

'Now, who's the bloody pro!'

He watches the credit meter tripping away, sees it stop correctly at two hundred.

He takes a deep breath, glances at the display above his head, sees the big prize looking down at him, sees that, with each wager on the ten machines linked to it, the jackpot is getting closer to the hundred thousand dollar maximum, where it will remain until the gods elect to spin a row of five big sevens on someone's machine. No, thinks Harry, not someone's machine, this machine, *his* machine.

He raises his fingers over the play buttons, lets them hover there for a few moments, waiting for the rush to sweep over him, through him, into his fingertips. He slaps his fingers down hard on the wide five-play button. The barrels dance their tune, and Harry is off, getting two nines straight away, a five-pay on the centre line for a five coin bet; only a small win, an insignificant win, but a good omen, opening a session with a drop.

He bangs again, watches the barrels locking in. Nothing. Then, three bars; a fifteen pay. Fifteen coins in, twenty out. Already in front. The rush again. Things are looking good. He feels confident—very confident; as usual, Harry knows that tonight's the night.

For ten minutes he plays, holds his own against Thirty-three, coaxing modest favours from her, taking things slowly; she likes it this way, likes Harry to get going gradually. But already he's getting as much as he's giving. His attention is beautifully focussed on Thirty-three; through well-tutored eyes he watches the fall of shot, adjusts the pressure on the play button— Harry's strategy for avoiding 'blockers', those pokie icons which, supposedly part of a winning combination, hardly ever pay at all, are harder to line up than the jackpot icons themselves.

He plays on, working into his rhythm, disciplining himself to play at cruising speed; no need to rush Thirty-three; she won't be rushed; all in good time; it will happen all in good time. Hell, he can sustain this effort until closing time. He glances at his watch. Yeah, until closing time, five hours away, until his stake money runs out, anyhow, or until he wins the biggie, yeah, the biggie.

16

R outines

The routines of the pokie freak.

Schedules of reinforcement. Like soft porn. Same effect anyhow. Maybe stronger. Rats running mazes. Pigeons playing ping-pong.

Yeah, man, smell those juicy schedules of reinforcement. They're visceral, man. Orgasmic, I'm tellin' yah...

Yes sirree, the biggie might seem to be the goal of Harry and his comrades, but it's the thrill of hoping to win the biggie that's the real prize, and it's the most democratic prize of all because it's won by every player, every night, every day, and it resides in every player's erotic dreams about that great big poker machine in the sky, the blissful agony of losing your stake, of seeing the biggie fade from sight at last behind the fast dwindling number on the credit meter, behind the last fragment of hope, behind the self-imposed, special form of carefully fostered, designer-style masochism enjoyed by all the Harrys and all the Waddling Thighs smacking their sweaty fingers down on those shit-hot play buttons.

No one seriously hooked on the pokies will pull out, even if they win the biggie they'll be back, the biggie'll go down the slot,

Everything'll be fine, matey, you just watch me, honey-child, I'll feed yah, sweetie, see if I don't, I'll see yah alright, I will, darl, I surely will.

The last coin, the last cashed cheque, the last of the loan from your scowling buddy sitting over there, wondering if the loan will ever be repaid, all disappear inside the big magic box.

No good of complainin', not if you wanna be respected as a true blue pro—come on my ever-lovin' sweetie, give it to me, you black-eyed bitch on heat, give it to me, why don't yer!

On the other hand there's a wonderful sense of well-being and social harmony inside Mid-City Leagues, a sense that is marvellously self-sustaining, by virtue of the endless resources supplied by the perfect labour force.

The drones.

The drones—the pokie operators—work assiduously at their task, by their self-sacrifice to the greater good of the membership, generating the fabulous wealth needed by the club for its numerous enterprises. They do this work tirelessly. So completely absorbed are they by what they do, they are blind to the fact it is work. They, and herein lies the genius of the system, are convinced it is recreational. What a wonderful economic system, where the labourers need no other incentive than the work itself, where the workers expect no reward but the privilege of paying management for allowing them to work. And there are no fringe benefits demanded or offered; no paid annual leave, no superannuation, no overtime rates—And no industrial disputes, no trade union officials making nuisances of themselves on the shop floor.

Harry punches away at Thirty-three, grateful he's yoked into its built-in reinforcement schedule—the perfect anodyne for all the Harrys otherwise fouling up their lives in the dangerous and unfriendly world outside.

Likewise, Harry can drink as much booze as he likes, provided he does so discreetly, for discreet drunkenness is another part of the environment of structured harmony maintained inside the club.

And Harry, the quite well-paid assistant manager of Gordie Sloan's Petersham furniture store, despite his origins at the lower end of this shallow pecking order—Sydney has a much shallower pyramid of social classes than Melbourne, pays not much more than nominal allegiance to the more outrageous aspects of north-of-the-border wowserism, and is thus thought of by its indigenous population as the ideal egalitarian city—has adapted very well to the lifestyle.

At least he gives this impression.

Anyhow the lifestyle is irresistible. The booze is cheap, the meals lower than cost—even a one-dollar lunch every Wednesday including choice of three deserts. And free bingo four times a week, with generous prizes of meat and poultry, and sausages and eggs and bacon, and even fruit and veg trays, and yes, hams at Christmas; and lobster tails in the Restaurant which overlooks Sydney Harbour and allows you to dine in view of the Sydney Opera House which statistics suggest you as inner-city working class are unlikely ever to attend, or desire to attend—on the inside, at least.

Then there's the sauna and spa and indoor heated pool and the work-out gym—which Harry, a mere drone, has never bothered even to inspect let alone make use of—and the squash courts free to members and guests, and the golf club, the darts club, indoor bowls, ladies euchre days and evenings, and bridge club tournaments, and day trips for seniors, and the Christmas Club, and the age-pensioners' holiday scheme, and free cocktail franks and fish pieces on Friday evenings, and classes in aerobics for mums and ballet lessons for the kids, and free raffles and cups of cappuccino, and new release videos in the viewing lounge, first run movies in the club cinema—

———

And of course the game of rugby league, around which this massive organisation of socially harmonious activity enfolds itself, and which provides the membership with its regular doses of spiritual sustenance including, in addition to the standard weekly form of worship on the playing field, a plethora of myth and legend and sainthood and martyrdom—Harry is of course himself a lesser martyr having selflessly offered up his left knee joint for the greater glory of the game.

Then there is the music.

Tons of it.

17

Music.

Lots of music.

Not far away from Harry's location at machine Thirty-three, on the narrow stage above the parquetry dance floor, the *City Leagues Four*, the regular 'Downstairs Band' as it is known, is playing an old song, something in strict tempo. The tempo isn't all that strict from a purely performance point of view, or so is the unwavering judgement of Fred Donaldson who, with his youthful partner, dances a very professional looking quickstep. Fred's assessment of the band is based on his prejudiced comparison of it with the great dance bands he remembers from the days when he'd given his glittering performances on the dance floor of the old George Street Trocadero. Fred, long retired as a physical education teacher, is giving his usual celebrity performance. He loves dancing—ballroom dancing, of course, not the new-fangled rubbish the kids go in for these days (by kids he means anyone under fifty). Right now Fred is dancing with a much younger woman, one of his old students in fact, a spritely widow of fifty-nine. But now, as the tune ends, Fred senses his moment is over. The band rearranges its music, takes a collective deep breath, replaces old-style with new-style instruments. For a few moments other club sounds become apparent;

the mechanical hum of working pokies, the click of colliding snooker balls over in the Members' Bar, the buzz of sound from a thousand voices, the breathy whir of exhaust fans. Fred stands immobile, his noble head drooping as he fears the worst. The band is about to play something the old purist regards as sordidly modern.

Fred's hunch is correct, for those youthful middle-aged couples seated around the dance floor seem suddenly expectant. Even Harry in the Pokie Lounge lifts his head because of it. Something new is happening under the dome. The tempo of the music changes. The band seems suddenly inspired, as though it has been waiting for this moment, as though everything it has already played were mere preliminary. Now there's new movement, a new urgency breaking out under the dome. Couples flood onto the dance floor; shoes stomp; floorboards quiver; the big speakers boom, the air trembles in response. Above all this movement, the chandelier wobbles dangerously, causes wild shadows to flash across the mirrored cupola of Don's Dome.

It's a big Beatles number one, an early Lennon-McCartney hit, a song full of early-sixties exuberance, primitive and profound, optimistic, infectious, pre-Sergeant Pepper, pre-1964 Aussie tour. Excitement bursts from the music, cascades over the dancers, makes them bright-eyed, eager.

The woman Harry encountered in the carpark is standing. She and her husband are playing a dollar poker machine just behind the screen forming the perimeter of the Pokie Lounge. On the other side of the screen is the dance floor, but, even while standing, the woman, who is just under five feet tall, cannot see the activity on the dance floor. So she stretches upwards, on tiptoe, lifting her body so that her back is very straight, her leg muscles very taut, her arms, as though she might be an aerialist preparing to launch herself into space, held vertically down the sides of her body, palms to the rear, and her head upraised on her arching neck so that she can just see over the screen wall and gain eye contact with the taller dancers on the floor. She can see the whole of the band, the entire ensemble of players, instruments and amplifier boxes, music stands, microphones, and upright chairs in front of which the band members now stand, their music far too rich in energy, in style, in nostalgia, to be played sitting down.

The woman hears a song of her youth. It is a song she has never shared with her husband, for he is more than a dozen years older and has different allegiances. Sometimes, like tonight, she feels amazed with herself that she is still married to Andy Simpson. Songs like this one reinforce her amazement. She feels the song's driving force, its primitive rhythms. She stands poised on the balls of her feet, a diminutive Venus, no longer a forty-two-year-old check-out girl at Coles Food Store married to Andy Simpson, retired bus driver with extinguished libido.

Harry's confidence is restored. He's in the early stages of his game on Thirty-three. Most of his stake is intact. Apart from the few dollars he's spent on beer and cigarettes, he has two hundred coins registered on Thirty-three's credit meter, plus a hundred dollars and change in his pocket. No need at the moment to feel edgy about his stake. It will last into the next hour and a half at least, he estimates confidently. Yes, thinks Harry, it's all here, all the therapy he needs, as he knew it would be: beer and pokies, music and sex, and yes, his mates, and Gordie Sloan, good old Gordie; yeah, good old Gordie, salt-of-the-earth Gordie; yes, it's all here, all the ingredients are here; maybe this evening he will make it happen; he's been a good little boy for a while, hasn't he? time for a bit of fun; yeah, why not? he could do with some fun, for a change—Harry knew he needed a change, was certain he deserved a change; a big win on Thirty-three, yeah a big win; and a big wad of money in his pocket, bulging in his pocket; and a big win with that woman over there, yeah, that really great looking sheila over there, with that cute little arse poking out as she stands up straight, like a bloody nude statue almost, the way her well rounded bum shows out so well inside her tight skirt. Yeah, yeah; why not?

He punches Thirty-three, lets the machine grind away as he eyeballs the woman.

And as she watches the musicians the woman is indeed thinking about Harry. Harry has been under her discreet surveillance since he wandered past her in the club foyer a half an hour ago. Harry is nine or ten years younger than Andy she's estimated, an age gap which, as she ponders it, makes her heartbeat faster, makes her body strain harder as she stretches upwards, gaining an extra fraction of height.

She fixes her eyes on the musicians, looking over the heads of the bunch of middle-aged rockers gyrating fleshily below them on the dance floor. Two of them are shiny bald; the other two with long 'Sixties hair, now wispy and thin and tied into horse tails. All of them notice the woman, see her shining eyes appearing above the screen which, like grotesque attire, hides, indeed distorts, the shape of her body behind the green frosted glass, yet encourages the same powerful interest, making all four players grin at her as they sway and play, and making the lead guitarist, the club Lothario, wink broadly at the woman as though, after her wait of twenty-odd years, he is Lennon inviting her to be his chosen groupie, and the woman is careless enough to acknowledge his wink, allowing herself to imagine it is handsome Harry who is winking at her, and the lead guitarist is inspired it seems, and he hears the voice in his own music, captures it, draws it magically out of his Rickenbacker, is suddenly inside the music, *is* the music, and he and his fellow musicians and the dancers and the woman, and Harry watching from Thirty-three, are united in their musical synergy, and suddenly, it is June, 1964, and the Fab Four are in Australia, and the words, those silly, stupid, terrific words, thinks the woman, the words must have been written just for me, why not? just for me, for I am important in my needs, I need these words, they help me through my life, even if they are silly, stupid words... *'So how could I dance with another... oh when I saw her standing there...'*

For a while.

And then, as if for comic contrast, Andy Simpson—the bus-driver husband—needs to be in on the act. Now he's at Harry's elbow, offering

Harry a fresh schooner, even at the instant Harry imagines he's enfolding the woman's unclothed body with his own.

'Here you are, Jack.'

'Eh? What?'

(Who the hell's Jack? wonders Harry.)

Harry turns, looks down at Andy, even blushes slightly, as though, for one of the few times in his life, he's been caught, vicariously as it were, red-handed.

'Eh?'

'Here, mate. I've got you a beer.'

He proffers the schooner, filled correctly with the dark coloured 'old' beer he's noticed Harry is drinking.

'Oh, right, thanks.'

Andy raises his glass, squints like an excited house pet at Harry through his thick lenses.

'For old times' sake,' he declares.

'Yeah; yeah; for old times' sake.'

Harry drinks deeply. From his height he can see Andy's wife. She turns her head, sees Harry and, even as her husband, oblivious of the infidelity occurring under his eyes, happily quaffs his beer in the company of the Balmain champion, catches Harry's eye and sees the big man with the slicked back hair, and turns away abruptly, for her cheeks are already burning and her heart is thudding as though she already feels Harry's hands straying over her body.

The music soars and Andy is shouting something at Harry.

'Bloody hard...' he begins.

'Eh?'

'Bloody hard,' yells Andy. 'Bloody hard to have a decent conversation with that racket going on.'

Harry nods. 'Yeah, yeah,' he says.

'Better get back to the old woman,' Andy calls out. 'See you later, mate.' He winks at Harry, taps his twisted elbow, and trots back to the woman who is now seated in front of the poker machine, her small-made body small again, small and secure, and basks in the joy of his acquaintanceship with Jack Irvine, ex-Tigers forward—Jeez! now he's a drinking mate of the big feller; and he's got a couple of hundred up on his machine (dollars, that is), and he's glowing nicely from his beer—good beer at this club, thinks Andy approvingly, and makes a decision to return here more often, even though he and the woman live in Ashfield and thus naturally barrack for the Roosters. Yes, life is sweet for Andy Simpson, now he's settled his mortgage and taken early retirement and can afford a hundred and fifty a week on the pokies if he wants to, maybe two hundred now his wife's back at work after being laid off for six months.

Harry watches Andy going back to the woman. He shakes his head slowly, wondering, as he has done so often in the past, what such a woman could possibly see in such a man as Andy Simpson. And his sense of disquiet has returned. His sense of harmony has been disturbed; his rhythm lost. As though the harmless little man with the bald head and thick-lensed glasses has some kind of power, maybe it's just the power of simply bloody well being the woman's husband, broods Harry, suddenly feeling jealousy as well as envy, as though he, Harry, had rights over the woman, and not that ridiculous little husband with those gaping big eyes.

Harry *is* troubled again. Like he was troubled back there—He can't remember exactly where it was that he felt troubled. When he was walking along Oxford Street? Yeah: maybe. He lowers his eyes, rests his fingers near but not on Thirty-three's play button. A memory insists on returning. It worms its way into his mind. It is a name; the name of a place, or of a street, perhaps? No, a road, a major thoroughfare—Parramatta Road? Harry's frown deepens. He thinks about this name. At first he confuses the road with the place, the place with the football team, the football team with something he remembers from his school days, something about Parramatta, something about his Great-grandfather O'Brien maybe? Something he'd been taught in Primary School, about convicts? No; none of these. His attention returns sluggishly to the idea of a road in Sydney, a long, traffic-swirling road, a corridor of noise and movement, heading east and west... Parramatta Road... Suddenly he starts, grips Thirty-three's cold metal edges. A door slams in his head. He feels it as a real event, a palpable, door-slamming bang inside his skull. He clings to Thirty-three, breathing heavily. His hand jerks downwards and triggers the play button. Four bells drop into line. Thirty-three sings her mechanical tune. She's dropped him a two hundred and fifty pay.

'Nice when you get 'em,' calls out a young bloke playing Thirty-two alongside Harry.

Harry manages a weak smile. 'You got to have the knack,' he says.

'Yeah, or plenty of arse,' grins the young man, at that instant pulling in four scatters for a hundred pay. 'See what I mean?'

'Yeah,' answers Harry, back in his deadpan mode, himself pulling a fifty pay which makes his credit meter whip along nicely over the four hundred mark. 'Like that, you mean?'

And he's thinking about the woman again. Yet he's not thinking about her. He's thinking about Joanie, his wife. Of course, it's Joanie he's reminded of by the woman. At a distance, the woman could easily pass for Joanie, has passed for her, has done sterling service in passing for her, in restraining his anxiety, his fear that there's something very important that he should be remembering, except that he knows that it mustn't be remembered, not yet, not while he's in this strange mood, not while he's playing Thirty-three, on the way to winning a hundred thousand, on the way to that holiday at Surfers he's promised Joanie when... when... He thinks about Joanie. He smiles, plays Thirty-three, has sweet thoughts about his wife. About his wife of more than twenty years ago, a Joanie created to be his perfect partner, so he believed then, believes at this moment. Yes, it's Joanie's young face that Harry sees, the face of his bride of three months, a face superimposing like a slow dissolve on the image of the woman's face; and the woman's figure, now Joanie's figure, with its gentle wobble, the gentle wobble as she works in the kitchen standing side on to him as he sits at the table half-reading the evening paper.

18

It's all inside his head. Clear as day. Happening now. As though real. More real than real, as Joanie taps her foot delicately to rock and roll music playing on the radio. She is very tiny, and shy yet not shy. She is so desperately in love with Harry, she is, in these early days of her marriage, sometimes not shy.

'Hey, guess what! Ringo Starr married that Liverpool hairdresser,' says Harry.

'Yes, love, I heard it on the radio.'

'Wonder if it'll last?'

'Oh, I hope so, Harry. Ringo's such a homely sort of bloke. He needs someone like her, don't you think?'

'A hairdresser?'

'Well, yes, Harry.'

'And him a rock and roll star?'

The tapping of Joanie's foot ensures that the gentle wobble flows into her hips making them sway but only perceptibly so. She is amazed with herself for doing this. She can hardly believe she is doing it.

'Yes, but he's really a very quiet type.'

'A quiet type! Joanie he's a drummer in a rock and roll band.'

She pauses, turns to Harry; there's that fluttering inside her chest again, making her feel faint, yet aroused.

'Oh, Harry, you know what I mean. He's from working class Liverpool. A nice home-town girl's just the sort he'd go for.'

Then she's ironing and wobbling again.

'Hey Joanie,' says Harry.

Oh, thinks Joanie for the thousandth time, Harry's so strong and young and beautiful. She congratulates herself for being confident enough to think that a man could be beautiful. And he's here, she tells herself, yes, here, with her, alone, in their kitchen. She can't believe it. But it's true. It's true. She turns again. The flutter continues. It feels dangerous, threatening, yet the heart seems so strong, is strong, like her body, like her desire. She smiles at Harry.

'Yes, love,' she says.

Harry's eyes are focussed on her teeth. Joanie feels so excited about the way Harry admires her teeth. She has such interesting teeth, he's told her. And teeth are such an intimate part of the body. They're always there, in front of you, white and flashing, always there, in your awareness.

'I've got three work shirts in the wardrobe, already,' he says.

Joanie's smile widens.

'Only one, Harry.'

'Nah; I reckon there'd be three at least.'

Joanie smiles again, shakes her head, runs her iron along the shirt sleeve. Now she feels power. It is a wonderful feeling. The flutter has gone. The sensation seems lower, in her belly. Lower than that. She has to catch her breath. She'd never really understood how sexy she could feel. Not before she met Harry, that is.

'There's just the one, love,' she says again, playing with him and enjoying it, sensing the trace of anxiety in his voice, the kind of anxiety she now knows young men cannot hide when they're aroused.

'You sure? You checked?'

'Yes, love.'

Harry turns his attention to the newspaper, pretends he's reading. Joanie smiles again, to herself. Harry sighs deeply, looks up, scans the ironing basket which seems full of clothes. He takes a deep breath.

'Joanie,' he says, 'Jeez, love! you're not bloody doing all the ironing in that basket, are you?'

Joanie pauses again. Outside, the daylight was almost gone. On the veranda at the front of the house she knew the old man would be dozing in his armchair.

'Oh, I reckon I can leave the rest until tomorrow,' she says.

19

For a full two minutes, Harry remembers. The memory is isolated, a separate thing, not part of other memories, disconnected. He is there, fumbling first with Joanie's, then with his own clothing, cannot wait until he is fully undressed, must take Joanie's body, as if terrified otherwise that sudden death will intervene, a young man so frantically sprouted near his woman, near her sweet cunt, her smells, her breath, the sweetness of her sweetness in his mouth, in his ears, in his nose, in his skin, being enveloped by her, absorbing himself into her, becoming her, trying desperately to become her, to become her substance, somehow.

Somehow.

As he pummels the play button on Thirty-three, Harry remembers. Until his memory fades and he relaxes, as though it had been real and he is now subsided alongside Joanie, or she is still astride him as he feels the shrinking of him inside her and knows with that deep sadness of all men following ejaculation that it is over until the next time for which he is now condemned to wait however long that eternity chooses to last.

Or is that truly what he remembers?

Calm again, he drains Andy's schooner, his third for the night. Three schooners give him a gentle flush, deepen the already dark oaky colour of his skin. He decides to play Thirty-three for a while longer before going for his fourth schooner. No need to make a welter of it tonight, he tells himself. He isn't really in the mood for a heavy night on the grog. Maybe six or seven schooners, that sort of thing, enough to relax a bloke nicely, without making you stupid.

Yet he now knows he's making a series of what Doreen would have called rationalisations. She'd studied psychology and was full of big words.

'Harry, there's nothing wrong with being homosexual,' she'd once scolded him after he'd admitted he thought men who 'did it' to other men were dirty mongrels. 'Maybe deep down we're all bi-sexual creatures, you know, like there's always a duality, never a singularity in nature.'

Yeah, love,' he'd replied, 'Yeah, that'd be right.'

Privately he'd tell himself Doreen had been reading her funny books again or listening to that Derek feller who wrote novels he couldn't get published. Anyhow, suddenly sick of what he did not understand, he'd grabbed hold of Doreen, who was small and tiny like Joanie, and lifted her off her feet as though she'd weighed nothing and had sex with her standing upright.

That was before he met Joanie, wasn't it?

He can't remember. Joanie before Doreen? Doreen before Joanie?

(There is something very primitive about fucking upright.)

Yes, it was Doreen, against the wall in the Paddington terrace. He'd held her tightly, she'd gasped but not tried to push him off her, even though she'd had trouble drawing breath, he remembered the gasps, he can hear her gasps now, Doreen's gasps, like little screams, her voice overlaying the gasp as air rushes from her mouth all over him, her voice a feminine whimper increasing his ardour, making him fuck harder than ever, remembers Harry.

Afterwards, on the bed upstairs, she'd fallen asleep in his arms, left him free with his dreams.

Harry sighs, remembering Doreen, how she turned him on. He returns to playing Thirty-three. Then, becoming aware that his knee feels tender, he pauses and shifts his position looking around for an unattended stool. He finds one which he then half-straddles, using the stool as a brace to take most of the weight off his left leg and some off his right one. It's a typical pose; Harry can be recognised by it—after the third schooner, that is, which, on the average, happens to be the time his knee joint begins to make its presence felt.

He gives his full attention back to Thirty-three. Slowly he strokes her vertical edges with his fingertips, allows his fingers to travel over the play buttons, touching but not yet pressing. Suddenly he jabs his finger down hard on the five play. Thirty-three spins her barrels. But pays him nothing. He jabs again. Nothing. He presses more gently. Still nothing. He pauses, then nudges the five-play button with the edge of his thumb. Nothing. He uses his left thumb. Nothing. He bangs his fist down hard. Nothing.

'Come on, come on.'

Three bells. A pay at last. Twenty-five. Harry breathes deeply, imagining as always that he's broken the drought. He punches again, scores three tens. Then Thirty-three pays nothing for nine straight games. He pauses, curses under his breath as he scans the credit meter. Eighty-eight coins remain. He's losing, but still playing on the first stake, still surviving on his first twenty bucks. Okay, above average, he assures himself. Better than most of the players around him are doing. Better than Waddling Thighs over there, sweaty under the armpits, pumping coins into a twenty-cent machine, a cigarette dangling from her lips, its smoke curling up over her face, making her squint heavily. He shudders, turns his eyes back to Thirty-three, presses gently.

A quick intake of breath. One, two... Christ! only two sevens. But enough to make something surge in Harry's guts, enough to tighten his stomach, make him feel the hardness of muscle under his belly fat.

Two sevens. On the first two reels. Only a ten pay. But they're around, those sevens. Look, there's another one on the top row; three in the window; and, yeah, see it, a fourth not quite out of sight, nearly in the window.

He plays on, thinking about the two sevens, confident it's only a matter of time now. He screws up his face in concentration, focusses all his energy on Thirty-three. He relaxes, then screws up his face again. He can feel the flesh gathered around his eyes, and his cheeks, bunched up and constricted. And it is as though Harry had done these very same things before, but that the doing of it this time has been a very significant event, so significant that the act of doing it now triggers more distant memory, the memory of himself as a little boy of seven, screwing up his face as he concentrates on the task of turning the big latch-key which pokes out of the lock on the back door of the house in Rozelle. He remembers he'd had sweaty palms; plenty of hot sweat. And that the key was difficult to turn. It was a key he'd tried to turn many times and had always failed. This time, though, nothing was going to stop him. His memory sharpens. He can see everything in the kitchen as though he's there now. Yeah, now he remembers why he'd been screwing up his face; because it was imperative that he turn that key; he'd had to conjure up that extra ounce of strength in those small fingers grasping the big key. And it had helped, the boy Harry's screwing up of his face, because the big key had turned, and he was out, out of the house, and in the back yard, the tiny paved back yard, and he could see flecks of green weed poking up in the cracks between the grey paving stones as he raced to the back gate. Then he was outside, in the lane—not the lane behind Marsden Street; there was no lane behind Marsden Street; Harbour Street, yeah, Harbour Street it was, down Rozelle, not Arncliffe, no, Rozelle, where he lived when he was a kid, yeah, the lane behind Harbour Street, behind his backyard, yeah, and he was racing away from the house, down-hill, towards the end of the block (no problem with his knee in those days), then up-hill, towards Darling Street and traffic and people.

He was out. He was this kid on Darling Street; this kid running for all he was worth towards Leichhardt. He remembers it now, the sense of freedom, he could feel the same sense now, the relief of it, in his chest, the lightness in his chest.

Jeez! there must have been a bloody good reason why he'd had to get out of the house, turn that big key? Harry hits Thirty-three's play button, swigs beer greedily. Yeah, there must have been a bloody fantastic reason for that. Thirty-three gives him a ten pay. He pokes around in his memory, ignoring the danger. His memory of the big latch key is very clear. The key is large and old-fashioned, made of wrought iron with a big ring on its end, and with the shiny, rust-coloured patina formed by thousands of fingerings down through the years.

Thirty-three distracts him. She hits him with a big hundred. Four scatters. He breathes deeply, watches the credit meter stop at 175, glances at his watch, twenty-five past eight, feels that same uneasiness about the time that he'd felt in the carpark, as though time has some special meaning tonight. Harry thinks about this. Nah, he tells himself shaking his head. Nah, it's just bloody well twenty-five past eight. That's all.

Then a fifty pay. 220 on the clock. Then a twenty-five. Three bells. The good old three bells. Got you out of trouble, the old three bells. 240. A ten pay. 245. The key again. Harry sees the key again. He sees the fingers of this kid, the kid's thumb and forefinger gripping the head of the key, straining, face all screwed up. The knuckles. Harry sees the kid's knuckles, sees them tight, sees them whitening. Then he can feel the kid's heart thumping, feel the kid's fear, feel the back of the kid's neck, weirdly, as though it's his own neck, feel the fear on the skin on the back of the kid's neck, yes, his neck, yes, his heart that was thumping, in his mind, on that screen, in his mind, something on the kitchen floor, lying on the kitchen floor? He's distracted again, this time by a commotion on the dance floor. Suddenly the image of the boy disappears. Something else is there, superimposing, as the dancers clap and cheer the band, urge them on, howl for more of the Beatles. 'Beatles, Beatles,' they chant, clapping hands, stomping feet. And the lead singer is grinning from ear to ear. He feels like he might be McCartney himself, on stage, before a hundred thousand screamers, yeah, yeah man. He turns his back to the audience, then spins round, flourishes his Rickenbacker extravagantly, sweeps the band into the same Beatles hit they'd played before. Harry loves that song. It does something to him. Lifts his spirits. He slams the play button. Christ! two sevens again. Surely to God he'll pull the biggie tonight, the super biggie. God! that Beatles song had been a big hit, hadn't it, when they'd moved into Marsden Street, 77 Marsden Street, Arncliffe? 77—must be an omen. Yeah, in 1964, a month after he and Joanie had been married. He remembers and feels a surge of energy, a sense of foreknowledge. This was it. The super biggie was on. He knew it. Just stay calm, mate. Stay with it. For God's sake don't run out of bloody money. Yeah, that Beatles song; and the number 77. Yeah, they'd been listening to the Beatles song on the car radio the day they'd arrived to view the half house that was up for rental on Marsden Street, Arncliffe.

20

They chose the half-house at Arncliffe because at the time there wasn't much else to choose from except for a few run down flats all within ear-splitting proximity of the electric train line, and because the southern suburb seemed far enough away from Lilyfield where Joanie and later, Harry, presently lived with Joanie's mother, Mrs Una Thomas.

Arncliffe straddled the Prince's Highway several miles from the Sydney GPO. Marsden street lay east of the highway. The house, standing on the high side of the street, with its galvanised iron roof, was made prominent by being surrounded by acres of roofs tiled in the Marseilles Red common to Sydney's inner ring of suburbs. From number 77's front veranda green glimpses of Barton Park poked through gaps between houses; now and then, filling those gaps, the disembodied tail of a jet liner, taxiing at Mascot Airport, would glide into view like a giant shark fin passing in calm water; most easterly of all, an isolated sliver of water, pinched between land and sky, glittered in the morning sun.

There was nothing glittering about the house. Once proudly able to hold its head high among its fibro-cement and brick veneer neighbours, it had become, when Harry and Joanie first set eyes on it, the weariest and most forlorn looking house on the street, a nineteen twenties weatherboard with drooping eaves and rotting window frames and paper-thin gutters held together by years of undisturbed leaf litter. And the paint, likewise weary from too much age, was grown mottled, its hue indistinct, and pockmarked as though disease had once inhabited the underlying timbers. A tin roof added its pallid voice to the murmurings of these dying colours, since it too had once been painted but had long since shed the last dried flakes of colour so that, undressed and uncaring, it exposed a patchwork of rust and weathered zinc to the outside world.

Yet something vaguely welcoming about the house transcended its run-down appearance. As if a kind of warmth, though sealed off inside, and thus unable to reach out and compensate for the physical dilapidation of the house, yet had managed to signal the outside world that useful life still survived behind those drawn and dingy curtains.

Even so, as Harry pulled the car up in front of the house they almost drove off straight away.

'It is a bit of a dump, love,' frowned Joanie.

'Yeah,' answered Harry, 'par for the course I reckon.'

They were already disillusioned with their morning's work.

'Probably been let already, anyway,' muttered Harry, leaning forward to re-start the engine. 'I suppose we could go back and have another look at that Kogarah flat, the one near the station,' Joanie said.

Harry sighed.

'The train noise'd raise the dead, I reckon.'

Joanie's frown deepened. After three weeks of marriage she was desperate for a place of her own. Mrs Thomas' behaviour had worsened immediately Harry had moved into the Lilyfield terrace; first she assumed total silence; after a few days she took to sitting in her bedroom, the door bolted, refusing to emerge while Joanie and Harry remained out of their bedroom. After they'd gone to bed, she would tip-toe to the bathroom or kitchen, and Harry and Joanie would hear creaking sounds as Mrs Thomas moved around the house performing whatever secret rituals her disturbed mind required. Joanie knew from past experience that her mother could sustain this behaviour indefinitely. As a tiny child she'd learned that this was her mother's way of inflicting punishment on both of them. Now, she was inflicting it on Harry as well.

Harry examined Joanie's face. She looked so worried, he thought, feeling suddenly angry at Mrs Thomas, silently cursing her for being so strange, so bloody weird. Brightly he said:

'Shall we have a look, then?'

Joanie was scanning the house, noting its run-down appearance, imagining what the inside was probably like.

'The place looks like it needs pulling down, doesn't it? But we haven't got a lot of options, have we, Harry?'

'Not a lot, love.'

Joanie poked her head out of the window, then put her hand on Harry's arm.

'Harry, look, there's someone there, on the veranda.'

Harry leaned his big frame over Joanie and looked up towards the house. He saw an old man shielding his eyes against the late morning sun as he squinted down at the car.

'You come to see the flat?' the old man shouted. The voice was surprisingly firm and clear, in curious contrast to the frail appearance of its owner.

'Yeah, that's right,' Harry shouted back.

They got out of the car. Harry called out: 'We're the O'Briens. My wife wrote to you last week, after we saw the ad in the paper.'

Slowly they walked along the short path towards the set of wooden steps leading up to the front veranda. The old man pulled out a ragged piece of paper from his trouser pocket. He stared at it, holding it at arm's length.

'Harry and Joanie O'Brien?'

'That's right,' answered Harry.

'I've bin' expectin' yer.'

Harry and Joanie were at the bottom of the steps. The old man peered at them. 'Any relation to Lofty O'Brien,' he called out.

'Lofty O'Brien?'

'Yep, that's him.'

The old man's voice might have moved up half a key.

Harry shook his head.

'Not that I know of.'

The voice dropped back again.

'Used to live on Windmill Street, down the Rocks.'

'My family come from Rozelle,' said Harry. 'Before that, Surry Hills.'

There was a moment of silence. While Harry and Joanie waited at the bottom of the steps, the old man studied the letter. At length he lifted his eyes. 'How about a Lofty Smith,' he asked. 'You wouldn't be related to a Lofty Smith, would yer?'

Harry exchanged a grin with Joanie.

'Lofty Smith?' he yelled back.

'Yep; Lofty Smith; a really big feller, bigger'n you.'

Harry shook his head. 'No mate,' he said. 'There's never been any Smiths in my family.'

The old man stared at Harry for a long moment. 'It don't matter,' he said in a voice which had lost much of its exuberance, 'anyhows, come on in,.'

The house was a modest three bedroomed place. Inside the rooms strong, organic smells and piles of litter gave ample evidence of too many years of unsupervised bachelordom.

'Place could do with a touch of the old broom,' admitted the old man as they entered the front door, then led them down the centre hall until they stood in the kitchen. 'This is the kitchen,' he announced proudly as he leaned over the marble-chip sink and, without success, attempted to turn off its single, dripping cold-water tap. Near the sink stood an old electric stove on which rested a couple of battered saucepans. 'Don't do much cookin' meself, these days,' explained the old man. Then, looking down at Joanie, he asked shrewdly. 'You like cookin', do you, love?'

Joanie gave the old man a shy smile. 'I can manage,' she muttered.

Harry said: 'She's being modest. Joanie'd have to be the best cook in Sydney.'

The old man grinned happily. 'That a fact,' he said, then added; 'kitchen needs a bit of a clean-up, I suppose.' Joanie caught Harry's eye. 'Oh, it's not that bad, really,' she said. Already Joanie was seeing possibilities in the house, hard work, yes, but there were definite possibilities. The old man patted the stove affectionately. 'Bought this one for Annie, me wife, in 1939,' he said. 'Cooked plenty of good hot dinners on it, too, she did.'

They continued with the inspection. To their astonishment, they discovered that every square inch of wall and woodwork was painted in the same fading China-blue water paint as had been the kitchen, and that the pungent, earthy smell which had made Joanie's nose curl up in mild disgust when she'd first entered the house seemed everywhere as they moved from one room to the other. The old man made no comment about the smell, but he did mention the colour scheme. 'Don't go much on that China-blue, meself,' he said, as he showed Harry and Joanie the larger of their two bedrooms. 'Got a real good special on it at Nock and Kirby's, back in 1949. Just before Annie died.' He frowned, sniffed sharply. 'The old girl had gone blind by then, so's the colour didn't matter. She liked the smell of fresh paint, though.' He turned away, then added. 'Put what was left of it on the weatherboards outside.' He turned to Harry, grinned. 'In my opinion, it weren't intended fer outside use.'

Although only half the house was for rent—a little more than half in fact because of the extra bedroom—Harry and Joanie had the kitchen.

Not the bathroom; that was to be shared. And, luckily as it turned out, the toilet was in the back yard rather than under the main roof. The toilet—'the little house' said the old man—was a quaint if dilapidated building, also of weatherboard and tin, painted in what Harry now knew to be faded China-blue, and, as a legacy from the days when Annie was still alive, surrounded for modesty by three giant Hydrangea bushes. And no longer on the pan system, noted Joanie, thankful for this mercy, but properly sewered with an elevated cistern from which hung a long chain fitted with a white porcelain handle shaped like a pear-drop.

The bathroom turned out to be the most interesting room in the house. It contained a scarred old claw-legged bath, and also the key to the mystery of the bad smell.

The bath was teeming with earthworms!

It blew their minds.

The old man—'the kids call me Maggoty,' he explained drily, 'yep, Maggoty Maguire, they call me, on account of the worms'—had a thriving earthworm farm in the bathroom. 'They like it in here,' he said, quite nonchalantly, as though a sea of earthworms in the bath was a commonplace. 'And they don't give you no trouble. Yep. They know their place,' he said, implying every single worm had graduated from good behaviour school. 'Never get out, they don't; well not so's you'd notice.' He looked up, saw the gaping expressions on Harry's and Joanie's faces. 'Anyway, there's a separate shower recess,' he announced, like he might have been a real estate agent about to grant his customers a privileged glance at the mansion's prize jewel, and he peeled open a sticky shower curtain to reveal a musty alcove with a galvanised shower pipe and a rusted shower head. 'Don't use it meself,' he informed them, tapping the oxidised pipe professionally but disturbing a dangerously large flake of corrosion which he stuck back in place with a lick of his finger, 'not much, anyways. Of course, yous two can, if yer want to.' He bent down low, breath rasping with effort, one hand on hip, his free arm dangling down like a loose fishing line with the fingertip swinging gently as he waited for his eyes to re-focus. Then, with practised skill, he picked up a long, thin worm which was half a body length into a reckless but now abortive escape bid down the encrusted shower drain. 'So long as you don't splash soapy water on me worms,' he added, carefully lifting a corner of the hessian sacking which covered the heaving mulch in the bath tub and placing the worm back among its wriggling brethren, 'they're not partial to soap.'

The old man slowly lifted his body upright. 'Well,' he said, 'that's about it.' He looked at Harry and Joanie, smiled. 'It's three pound ten a week if you were wonderin' about the rent. And you pays extra for electricity. There's no telephone. There's one up the street about five minutes away. Oh, yep; and you put out the garbage for both of us. Saves me back. On Thursday nights; they come early Friday mornin'.' He paused and looked quizzically at Harry. 'You sure you're not related to a Lofty O'Brien, or a Lofty Smith, as he reckoned he sometimes called himself.' Harry shook his head. 'No, mate,' he said. Maggoty frowned. 'Well, that's a real pity,' he said, ' a real pity.'

Harry and Joanie took the half-house.

'We'll only need six months, Mr Maguire,' said Joanie. 'We'll have enough for a deposit by then for our own place, won't we, Harry?'

Harry nodded.

'No problem,' said Maggoty.

They stayed fifteen years.

They stayed fifteen years because Maggoty—his proper name was Colin—died five months after they moved in and left Harry the house in his will.

Harry remembers, and smiles. He smiles because he remembers the cheeky note in the old man's voice:

'Pretty little thing, your wife,' he'd said, as Joanie, a little way off, cast her sceptical eye over the aged sink and stove. 'Reminds me of my Annie, she does, your Joanie.'

21

Joanie O'Brien, née Thomas, *was* a pretty little thing. Everyone in Lilyfield said so.

'Definitely got her good looks from her dad,' they said.

'Lucky for her she never took after her mother.'

'She were a funny little woman, that Una Thomas.'

'With funny eyes.'

'Narrow little eyes, they were.'

'Like they weren't never prop'ly open.'

'Never looked at yer, them eyes.'

'An' 'er funny little ways. Like the way she'd scuttle back in her house, real sudden, just before you reached 'er front gate.'

(Una had one of those narrow strips of garden in front of her Lilyfield terrace. With hydrangeas and rose bushes mixed up together struggling for living space. And a fence with a gate which she always kept secure with a piece of coat hanger wire. She felt safe behind the fence. Then there was the bullnose veranda, painted in spiritless grey, which hung low and dowdy over the front of the house like permanent mourning. Sometimes, when the street was empty of people, she would stand just outside the door, waiting.

Sometimes, just on dusk, she would emerge from under the veranda and creep to the front gate and peer up the street, motionless, her body held as though frozen, as she watched for the first sign of her husband's return.)

'It were a wonder that Keith Thomas ever married 'er, if you ask me.'

'No way 'e would have, I reckon, if the war weren't on, an' 'im in the army.'

'Shameful, weren't it; 'er seducin' 'im, like that?'

'An' gettin' 'erself in the family way.'

'So's they'd have to get married.'

'O' course, there weren't none o' that livin' together in them days.'

'That's why you got married.'

'So's you could; you know—well —get together, like.'

'Yearse...'

'It were a bit rough on Una, though.'

'When Keith Thomas went off to the war.'

'Yearse, an' 'er up the duff.'

'An' everyone around 'ere talkin' behind 'er back, like.'

'Terrible, weren't it?'

'Mind you, it weren't easy to feel sorry for Una.'

'No it weren't.'

'She was a bit of a loner. Never mixed with any of us.'

'An' as I said, she 'ad 'er funny ways.'

'All them airs and graces.'

'Yearse; like she was a cut above the rest of us.'

'Especially when she married Keith Thomas.'

"E were a good catch.'

'Real 'an'some 'e was. With 'is little brown mo, an' all.'

(Corporal Thomas wore the moustache to make him look regimental. He had the idea that to look regimental would strengthen his hand with the troops, compensate for his shortness of height.)

'Shame 'e got 'is 'ead blown off, up in New Guinea.'

'An' six months before Joanie was born, too.'

'She was somethin' diff'rent, that Joanie.'

'She weren't no Bradley—Bradley were Una's maiden name, y'know.'

'A Thomas through and through.'

'She was short though, like 'er mum.'

'Oh, real short; stunted you could say.'

'Almost a dwarf.'

'Well, not one of them real dwarfs; you know; them real ones, them real midgets, with stubby arms and legs, that look like they've bin' cut off short.'

'That's right; Joanie weren't nuthin' like that. She wus a pretty little thing; more like a normal sort of girl, but in a pint-sized body.'

'With all the right proportions.'

'An' all the right equipment, too.'

'But real small.'

'Oh, yearse, real small. Like one of them China dolls, she was. A real cutey.'

'Mind you; she 'ad her own little ways—later on; when she grew up.'

'Oh, she did. There was even talk she liked girls better'n she liked boys.'

'I never heard that.'

'Well, it weren't never proved or nuthin', just talk.'

'Anyhow, she turned out alright in the end, didn't she?'

'Oh, yearse; married that real good-lookin' feller, Harry O'Brien.'

'Yep, so she did.'

'Strange though, how a shy little thing like that'd catch a really big bloke like him.'

'Yep: six feet four that Harry'd be, if he's an inch.'

'Makes you think, don't it?'

'What does?'

'You know, 'ow they managed, like'?

22

Joanie *was* very petite and, as described by Harry, an 'extra good sort'. Her hair was the colour of dark honey, her skin was fair and unblemished by sun since she was very much the indoors type. She had big, blue-grey oval eyes and a really pretty mouth with soft, plump lips. Though her nose was long and sharply ridged—a Thomas feature—it wasn't an ugly nose as noses go, nor a particularly attractive one, but it suited the long, oval (Thomas) face and complemented the high cheekbones which stretched over her delicate skin and transformed her prettiness into an urgent beauty when she was in the mood for sex with Harry.

She really was very short, a fraction over four and a half feet; on tip-toe, she remained inches below Harry's shoulder; next to him she truly seemed doll-like; encircled by his arms she disappeared from sight; on his lap, she rested like a child; when they danced Harry had to stoop until he was bent almost double; when they made love, well, then, of course, they managed as all such couples have managed from the dawn of time, they made sure Joanie's size and Harry's height made no difference at all.

There was insatiable speculation on the reasons why Harry should be marrying at all, for Harry had, so to speak, never been short of women; and all the women in Harry's life had, by definition, competed well with Joanie in the category of good looks. It was a certain fact, as most of Harry's friends knew, even if none fully understood the reason why, just as it had been critical for Harry's other women, that Joanie's shortness of height was critical to her success with him. All Harry's women had been small, one or two even smaller than Joanie. Among them, Brenda Williams (who Harry used to work with at Pollards in the city) nearly snared Harry into marriage when he was nineteen—at least that was the story Brenda later spread around the store. In the end, Harry defied all the theories and married Joanie Thomas. None truly could claim they understood why. To most observers Joanie seemed not much different from many of Harry's girlfriends—'including that stuck up little North Shore bitch Doreen Wilcox he'd shacked up with; well, all but shacked up with; she was running a regular little business up there, you know. Too right she was!' And Harry hadn't put Joanie 'up the duff', as the jealous Brenda tried to spread it around. Nor was there any objective evidence that Joanie 'dropped her pants' more readily than any other of Harry's girlfriends, or that she was any the better in bed. Some of the more ignorant claimed Joanie reminded Harry of his mother—Joanie looked and behaved nothing like Raelene O'Brien.

Yet Harry had desperately wanted to marry Joanie. But why, everyone asked, get married at all? Not for the regular sex. Surely he hadn't needed to get married for the regular sex? Harry had never had trouble getting sex. Not like his mates. They'd always complained to him about how hard it was to get sex. But not Harry. It was always there, always available. That's what they said about him. Always available to Harry O'Brien. Just like it was available here. Here in Mid-City Leagues. With the woman over there next to her husband on the dollar machine. Just like it had always been...

...A smile grows over Harry's face. For a while he pauses, forgets Thirty-three. Since he'd turned thirteen, at any rate, he recalls; not long after he'd started having wet dreams and then discovered he could, by his own hand, replicate the experience at will, and compared with such private ecstasy, his first experiences of sex with girls had been somewhat disappointing.

The young girls willing to do it with him were just as amateurish as himself, there was no such thing as love-making, no use of technique, just a quick and giggly connection, then him coming almost straight away, and the girl saying something stupid, like, 'Did you do it, Harry?' or something pathetic, like, 'Was that good for you, Harry?' mimicking something they'd read in what in those days they called 'dirty magazines', and Harry, expended for the moment, suddenly having no further interest in Betty, or Donna, or Fay, or whoever, but finding out he was something of a celebrity around Rozelle and that the girls were coming after him so they could boast that they'd 'done it' with Harry O'Brien.

Then there was Tanya. His famous love affair with Tanya. His first serious love affair involving physical sex. All forty-eight hours of it. Made a man of him, though, it had, that affair with Tanya, scrawny-shanked, hot-breathed Tanya, who had the biggest breasts he'd ever seen, who was sixteen going on seventeen and an impatient temptress who'd heard about Harry and sought him out, and now had him inside her without his Frenchie on because she said it was her safe time of the month and anyway she enjoyed it better that way, and she was suddenly moaning even as he felt himself coming and worrying irrationally at the same time that Mrs Reilly, who he knew had been dead for nearly three years, might still hear Tanya's snorting sounds and walk in the bedroom he'd sneaked into with the girl, and catch him with his cock sprouted and his backside pointing skyward, and the girl under him with her scrawny thighs spread wide, and drag them apart like they used to try to drag poor yelping dogs apart in the street. Then, just as he was about to come, he'd convinced himself he definitely had heard the door opening, and he'd jerked himself out of her like a recoiling rifle because he respected the dead Mrs Reilly too much to have her see him doing this to Tanya, and it was too late anyway and he'd sprayed himself all over Tanya's legs, and she'd berated him for being gutless and a mongrel for cheating her out of her fun, which, despite all the moaning, Harry could not then comprehend since he had no idea girls had fun when they had sex, and Tanya had grabbed at him and peeled back his glistening foreskin and rubbed him hard and made him gasp in a kind of sweet unbearable agony and he'd sprouted again which he'd thought at the time was truly remarkable and she'd put him inside her and then had stopped shouting for a while but had begun breathing heavily and slobbering all over his face and squirming like a wild, snake-like creature under him until she began shouting again and gave Harry his first experience of a female going off with him tight inside her.

That night, as he lay in bed, he knew he was in love with Tanya. It had to be love, the feeling he had for Tanya, the wonder he felt as he recalled the experience of her coming like that. Yeah, it was love alright, his initiation into real love, real sexual love of a man for a woman. He'd been in love before. Sure he had. A number of times. Well, one time, at least, before Tanya. But that was different. Wasn't it? Harry reassured himself that it was different. That one time. Whoever the girl had been. Yeah, 'course it was different. There'd been no sex, no physical sex anyhow, not even the desire for physical sex, not like with Tanya, it hadn't been like it was with Tanya, though she'd been special enough in her own way, she'd been the first, the first girl with truly full-sized breasts, breasts with enough weight to make them show they were mature, womanly breasts, you know, beginning to droop slightly (which idea represented the popular wisdom shared by Harry's peers), yeah, Tanya, the first girl who'd ever taken real pleasure from him, from his body, from his stiff cock which, though it isn't stiff right now, quivers inside his pants in front of Thirty-three as he recalls again his boyhood frenzy, and his eagerness, and the power of his desire to empty himself into female bodies, and Tanya, what Tanya had done for him, he could never forget Tanya, never forget her for making a thirteen year-old kid feel he was a man, whatever the hell that meant!

Harry punches Thirty-three hard.

It was all a big joke. She was already pregnant. That's why it had been safe. She was in the family way. That was Tanya's style; how she exhibited her pride, that pregnant or not, she could still seduce any bloke in town. Harry smiles ruefully as he remembers Tanya, how he'd been in and out of love with her in the space of two days. Yet she'd settled down, turned out okay, when the kids came along.

Kids? Tanya's kids. Tanya's five kids. Harry shudders. Five kids! And probably five different fathers! But then, he'd been damn lucky. He'd met Joanie. Much later on, of course. Oh, he was still seeing Doreen Wilcox at the time he met Joanie—well, more or less seeing her. But there was never any question of marrying Doreen.

Hang on. Marrying Doreen? He would have married Doreen. He wanted to marry her. She wouldn't have wanted kids. Well, maybe she might have wanted kids. The fact was, she couldn't have them. Could she? Not after that mongrel of her first husband wrecked her insides.

He punches Thirty-three.

He breathes deeply. Poor Doreen, he thinks. Then he corrects himself. Doreen had had kids. Hadn't she? Harry thought he could remember that Doreen had had kids. Not his kids, of course. Derek's kids. After she'd had that special operation.

But Joanie. Things were different with Joanie. You could respect her. Yeah, you could respect Joanie Thomas.

Lazily he plays Thirty-three, falls into a kind of reverie, thinking about Joanie.

Even the very first time he saw her there was something about Joanie Thomas that touched Harry deeply. He sensed immediately how fragile she was, that this was the real truth about her, that all her other characteristics, all her imagined strengths, were somehow contradictions, disguises, that she had to be always brave because she was so fragile, so precious. He pauses. Was that the truth? Was it fact? Or something existing outside his memory of fact? Yet it seems so true, so matter of fact. He sighs deeply, he was doing a lot of sighing tonight. Punching the reserve button, he heads for the Long Bar.

Around him the club seems normal. The faces of the pokie players seem normal, their muted emotions, their calm exteriors, betraying little of what they truly feel inside themselves—anger, frustration, resignation, pretended indifference, smug satisfaction, here and there—like on the crabby face of Waddling Thighs over there who'd just missed winning a hundred—poorly disguised desperation. Everything normal, decides Harry. Normal on the dance floor where music plays, a soft jazz-waltz and the sedate movements of couples on the dance floor, the sedate but stately Fred Donaldson, still gliding around on his velvet feet. Normal because he can see the lead guitarist resting while his three colleagues skilfully carry the tune, the lead guitarist with the weather-beaten Rickenbacker and the McCartney style, sitting quietly behind the band, dragging on a smoke, swigging a beer. Normal enough to permit Harry to think about Joanie, about the reasons he'd been attracted to her, about her face, why her face had seemed so different, so important, why she was special enough to make Harry willing to risk marriage.

23

Apart from the fact that he preferred his women to be petite, Harry would never tell his mates what really turned him on about Joanie. Harry's romance with Joanie developed more than anything else out of his fantasy over her crooked front teeth. Amongst all the things he loved about her, he loved Joanie's front teeth most of all; the thought of them aroused him, they were the critical factor; the sight of them made him breathless, the feel of them made him fully alive. He spent hours thinking about Joanie's front teeth. He dreamed about them. All her vitality, her beauty, her sexuality, her person, seemed to find their focus in those front teeth, how the right tooth crossed over the left one, how this formed the tiny vee-shaped cleft where they met, how, when they kissed, he could feel the gentle imperfection with his tongue.

(Thirty-three gives him three bells. Then a fifty pay. Don't knock it, he reminds himself, they all count, even the small pays, they're the ones that keep you alive, keep you in the race, yeah, he mutters under his breath, eyeing the three lined-up purple crowns with the fourth crown (mini-jackpot level) mocking him (so it thought) from its neutral (useless) position on a different row.)

He laughs. Yeah; Joanie's front teeth.

(Thirty-three hits him with three kings.)

Yeah, how he'd loved those front teeth.

(Then with a hundred scatters.)

Those front teeth had really done it to him.

'Jeez, you're doing alright.'

It's Gordie at his elbow, eyeing Thirty-three's credit meter, Gordie putting his arm round Harry's shoulder, squeezing Harry's shoulder, this good old mate who he's known for over thirty years.

Thirty years?

'How's it goin'?' asks Gordie conversationally.

'Alright, mate.'

Gordie's hand is still on Harry's shoulder.

'Wouldn't be your shout, would it, Harry?'

Harry drags his eyes away from Thirty-three, looks at Gordie. He shrugs Gordie's warm hand off his shoulder.

'Yeah, yeah, mate,' he says, fumbling in his pocket for money. He hands over a bill. 'You get 'em, will you, Gordie?'

Gordie smiles weakly, stops himself making a hand gesture. He swivels quickly on his heels, heads for the Long Bar.

Harry watches his friend go, watches the lowered head, the back of the neck, the wispy hair. Gordie seems so old tonight, so round-shouldered. And that scar on his face. And Joanie, he's thinking about Joanie again, and about the woman, the thoughts are jumbled, their visual content confusing, the two faces changing places, flip-flopping in his mind, Joanie, then the woman in the carpark, then Joanie, then Gordie, and Gordie's new scar, and Gordie's hand on his arm, Gordie's warm fingers, then Joanie again, then the woman, their images flip-flopping; and all the while he plays Thirty-three, slowly, again absently, as though purely from habit, pressing the play-button, automatically registering the results, automatically registering his successes, assessing the favourable odds he believes control the outcome of the spinning barrels, automatically ignoring the cold logic of the poker machine.

Joanie? Was it something to do with getting married? Yeah, that must be it. Were they too young? Or was Joanie pregnant? Nah! no way she could have been pregnant; not like Tanya. Maybe they'd been too young, he'd been twenty, Joanie nineteen, when they'd married. But all his mates were married, well, just about all of them, by the time they were nineteen or twenty; and most of them fathers. Anyway, it was the way things were, in 1964. Even though living in with the girlfriend was more common than it had been back in the fifties it was still frowned on in working class Sydney and, because the comfort of a legally shared bed was preferable to the back of the Holden or Ford, or even the family lounge, specially when it was within earshot (as it usually was) of the girlfriend's parents who you could bet your last quid were lying wide-eyed awake on their innerspring, you got married and enjoyed your own brand spanking new innerspring, right?

He laughs inside himself at the thought of the innerspring mattress, the comic picture of himself, rump skywards, cheeks squeezed together, thrusting, as though the existence of the whole fucking universe depended on him thrusting like that!

Suddenly he feels angry with himself. It is as though he suddenly hates the young man he knew was once himself, as though he sees the pointlessness of all that fucking, all that sweating, all that useless shedding of semen.

Love? Was it because of love? Harry suddenly, desperately, hopes it was because of love. He sensed it was because he was in love, truly, deeply in love. Yet love? What the hell did it mean? Was it just some kind of fucking delusion? Was love only something you imagined, not real? And here he is, playing Thirty-three. That's love, isn't it, he says to himself, giggling softly?

There's a sense of something going wrong inside Harry's head. 'Something wrong,' he says out loud. 'Eh? You say something, mate?' a voice nearby says. 'Get fucked,' mutters Harry to the voice. The voice falls silent.

'Something wrong,' repeats Harry under his breath. Yet he does not understand. Suddenly he does not understand. Hell! he'd always thought he'd understood.

Yeah, I understand, he'd said, often enough, to Gordie, to Joanie, to … to … He's angry. There's a dangerous feeling of rage in the front of his brain. Yet quietly he plays Thirty-three. Must pull himself together, he tells himself again. Must get out of this mood, get back inside his proper self again. Remember things. Yeah, must do that. Memory? What the fuck's wrong with his memory tonight? Sees himself reeling along the rain-soaked path in Centennial Park. What the bloody hell was he doing in Centennial park? Having a fucking nervous breakdown, that's fucking what! Yet he does not know why. Doesn't know why, what, for Christ's sake? His anger? Why is he angry?

A moment ago, he knew why. Now, it's gone, the reason for his anger. But there'd been so many causes of his anger. Quietly he plays Thirty-three, but the anger persists, grows, now he angrily expects, demands, his memory to be immutable, unforgettable.

Memory? He has memory. Now he has floods of memory. A fucking deluge of memory. As if there is no time, just existence, and memory and experience truly are indistinguishable. As though, for example, Una Thomas is part of the scheme, creating Joanie in her one moment of ecstasy with poor, fucking, doomed Corporal Thomas, as poor, fucking, doomed Una vividly remembers, or would be remembering if she was still living, maybe is remembering, as she lies sleeplessly in bed and switches on the bedside lamp, and stares dully at the nineteen forties wedding photo of herself and husband Keith on the bedside table. It is a badly composed shot, the spaces are all wrong, the couple, with apprehensive eyes, have been caught unawares by the camera, Keith, the moustachioed corporal, wears Service Dress uniform complete with slouch hat, Una, short and already dumpy, her pregnancy with Joanie just visible if you knew it was there, her plainness cruelly emphatic against the slim good looks of her husband, her wedding dress a cream two-piece suit in artificial silk and a tiny hat sitting flatly on her new but flatly rendered permanent wave, a posy of orchids in her hands as she stares out at you in her confusion. Then, twenty-five years later, she dies, as though heroically, thinking of Keith, and Harry remembers watching Joanie destroy the wedding photo the day after the funeral, and understood her anger, he was angry too, is angry now, as he thinks about his own wedding photo, his own wedding, himself dwarfing Joanie, the jokes about his size, about the size of his cock, the way they 'did it', jokes of this kind from his mates, his rellies, in Mid-City Leagues, in church, anywhere, then, now, it wasn't (isn't) the jokes, why he was (is) angry, he expected (expects) them, but it all seems the same, memories and now, as though everything is *now*, like in his dream, what dream? now he plays Thirty-three angrily, feels angry, truly cannot understand his anger, understands it fully, flip-flop again, as though wasting away, like poor, fucking Flan O'Brien, so much confusion, on the kitchen floor, straining to empty his whole being into Joanie, as though desperate to crawl everything he is into her, crawl back into the womb Doreen would have explained to him as though he really was stupid and ignorant, which he was, wasn't he, punching the five-play button, now, last week, last year, pulling the pokie handle, watching kings and queens, and those jokers, watching for five jokers on the two bob machine up the Dragons, he's a youth of twenty-one, might as well be, wouldn't mind being fuckin' twenty-one again, waltzing blindly into marriage, only way to do it, blindly, only way you can do it, sees everything as they all couldn't see it then, he thinks, as though everything is cocks and cunts, nineteen sixties, naked girls and glimpses of hairy crotches on TV, just like that, they call it the sexual revolution, sounds really good, as though it has anything to do with them, war and sex, sex everywhere, everybody having sex, on the street, up the park, on the deck of the Manly Ferry for Christ's sake! some kind of protest about the war, a pair of kids with naked arses, fucking like that as the ferry crosses the harbour heads while some idiot crew member stands watching and giggling and some stern-faced woman with the light of Christ in her eye throws a raincoat over the wriggling bodies and the passengers cheer madly as the ferry plunges in the open swell...but—made their point, didn't they, if you see what I mean, Ha!...and then, as though mocking those two poor naked kids, they'd watched brains spurting like jism on a Saigon street that night on TV, yeah, from his fucking head! Jesus! no protest that, just bloody murder on the TV screen, and he is angry, wasted angry, as though it has anything to do with them, Harry and Joanie, missed the ballot, lucky bastard, of course it has to do with them, these working class kids, that's the point, inter-connections, all is inter-connections, Joanie and Harry, dragging their upbringings behind them, the dross of their family histories stretched out behind them, clinging, as they grope forward, feel fears, anxieties, feel in love, what else can they feel? which is not the contradiction it sounds, as they stand together, giant alongside tiny woman, in fancy dress, in central position, so vulnerable, so strong, so strong in church, so young, so angry with hope, mouthing strange words, 'I do', seeing stained teeth in the mouth of a strange priest, little man, bald head, bad breath, (a bit like Andy Simpson over there on the dollar pokie), and cousin Kevin, family larrikin, in the pew behind, says words which sound like 'fuck' and 'shit', so what's new? he's pissed already, and Harry wondering why he is getting married at all, must get married, must have Joanie, need Joanie, then blushes, thinks, wants to giggle, 'I do', remembers his first wank with Gordie and the boys, and them coming like that, looks of concentration, gaping eyes, in unison almost, except for poor bloody Frankie Jones with his stubby little cock, going like hell but nothing doing while the rest spurt like young stallions, wasting seed, lavishly, and Gordie looking at him like that, even then, fuck Gordie, best mate, love him, hate the bastard, strange feelings, can't help his strange feelings, everyone has strange feelings, now and again, especially when you're out drinking like this and you've got a lot on your mind, it's only natural, can't be natural of course, dangerous, not allowed, got to have rules; like when you get married, yet he knows why he's getting married, he knows why he's here, in front of his rellies, 'Fuck them before they fuck you!' said Mackenzie.

Suddenly he feels very calm. He breathes in deeply, feels the warm club air filling his lungs, the heady taste of other people's cigarette smoke. He breathes again, pauses his fingers above Thirty-three's play-buttons. He remembers Joanie's voice, hears it inside him. It's a soft voice, set a little higher than the voices of most young women he knows. He likes this, this set of Joanie's voice, this girlish quality in her voice. Like the front teeth in a way. Yeah, now he thinks about it, like the front teeth. He'd listen to Joanie's voice and gaze at her teeth all night long.

'My mum's very funny with people,' she'd said one night.

'Some of my relatives are pretty funny,' Harry had smiled back.

'She won't be any trouble once we're married.'

'Yeah, right,' he'd said while watching her face closely, waiting for her mouth to open.

'We've never really got on, mum and me.'

He'd leaned forward, touched her cheek. 'It doesn't matter, love,' he'd whispered, and Joanie's expression had brightened, and she'd opened her mouth, smiled broadly.

'Anyway, I'm more like my dad,' she'd said blushing.

'Oh, you are?'

'Yes, Harry.'

'Then he must have been really good looking, your dad,' he'd said, then Joanie had taken hold of his fingers and squeezed them hard. She had tiny hands with slender fingers and tiny, oval fingernails. Joanie's fingernails had seemed perfectly formed, perfectly shaped.

'Oh, he was, Harry,' she'd said, gazing at him with wide, earnest eyes. 'He was a very handsome man, my dad.' Then she'd dropped her eyes, blushed,

'Just as handsome as you, Harry, darling.' she'd murmured. Then he'd stood up, still holding her hands, guided himself round the table until he reached her, leaned down, and scooped her into his arms. And the closeness of her had overwhelmed him—

And suddenly they are lowering themselves on to the kitchen floor, struggling to loosen clothing, and then she is straddling him, gazing into his eyes, hers blue and widely spaced, unblinking, full of urgency, concealing other, less carnal motives which now, as her ardour swells, she abandons, and is no longer shy, and seeks out his eyes, wants to be his woman, it is her only idea, wants to absorb him, be absorbed by him, yes, seeks out his eyes, his dark, Spanish eyes, as though she might be Mary Cathleen, as though they have just a few desperate moments left before discovery and violent separation; and she opens her mouth, raises her upper lip, widens her thighs...

As though it could be so simple thinks Harry as he remembers that time with Joanie, remembers how grateful he was to her, how easily she'd been deceived.

'Oh, Harry, dearest, I'll love you forever.'

'I'll always love you, too,' he'd lied.

Though he was sure he was telling Joanie the truth, he knew he was lying.

'This is the greatest sex in the world,' he'd told her.

'Oh, Harry,' Joanie had sighed.

'Greatest sex, bar none,' he'd said.

'Oh, Harry,' she'd said.

24

Nor was it so simple for Joanie, even though she was so sure she was in love with Harry. Yet being in love with Harry frightened her. Everything about it was so new, so strange, so different from anything she'd ever imagined it might be. Being in love was such a physical thing. Such a gut-centred, physical thing. As though lodged inside her organs. Inside her. Physically located inside her guts. As though it was flesh, and guts, and great spasms of feeling in her belly, and great soarings inside her vagina, such great soarings, making her feel as if something was about to explode inside her, as though her body was about to go up in one great big banging explosion. And it was so unchildlike, so ungentle, so hard and not soft, although she knew it was her softness which made Harry shudder the way he did, as his fingers felt her softness. But yes, so physical, so exhaustingly physical, not subdued, not shy, affirming, throbbing, and the fierceness of it, and sweat covered sheets, and breathing hard, and bodies smelling, and stickiness everywhere belonging to both of them, and gasping for breath, and grasping, and gripping, about surviving.

So unchildlike. This sexual being she had become. And being in love with a man was such an unchildlike thing to be. So unlike what she'd imagined. Maybe she was feeling like a woman, she told herself. Being a woman.

As though this was all there was to it. This awakening of her body.

'You just know when you're in love,' she told Harry. 'Oh, I do love you, Harry.'

Joanie liked the sound of herself saying: 'I do love you, Harry.' The sound seemed so complete in itself. Sometimes, despite the sexual power in her body, she imagined all she needed was the sound of her voice saying, 'I love you, Harry.'

And she was sure Harry was in love with her. She could tell by the way he would gaze at her teeth. It was funny, and exciting, the thought of it raised Joanie's goose bumps, that Harry never seemed to tire of gazing at her teeth.

'Why are you always looking at my teeth, Harry?'

'I just like them.'

'You like my teeth?'

'Yeah, they're nice.'

'Nice?'

'Really nice?'

'Sexy?'

'Yeah, real sexy.'

'Oh, Harry, I really want to marry you, darling.'

'I want to marry you, too, Joanie.'

'Oh, Harry, do you, do you?'

'Yes, Joanie, I do.'

Then they would clutch each other tightly.

'Oh, I love you, Harry, my darling.'

'I love you, Joanie.'

As she would feel him thrusting.

'Oh, I love you, Harry.'

As though the words had become the deed.

'Oh, ohhh, Harry...Ohhh,' as it happened with Harry for the first time, 'ohhh...ohhh.'

Joanie was so sure that she loved Harry. She loved him so much she felt as though she'd always loved him, that her love was so strong that it must have existed before they'd met, that it must have existed before either of them had been born.

Once, she slowly undressed herself in front of the mirror. She gazed at her nakedness, seeing yet unseeing, trying to imagine how her flesh might appear to Harry, trying to imagine how his erect penis might feel to him as it entered her, if it was like the feelings she had, and then, as if merely trying an experiment, she touched herself, and began rubbing gently, rhythmically, as she'd learned in her girlhood, rubbing, feeling, arousing, pushing her free fingers inside her as she rubbed, imagining her fingers were Harry himself so that she brought herself quickly to orgasm and caught sight of the strange, young, serious-faced woman watching herself nakedly climaxing in the mirror.

Joanie was certain she loved everything about Harry. Much of what she loved she'd made up in her mind. She'd made it up years and years ago. Some of it she'd made up so long ago it seemed as though she hadn't made it up at all, that it had been like revelation, yes, that was it, revelation.

She loved all the strong things about Harry. To Joanie it was evident that everything about Harry was strong; his voice was strong; it was a manly voice, deep and rich, and full of reassurance; its qualities of hesitancy and querulousness she did not see, she saw these as endearments, embellishments of his strength, signs of his inner tenderness. She loved Harry's eyes, his dark, sometimes liquid eyes, his strong and beautiful eyes; she did not see the sadness behind Harry's eyes, the sadness which sometimes looked out on the world, as though unable to comprehend what it saw. She loved his mouth, his strong, sensuous mouth; she did not see that Harry's mouth was unsure of itself, that there might be weakness there, a betrayal of a weakness she could not see. And so Joanie saw Harry held there, inside Joanie's head, carefully defined, carefully created, Joanie's perfect creation.

Joanie really loved Harry. She was so sure of it. Yet there were times, even as she felt his hot seed spurting in her, when she worried about Harry's love for her. Sometimes she knew he used her body merely as a corridor of pleasure—as Harry's woman, she realised this was the way men were; that they were always anxious, that their bodies were difficult to control, that it was not their fault, that it was the way nature had made them. Sometimes, though, as she lovingly provided him with that pleasure, a great fear would possess her, a fear that she was detached from that corridor, no longer its owner, that Harry might even be imagining she was someone else, and the fear would become horror, horror that she might be losing Harry's love, that he preferred some stranger's body, and then she would grab hold of his thighs and make love to him fiercely, and make him lust after her so violently that he would come quickly and jerk his body in those giant convulsive movements as she lay suddenly still, enjoying her moment of reassurance while he enjoyed his moment of release.

'Was that good, Harry?'

'Yeah, really great, Joanie.'

'I love you, Harry.'

'I love you, too, darl.'

Sometimes it was as though their lovemaking was ritual, a duty to perform. Yet Harry seemed always enthusiastic. He always achieved orgasm. Sometimes twice. After their love-making, as she lay on his body, filled by his sperm, feeling the rise and fall of his chest, she would seek his hand and cradle as much of it as she could in both of hers. Then she would sleep, and be a child again, a child dreaming of her wedding day, dreaming of the dreams she'd had before her wedding day, and feeling suddenly cold in her dream, and shivering as she slept, and moving against Harry's body, and making him stir and complain as he slept, and feeling cold against her back, despite the blankets, despite the hot furnace of Harry's chest beneath her, and dreaming herself lying on a cold surface, a hard surface, like stone under her naked body, cold and hard, covered by sheeting, as though tightly bound and unable to move, and now Harry is standing nearby, but is oblivious of her presence, and, though her mouth opens and she desperately wills herself, she can make no sound, and she sees Harry being married to a tall, regal woman, with a proud head held high, and a veil flowing down her back and trailing towards where the tiny Joanie is lying, the veil suddenly curling itself into a long, writhing, living thing, a serpent coiling itself around her neck, making her gasp, making her eyes bulge, so that she is dying, and struggling with her own death, as though her death is the serpent, yet no, it is the tall woman, and now it is the tall woman who is unable to move, and Joanie strangles the neck of the serpent which is suddenly the neck of the woman, and feels the woman's flesh crumbling between her fingers, and dissolving, and disintegrating into nothingness, and Harry is there, and smiling, and she has risen in height, and is looking him in the eye, and he is smiling at her, and they dance the nuptial dance, and she feels her proud breast straining against Harry as they dance, and the powerful lustful feeling growing between her thighs, and Harry's big frame seems suddenly fragile, as though she is the stronger of them, providing all the strength, and she pulls him to a halt, and throws her arms around his neck, and people are clapping and cheering, and she can hear an O'Brien cousin yelling obscenely and she does not care...

One day a few weeks after the wedding Joanie was the first to awaken. She lay on her side gazing at their wedding photo on the bedside table. She and Harry were both smiling, both looking so happy. It was a good likeness, and a nicely framed shot. The photographer had managed to select an angle which had cleverly removed much of the emphasis of their difference in height. Joanie seemed to have grown taller; as though the act of having her photograph taken alongside Harry had given her new height.

They rose early, quickly ate breakfast. They knew Mrs Thomas would be awake, listening, waiting for them to leave. Quietly they washed up the breakfast dishes, left the house. By eleven that morning they had found their way to Col Maguire's house on Marsden Street.

Later, when old Col, the worm farmer, feared they mightn't take the flat he went up close to them. They could tell he was keen, even anxious for them to take the flat. 'O' course,' Col had said, 'if yerse agree to paint the house, I'll give yerse the first six months rent-free.' And, imagining they still hesitated. 'Oh, yep; an' I supply the paint, naturally, an' the brushes.' Then, catching Joanie's eye, and believing it was time to play his trump card, he added, 'An' I'll move the worm farm out' the back yard.'

25

Carelessly Harry misses a hundred-dollar mini jackpot, but scores a nice consolation prize of two hundred and fifty coins (twenty-five dollars). For a while he gazes at the line of four bells—'twenty-five dollars would have been a good 'pull-out' jackpot twenty years ago,' he muses. Skilfully he depresses the play button, pulls three sevens—Haa! breath escapes as the three sevens appear giving him a hundred pay—his fingers trembling he plays on, passes three hundred credit, ah, ha! three hundred is important, three hundred and above, so his superstition goes, means a better chance the biggie's in there, ah, ha! four bells, another twenty-five bucks, amazing stuff; now he's fifty bucks in credit, and forty-odd in his pocket; going well. Three sevens again. Jeez! three sevens twice. He stares at the three sevens. They remind him of something. Worms? Yeah, worms, for Christ's sake! Worms with their necks bloody bent. Bent worms and sevens, he thinks, Old Col Maguire and the biggie. And seven hundred in the window. He smiles. 'Those bloody worms,' he says. 'And old Col: bloody good mate, the old Col,' he chuckles, 'old Maggoty,' and smiles at the memory of the earthworm farm in the bathroom, the warmth of Col's cheeky smile—the shrewd old business man had agreed to transfer the worm farm to the backyard, Harry sees himself and Col scooping the worm mulch out of the bath, tipping the wriggling muck into buckets, re-housing the farm in two cut-down forty-four gallon drums under Col's window, 'So's I can keep an eye on the little buggers without havin' to go outside.'

His smile widens. Now he can see Joanie's face, how it lights up when the last of Col's worms has departed. He remembers her enthusiasm as she cleans the bathroom, obliterates all traces of the former occupants.

She asked Harry to put a lock on the bathroom door. 'No need to risk the old bloke catching me in my birthday suit, is there, Harry?' He pauses, remembers, Joanie in her birthday suit, at nineteen, or was it twenty, what a sight for sore eyes; yeah, he remembers installing the lock on the bathroom door, making love to Joanie under the shower. He shivers; Harry shivers because he feels Joanie's fingers touching him, caressing him, her wet skin pressing lightly on him; he shivers because he remembers the feel of her weight in his arms, the feel of the softness, roundness, firmness of her, the feel of her wet body sliding along his wet body, sliding until she is able to slide herself into him; he shivers more as he remembers how they make love a second time, almost a third and then, exhausted, lie in the shower recess, under the falling water, clutching each other, almost sleeping. And he pauses in front of Thirty-three. His eyes flutter behind almost closed eyelids. 'Almost sleeping.' He and Joanie together, 'Almost sleeping.' They had slept, fallen asleep, until the water began to run cold and they'd awoken, spluttering, Joanie squealing, he laughing, she hurrying to get out of the shower recess, he struggling to turn off the water, standing on the cold bathroom tiles, shivering, rubbing himself down, watching Joanie who is doing likewise, both of them curiously embarrassed, two naked bodies wriggling into underwear, like a couple of kids.

There'd been a problem, though. Earlier in the evening. When he was putting the lock on the door. He'd had difficulty lining up the striking plate and the key had jammed inside the lock. He'd had all kinds of trouble moving the key.

Suddenly he feels giddy. He steps back from Thirty-three. The images in the window swim in front of his eyes. He stumbles, grabs at the stool just behind him, sits on the stool. He breathes deeply, sucking air. He fumbles at his cigarette packet, manages to get one out, to light up. The smoke tastes acrid and hot, unfamiliar. He coughs, stubs out the cigarette, stares at its remains in the ashtray, wondering why the thing had made him feel so sick. He picks up his beer glass. A few inches remain. He drinks them off.

The bathroom. Yeah, the bathroom. Harry remembers the bathroom. And the lock. He was struggling to unjam the key.

He couldn't move the key.

'Rosy,' he says.

'What's that, mate?' It's the voice of a young man playing Thirty-two alongside Harry. 'You say something?' he repeats affably.

Harry frowns. He thought he'd said the name inside his head: 'Rosy.' There'd been trouble with Rosy. Big trouble. That was why he'd had to get out of the house. Because of Rosy. Out of the house at Rozelle.

'Rosy.'

The young man throws Harry a quick, nervous glance.

Harry says again: 'Rosy.'

'What you say, mate?'

Harry turns to the young man.

'It was Rosy. That fat bitch, Rosy.'

The young man sees Harry's far-away expression. 'Yeah,' he says, humouring Harry, 'it was Rosy, mate.'

Harry looks away. He leans forward, gripping the sides of Thirty-three.

'Yeah, Rosy.'

There'd been trouble between him and Rosy. There'd always been trouble between them. This time it was real bad trouble; real bad. They were fighting. He'd attacked Rosy. Or she'd attacked him. He wasn't sure which. He'd grabbed her, grabbed her hair, pulled out her hair, kicked her in the stomach, bitten her, bitten her on the shoulder, he'd made red marks on the shoulder, red teeth marks. They'd fallen to the floor. They were both screaming, both spitting, both crazy mad. They were fighting. Then those thighs again, huge thighs, straddling him, suffocating him. Then the big woman's convulsions. And Harry under her, feeling the big body jerking above him, and the thighs again, pinning him again, him struggling. Then the fat bitch must have become unconscious. She wasn't moving. She was still breathing. He could hear her shallow breathing. But her eyes were nearly closed and he could see the whites showing and the dribble running out of her mouth. From his position he could see the dribble. It was thick dribble, full of tiny bubbles, thick and sticky. And he pushes and heaves at the dead weight, and he panics because she won't move, she won't bloody move, and he strikes at the great mound of pudgy flesh, and he thinks he's passing out, but he's got one leg free, and he uses it as a mad striking piston, pushing, striking, coiling that free leg like a spring, releasing it, pushing, kicking, until he's free, he's free.

And Harry sees the small boy leaning over the big body of the woman, the big body with the big thighs, lying there, quietly, but breathing, yes still breathing, he hasn't killed her, he wants to kill her, he kicks the body, kicks the fat thigh, sees the fat thigh quiver like soft jelly, kicks it again and again. Then he stops kicking. She's unconscious. Can't stop him leaving the house now, he suddenly realises, suddenly feeling the thumping of his heart. If he can open the kitchen door, get the door open. Not the front door. There's no key in the front door, no key in the turned deadlock. It has to be the back door. Not the windows. He can't open the windows. No one can open the jammed windows. He pauses and stares at Rosy's face. He hates that face. He kicks the face, sees his shoe connecting with puffy flesh under the eyes, beady eyes, Rosy's beady eyes. He sees the face swelling before his eyes. He enjoys the swelling, sees redness forming, the swollen flesh now covering the eye, as though Rosy is one-eyed, has only one beady eye, he kicks at the other eye, viciously, remembers the back door, the back door, he turns—the boy turns. The key is in the lock. The big latchkey. He stares, the boy stares at the key, cries, tears flow, rage, he feels the boy's rage, feels the rage exploding from the boy, feels it grabbing the key, feels the rage wrenching at the key, wrenching, turning, turning the key...

Harry slams his fist down hard on Thirty-three's play button.

He slams again.

'Jeez, mate!'

Harry turns, sees the young man gaping at him.

He snarls.

'What's yer problem, matey?'

'Nuthin', mate, nuthin.''

He bangs Thirty-three.

Bangs again, and again, and again.

'Harry! Harry, mate!'

It's Vincenzio, the club official.

'Harry, take it easy, mate, okay.'

'She was a big bitch.'

'Yeah, yeah, Harry.'

Harry breathes heavily. 'But I turned the bastard,' he says. 'I turned her.'

'Yeah, mate, yeah,' says Vincenzio uncertainly.

Harry feels calmer. He'd turned the key. Yeah, he'd turned the key.

He smiles at Vincenzio.

'A proper bastard she was, too, mate, the key, I mean.'

Vincenzio frowns. The young man alongside Harry studiously plays Thirty-two. Other players shift from one foot to the other. Vincenzio wonders what to say. He gives Harry a friendly pat on the back.

'Win the big one for me, will you, Harry?'

Harry punches Thirty-three, more gently now. His features seem more relaxed, thinks Vincenzio.

The barrels spin.

Three sevens.

For the third fucking time, thinks Harry. Where's the other fucking two of the bastards, then?

'They're around, tonight, mate,' encourages Vincenzio.

'Yeah, they're around,' mutters Harry.

'Just a matter of time, Harry.'

'Just a matter of time.'

Vincenzio moves away.

Harry hears sounds. New sounds. Musical sounds. Streuth! It's the random mini jackpot, going off somewhere to his right. He stares in disbelief, sees the old couple. Christ! They've won the random mini jackpot. Two hundred and fifty dollars. Fuck! How'd they do it? How'd they bloody well do it?

Vincenzio's paying out money in crisp fifties. For a moment the old girl clutches the notes, then hands them to the old boy who buries them deep in his trouser pocket. Very business-like, observes Harry, worrying at what he sees; very business-like; a couple of old pros for sure, not a sign of emotion on either face—well maybe the old girl's smirking—but the old boy? old gummy fish face, not on your nelly! And Harry knows the couple are far from finished. Not them. Not now they've got such a good stake. Jeez! the old girl's back into it already, punching Thirty-nine's play button. Harry smiles grimly. Thirty-nine's a real dummy of a machine. Never done a thing. There for the mugs. A club machine. But they'd won the mini jackpot, hadn't they? Maybe Thirty-nine's on the boil. Jesus! he'd better get on with it then. He punches Thirty-three. 'Come on, sweetheart,' he says quietly.

26

A little while later. The club is much busier. Young people coming in. Some of them drift into the pokie lounge; most loiter in the open space on the Mixed Lounge side of the Long Bar—the 'Meat Market' as it is called. The smell of young women is on the air, invading Harry's space; alertly he lifts his head; it is a light musky sweaty wetness kind of odour, a familiar friendly sexy sensuous odour, an odour enhanced by the odours of skin lotion and perfume and volatile hair sprays and glistening sexy-smelling lipstick and black sexy mascara; a smell guaranteeing action tonight, for the lucky few at least, frustration for the rest, for most of the young stags, as though rutting now as they mill round the bar washing the aroma of young women into their nostrils, brushing against their passing bodies, those hips and thighs, firm and young, firm young flesh, thinks Harry, plump, erotic, sexy, erect erotic flesh, bodies in tight clothes, tight arses and tits and thighs, swinging by, and calves, taut and swaggering on high heels. And the young men, those with girlfriends, the least anxious, crotch-confident, idly drinking Victoria Bitter in green cans, standing in small male clusters; their womenfolk chattering and their dark devilish eyes darting around the room, appraising other young women, brazenly, scornfully, making comparisons, pouting warningly at a competitor here, an old flame of their guy's there, watching for prowlers, and other young men, men without women, dragging on cigarettes, swigging from cans or schooners, trying to seem calm, to seem macho, but with anxious eyes, watching, assessing.

'Yer reckon Wendy Williams'll be comin' in tonight?'

'Fuckin' hope so.'

'Yer seen her this week?'

'Seen her up the markets.'

'Jeez! she still runnin' that handbag stall?'

'Yeah; reckon's she can make three hundred clear on a Sunday mornin'.'

'Yeah?'

'Yeah.'

A quick, nervous drag, and a swig of beer.

'Top fuckin' chick, Wendy.'

'Yeah, fuckin' tops.'

'Bit of a bitch though.'

'Fuckin' good screw, but.'

'Yeah.'

Or the two young guys playing Thirty-four next to Harry, evoking Harry's contempt.

'Jeez! Smithy; these link machines don't give yer shit! Ten bucks without a pay!'

'Yer not wrong, mate.'

'Piss it off.'

Smithy slaps his hand on the pay button.

'Mate,' he says in mock disgust as Thirty-four takes the last five coins, 'this one's harder to fuck than Friday-night-Freda!'

They move away, laughing. Harry wonders about Freda, shakes his head. Freda who?

Two young women arrive, pause in front of Thirty-four which is free again.

'This one do, Tina?'

'Why not, love. All the bloody same, aren't they?'

Harry glances at Tina. She's the shorter of the two, the only one he sees, as though her friend mightn't be there. Tina is short, and red-haired, maybe twenty-one, twenty-two, with round cheeks, flushed already, and a tiny mouth, not a bad little mouth, and a stub of a nose. Not real pretty, but has something. Young, yeah, young. Fresh-featured. No lines. And clean smelling, smelling clean and sexy.

Tina hitches herself up on to a stool. Harry feels her thigh brushing against his leg. She smiles at him. 'Not much room to move around, is there, mate?' she says cheerfully.

Harry returns her smile.

'That's for sure.'

'You winnin?' she says.

'Nah,' says Harry.

'Got to come up some time, I reckon. The biggie, I mean.'

'Yeah, love, you're not wrong.'

Tina grins at Harry, flashing teeth, straight teeth he notes, very straight teeth, the kind of teeth you see a lot more of these days, compared with when he was that age.

'You come here regular?' she asks.

'Yeah, pretty regular.'

'Ever done any good?' Tina seems at ease, as though she and Harry might be old friends. Harry thinks to himself how easy it would be.

'Won five hundred last week.'

'Coins?'

'Dollars.'

'Jeez! that's alright. Best we've ever done is fifty bucks.' She turns to her friend who Harry sees for the first time, a weedy girl with a pimply nose doused in make-up, 'Right, Cheryl?'

'Right, Tina.'

Tina presses Thirty-four. She and her friend play their twenty dollars, finally lose. They stand. Harry pauses. He picks up his empty beer glass, examines it.

'Think I'll have another,' he says, then fixes his eye on Tina. 'You and your mate like something to drink?'

Tina smiles. Her friend giggles.

'Thanks,' says Tina, 'we can't, mate.' She has friendly eyes thinks Harry. 'Our husbands are over there,' she explains.

The two young wives depart. Harry's eyes follow Tina. She wears a tight black skirt and a red top, one of those tube tops that shows everything. And a deep nostalgia wells up in Harry, and he feels a rush of envy for Tina's husband whoever he is, Tina's young husband, lucky bastard. He feels sad, very sad, very sorry for himself.

Then dizzy again. Suddenly Harry feels dizzy. The light dims. He has trouble breathing. Images of Centennial Park flash across his eyes...

'You alright, mate?' says a voice.

'Wha...Whassat?'

He is shaking, trying to catch his breath.

He breathes, recovers enough to see the consternation developing around him.

'I'm okay, I'm okay...'

The light brightens.

'I'm okay.'

'You sure, mate?'

'Yeah, yeah...'

He's leaning forward, his hands clutching Thirty-three.

Hey, Harry.'

It's Vincenzio.

'Harry.'

Harry hears a tune playing. Thirty-three is playing a tune, 'Waltzing Matilda'.

'Hey, Harry.'

Harry sees the four sevens. His mind sees the biggie. His eyes register four sevens.

'The biggie?' he says.

'Big enough,' says Vincenzio.

Harry sees four sevens.

'Four sevens,' he mutters. 'Four lousy sevens.'

'A nice hundred bucks, Harry,' says Vincenzio.

Vincenzio leaves to get the jackpot register. Soon he's back at Harry's elbow. He switches off the music.

'Sign for me, will you, Harry?'

Harry signs.

Vincenzio hands him a crisp new hundred.

'We're giving them away, tonight,' he jokes.

Harry presses the play button. The four sevens vanish.

'The big one next time, Harry,' consoles Vincenzio.

'Yeah, mate,' says Harry tiredly.

'Yeah, mate,' says Vincenzio, 'saw a sheila do it last week, up the Bulldogs. Pulled off a hundred dollars first, just like you did; then five sevens, straight up, ten minutes later; a hundred thousand; no shit, Harry.'

Harry sucks air. He feels strangely calm; deadened but calm. He lights up a cigarette. Vincenzio moves away. He draws on the cigarette. The smoke tastes good. He draws again, deeply.

'Thought you'd given them up, mate,' says a woman's voice.

It's Trish, the barmaid, collecting empties, wiping down the shelving around the poker machines. Harry looks at her. She seems different, older, much older. She stands up, straightens her back, looks up at Harry.

'You feeling alright, Harry,' she says.

Harry stubs his cigarette, gestures towards his empty glass which Trish has just picked up.

'Beer must be off,' he says.

'Maybe you ought to go and sit down for a bit, Harry.'

Harry frowns, thinks, punches Thirty-three.

'The pokies'll still be here when you get back, love,' adds Trish softly.

'Yeah, right,' says Harry, punching the reserve button.

Trish watches Harry move away. She can see the back of his head, the hair dry now, the wisps of grey showing, the skin on the back of the neck beginning to wrinkle, the horizontal axis of the shoulders beginning to sag as though bearing heavy weights.

27

Harry rounds the green glass screen. His body is slumped and his head hangs low. He feels cheated. He is thinking that his hundred-dollar win isn't a 'real' win, just stake money, enough to help him keep on trying for the biggie, that was all. 'So what's new,' he snarls to himself, then hears himself mutter: 'Rosy,' and feels surprised that he has said the name, and allows the image of the big woman to appear in his mind's eye; and her smell, allows himself to conjure up the smell of her body; and her mouth. 'Bitch,' he says. He glances over to Waddling Thighs, sees her, hears her voice as she speaks to the player next to her. The voice is deep, carries over to him. She's cursing her bad luck. He shudders. He feels hatred for Waddling Thighs, sees the small boy again—himself?—squashed under Rosy's weight on the kitchen lino.

He takes a deep breath, heads towards the dance floor. The same people are dancing—veteran rockers mostly, paunchy men and sagging women, Nineteen-fifties teenagers dancing a slow foxtrot; plus a handful of youngsters shuffling awkwardly to the unfamiliar tempo, their heads already turning towards the upstairs disco; and, besides these, a few couples in their sixties, including the spritely Fred Donaldson, older than that.

Harry is almost at the Simpson woman's table before he sees her. Instantly his mood lifts. The woman is alone. She sits with her knees crossed. Harry can see her right foot; it hangs loosely over her left leg, swinging gently to the beat of the music. Between her fingers she holds a cigarette which she's smoking lightly, puffing pale blue smoke into the air. For a few moments that's all there is, all that's in his mind; for these moments there's no complication, nothing to disturb his well-being, just the presence of the women and himself. And then, curiously, he's in another reality, and has to catch his breath, and suddenly he's inhibited, uncertain about whether to act, how to act; and anxious; and afraid; and his feet want to tip-toe away, like a guilty child come upon adults engaged in adult behaviour, as though he truly is a child, a child struggling to turn a big latch-key, a child awakening from a dream, fearing the dream is reality. Then the woman turns her head, but only slightly and not yet far enough round that her eyes fall naturally on him, and so he pauses, then freezes in his step as the women holds her position and still does not see him. For a few seconds both he and the woman remained unmoving, he, his instincts confused, she, her head held high, like a cat poised, waiting for instinct to trigger response.

Harry almost returned to the Pokie Lounge. He wanted to scurry back there, back to Thirty-three. He wanted to giggle, to break out into a giggle, like a kid, giggling like a kid, giggling at his idea that Thirty-three was like his mother. Yet she was like his mother, hard-edged, like his mother, and cold, and did not care about him, did not care enough about him to give him what he really wanted. Four sevens. That's what she'd given him. Four lousy sevens. She'd paid him off, just like his own mother had paid him off with that lousy three hundred quid from the sale of the Rozelle terrace. No, Harry didn't want to go back to mother. Or father. But Flan was dead. His father was dead. That part of him was dead. That part of him? What part of him? His dead father. He remembered his father's dead face. The dead mouth. He remembered the dead mouth. In 1963. The year after he'd met Doreen—Jesus! could this woman be Doreen? Did Doreen smoke cigarettes? He couldn't remember if she smoked cigarettes. But the woman looked like Doreen. Maybe he wanted her to look like Doreen, to be Doreen. Jesus! she looked like Doreen. From the back anyway. Maybe that was why she'd made him think about his father, about Flan O'Brien? Why was everything so confused? Why did he feel so confused? Standing there. Behind Doreen. Doreen? She wasn't Doreen. Then why was he thinking about Doreen? Jeez! he hadn't seen Doreen in over twenty years.

1964. The year he'd last seen Doreen. But he'd met her in 1962. He was sure of that. 1962. The year they discovered his father's illness. The illness which finally killed him a year and a half later—helped to kill him, anyway; illness or not, Flan was quite capable of killing himself. The illness just brought the event on a bit sooner, that was all. '...Nothing to be alarmed about at this stage, Mr O'Brien, but make sure you take this course of anti-biotics—it ought to shift the bronchitis—and then rest in bed for a couple of days at least—I'll give you a note—and, er, yes, try to ease up on the smoking, and, yes, the drinking. Oh, and maybe we should book you in for a chest X-ray; you know, just to be on the safe side,' so advised the busy GP with the deadpan expression who Flan was compelled to visit one morning when he'd had more trouble than usual catching his breath, and had brought up red-stained phlegm for the first time as he coughed and spluttered and cursed, and, judging by the sound it made as it struck the cement-rendered bathroom floor, broke something made of glass—deliberately because of his rage—in between pauses when he had to hawk into the toilet bowl, or cling to the wall as he heaved to catch his breath: and—before the need for the GP had become obligatory—all of which having more or less become routine performance (except when Flan found himself still drunk when he awoke in the morning which discovery placated the demons inside him somewhat), therefore did nothing to permanently dampen his bad temper; or convince him of his certain mortality; or thus ('Fuck the doctor! What would he know'?) encourage him to stop chain-smoking unfiltered cigarettes, a number of which he somehow managed to consume as he floundered like a beached sea elephant all over the bathroom; or to refrain from staying out late drinking his usual fill which would have pole-axed a dozen average boozers; or from bringing home some worn out old tart now reduced to cadging hand-outs from has-been lady-killers like Flan O'Brien who want to but haven't a hope of getting it up and so are forced to make do with the comfort and security of a warm female body while they sleep it off.

A warm female body? Harry knew all about warm female bodies. He clears his dry throat. The woman turns, sees him, then betrays herself by blushing deeply and fumbling with her cigarette, trying to stub it in an ashtray but managing, in her nervousness, to drop it on the edge of the dance floor. Harry bends down and quickly picks up the cigarette. He sees the sexy red smear of lipstick on the filter tip. He fingers the still smouldering cigarette for a moment, drops it into the ashtray.

'Oh, thanks,' says the woman.

Harry smiles.

'Saw you were on your own. Thought you wouldn't mind if I said hello.'

Harry has sudden fear she was going to refuse.

'Why not?' says the woman. Her voice is less hesitant than her face.

He sits down, offers the woman a fresh cigarette, helps her light up.

'Sorry about that mix-up in the carpark,' he says lightly.

'That's alright.'

'Caught my shoe in a snag.'

'Oh, right. Er, your leg...'

'My knee—it's okay.' Harry recklessly slaps his knee. 'It's nuthin; right as rain.'

'That's good.'

She looks away, suddenly blushing again, as though her comment was more intimate than she'd intended.

Harry says: 'Met your husband—er—Andy, right?'

'Yes.' The woman utters the word without emotion. And the blush is fading.

'Nice bloke, real friendly.'

'Oh, he's always been a friendly bloke.'

'Met him in the change booth queue; had a chat with him.'

'Yes, he told me.'

'Won't bother him...' says Harry—the woman's eyes lift—'I mean, if we have a little chat ourselves.'

The woman smiles, shows Harry her teeth. Harry feels his heart leap.

'No, it won't bother him.'

'Or, maybe have a dance?'

'No, he won't mind.'

'And you? Would you like to dance?'

'Yes, okay.'

Harry stands up, gallantly taking the woman's hand, noting her palm is moist—a dead giveaway, he reminds himself. The woman rises out of her chair. She is more petite than he'd realised. She misses his shoulder by a good nine inches. He feels good to be so much taller than the woman.

They both pause to stub their cigarettes.

Then they dance. Despite the incongruity of their sizes they dance well together. They dance in silence. For the time being the music and the movement seem enough. Later, perhaps, it will be time to pursue risk. For the moment, both seem content to let McCartney play the tune, to let him drift them into the pleasure of their still uncommitted intimacy—'*Yesterday... all my troubles seemed so far away...*'

Harry closes his eyes. The music is so familiar, the song so reminiscent of another time in his life, his mood, now he is holding the woman to him, so changed, that it seems natural for the delusion to insinuate itself into his mind, behind his closed eyes, that it is 1964 again, and that it is Doreen here, in his arms, the sexy little Doreen. He dreams up the image of Doreen. She was a hellcat alright, that Doreen, a grown-up version of Tanya, better than Tanya, softer, softer in the body, but firm, not bony, not bony-shanked, bony-hipped, like Tanya, soft but firm, and round, like the feel of this woman's hips, the roundness just below her hips, which he can feel moving under his hand as they dance; and her breath, warm breath, slightly smoky, and her smell, the odour of female sweat, and her hair, smelling freshly washed, hair, smelling like, like... Harry sighs, frowns, then smiles, then thinks—like Joanie, yes, Joanie, not Doreen, Joanie, yes, Joanie, it is Joanie's hair, the smell of Joanie's hair, the same smell, the same fresh smell, the smell he remembers filling his nostrils as she comes out of the bathroom, smelling so fresh, her hair in wet ringlets, wet honey-coloured ringlets, Joanie's hair, Joanie's smell, Joanie there... And she is happy; Jesus! they were both happy. He holds the woman closer, tighter, feels her stiffen, then relax, surrender—just like Joanie.

'Like old times,' he says softly.

The woman does not answer. She thinks the big man's comment strange; it does not occur to her that she is being transformed into Harry's wife.

28

It's 1964. Spring almost become summer. November warmth, still pleasant, still mild, the air not yet so humid it stifles breath. The day Harry and Joanie moved into Marsden Street.

It was good for them to move, to get away from Una Thomas, from that demented silence. Mrs Thomas remained unaware they were leaving. She hadn't spoken for three weeks. There seemed no point in making further effort.

They took everything they owned with them. Their belongings, mainly wedding presents plus extra linen and kitchenware collected by Joanie in the months before the wedding, just fitted into the backseat and boot of the car. They needed no bed, no table and chairs. Marsden Street was furnished with the accumulations of Col and Annie's forty-odd years of married life. Col wanted Joanie and Harry to use the furniture. 'It'd make Annie real happy,' he said cheerfully, as if she was still there.

It was time for a new start; time, so they both thought, time to abandon their pasts. And so they could not get away fast enough. Both shared the same urgency as the car toiled away from Una's Lilyfield house. The car was low on its springs, fighting against its own age and the weight on its back axle. Yet the car, too, might have been collaborating in the escape, for it picked up speed quickly, quickly allowed Harry to change into second gear, reached the brow of the hill, seemed to sigh, then, as though happily, plunged down the hill past the university towards the city and the turn-off to the south which would, after the twenty minute drive, bring them all to Arncliffe.

Then they plunged into the task of renovating the house. They plunged into work, beavering away with mop and broom, with Bon Ami and Sunlight soap, and DX detergent and Gumption paste, and steel wool and paint scraper. They attacked the grime that had settled and solidified all over the house. They scraped and scoured, they shined brass and chrome, and polished wood, Col's dining room table, making it gleam with pride, and Annie's walnut china cabinet, and the floorboards in the dining room, and in the hallway. They removed faded lino from the kitchen, discovered old newspapers used as underlay by Col back in 1932, and read that Sydney's 'coat hanger' was opened in March that year, that, in April, the 'Nation [was] shocked' by the death of Pharlap... They tackled the painting, Joanie choosing the colours, Harry and Joanie applying paint, Col watching with shining eyes as the house was slowly transformed—dove-grey in the kitchen, chequered black and off-white tiles to replace the lino, pale saffron in the dining room, a warm gold satin finish in the lounge room, the bedrooms a soft lilac pastel.

Then the outside. They cleaned the gutters, and mowed the grass, and trimmed the shrubs, and weeded the garden, and pruned the hydrangeas that encircled the little house, and repaired the fence, and oiled the gates, and re-hung the lop-sided door of the garden shed.

And painted 77. And felt the house respond, felt it shedding dross, shedding neglect, felt it pulling itself together, straightening its shoulders, lifting its head up high. And Col's shrill falsetto, ringing out in glory as he sang the most wonderfully sentimental ballad under the shower in the now sparkling bathroom.

She was young and I was handsome
and she lived not far away
And I wooed her and I won her
My Annie, my Anneeee...
Oh, I wooed her, and I won her
On that fine St Patrick's day.

By Christmas number 77 was a house transformed. Col gazed open-mouthed at the new guttering, its unweathered galvanising glittering in the sun, and the fresh green roof, and green-framed windows like wide open eyes gazing out between white gleaming weatherboards, and post-office red paving paint on the steps leading up to the front veranda, and said dreamily, 'Annie would've bin' real tickled, so she would, real tickled.'

In those first months Harry was a new person. He was so enthusiastic, so passionate, so desperate to do Joanie's bidding. He wanted to please her, to make love to her desperately, sexily, sexily enough to risk embarrassing both of them in front of Col. He would arrive home from the store and bound up the red-painted steps, past Col who reclined, as he always did in the afternoons, almost horizontally on his deck chair and to whom Harry would throw a cheery 'G'day, mate' as he raced into the house, his boots shaking the veranda boards, then scoop up the tiny Joanie in his arms, and, without pausing, bundle her into the bedroom where he would make love to her behind the closed door, trying (usually failing) to avoid making tell-tale noises.

Harry's passion was not limited to sex. He liked his beer. Yet he wanted to do things which would prove how much he respected Joanie, how much he wanted, by his behaviour, to please her. So he would make the rashest of promises. He declared on one occasion, for instance, that he would give up drinking beer.

'No sweat, Joanie, I'll do it. Tell me you want me to stop drinking beer, and I'll do it.'

'Oh, Harry, you can't do that,' answered Joanie.

He loved her for saying this and felt wonderfully relieved.

Yet he did promise to cut down on his drinking. He knew he drank plenty, only as much as his mates though, not more than a dozen schooners in a session, not that he ever got really drunk, not roaring drunk like his father, never like his father, he could always walk straight and unaided after a session with his mates, and he never abused Joanie; Hell! he would and often did bed down on the couch rather than disturb Joanie's beauty sleep. And he'd shown his true mettle, hadn't he, right through 1965, by getting drunk only once (strictly speaking twice, except that the second time hadn't seemed to count), and that was totally justified, for it occurred aboard the boat they'd chartered to go up to the Hawkesbury in celebration of the Dragon's tenth consecutive Grand Final win...

'I've finished with the races,' he declared to Joanie. '

'That's good, Harry.'

'They're all bloody fixed, anyhow.' (He was pumped up with virtue after losing thirty pounds at Randwick.) 'A mug's game, betting on the horses.'

Yet he'd had it in his blood. But he kept his promise. He never did bet on the horses—well, only on Melbourne Cup day, which didn't count since betting on the Cup was like putting money on the plate on Sunday, wasn't it? So that explained the pokies, which, even though one form of gambling had been substituted for another, wasn't really the same thing, just a way of supporting your club and ensuring you got cheap grog and T-bone steaks— right? Anyhow, all he did was have a few quid on the two-bob machine, with a couple of mates, at the end of the week, on Friday night, when they were all relaxing over a few beers.

Then there was the war. They'd been real lucky. Harry missed out on the National Service ballot, was not invited to serve in Vietnam. The war, as for so many of his countrymen, merely passed him by. Except for a few troubling incidents which touched him personally like the one about

Gordie Sloan's cousin, who Harry had met a couple of times and heard had become transformed into a gung-ho soldier with no hope of reaching old-age, and whose mother had been flown to Saigon so she could be with him when he died of his wounds, then she'd died a couple of months later, and Gordie's uncle, the soldier's father, not long after that, and all that was left of that family was a name in bronze on the wall at the Canberra War Memorial.

Besides, Harry was married. And they'd met Col Maguire. A real lucky break that was. Meeting the old man who thought he knew Harry's great grandfather. Well, maybe so, maybe so. It was possible. Somebody had to have been Harry's great-grandfather.

29

Col Maguire only acted the comic role. It was his way of coping with life without Annie; hence the worm farm in the bath, which, though recognising its practical value, his neighbours thought hilarious, and his other eccentricities, making up the reputation—though perhaps not always as wittingly as he believed—he encouraged Marsden Street to accept, that he was an old man showing the physical effects of his age and maybe the symptoms of dementia as well. Privately, so far as his mind was concerned, Col believed he was unchanged from the days of his young manhood. It was his dilapidated old body that was the bloody problem.

The old man was a widower and childless; and lonely, and not thrilled about being eighty-seven years old; and despite his aching hips and his terrible wind problem and his fluttery old heart, given to imagining, as he lay in bed at night, that he'd still be able to manage a tumble with his Annie if only she were lying with him; and regretful that he had no children, no living relatives, that his few friends were dead; and himself, fast changing into an old fossil, left there like a memory of the distant past. And so, he was utterly delighted when Harry and Joanie moved in with him. 'Really glad yous two took the flat,' he mumbled self-consciously one evening after his meal of grilled chump chops and vegetables cooked by Joanie. He'd pulled himself to his feet, patted the tiny bulge of his stomach. 'Nice meal, Joanie,' he said. 'Just like Annie used to cook. Yep. Just like my Annie.' He stood still for a few moments, remembering. Then his eyes brightened as he thought of something. 'Don't go away,' he said. 'I'll be right back.' He shuffled over to his bedroom and Harry and Joanie could hear him rummaging in there. At length he reappeared, dusting off an old family photo album. 'Thought you might like to see some pictures of me and the wife, when we were younger, like.'

He had grown to love Harry, and 'little Joanie' as he called her. 'Yep: remind me of my Annie, you do,' he told her. 'She was a whippersnapper, too. Yep: nothing to her—a man could lift her up with one hand, easy like.'

Yet there was something on the old man's mind. The more he saw of Harry, the more he was sure Harry was old Lofty's descendant. His memory of the Irishman's features had grown dim, yet, as soon as he'd set eyes on Harry, he was sure he was looking at a young version of the old Irishman.

One afternoon in January 1965, as they sat together on the side veranda, enjoying the cool side of the house, it's north easterly aspect, with a whisper of sea breeze on their brow, Col talked to Harry. Harry was drinking beer. He'd just finished mowing the lawn. His skin shone with sweat. He sat with his back against the shaded veranda wall, alongside Col's deck chair.

'Strange thing, the way things turn out in life,' Col had said.

'Yeah,' answered Harry.

'Especially the way you meet people.'

'Hmm,' murmured Harry, 'that's for sure.'

'Like someone was directing it all.'

'You mean, like God, or something?'

'Well, maybe. Some people would say that, wouldn't they?'

'How about you?'

'Yep, it's possible. Take my Annie, for example; I mean the way we met.

That could have been His handiwork.' He turned, grunted as the movement triggered pain in his hip. 'You remember that Irishman I told you about once, the one who used to live down the Rocks.'

'Lofty?'

'Yep, Lofty O'Brien. Met him back in 1898; the year I moved to Sydney.' Col shifted in his chair. 'Yep, the tallest bloke I ever knew. Taller'n you, he was. Poor bugger was ill, though. Had a weak heart. A real shame; a big feller like that. Made him pretty useless for anything. Oh, he could still get around, and there were rumours he was still handy enough with the ladies.' He laughed, threw Harry a sly wink. 'Last thing to go, they reckon.'

Harry grinned. Even at twenty-one it was good to have such a widespread rumour confirmed by experience.

'Yep, well,' Col went on, 'as a matter of fact it was over a woman that we got into trouble the night I met the old feller. Down the Rocks in the 'Hit and Miss' pub. A rough old place it was in them days. Full of crims and guzzlers, real hard cases. Anyway, these two blokes came in, looking for Lofty. Two brothers they were, big fellers, and real mad. The biggest of them, the eldest, had this ugly looking knife. And he made it clear he was going to use it. He went straight for Lofty. Reckoned Lofty'd been at his sister, you know, against her wishes.'

'You mean, raped her?'

'Yep, that's what the brother claimed. Of course Lofty denied everything. Said he'd never ever seen the bloke's sister, that he wouldn't recognise her if she was standin' there in the bar.'

'D'you think he did it?' Harry asked.

Col shifted in his seat, took a deep breath.

'Well,' he said, 'he weren't no angel. That's for sure. Anyhow, without any warning the feller with the knife went for him.'

'So, what happened?'

'I hit him with a chair.'

'Yeah?'

'Knocked him out clean.'

'And the other bloke, the brother?'

'Oh, evidently he was only there for moral support. He took off.'

'What about the bloke with the knife?'

'Yep, well; I thought I might have hit him just a touch more'n necessary. He didn't move; didn't even twitch.'

Harry eyes widened.

'You didn't, you know...'

'No, Harry,' smiled Col, 'I didn't kill him. Just gave him a bloody good headache. Took his mind off Lofty for a day or two, though, I can tell you.' He paused to catch his breath, then turned and squinted at Harry. 'What I wanted to tell you was that Lofty gave me all his money.'

'He gave you money?'

'Yep. Fifty quid. Had it in a pouch under his shirt. Didn't like taking it; you know, him bein' ill, like. But he insisted. Said he'd only be robbed if I didn't have it. Anyhow, I bought a horse and saddle and some camping gear. You see I went out bush.' Col frowned. 'I weren't no angel myself, you know. And the cove I hit with the chair had friends in the police. So going bush was sort of obligatory, you see. Anyhow, I finished up boundary riding for a cocky out near Cobar. Yep. And managed to save a few quid doin' it. Never saw a pub or a sheila for weeks on end.' Col paused, sipped his beer, smiled. 'Helped straighten me out, doin' that boundary ridin',' he said. 'Gave a man time to do a lot o' thinkin'. Out there, where there weren't no-one except you and your horse, and your dog, and the fence. I had this beaut little cattle dog bitch, name 'o Lady, real intelligent—would bark at me when she saw a fallen post or a broken railing. Yep, you could do a lot o' thinkin', ridin' the boundaries.' Col smiled at Harry. 'Yep, owed the old Lofty quite a lot,' he said earnestly. 'And not just the fifty pounds, neither. You know, if I hadn't bought that horse and saddle, I'd 'a never met my Annie.' Col shook his head firmly. 'Truthfully. I'd 'a never met her.'

Harry swigged beer.

'How d'you mean?'

'She was the fifth daughter of the farmer I worked for. Reckon that's why he never made any fuss when I asked him if me and Annie could get married, him havin' just the one boy and six girls, like.' He eased himself from one hip to the other. 'Prettiest woman I ever seen,' he said. 'Pretty as a picture. Anyhow, whatever bad things old Lofty O'Brien might 'a done in his life—an' I reckon he'd 'a done his fair share o' them—he done a real good thing when he gave me that fifty quid. Helped me set up, it did. And find my Annie.' He cocked his head, looked earnestly at Harry. 'Yep. I reckon if it hadn't 'a bin' for old Lofty, I'd 'a never found my Annie. And, you know, I only knew him for that one night. Never saw him again. Heard they'd found him dead in his room. Just before I took off for the bush. Don't even know where the old feller's buried.'

———

He is in City Leagues, remembering—Lofty giving Col his fifty pounds, then the chain of events, Col meeting Annie the farmer's daughter, Col's marriage, the couple buying the house on Marsden Street, then, twenty years after Annie's death, Col renting Harry and Joanie the half-house.

Then, as though it was all a joke, a meaningless joke—

There is an old television set. A black and white set. It is in the lounge room. It flickers and makes flickering shadows on the walls. They are watching television together, he and Col, being intimate.,

They're laughing. They laugh together. It's fully shared laughter, a synergy of shared laughter. While he still laughs, Col starts coughing, coughing and laughing, and Harry is laughing, both are laughing, Col laughing with a blue face—for Christ's sake! a blue face; why the fuck would he have a blue face?—

coughing and laughing, Col trying to gulp tea, not even aware of danger, gulping hot tea, gagging, gagging on hot tea, coughing more urgently, not laughing, eyes bulging, coughing, bulging eyes staring, eyes staring at Harry, through Harry, not seeing Harry, Col's body crumbling, tilting forward, Col's arm outstretched, Col falling, Col falling before Harry can move to catch him, falling on the scatter rug in front of the couch, the rug Harry has bought Joanie for her birthday, the rug with the dark red roses and the green edging, and the white spaces, no—yellow spaces, pale yellow spaces, pale yellow spaces staining, turning brown, turning brown from tea drooling like thin spittle from Col's mouth, hearing that sound, the sound of a stick cracking, Col's outstretched arm breaking, as his body spreads itself, spreads itself over the rug, Col lying on the side of his blue face, the eyes open but extinguished, switched off, Col no longer there.

That was Harry's second big drunk of 1965. On the occasion of Col's funeral. Wilfully he'd drunk himself into his biggest ever stupor.

Later that night of Col's funeral he'd awoken to find himself in bed. It was dark. He could smell soap. Joanie had washed his body, somehow put him to bed. She was there, lying quietly beside him, he could hear her breathing, he could smell her hair.

'Joanie.'

'What time is it?'

'Three-o-clock, love.'

'What happened?'

'You fell asleep.'

'I passed out, didn't I?'

'Harry, it's all right, love.'

Then he remembered.

'Joanie, why'd he have to die?'

'He was a very old man, Harry.'

'But, but he wasn't even sick.'

'They go like that, sometimes, when they're very old.'

'But he was alright. He was drinking his tea.'

'Yes, I know, love.'

'He was laughing. We were watching TV. Christ! we were only watching TV.'

'Yes, Harry.'

'I had things to talk about, things to tell him.'

'Yes, love.'

'Jeez, we only met him six months ago.'

'I know we did.'

'I felt really comfortable with old Col.'

'So did I, Harry.'

'He was a bloody fine mate.'

Joanie moved; she cradled Harry's head in her arms. He was shaking, sobbing like a child. Joanie trailed her fingers lightly across his chest, soothing him with the touch of her fingers. 'Try not to worry, darling,' she said. She stroked his belly. She could feel the movement of him, tiny spasms of movement. Then they were both pushing, were joined, and Harry was sobbing, then coming, wantonly, like a young boy, doing it like a young boy, the miracle of the first time.

Soon, as though he truly is a child, she hums him to sleep.

An hour later, he awakes. It is very dark; he feels very strange, lies very still, strains to hear Col's breathing in the next room, as he has done before, often, fearing the old man has died in his sleep, as he has feared before, as he does now, his mouth is very dry, he cannot swallow easily, he gags, he licks his lips, has no spittle, he tries to lie very still, hears Joanie breathing, thinks he hears the familiar tiny snores in Col's room, the house is so quiet, he hears a board creaking, his heart leaps, Col is moving around, he listens for a while, hears more creaking sounds, he moves, he rolls out of bed, he crouches on all fours in the darkness, hearing the almost-quiet outside of the sleeping city, he shivers, pulls himself to his feet, stands still, feels the cool boards under his feet, 'Col,' he calls out in a loud whisper, 'Col, is that you, mate?'

He is dancing under the big chandelier, and music is playing, and a warm, sweet smelling woman is in his arms, and he is remembering more, confronting memory, calling it to him, recreating himself, in an act of will, forcing himself to remember Col's funeral, the cold wind blowing up from the south, the few mourners at the graveside, the surprising lightness of the coffin, the mixture of anger and fear and honour and pride as he'd carried the coffin from the church, as though Col was with him then, with him now, is it possible, is he drunk, as though his memories are his life, all he is, feeling the woman's warmth, feeling calm, able to think, to remember, face memory, discover memory, discover himself, remembering suddenly he is on Parramatta Road, on foot, heading for the city...

30

It was morning. There were trams. They squealed on their tracks. As though they were alive, and complaining, thought the boy Harry. There were people, mostly men, in worn suits with shiny elbows and shiny backsides as they rose up off the wooden seats, and polished shoe leather, and felt hats, on their way to work, clutching newspapers, trying to read in the wind. There were tram conductors, circus performers straddling the running boards, pulling tickets, calmly, as traffic whizzed by inches from their coattails. And cars and delivery vans and drivers wearing navy blue singlets and sweat-stained overalls and whistling at young women jumping off the running boards and hurrying away to become invisible in the crowd. And honking, and back-firing, and the smell of burnt oil, and diesel, and the groaning of springs, and the smarting of eyes from all the fumes.

He was on foot. Why was he on foot? He saw a motorcycle and sidecar combination gliding past him, its rider wearing a Second World War pilot's helmet. The bike was a 600cc BSA. He was on Parramatta Road, just below the Norton Street intersection at Leichhardt, then Annandale and Camperdown, then passing Sydney University, he stopped near Grace Brothers' Store on Broadway, he was hungry and thirsty, he hadn't eaten breakfast, and it was nearly mid-day, why hadn't he eaten breakfast? why was he so far from Rozelle? Was he running away from home?

At a Milkbar, he bought a packet of Smith's crisps and a Caramello roll, and a bottle of Shelley's Lemon Delight, exhausting his money supply; but he'd slaked his thirst, and the Caramellos gave him energy; the crisps he stuffed into his pockets for later. Soon he was passing St Barnabas' Church, then the Brewery, and looking up at the big clock on the tower at the Station, and crossing Railway Square, and entering the long tunnel leading to the electric trains. He found a men's toilet, felt very small against the big men urinating alongside him, for a while his stream wouldn't come, but then it had come and he watched it proudly and didn't feel so small as he splashed happily against the stained porcelain. He felt even more grown up as he washed his hands in the big hand-basin and dried his hands on the big roller-towel before heading outside onto the concourse, his hands now jauntily thrust into his pockets because he'd temporarily forgotten why he was alone and seven years old in a men's toilet at Central Station.

Then he was crossing Eddy Avenue and entering Belmore Park, and eating crisps as he sat on a park bench dangling his legs, letting the sun warm him, and feeding some of his crisps to the dusty pigeons which cluttered the path under his feet. An old man sat next to him. The old man smelled of sweat and stale wine and was dressed in stained clothing. He saw that the man wore two overcoats, a grey one and a blue one on top. He could see blotches of dark shiny stuff like dried cooking fat on the man's pants. He could see the top of a bottle sticking out of the man's jacket pocket. The man looked sideways at Harry.

'You by yerself, mate?' asked the man.

'Yes, mister,' answered Harry.

'Yer not with yer Mum and Dad, then?'

'No.'

'You got any money?'

'No.'

'You sure?'

'Not even a couple o' bob?'

'I spent it.'

The old man sighed.

'How come yer on yer own in the city?'

'I walked here.'

'Where from?'

'Rozelle.'

'That where yer live, is it?'

'Yes, mister.'

'You runnin' away from home, are yer?'

Harry stared at the man. He seemed very old to Harry. His eyes were red-rimmed and his hair wispy and thin, and his hands, clasped on his lap, were trembling slightly and covered in purple blotches. The old man took the bottle from his pocket. Harry could see it was wrapped in newspaper except for the couple of inches at the top of its neck. The old man drank deeply. Harry could hear the liquor gurgling down the man's throat. He'd heard that sound so often before.

'That plonk?' he asked.

The old man looked down at him in surprise.

'Yeah,' he answered. 'Port wine, mate.'

'My dad drinks stuff like that.'

'Yeah?'

'Makes him drunk.'

'Does it?'

'My dad's always drunk.'

'That why yer run away, is it?'

'No.'

The man drank again.

'He knock you around, does he?'

'No.'

'Feeds you well, does he?'

'Yes, mister.'

'Don't seem to me like you've got a good reason to be runnin' away from home.'

'It was Rosy.'

'Who's Rosy?'

'She comes home with my dad.'

'She's the girlfriend, eh?'

'She stays all night.'

'Yeah, I see.'

'She frightens me.'

'How's she do that?'

'She does things to me.'

'What sort o' things?'

'Things.'

'Things?'

'Bad things.'

———

He remembered the bad things. He remembered the bad things about Rosy and about his father. He remembered how, as Flan O'Brien grew older, Flan's taste in women grew coarser, how he began to bring home women he'd picked up in pubs, or on the street, inner-city tarts, the dregs of Sydney's low life, women who, while their legs were open, sometimes smoked cigarettes and drank liquor, who, while Flan snored on the couch after he'd done with them, often unclothed, sauntered shamelessly past young Harry's staring eyes. And they were all big women, women with painted mouths and dyed hair, women with swinging breasts, degenerate women with dried up fluids smearing their underwear.

'Ooh! there's a little kid,' one of them leers at the nearly seven-year-old boy who sits on the floor with his back to the wall.

'That's Harry,' says the father.

'Mother of God! What sort of a name's that for a little tyke?'

The woman is about thirty, big and buxom, with fat cheeks and beady, short-sighted eyes, and sweaty armpits, and smeared lipstick, on thick lips, the colour of bull's liver. She's drunk. She sways above Harry like a giant, rolls her eyes at him.

'G'day, Harry,' she says as her outstretched fingers stray towards his crotch.

'Bet you ain't got one as big as your dad's, have yer, sweetie?'

Harry squeezes against the wall.

'Got what?' he says and the woman bursts into a cackling laugh which sets her breasts wobbling and sends the smell of her breath all over the boy's face.

'Ooh, he's a regular comedian, ain't he, this son of yours.'

She moves closer to the boy.

'Maybe the little bloke needs a bit of comfortin'.'

She pushes herself even closer to Harry, presses him against the wall. Then she is pressing her swollen nipple into his face. She pants like an animal. She tries to make him take the nipple into his mouth. Suddenly he cannot breathe. The light grows dim. He tries to push himself away.

'Hey, don't yer like it'? shouts the woman. 'Hey, Flan, this kid of yours don't like me titty?'

'Let me go,' he manages to yell. Now he is trying to slide away, under the woman's body. Her backside seems enormous, she sits on his legs, pins them on the floor. Her crotch is open, he can see black hair and the loose flab of her thighs flattened on the linoleum floor. Then he is suffocating. His lungs claw for air. On the couch he sees his father, clutching his bottle, leering at him through sodden eyes.

'Give it to him, Rosy. Give it to the little bugger.'

Harry faints.

When he came to he was lying in bed. Rosy was bending over him. He could smell her; it was strong and pungent and made him feel sick.

'He's alright,' she was calling out.

'Come back in here, then, will yer?' yelled his father.

Rosy looked down at Harry. She towered over him. She had a hard face and hard eyes.

'You stupid little bastard; why'd yer go an' faint like that? Scared us all shitless, yer did!'

The next morning she said to him: 'Listen, kid, do as yer told an' yer'll be alright. Otherwise, look out. 'She glared warningly at him, 'I'm livin' here, now, mate; at least while yer mum's gone. An' what I say, goes, okay?' He didn't reply and she leaned her hand on his chest, pressing him against the wall. 'An' don't you go gettin' no big ideas, matey; I don't want no trouble with you.' They were in the kitchen, near the back door. Rosy reached out to turn the big back door latchkey. Even she had trouble with it and she squeezed and grunted until the big key turned. 'There,' she said, 'An' don't you think about leavin' the house unless I tell you.'

Once he tried to talk to Flan.

'I don't like Rosy,' he said.

Flan had looked at him. He wasn't drunk. He'd just arrived home from work. But he'd opened his first bottle.

'What's yer problem with Rosy?'

'I just don't like her.'

Then Rosy came into the lounge room. She saw the look on Harry's face.

'What's the matter with the kid, Flan?'

'The little fella doesn't like you, Rosy,' he said.

'Don't he, then!' She turned to Harry. 'Oh, and what don't yer like about me, kid?'

Harry was close to tears. He was frightened. And he hated his father for not sticking up for him.

'I don't like you staying here,' he said. 'I want you to go.'

Rosy's eyes opened wide. 'Why, you cheeky little bugger,' she said. She turned to Flan. 'Flan; tell the kid I'm stayin', right? As long as I want to.'

Harry remembered standing in the room that day, looking at his father. He remembered his father's eyes, how dead-looking they seemed. 'Just do what Rosy tells you,' Flan said, then sat down and began the night's serious drinking.

Harry began to believe he would never escape from the prison Rosy had built around him at home, which he had to come back to every day after school, for she stayed in the house all day, in the morning drinking coffee, chain-smoking, watching TV, then getting into the liquor and drinking half a hip-flask of whiskey as regular as clockwork every afternoon so that she was all sexy and ready for it when Flan arrived home from work.

He watched them having sex. Through the keyhole of the lounge room door. Rosy liked it on her back; he watched her with her fat thighs wrapped around Flan's backside, and heard all the weird squelching sounds they made, and wondered why they were doing what they were doing.

And then he came down with measles, and had to stay home in bed, in a darkened room, and he discovered Rosy had locked his window and that all the other windows were locked, too. Then, one afternoon, when the illness had all but run its course, she'd come to him and flopped her huge body down on the bed alongside him. For a minute she lay there in silence, watching him, not yet touching him, just watching, and looking, and looking at him all over so that he began to understand what was on her mind.

Then she'd played with him and tried to put him inside her, and he'd just had this little stub of a cock without any strength in it, he remembered, and she'd got angrier and angrier and more and more frustrated as she tried to get him on top of her then got herself on top of him so that he had that horror of suffocation again and struggled and wriggled while she tried to get a feeling off him.

After a while she went away, and he'd dressed himself. He could see himself getting dressed in the Rozelle bedroom. He could remember how shaky he'd felt from being in bed for a week. Then he'd gone downstairs and tried to get out of the house, and the key seemed so tight and as he wrestled with it Rosy came in holding her bottle and she was getting drunker than usual and she put the bottle on the kitchen table and stood there swaying with her hands on her hips and a look of pure hate in her eye.

'An' where the bloody hell d'you think you're goin?'

'I'm just going outside,' he'd whispered.

Rosy thrust her face close to Harry's.

'I thought I told you, you weren't goin' anywhere 'less I said so.'

Then she grabbed his shirt collar and yanked him forward. He lost his footing and fell against her body. He could smell her whiskey breath, and he felt sick, and struggled to escape and pulled back from her while she tried to grab him with both hands. Again he remembered kicking her shin, hearing her scream, her cursing him, him head-butting, biting, them falling, wrestling, then underneath her, the way her body smelled, him swooning, struggling to escape, escaping, on his feet again, kicking, kicking her face, her eyes, her limp body, her shallow breathing, the sticky dribble on the kitchen lino, him realising she was unconscious.

He was half a mile past the Victoria Road intersection on Darling Street before he pulled up. His mind boiled with anger and fear. He started walking. He walked all the way to Belmore Park in the city.

Later, as he walked back along Parramatta Road, he saw someone who reminded him of Rosy coming towards him. Panicking, he darted away, wanting to escape, intending to cross to the other side of the busy road. In his haste he crashed into the side of a car which was just pulling to a halt. He fell stunned on the roadway. He awoke in hospital with Flan and Raelene standing near his bed. There was no sign of Rosy and no memory of her remaining in Harry's mind—Except for now—

'Is everything okay?' says the woman he's dancing with. He looks down at her. She's frowning. Suddenly he realises how tightly he's holding her. He slackens his fingers, feels her relax in his arms.

'Yeah, everything's okay,' says Harry.

31

Everything could have been okay thinks Harry, everything was okay, long before old Col died, before he'd met old Maggoty, when Harry was just a kid, living in the Rozelle terrace, after Rosy had gone, wherever she'd gone—maybe he hadn't kicked her to death that afternoon in the kitchen after all? And old Col? poor old bugger dying like that, his arm cracking like a dry twig poor old mate, falling on the floor, tea spilling on Joanie's scatter rug, the rug he'd bought her for Christmas, or was it her birthday, Mrs Reilly coming to the house like that, that morning, and the helmet...

Harry did get a flyer's helmet. The helmet belonged to Mrs Reilly's son, Tom, who'd been a rear-gunner with Bomber Command and what was left of him buried in Holland. His effects had been sent to his mother, among them the leather helmet which, though Harry never found it out, wasn't Tom's issue helmet, but a First World War souvenir Tom had bought for good luck in London's Soho. He was given the helmet in 1951, when he was seven years old, on the day after he was brought home from hospital. He'd had a white bandage around his head, and his head was still sore, but he felt important, he knew the goings-on in the house were about him. There were people in the lounge room, Flan was there, and Raelene, and a lady with grey hair and a friendly face who he found out later was Mrs Reilly, and a grim-faced man dressed in a dark suit holding a felt hat in his hands and listening to another woman who was dressed in some sort of uniform and who was doing all the talking and saying things which seemed to make Flan's head hang lower and lower and his mum's eyes stare harder and harder through the window.

After a while Mrs Reilly had taken Harry from the room. While Harry and Mrs Reilly waited in the kitchen, the sounds of voices rose and fell in the lounge room. Harry could hear the woman in the uniform speaking. She was saying things to his mum and dad, and they were responding, Flan loudly at first, his bluster echoing round the house, then, like a squall subsiding, dropping to a murmur. Finally, the man with the hat spoke. He had a deep voice and he spoke slowly, deliberately, as though he was reading out a list. Then there was silence, and out there, in the kitchen, Mrs Reilly was rummaging in the big black handbag she always carried and pulling out the flying helmet.

'How would you like this, Harry?' she said.

Harry stared at the helmet. It was dark brown, and stained, and had leather straps. It seemed such a wonderful thing to him.

'Yes, thanks, Mrs Reilly.'

The old lady gave him the helmet. Harry felt its softness in his hands. The softness made it seem warm and friendly.

'Now you have to take good care of it, love,' said Mrs Reilly. 'That helmet belonged to my Tom, you know.'

Harry looked up at Mrs Reilly. She was a slightly built woman in her fifties, with sad kindly eyes. Today, though, as she looked at Harry, saw how he held the flying helmet, saw how he curled his fingers round it as though he was already aware how precious it was to her, she was smiling, and her smile all but made her sadness disappear. And she made Harry feel suddenly secure, as though this older lady had been sent to him, to give him the helmet.

'Gee, thanks, Mrs Reilly,' he said.

Mrs Reilly's smile widened.

'You know, Harry, you remind me of my Tom. Just like you, he was. Just the same sort of really nice young boy.'

She touched Harry's forehead gently with her fingers, below his bandage. The fingers felt really soft to Harry, and warm, like the flying helmet.

'And how's your head feeling, you poor young feller?'

'Real good, Mrs Reilly,' said Harry.

Raelene had employed Mrs Reilly to look after Harry. Later, after the others had left, his mother came out to the kitchen.

'You'll be moving in with Mrs Reilly, Harry,' said his mother. 'She'll be looking after you from now on. And don't worry about your father. I've spoken to him. He won't bother you.' Then she handed Mrs Reilly some money and a piece of notepaper.

'That's where I'll be,' she said. 'I'll send you another fifty pounds in three months.'

And that was it. That was all she said, her speech, like her manner, peremptory as always. Then she was gone, his mother, a stranger to him then, a stranger now, a tall, handsome woman more shadowy than real.

———

Mrs Reilly lived a few streets away from the O'Briens. She was a widow. Her husband had died in 1918. He'd been killed near Villers Bretonneux in Northern France. He was buried there. On the mantle-piece in her lounge room she kept a photograph of him alongside one of her son. He was dressed in khaki. He looked very young. The photograph had been taken in Sydney in 1915. The face was smooth, boyish, smiling. The father and son might have been brothers.

'Do you like ice-cream?' Mrs Reilly asked Harry that first morning.

'Rather have Caramellos.'

They bought Caramellos at the corner shop. As they stood outside the shop Mrs Reilly said: 'Harry, why don't we go into town?'

Harry's eyes lit up.

'On a tram, Mrs Reilly?'

'Yes, dear, on a tram.'

They sat next to one another on a tram, all the way from Rozelle to Circular Quay, stickily sharing Caramellos, watching the inner suburbs going about their business, enjoying the wind on their faces as the tram ploughed along its shiny tracks. Harry's cheeks were glowing. He felt so full of freedom; it welled up inside him as the roadway swept by under his feet. He forgot the soreness in his head. He felt so good to be alive. He found his eyes looking at Mrs Reilly. She was already smiling at him. When she smiled her face seemed very soft. Harry suddenly knew he would be very safe with Mrs Reilly. She was slightly built, just a slip of a woman, not strong, even to the small boy she seemed a little fragile. Yet he felt very secure next to her, and the feeling was very new and satisfying. Harry offered Mrs Reilly another Caramello. Her smile broadened. 'Why, thank you, Harry,' she said. The chocolate coated sweets had softened in the heat of his palm and Mrs Reilly had trouble freeing the one which poked out of the top of the roll. Harry pulled the sweet out for her. Mrs Reilly popped it in her mouth. 'Mmm,' she said. 'These are really good, aren't they, dear?'

They went to Luna Park on a white-painted ferry. It was a gloriously bright day on Sydney Harbour. Harry gazed upwards as the ferry sailed under the great bridge. It seemed as if the great iron thing was slowly moving, slowly moving across the blue sky. Harry's heart soared. Inside the fairground he went on all the rides which Mrs Reilly allowed him to. She watched him as he sped towards her down the giant slippery dip, as he squealed with pleasure inside a tumbling barrel, as he greedily drank a bottle of Lemon Delight in the great hall of the Fun House where they sat surrounded by kids and teenagers screaming with excitement.

Harry lived with Mrs Reilly for three years. They were happy, secure years, years he would always cherish. During this time he saw little of

Flan O'Brien. Their only contact was accidental, their only conversation a muttered acknowledgement on the rare occasions they passed by one another on the street. Raelene O'Brien supplied the money for Harry's upkeep. That was an obligatory part of the deal.

And then the illness, which Mrs Reilly had so carefully concealed from Harry, worsened. To Harry, she seemed just a little more tired than usual. Harry began to do new chores at home. He made freshly squeezed orange juice for her. She loved oranges. He would get up early and prepare the juice, then take it to Mrs Reilly still lying in her bed. He would watch her as she sipped the juice, and wonder at the expression in her eyes, the look which even to his then ten year-old experience seemed different from usual—maybe the eyes were a little more heavy-lidded, filled more evidently with sleep—but as he looked at her and Mrs Reilly smiled back at him and sent him messages of reassurance and love with her eyes he thought all was well and that her tiredness would pass and was nothing. He did not know how much energy she consumed to manage him that smile.

Then, one day after school, Harry arrived home and she was gone. He never saw Mrs Reilly again. A woman who he did not know was waiting for him, trying to tell him, yet not really telling him, saying something to him about how sad it was, that Mrs Reilly had had to go away because she was very ill, not telling Harry that Mrs Reilly was already dead, had been dead since nine-thirty that morning.

On the day Mrs Reilly died, Raelene hurried back to Rozelle, already anxious to set up alternative arrangements for him. She was all business-like and unsympathetic, made no reference to Alice Reilly, seemed oblivious of the small boy's anguish. 'You'll be living back home, with your father' she said, 'I'll get someone to do the house-keeping.'

In time, after the pain had eased, the boy would conjure up a picture of Mrs Reilly's face in his mind. Sometimes he would don his flying helmet as well and the feel of the softened leather on his head gave him extra consolation. He would remember that for three years he'd been Mrs Reilly's son, and he would imagine the soft leather encasing his head was the touch of Mrs Reilly's hand.

32

And then, suddenly, everything was Judy. Harry's whole life was Judy. She was everything to him. His friend, his companion, his mentor. Everything. Everything except his lover. Not yet. Not the lover of a boy of ten going on eleven. Not a lover like the lovers of his father who still came late at night to the house and carried on with Flan downstairs, while Harry lay awake, listening, and trying not to connect what Flan was doing with the thoughts he was having about Judy, and sometimes dreaming terrible dreams about Flan and Judy, and awakening in a sweat and crying into his pillow and clutching his flying helmet and chewing the end of the leather strap, and not understanding why he felt so lonely and afraid, and dreaming of Mrs Reilly sitting next to him on a tram going towards the city, and seeing her face and Judy's face becoming the same face in his mind, and wanting Mrs Reilly back and wondering what it was like for her in the box under the earth and whether she was alright, or wanted to get out, or was really dead and a skeleton.

Then, as though his grieving was truly ended, one night he dreamed a different dream. He dreamed about Judy, and she touched him, and their bodies were close, and he felt safe in his dream, and he saw Mrs Reilly smiling as though she was happy too, and he awoke feeling at peace, and he lay in bed for a while with his eyes closed, breathing easily.

Judy Connell was sixteen years old when Raelene hired her to housekeep for Harry and Flan. Except for the great difference in age, she might have been Mrs Reilly sent back to him, for she had the same nature, the same zest for living. She didn't just smile—she laughed; a bubbling, effervescence of a laugh that rippled joyfully out of her mouth and grabbed hold of you so that you became intoxicated by it and began laughing with her, laughing as though your body would break into pieces, as though laughter was the only purpose in being alive.

'I'm Judy,' she said on the day they first met.

Her voice was set high and it seemed to Harry as though tiny bells might have been placed in her throat for her voice tinkled joyfully when she spoke.

'G'day, Judy,' whispered Harry.

Judy laughed her laugh.

'No need to whisper, mate,' she said. Her eyes roved around the kitchen. She opened the kitchenette doors, scanning the contents. She leaned down. She was short and small-made, like Mrs Reilly, but young, so young, and the curve of her buttocks seemed so fine to the eyes of Harry as he watched her that morning, so fine that he felt strange new stirrings which made him shy and embarrassed so that he had trouble looking Judy in the eye.

Judy pulled out a brown paper bag. She peered inside it, took out an unwashed potato. She held it up, smiling.

'Hey, d'you like chips?'

'Yeah.'

'Then we'll have chips.'

She cooked chips and they ate them together. And Harry kept sneaking glances at Judy, amazed at how much she reminded him of Mrs Reilly, allowing himself to imagine she had come back to him, that she, Judy, was a young Mrs Reilly.

At the end of the week he bought her a roll of Caramellos.

'They're my favourite lollies,' he said.

'Mine, too,' grinned Judy, and she unwrapped the chocolate caramels and gave him one and it was the sweetest taste Harry had ever experienced and he let the taste remain in his mouth as long as he could.

'What do you do during the day?' he asked.

'I'm doing a full-time course at the tech.'

'What's that?'

'It's a business course. I'm learning about book-keeping, and office procedure, and typing, and shorthand.'

'Is it interesting?'

'Not too bad. I don't mind it.'

'What's it for?'

'Why, so's I can get a good position in an office.'

'Doing what?'

'Well, I'd start off as an office junior, doing filing, answering the phone.' Judy laughed. 'And probably making tea for the boss.'

'You make pretty good tea, Judy,' said Harry, blushing.

One Saturday they went out together to Drummoyne swimming pool. Harry saw Judy in her swimming costume for the first time. He saw how beautiful she was. And she could swim. Like a fish, he realised, like a wonderful, stream-lined fish, cutting through the water without effort, her head bobbing up at the end of the pool and she yelling out to him merrily:

'Come on, Harry. Get in. The water's great.'

He dived in and swam towards her. And when he reached her, they splashed each other, and laughed, and raced each other down the pool and touched at the same instant so that he felt he could match her at least in one thing, and this made him feel good.

Afterwards they drank milkshakes and ate ice creams at a milkbar in Drummoyne.

'How's it going at school?' Judy asked.

'It's okay.'

'Try to stick with it, Harry. You'll need it, your schooling, later on.'

'Yes, alright, Judy.' Secretly Harry knew he would do anything for Judy.

'Promise me.'

'I promise.'

'And make something of yourself, okay, mate?'

She was always doing this, trying to make him feel important, as though he had worth, as a person.

'Okay.'

'Like an airline pilot.'

'An airline pilot?'

Judy grinned.

'You've got the flying helmet already,' she said.

'That was Tom's.'

'Tom's? Who's Tom?'

Harry's expression clouded and Judy, seeing this, leaned towards him touching his hand gently. It was a strange experience that touch of Judy's hand, while they were talking about Mrs Reilly's son, and the flying helmet.

'Mrs Reilly's son. He flew in bombers. During the war.'

They fell silent. Self-consciously Harry pulled his hand away.

'She was really good to you, wasn't she, Mrs Reilly?' said Judy softly.

Harry nodded his head.

'I guess you'll always have really good memories about her.'

Harry nodded again.

'She was like my mum,' he said.

'You really loved her, didn't you, Harry.'

'Yes.'

Judy took his hand again, more firmly this time.

'And she'd be real proud of you, Harry, if you did something with yourself.'

'Like flying an aeroplane?'

Judy laughed out loud.

'Yeah, why not.'

As they walked back towards Rozelle, Harry asked: 'How long will you be coming to the house?'

When Judy answered his heart leapt.

'Your mother said as long as I like,' she said lightly. 'That alright with you, Harry?'

That night Harry lost himself in fantasies of the girl. She was like a warmness inside him. She was the most perfect thing he had ever known. That night, in his mind, he explored his way around her body, he became part of her; she became part of him; they became each other; her lips were his lips, her eyes, her face, her arms, her legs, her mouth, her teeth, her lovely crossed-over front teeth, Judy's teeth which she showed him so often, every time she spoke, every time she smiled, every time she laughed her laugh. He touched her in his mind, embraced her, held her to his breast. And he slept in her arms and felt so safe and so calm. And the great disturbances in his mind began to fade and he began to heal and he thought, even as a ten year-old boy going on eleven might think, that all was well, that his troubles were going away, at last.

Once, when he was eleven years old, he had to fight for her. Flan O'Brien had tried to take her from him. She'd arrived before Harry got home from school. They were in the lounge room. Flan had been drinking.

He was drawing on all his charm. He was flattering Judy, telling her how pretty she was, offering her drink, standing close, towering over her.

Harry saw them through the open lounge room door. He rushed into the room.

'She doesn't drink, dad.'

'What's that?'

'I said she doesn't drink.'

Flan stared at Harry for a moment, then spoke in a quiet, menacing voice: 'I'm going to have a little drink with Judy.' Harry stood his ground, saw Flan's face turn crimson with anger. His father raised his voice. 'With the baby-sitter,' he sneered.

Harry held his father's eyes, spoke to Judy.

'Come on, Judy.'

Flan crashed his bottle down.

'Why, you cheeky little bastard—' he shouted.

'It's all right, Mr O'Brien.' Judy broke in, speaking very firmly. 'He'll go.' She looked warningly at Harry. 'Won't you, Harry?'

'Not without you,' said Harry.

Flan looked first at Harry, then at Judy. Slowly his lips curled into a knowing smirk 'Aha; so that's what it's all about. You're having it off. You and the kid.'

Judy stepped forward. Her eyes blazed. She breathed in sharply through her nose, crashed her hand into his face. 'You mongrel,' she shouted, then slapped him again as he stood there, caught by surprise, his face smarting and his eye already bloodshot, but then he moved, lunged at her tiny body, grabbed her wrist and twisted it sharply so that she cried out in pain, and Harry jumped forward, his fists pumping even as he flung his body forward, his mind full of hate and murder. He slammed his body into Flan's back, smashing his fists into the soft region below the ribs. He struck again and again, hardly aware of anything except the redness in front of his eyes and the rage which now tried to burst out of his chest and gave him so much power. Vaguely, he was aware that Judy was crying out in pain. He kicked Flan's legs, searching for sharp bone, connecting. 'Let go of her,' he screamed. 'Let go of her, you mongrel.' And Flan was screaming and trying to fend off Harry with his free hand. Then Judy kneed Flan in the groin and he yelled out in pain and released her, and Harry hit him in the stomach and this made Flan double up in pain so that he reeled back, his face grey, his eyes popping. Suddenly the older man was done. He had no breath and his legs were bending at the knees.

'Okay, okay,' he whimpered.

He lurched forward and collapsed onto the couch. He groaned and began retching. He seemed very ill, yet Harry could feel nothing for him except the purest hate. 'And leave her alone,' Harry shouted. 'Leave her alone, you bastard. If you ever touch her again, I'll kill you!'

That night, Harry decided he was going to marry Judy when he grew up. He would become a pilot and marry her. He would wear his leather flying helmet as he piloted the aeroplane, and Judy would be sitting alongside, and he would be happy forever, and Flan would be dead, dead and gone, and all his women with him, and Rosy would never come back, and Judy would be with him, he would fly the plane, and Judy would be there, always, and he would take care of her, and marry her, and she would be his best friend, and she would take care of him.

33

There was the afternoon Harry waited for Judy. Everything seemed normal. He had no premonition of disaster. He was in love with Judy in the way an eleven-year-old boy, still to discover his sexual powers, expresses love. He would have gladly sacrificed his life for her. He would have thrust a dagger in his breast for her. Anything.

He expected her any minute. Normally she arrived about ten past four, after her last tech class, and they spent the next couple of hours together preparing and eating their evening meal. Flan was never home at this time. He had taken to staying out drinking late. Of course there was never any sign of Raelene.

At 4:30 Harry went outside and scanned Harbour Street for signs of Judy. There were none. He went back inside. Twenty minutes later he was back outside. It was a cloudy mid-August afternoon and already growing dark and it was difficult to see very far in the gloom. So he walked a hundred yards in the direction he knew she would be coming from, then another hundred yards, until he arrived at the busy Darling Street intersection. And saw no sign of Judy. He ran back to the house, thinking she may have come from the other direction. There was no one there. He went inside and turned the light on in the kitchen, and sat down, and waited.

At 6:00 he took out potatoes, washed them ready for cooking. They were having chips tonight. Harry had promised to fry chips for Judy. It was becoming a ritual; eating chips with Judy, as though to commemorate their first meeting, create a special intimacy, intensify their friendship.

Harry put the frying pan on the stove. He placed a slab of cooking fat near the frying pan. He opened the ice box, took out three lamb loin chops. Two for him, one for Judy. He took out the chops. Now that she was running so late, Judy would appreciate all his preparations.

Harry kept his vigil until 9:00 pm. He sat quite still, waiting. He remembered something. Yes, the uncooked potatoes were turning brown. He washed them under the tap, left them submerged in cold water. They seemed less brown. He stirred the water with his fingers. He decided the potatoes would still be alright. He examined the lamb chops. They were drying out as they sat on the wooden cutting board. He put them back in the icebox on a small white plate. He waited. He made himself stay calm. There was nothing wrong. She'd been delayed. That was all. There was nothing to worry about.

At 10:30 pm Flan arrived home. He let himself in by the front door. Harry was seated bolt upright, his ears tuned-in to every sound Flan was making. He listened for evidence that someone was with Flan. It was clear he was alone. He heard his father enter the bathroom, heard him coughing. He got a whiff of Flan's cigarette smoke. He heard Flan return to the lounge room. He did not expect his father to come to the kitchen. Nowadays there were no more attempts at communication. Not after that night. It was over. There was just a deadness between them.

At 11:00 pm the house was in silence. Harry sat alone. Flan was probably asleep on the couch. Soon he would begin snoring. Soon after that he would awake and need a drink, two drinks, then he would be asleep again. It was the pattern Harry knew well, the pattern of behaviour of his alcoholic father.

At 11:30 pm he heard a car pulling up and then the sound of footsteps on the street in front of the house. Then there was a knock at the front door. Harry rose to answer the door. He knew his father would have passed out and would not stir.

The two policemen were making enquiries about the whereabouts of Judy Connell. Her father had called the police. He thought she might still be at the O'Brien's where she helped with the cooking and cleaning. No, Harry heard himself saying, she hadn't been there that night. No, he hadn't seen her all day. Yes, he had seen her yesterday. Yes, he'd expected her earlier that evening. No, there hadn't been any misunderstanding.

The policemen thanked Harry for his help and left.

Harry returned to the kitchen. He sat down. His body was trembling. A kind of whiteness was forming in front of his eyes. He stifled the urge to cry. He wouldn't want Judy to come in and catch him crying. Not an eleven-year-old boy, going to high school next year.

Later he went to bed and lay awake all night listening to the sounds on the street, waiting for Judy to arrive.

She was never found. She simply vanished. Like a zephyr. Without trace. As a dream. As though there'd been nothing of substance. Only thought. Only imagination.

There was a big effort to find her. They put her picture in the papers.

It was as though Harry began to die on the night Judy disappeared. He is there now, still waiting in the kitchen, still hoping, still expecting to hear Judy's voice calling to him as she comes through the door:

'Harry, Hi, Harry, love. Are you there? Harree, I'm back.'

'Here, Judy. I'm in the kitchen, Judy.'

Except that he'd already be on his feet, running towards the front door, running to meet Judy.

'Gee, Harry, I'm sorry I'm late, love.'

'That's okay, Judy.'

'Hope I didn't worry you, or anything.'

Like an old married couple they were, he and Judy.

His Judy. Harry's Judy. Harry and Judy. Mr and Mrs Harry and Judy.

'No, she's apples, Judy. I knew you'd been held up or something.'

'That's right, Harry. Now, what are you giving me for tea, my love?'

My love! Oh, Judy, Judy, Judy!

But he's having a night out in City Leagues. How weird it all seems to him, that he's here under Dom's dome, dancing under the fluttering shadows, and re-living all of his life; as though instead of a handsome got-it-all-together dancing man he's really a small boy drowning inside himself. He wonders as he'd first wondered the night Judy disappeared if it is true that you can be partly dead while you are still alive; he wonders how much dead you can be before you finally stop being alive; he wonders this as he feels the warm female body next to him, as he senses her compliance, as he imagines first she is Joanie, no, no, not Joanie, Judy, oh, if only she were Judy, anguishes Harry to himself, dancing man, dancing under the dome, while he watches himself, or at least is watched by something which he senses is part of himself, as though there are those two of him there again, one who watches, one who acts; he wonders again how dead you can become before you stop being a real living person. He sighs. Yes, he truly is in Mid-City Leagues, moving with the woman, to the slow beat of a jazz waltz. He wonders who that different person is, if it is himself, or is he imagining everything, living through some kind of vision, this sense of something beyond his comprehension, beyond his grasp, memories of the boy, waiting that night in the empty kitchen, of the boy hoping against hope—

'I reckoned we'd have lamb chops,' he would have said.

'Terrific,' she would have said.

'And chips.'

'Yes, chips, Harry. Oh, I'm hungry. I had a really hard day, Harry.'

'And tinned peaches.'

Harry knew how much Judy loved tinned peaches.

'Peaches? Fantastic, Harry.'

Tears begin to well, and he feels ashamed, and alarmed that he might betray himself to the woman, and so, urgently, he holds her closer to him, feels her body touch him, yield, groove itself into him, insists to himself that she feels familiar, that her smell truly is familiar, the sounds of her breathing, the special way she has of inhaling, exhaling, the tiny tremors of movement in her living body, her beautiful small-made body, and yes, almost with a laugh because it is such a trivial yet so necessary a detail, the shape of her teeth. And yet.

And yet so much of what he had once been had been destroyed on the night Judy disappeared. He knew it now, as though it had just happened, as he'd sat quietly in the kitchen, waiting, listening, knowing that if he stayed calm Judy would be pleased with him. He sighed. He can feel the pain of that waiting now, and he groans a little. The woman's eyes narrow, flick briefly up at him. He does not notice her doing this, but continues to stare, and the woman drops her eyes, puzzled yet not questioning why she is puzzled, afraid that to do so might break the spell.

'Started playing league,' he mutters under his breath.

The woman frowns.

'Did you say something?'

'Started playing league.'

'Oh—I see, Rugby League—right.'

'Best thing to do.'

The woman does not think Harry needs a reply.

He'd begun playing football. Somehow he had to set free his rage. He thought he could do this through the brute physical violence of the sport. And he was growing tall, and thickening, adding muscle, his voice deep and man-like. Because he was fearless, on the football field he became feared. To suffer one of Harry's diving tackles became an experience worth boasting about. In the attack, the ball, once safely in Harry's hands, spelled doom for the opposition. He was unstoppable.

He was unstoppable in other ways. He became a much in demand stud, sought after by the best looking girls in town, girls like Tanya; Tanya who had become significant to Harry in so many ways, most of all because, on that day in his Rozelle bedroom, he'd secretly transformed the snorting scrawny-shanked Tanya into Judy Connell.

'Great band.' Harry hears the woman saying.

'Yeah.'

'Real sixties sound.'

'Yeah.'

He allows his right hand to move down her back, not too far down, maybe a couple of inches lower than before. He feels perfectly free to do this, as though it is his right, to stretch his fingers downwards so that they make contact with the pad of softer flesh around the hips. He feels the woman's body stiffen, move away a fraction. He pulls her back to him. She yields, he can feel her body relaxing, losing its stiffness.

He holds her even closer, close enough for intimacy. He is sure that, like his own, the woman's mind is made up, that all that remains now is to end the brief liaison in the usual way. And then, suddenly, making him nearly laugh out loud with the discovery of it, it is as though his lustful thoughts are of no consequence, which he marvels at, yet does not feel distressed by, and he begins to remember other things, as though the security of the woman's body, her nearness, the envelope of comfort and security she's created around him, has empowered him, given him back his strength. He resumes the exploration of his memory, putting more of the pieces together, reappraising all that he was, all that he'd feared he might yet become, had hoped desperately he would never become.

His father. He was just like his father. This was just what Flan would be doing now if he was Harry. Dancing with a woman he'd chatted up and expected to be having sex with soon—Yes, maybe he had grown to be just like his father? Maybe he'd failed to break away from his father's influence; maybe the family ties were too strong, the blood too thick? Yet it just wasn't true! Of course he hadn't become like his father! Not Flan O'Brien! Not like him! He, Harry, hadn't married a prostitute; a prostitute who'd stupidly (as she once told Harry in her cool way of speaking as though telling him it was raining outside) fallen pregnant with Harry after which Flan, poor, misguided Flan, had threatened bloody murder if she went ahead with her plans for an abortion, which she'd thus abandoned, and which explained why Harry was around instead of in Limbo waiting for eternity to end, and why Flan allowed himself to be destroyed by Raelene, who he wouldn't divorce, even though she promised him fifteen hundred a year for life, because, although he was a lapsed Catholic and probably excommunicated for all he knew, he had this crazy mixed-up idea that if he ended his marriage it would be like sinning against the Holy Ghost, for which sin Flan could never be forgiven even if he whipped himself day and night for the rest of his life, and which was why he stayed drunk nearly all of his life and hated Harry until his power to hate died from the exhaustion his body suffered from the drink and all the other abuses he visited on himself, and all he could do was pick up worn-out tarts looking for a warm bed on a cold and lonely night—Hell! he was nothing like his father, nothing at all. And he was sure as hell nothing like melancholic old Grandfather Denis, in his grave at forty, dead at thirty, depending on how you looked at it, yet in his heart of hearts he felt like his father (Why?), and his Grandfather Denis, and all the other O'Brien men, in so many ways, thinks Harry, with insight which is so vividly clear to him, and thus so full of threat that he stops abruptly in the middle of the dance floor, and the woman, caught by surprise, continues to move, and is almost separated from him, but then she swivels on her heel and recoils back into his arms with a sharp intake of breath, and he apologises, and they move off together, but Harry is thinking, and thus dancing like a machine, yet the woman is so bound up in her own reverie that she does not reflect on the possible meaning of his behaviour, but settles back into the gentle rhythm of the slow waltz, and allows the music and the mood and the nearness of the big man to continue their seduction, and she snuggles closer to Harry, and feels the warmth of their touching bellies, and feels her breath coming suddenly in shorter gasps, as though she's been running hard, and she makes an effort to hide this sign that she's becoming aroused, but Harry is in a different world and thinking about his insights, and trying to understand what they might mean, and becoming aware, as in a synoptic vision, that we are all part of each other, which after our anger subsides thus makes us so sad and inconsolable, even when our enemy let alone our friend dies, and we are left confused and wondering why we pulled the trigger, or dropped the bombs, or stabbed with the knife, or simply chose indifference.

As he dances with someone whose name he still does not know but is thinking this moment about Judy's hands with those lovely tiny fingers, then suddenly, disjointedly, about Doreen Wilcox one-time lingerie girl at Pollards, bit of drama queen that Doreen, but tremendous in bed, better than Tanya, more subtle, made him think he was dying with pleasure (Dying?), Doreen who'd loved him fiercely but not unconditionally, who he'd never married, even though, like Tanya, she'd reminded Harry of his dead Judy, and for all he knew, when he dreamed about it, was Judy O'Connell, and of Joanie Thomas, who he'd married just before his twenty-first birthday, Joanie who might have been Judy's twin sister, Joanie who Harry desperately wanted to be Judy's twin sister if she couldn't be Judy come back from her watery grave (somehow he'd always believed it was a watery grave, admitted to himself she was long gone to a watery grave, yet she swam so strongly, remembered Harry, seeing her lovely body cruising effortlessly down the

Drummoyne pool, and his hope soared again, that Judy was still alive, that she would come back to him, end all his waiting, come back to him), Judy who was now in his arms he wanted to believe, here in City Leagues, under Don's Dome, under the crooked chandelier, as they dance inside the crooked shadows which Harry thought he'd escaped from that day in the park, in Belmore Park? no Centennial Park wasn't it? an old man with a stink like fish guts, wasn't he? was he? and, and...

34

There are other, less visible, shadows under Don's dome. Despite her reverie the woman from the carpark feels them, they penetrate her space, shadows vaguely real, vaguely unreal, shadows she'd thought she'd be able to ignore, at least while she dances with the stranger.

Harry says:

'Your name wouldn't be Judy, would it?'

She likes his voice, the way it thrills her.

'No,' she says breathily.

'Oh,' he says.

'It's Joanna.'

'Joanna.'

Harry thinks: 'Joanna, Joanie, Judy.'

He holds the woman closer. She is like all his women; warm, desirable. She smells like women should smell. A soft sweet smell. Like Judy.

'Judy,' murmurs Harry as they dance.

Joanna,' she corrects him.

Joanna,' says Harry.

He closes his eyes. He is dancing with Joanna. He is dancing with Judy, with Joanie; it's all the same, Joanna, Joanie, Judy.

He whispers: 'It's hot in here.'

The woman laughs shyly.

'Yes, it's very hot.'

'We could take a walk outside, get some fresh air.'

The woman knows she's going to agree.

'Er, yes—yes—alright, then.'

Harry pulls her even closer, feels the strong softness of her between her hips.

And they're on the point of moving off the dance floor except that there's a man at the stranger's elbow, the little man with the olive complexion and the bow-tie who pays out the jackpots, a dapper little Italian-looking man speaking to the stranger.

'Harry.'

So that's his name, she thinks, Harry, not Jack, as he'd told her husband.

Now the little man is stammering.

'Harry...'

'Vincenzio, for crying out loud!'

Suddenly they're a grotesque trio dodging couples on the dance floor.

'Mate, it's Thirty-three; machine Thirty-three.'

Harry pauses abruptly. The woman, suddenly aware of people swirling around her, of eyes watching, pauses with him, her right hand still held in his left one, still connected with him, she deludes herself, still with him.

'Thirty-three?'

'Yeah, Harry. Someone wants to play Thirty-three.'

And then the stranger is pulling away from her.

'Harry,' says Vincenzio, 'twenty minutes, mate. You've been off the machine twenty minutes. They've been watching. This old couple.'

'Old couple?'

'Yeah, an old couple. A bloke and his wife. Visitors. Don't know 'em.'

Vincenzio is already hurrying away. 'Harry,' he says over his shoulder, 'make it quick, okay, mate.'

Harry turns to the woman. She's frowning heavily. 'Listen, love,' (Christ! now he's escorting her off the dance floor), 'I've got this machine, see.'

Oh, so he's got this machine, she thinks bitterly. She's being discarded for a bloody poker machine. She's just made the most daring, the most dangerous decision of her life and this bastard's telling her he has this poker machine. She's just agreed to throw away all constraint and fuck this stranger in the Hi-Ace and he has this machine! She should have known. She should have bloody known.

'Give us a few minutes, will you Joanie?' he says.

'Who the hell's Joanie?' snaps the woman, loud enough to make the heads of nearby dancers turn. What a bastard! What a mongrel! And then he has gone, and she's walking back to her table, and her fingers tremble and make the match flame quiver and then go out as she tries to light a cigarette, and she curses silently again because she's totally pissed off with Jack, Harry, whatever his bloody name is, and because she can now feel the eyes of other women smirking at her as she sits down, crosses her legs, wipes all expression off her face, lights up, sucks cigarette smoke deep into her lungs. 'Fuck you, Jack, she says under her breath, 'fuck you, Jack, Harry, whatever your fucking name is!'

35

The pokie lounge is going full bore. On the link machines, only Thirty-three stands silent. Harry's keys and handkerchief rest in the money tray and the credit meter shows his coin balance, but the reserve light has long since stopped flashing. As Harry arrives, Vincenzio is trying to placate the old couple now standing proprietorially in front of and close up against Thirty-three's window.

'I'm sorry love,' the club official is saying.

'He's bin' away nearly half an hour,' protests the old girl.

'Yeah, yeah, love,' replies Vincenzio. 'I'm real sorry.'

'Had to make a phone call—long distance,' mutters Harry.

The old girl's eyes flash suspiciously.

'Thought I saw you dancin' back there?'

Harry shrugged his shoulders.

'That was my wife,' he says matter of factly as though it's really the truth.

'Three minutes, Harry,' says Vincenzio unhappily. 'Then the machine's free; okay, mate?'

Vincenzio leaves but the couple stand their ground, close to Harry.

'We oughter be on that machine,' whinges the old girl to the back of Harry's head, then turns to hubby. 'Owes us a few quid, that number Thirty-three, don't it love?' As she speaks, the man playing Thirty-four alongside finishes off. The old girl swoops on the free machine, punches the reserve button. She smiles grimly at hubby, shrugs her shoulders. 'Okay, maybe this is the one, then, eh, love?' she says kindly to him. Hubby moves his silent lips as usual.

They all punch away. Surrounded by all the other punching players. As though their lives depend on it. Like breath in their bodies. For a few minutes Harry plays Thirty-three, carves his way through a few hundred coins, knowing he's in a dead spot, knowing he could easily run out of stake before the old couple. He squares his shoulders. Nah, he decides. Thirty-three would never give anyone else the biggie. Even if he runs out of money and they take the machine off him. Nah, 'course she wouldn't. Yet his nagging fear that she might persists. He speeds up his game. He counts his plays; estimates he's punching at a rate half a game faster than that of the old couple. He pauses. He's being stupid. He's using up his stake faster than they are. He slows down. They seem to slow down with him. They're pacing him, stalking him, hunting him. He slows down more. They slow down too, silently mocking him, intimidating him. A stool becomes free nearby. He grabs it, straddles it as before, feels the sudden relief as the pain in his knee subsides. Then he punches the reserve button. Suddenly he needs a drink. A good, stiff drink.

But he daren't leave Thirty-three. Not even for his allowed three minutes. Jeez! with the number of people at the bar, he'd need more than three minutes to get there, get served, and get back. He begins to feel panic. He feels himself breathing rapidly. Sweat forms on his palms. Jesus! He's leaving wet marks all over Thirty-three's play buttons. He makes an effort to control himself.

Then he scores a hundred pay.

He pauses, sucked in a deep breath, watches the credit meter trip over the three hundred mark—the safety margin.

He has an idea, turns to the old couple.

'Hey! How about I buy you both a drink?'

The old girl's eyes are glued to Thirty-four. Surprisingly it's the old boy who responds. He nudges his wife gently in the ribs. Without turning she speaks. 'I'll have a brandy; he'll have a middy o' new.'

'How d' you want the brandy?' asks Harry.

'As it comes,' replies the old girl without altering her rhythm.

'Half or full nip?'

'Whatever you can afford, matey.'

Harry punches the reserve button on Thirty-three.

'Keep an eye on this for me, okay?'

The old girl nods.

He hurries across to the Long Bar and orders the drinks. Trish, as usual very busy, moves her fingers quickly, from bar tap to new glass, to cash register, to customers with outstretched hands grasping change, grasping glasses, licking foam tops.

'How's it goin', Harry?' she yells.

As Trish speaks and Harry stands in the frantic swirl at the bar, the light behind his eyes grows dim, then a dizzy spasm smacks him hard inside his head and he falls forward, hands outstretched, grabbing at, mercifully finding, clinging to the bar rail. He closes his eyes, squeezes the eyelids tight, sees strange lights, strange shapes.

'Harry! Harry, love. You alright?'

Trish is staring at him. Customers are staring at him. But the light is returning. He looks at Trish.

'Think I've had a turn, or something.'

Trish pushes a liquor glass towards him.

'Brandy,' she says. 'Drink it.'

Harry drinks the brandy. The liquor hits the back of his throat. He feels better, then pushes himself upright, finds he can stand unaided. He looks around him, sees eyes, watching him.

'Gimme another one,' he says to Trish.

He clutches the second brandy, looks around the club, wonders why it all seems suddenly strange, distant, as though he's the only real thing present, as though all the activity he see's happening around him is happening on a movie screen, a screen inside his head, projecting all these images... God! the light. The bloody light's dimming again. He senses that the light is fading behind his eyes. He leans forward, slumping, grabbing at the bar rail again. He makes a tremendous effort to control himself.

He downs the liquor, shudders his big frame, closes then opens his eyes. The light is back, brightly, as bright as usual, yet now he has a feeling of intense fear. It is in his guts, in his kidneys, in the icy sweat on his palms.

'Where's Joanie?' he says in the strangest of voices.

He looks at Trish.

'Where's Joanie?' he repeats.

Trish is serving. She's missed what he said. 'Hang on, Harry,' she calls out.

Harry's eyes dart around the mixed lounge, searching faces. He cannot see Joanie.

'The pokie lounge,' he says out loud to himself. 'Must be in the pokie lounge.'

He picks up his tray of drinks, heads away, repeats, 'in the pokie lounge,' over and over again.

36

He's back at Thirty-three. That's Machine Thirty-three at Mid-City Leagues Club. Not up the Dragons. No, not the Dragons. Not St George Leagues. Not with all the old crowd. Only Gordie Sloan and Tubs Mackenzie, his old school mates, the only ones of the old crowd down here at Mid-City, fuckin' old Tubs, never smiled in his life, like his father before him, Tubs senior, the one with the clapped out Vanguard, no money for his own fuckin' funeral. Harry laughs, a thin, high-pitched laugh, not like his own laugh. Must be slumming it, he tells himself. That'd explain the brandy. He only drank brandy when he was out slumming it. With Joanie? That felt odd. Out slumming it with Joanie? He wonders. Yet how relieved Harry feels. A bit drunk, for sure, Hell! he'd had four nips of brandy. Or was it five? And God knows how many schooners. He giggles. Nah, he wasn't drunk. Only relaxed, That's it. Relaxed. Relaxed because he can see Joanie over there. She's at a dollar pokie, sitting down, next to some old bloke with a bald head and thick glasses shining like flamin' car headlights. Anyhow, she's being sociable. That was good. Help her with her shyness. Yeah, about time Joanie got out and met people. Blokes too. Harry isn't worried about blokes. So long as they're old blokes. He giggles. Old blokes who can't do nothing more'n talk about it. Ahh, breathes Harry, then tells himself, no need to worry any more. No need to worry.

He gives the old couple their drinks.

'Thought I'd lost the wife,' he says, grinning broadly.

The old boy snorts.

'Cheers,' says Harry.

'Here's lookin' up yer kilt,' says the old girl, knocking back the brandy.

The old boy sips his middy pensively.

Harry quaffs his schooner. He feels conversational.

'Wouldn't want to lose my wife, would I?' he says.

The old boy throws him an extra loud sniff.

The old girl smiles at hubby. 'You never lost me, did you, matey?' she says. This time the husband's sniff sounds different, more affable. 'Prob'ly because we never had no kids to mess us around, eh, love?' says the old girl as she punches Thirty-four. The tip of hubby's tongue moves out of his mouth tentatively, goes back inside. 'Or because we've always bin' good at havin' fun together,' continues the old girl, sucking her cheek. Then she pauses, and turns. The brandy is at work. She still speaks in the same sandpapery voice, but the voice is less coarse-grained, softer, more like a finishing paper, no longer interested in ripping off hunks of wood.

'You got any kids?' she asks.

'Yeah, I got a kid,' Harry says. 'I got a kid.'

He finds he had no trouble saying this—'I got a kid,' he, Harry, saying, 'I got a kid.'

'Yeah, a boy.'

He makes the barrels spin. Light from Dom's dome flashes on the spinning icons.

'What's his name?'

Harry turns to the old girl.

'Keithy,' he says easily.

'Keithy. That's a nice name.' She looks at hubby. 'Isn't it, love?' Hubby blinks twice. 'He likes that name. Don't yer, sweetie?' She puts down her empty glass, reaches into her bag, pulls out a fifty-dollar bill. 'Get us all the same again, love,' she asks her husband. 'We're not havin' too bad of a night,' she winks at Harry as the old boy glides away.

Harry sees the old girl's eyes are friendly, that she's smiling.

'Your name wouldn't be...' he begins.

'Johnson. We're the Johnsons.'

'Oh.'

Not Maguire, registers Harry, not Maguire. Not Annie Maguire, he thinks stupidly, drunkenly.

'O'Brien,' he hears his voice saying. 'Harry O'Brien.'

They shake hands like a couple of men. Mrs Johnson's palm is warm but dry, her handshake firm.

'How're yer goin'?' she says affably.

The machines wait while Harry and Mrs Johnson chat. They chat about pokies, about winning at the pokies, about their triumphs, not a word about their losses this time, not at this stage in the night's game—no point in upsetting lady-luck, not when both of them secretly know the biggie's real close.

'Saw thirty-eight thousand go off the other night,' says Mrs Johnson. 'Out the Sharks. That's our club. A couple of kids. My Gawd, you should of seen 'em. I'm tellin' yer, mad they was; went off their brains.' Mrs Johnson rasped out a chuckle. 'Jumpin' and yellin' all over the club. Turned out both of 'em were unemployed, and up to their ears in debt. Yeah, thirty-eight thousand dollars they won.'

Then hubby's back. Mrs Johnson hands Harry his beer, picks up her double brandy, winks at Harry, winks at Hubby.

'Here's lookin' at yer,' she says and downs the liquor as though it might have been lolly water. She smacks her lips. 'This here big feller's Harry O'Brien,' she says to Mr Johnson.

Mr Johnson makes some friendly shapes with his mouth.

'Don't say much, my old Tom,' explains Mrs Johnson.

They resume their games.

'Keithy,' says Mrs Johnson in her new conversational style, 'How old is he?'

'Thirteen.'

'A big bloke is he?'

Harry smiles. 'Keithy? yeah, he's a big bloke.'

'Look like you, does he?'

'Not really,' answers Harry.

'More like the wife, then?'

'Yeah, more like the wife.'

37

In fact, just about everyone at the Dragons said that Keithy had his father's looks. Only Harry seemed certain that they were all mistaken, that Keithy favoured Joanie. 'What's wrong with yer?' he would say in genuine consternation. 'Jeez! he's the image of his mother.' And he would peer at his son, and see Joanie's replica before him, the same Joanie eyes and nose, the same long oval face buried under the chubby cheeks, the Joanie eyes staring upwards, the Joanie lips forming the same Joanie mouth. And he knew that Keithy would have the same Joanie teeth. He longed for the time when Keithy would have teeth; he was convinced the front ones would be crossed over.

Then, as the months passed, as though Joanie's features did not count, were not needed, as though they were still guiding the fortunes of their descendants, Roderigo and Mary Cathleen began to imprint themselves on the boy's features. And Flan O'Brien. Keithy began to develop into a replica of Harry's dad.

Harry insisted the boy resembled Joanie.

'Course he's like his mother,' he pronounced to the blokes at the club.

'That's a relief,' they joked.

'I don't reckon you can tell,' said the resident expert on these matters.

'What do you mean?' growled Harry.

'Takes at least a couple of years,' said the expert.

'He looks exactly like Joanie,' insisted Harry.

'Nah, mate, takes a couple of years,' insisted the expert.

'Listen, mate, he's got her eyes, blue-grey ones.'

'Eyes can change colour.'

'And her nose. He's got her long nose.'

'Harry, the kid's too young, I'm tellin' yer,' said the expert. 'It's because of their bones. Their bones are like a kind of stiff jelly. Don't have any permanent shape in them. That's why they all look the same—new babies, I mean. That's why they sometimes get 'em mixed up in the hospital.'

Harry was unconvinced. 'No chance Keithy got mixed up,' he said. 'The kid's the spitting image of his mother.'

An hour later, when nearly everyone had gone home, Harry said:

'Still reckon the young bloke's the spittin' image of Joanie.'

'Important to you, is it, Harry?' asked Gordie.

'Nah, 'course not,' said Harry.

He remembers he'd been dozing in front of TV. The baby was asleep in Col's old bedroom. The house sparkled with new paint and varnish. Joanie had recently bathed the baby. The smell of talcum powder and baby oil was still strong. Joanie had her figure back. She was as gorgeous as ever.

'Harry, you're right, darling,' she'd said.

'What about?'

'About Keithy.'

'I am?'

'Yes. He does look like me. Like a Thomas. Like my dad.'

196

38

Joanie had only ever had the one love affair. It was all she'd ever wanted. A love affair with someone like Harry. A tall man, big, strong, protective. She'd always wanted to be married. Being married was, to Joanie, the reason for her existence. And to have a child, to be a mother, oh, she just knew she was going to be a good mother, a good wife. She just knew this, as though the knowledge was there, inside her bones.

'I'll get married one day,' she'd said to Una Thomas one morning as her mother sat silently eating her breakfast.

Her mother hadn't replied, and Joanie, talking to her as a child might talk to a child's toy, carried on, 'And I'll have a baby boy, and I'll call him Keith.'

Una dug cereal from her bowl.

'I'll call him Keith,' repeated Joanie who was eleven at the time. 'After my dad.'

Una's mouth chewed but she did not look up.

'Keith's a nice name,' said Joanie.

Una, inside her impenetrable reality, merely continued eating.

'And he'll grow up to be tall and handsome; just like my dad.'

Una stood up, carried her empty bowl to the sink.

'Just like my dad,' said Joanie again.

Una, her dressing gown rustling around her stubby figure, left the kitchen.

'Just like my dad,' said Joanie to her mother's back. 'And I'll love him,' she said, her voice rising loudly as her mother's bedroom door slammed, and she heard Una's muffled voice saying things she couldn't understand but knew that she was having one of her arguments with Corporal Thomas who Joanie knew truly was dead because the few bits of his body left over after he'd been blown up were lying buried somewhere in New Guinea.

'And I'll be a real mother,' whispered Joanie to herself, 'and I'll have a husband who'll love me and stay with me all my life.'

———

Joanie was convinced she was handling things well. She'd made all the right decisions, all the right adjustments to marriage and motherhood. Things were working out as she'd planned. She'd been especially submissive to Harry's needs; she'd learned how important it was to humour him, like when she'd assured him Keithy favoured her side of the family. Not that she didn't feel annoyed—quietly to herself, of course—that Harry needed humouring so much these days. But she could cope with it. Goodness, she'd coped with her mother for all those years. Yes, Joanie reassured herself, anyone who could cope with Una Thomas for twenty years could cope with Harry O'Brien.

Besides she loved Harry desperately. Every day she reminded herself of this important fact. Not that she ever said it out loud to Harry. Not anymore. Not like when they were first married, before Keithy was born, before old Col died on the floor in the lounge room.

She wasn't as upset as Harry over Col's sudden death. Oh, she was shocked, of course, but then, shock's one thing, being upset's another. She thought it must have been the hard part of herself coming out.

Because Harry needed her to be hard. Because if she hadn't been hard, then maybe Harry wouldn't have been able to cope with the loss of the old man. Anyhow, good had come of it. They'd had Keithy. They'd managed to make new life out of old, in a manner of speaking.

It was exciting that everything was working out as planned. It was crystal clear to Joanie that those years of waiting for the right man to come along hadn't been wasted. They were part of the plan. Without them there would have been no plan, no purpose, no Harry. Oh yes, Joanie now realised, you had to put up with a lot in life if you wanted to achieve something. That was how it was. Nothing good would come without effort, without sacrifice. All those years of living with her mother. They were the years of her sacrifice. Now she was enjoying her reward. And she loved Harry so much. And Keithy. Both of them were hers. Her two great rewards for keeping faith. Yes, Joanie had everything. Including friends. Especially Gordie and Jen Sloan. Of course Gordie idolised Harry. But that was okay. Men needed their mates. Anyhow, Jen Sloan was just as good a mate to her as Gordie was to Harry. So everything was evened out, wasn't it?

Today she was at home, with her friend Jen Sloan. Joanie loved having Jen over to visit. She could think of nothing more satisfying than to hold baby Keithy on her knee while chatting with Jen.

It was different however if Jen was holding the baby. Normally, because she was breast-feeding, Joanie always held him when he was awake. She'd developed the habit of putting Keithy immediately to bed when he'd finished his feed, been burped, and had his nappy changed. Normally Jen just watched and sipped a glass of white wine. Sometimes, Joanie caught Jen's eye. There'd be an instant of shyness between them, as though the exchanged glance meant more than either of them had intended.

They were in the kitchen. Joanie had finished breast feeding the boy and for once, and inexpertly, Jen was holding him. Keithy's face broke into a smile. Joanie felt a sudden twinge of jealousy. She knew how much Jen wanted her own baby, that there was great doubt about her friend's ability to fall pregnant, yet she resented her child smiling at the other woman, as though she might be trying to steal Keithy's affections. Yet she knew this was absurd. Maybe it was the other way around. Maybe she resented Jen for smiling at Keithy. She frowned. Keithy's fingers were waving in front of Jen, his fingertips brushing the place where Jen's nipples would be. Joanie's frown deepened. Now she felt jealous of Keithy, of her own child, whose fingers were straying so close to her friend's breasts. She thrust the silly idea from her mind, thought about Harry. Okay, so she and Harry hadn't had sex for five nights. Well, sex wasn't everything in a relationship. Sex was important, though, for men probably central. But not for women. Women bore children. Women had other uses for their body. Men had to make do with sex. There was no option for them, thought Joanie. She knew that sex was Harry's way of being Harry, just like motherhood was Joanie's way of being Joanie. And she was in love with Harry. That was the thing. She was in love with the man who was the father of her child. That was the great anchorage in her life, her love for Harry, her mothering of his child. It was going to be alright, her marriage. She was doing it right. As long as she understood Harry and his needs. And she did understand. And Harry was really and truly the most perfect thing in the world. Well, anyhow, his body was the most perfect thing she had ever seen, ever touched. She felt reassured. She smiled at Jen. Jen smiled back. Keithy made a gurgling sound, lunged at Jen's breast, grabbed the material of Jen's blouse, let out a chuckle. Joanie busied herself pouring tea, remembered again it was five days since she and Harry had had sex. And Harry's ardour had seemed subdued. Oh, he'd had a really exhausting day at work; poor man he'd had to load the truck three times in the one day because of all those rush orders. And he'd not arrived home until after ten. And he'd hardly eaten anything, which was surprising, even worrying, because Harry's appetite was unequalled among his mates, and for him to eat only a couple of mouthfuls of best grilled sirloin was really unusual.

Later she mentioned it to Jen.

'He's really pushing himself at work, Jen.'

'It's that time of year, love. People are spending. It's our busiest time. Things'll slacken off after Christmas.'

It was early evening. The men were still at the store. Keithy lay asleep in his bassinet near Joanie's chair. Soon the bassinet would be too small for Keithy's lengthening body.

'And he's been so tired,' said Joanie.

Jen's eyebrows lifted.

Joanie continued: 'Harry's always been, well, so full of energy. You know, so, well, so physical.' She lowered her eyes. 'Well, I was wondering— well, if it was me.'

Jen snorted.

"Course it isn't you, love. Listen; how long have you been married now? Nearly two years, right?' Joanie nodded. 'Well there you are,' said Jen. Her cheeks were bunched up into a grin. Though she was on the short side, she was plump and rounded in all the correct places. 'You know what they say?'

'What do they say, Jen?'

'Oh, you know. That at first, they, men, I mean, want it for...' She paused as she saw the mystified look on Joanie's face. 'Sex, darlin'—s-e-x, sex, I'm talking about—they, men, want it for breakfast, dinner, and tea. Then, later on—and not much later on it seems for most of them—well—' She threw Joanie a sly grin, shrugged. 'You know what I mean.'

Joanie smiled. 'Harry's not like that,' she said.

'Then he's different from all the men I know,' replied Jen with a shrug of her shoulders. Her grin faded. 'Sleep's what's important to men. Sleep. If you ask me, nothing competes with sleep. Five minutes of sex then ten hours of sleep. That's what they want. And sometimes you can forget the five minutes of sex.'

'It's not like that with me and Harry,' persisted Joanie.

'Oh, come on, love.' Jen said impatiently. 'Harry's just a bloke like the rest of them?'

'Jen, he isn't. He's different.'

But Joanie sensed her voice might not carry its usual conviction.

'He is different,' she repeated, imagining the firmness was back in her voice.

Then she gazed at Keithy who was asleep in his bassinet.

'I never really had a proper boyfriend until I met Harry.'

'Proper?'

'Yes, you know...'

'You mean...'

'Yes.'

'Hummph! You waited a long time, didn't you?'

Joanie had waited a long time. That was part of the bargain she'd made with herself as a girl, living in the Lilyfield house with her weird mother, part of her task of keeping the faith. And she'd been rewarded beyond measure. She'd met Harry.

She met Harry on the night train from Melbourne. She'd boarded the train at the Riverina town of Junee after visiting her mother's widowed cousin there. She was feeling in low spirits as she said goodbye to her relative, for she was worried about going back to Lilyfield, wondered if she had the courage to endure her mother's silence for much longer. And in this mood she'd taken the seat next to a young man about her own age; there'd only been opportunity for a fleeting glance as she settled into the crowded compartment for the long and uncomfortable journey to Sydney, but immediately she became aware of his great size and felt the warmth of his body her gloom lifted. Then the train jerked into motion and she felt her hips pressing momentarily against the young man. Her heart raced;

she could feel it working away inside her, sending hot blood rushing around her body, flushing her cheeks, making her feel gloriously alive, more alive than she'd ever felt before. She knew that the stranger had been guided there, that it all had so much meaning for her life, as though it was preordained, that everything was going to be alright, that here, on the train, among all these ordinary day-to-day affairs, like that man over there snoring gently, and the woman every couple of minutes who pulled a travelling rug over her sleeping child; oh, yes, Joanie knew she was being drawn into some long-awaited, long hoped-for ritual ceremony involving the young stranger, the beautiful stranger, who'd appeared in the railway carriage straight out of her most vivid fantasy. Yet this was no fantasy, this was real; the eighteen-year-old girl knew it, the young man fitted so perfectly the image of the man she was searching for. She turned her head slightly, catching her breath as she did so, seeing his head turn likewise, seeing his eyes... Oh, he was so flawless, so perfect, a beautiful, beautiful man.

But what was she to do? She was no trollop. And she was so shy. And she'd had no experience at this kind of thing. How do you pick up a young man? Do you do something? What do you do?

She did this. As the journey lengthened and the talking in the compartment gradually died away, she pretended tiredness. Slowly, imperceptibly, she allowed her head to fall to the side until, after several minutes, it lay gently against the young man's body, below his shoulder, close to his heart. After a while, the young man shifted in his seat and carefully withdrew his arm from where it was trapped between his body and Joanie's head and, without attempting to speak, gently moved his arm up and around her shoulder until he enfolded her body.

In the dawn, as the train clattered wearily into Sydney Central, they moved apart. They moved reluctantly, as though to move apart was already too painful for them. And, as they did so, she caught Harry's eye, and the signals flashed back and forth, and he was smiling.

He helped with her suitcase and bought her tea and raisin toast in the railway cafeteria. She learned his name, that he lived only a mile and a half from her, that he worked in the city, that, that...

She told Jen:

'We met on the train. I was on my way home from Junee. Harry had been to Albury.'

Jen grinned. 'I know, and you had really great sex in the carriage.'

Joanie blushed, dropped her eyes. 'Well, not exactly; the train *was* packed, Jen.'

'But if it had been empty?'

'Well, then, who knows?' replied Joanie with a trace of wickedness in her smile.

Jen glanced at her watch.

'I guess those two men of ours will be a little while yet.'

Joanie rose, refilled the kettle. She switched it on, went to the baby. He was awake, lying on his back with his eyes on her.

Jen said, 'Can I nurse him?'

'Of course,' said Joanie.

Jen leaned down and picked up the baby.

'My, my,' said Jen, 'aren't you the big feller, then.'

'He is getting to be a big boy, isn't he?' said Joanie.

'He certainly is,' agreed Jen, 'a big, big boy, aren't you,' she added, holding Keithy out from her and giving the baby boy a smile. 'And doesn't he favour Harry?'

'Oh, I don't know, Jen,' said Joanie, now making fresh tea. 'Sometimes I think he looks just like my dad, just like a Thomas.'

Jen studied Keithy's face, looked up, studied Joanie's face, shook her head.

'No,' she said, 'he's definitely got Harry's eyes, and Harry's mouth.'

'Oh, do you really think so?'

'Yes. No doubt about it, Joanie. He's another Harry,' said Jen.

39

They'd said the same thing about Harry.

'Bloody hell! he's another Flan O'Brien!'

'Yearse; definitely another Flan O'Brien,' they sighed, dolefully noting how history had repeated itself.

'Maybe it's only 'is looks,' said the optimist.

'Time'll tell,' said the oracle.

'Like father, like son, I always say,' said the pessimist.

—

Whatever else he was Harry was a big child. And strong. In time he grew up to be the biggest kid on the street. Much was expected of him by his peers. There were four in Harry's Rozelle gang—himself, Gordie Sloan, the two Mackenzie brothers. He knocked around mostly with Gordie, but allowed Tubsy and his young brother, Gerry, to hang around when it suited him. He wasn't fussed about gangs. Other kids thought gangs were essential. Every kid belonged to one. Harry formed his gang more to conform with the inner-city norm. It just wasn't smart to ignore convention. When you had a gang you were respected. It was about that simple.

Not that he hadn't had to subdue big Tubsy. They didn't like each other, but no other gang would accept the fat boy, and in the end, it was soft-hearted Gordie who talked Harry into taking him and his brother on. And then, to show his gratitude, Tubsy said he ought to be the boss cocky himself because he was the eldest by a few months.

The crisis developed in the school playground. Tubsy jumped Harry from behind. It was the fight that finally clinched Harry's position as boss, the fight which ended with Tubsy breaking his finger and Harry scoring a ripped nose.

The problem for Tubsy was that Harry wasn't only the stronger of the two, he was also the angrier. Harry's anger had almost nothing to do with Tubsy, and almost without exception he kept it under control. This made Harry an even more dangerous adversary, for it gave the impression that he didn't have the push to exploit his size and strength. Which mistake Tubsy made for the last time with Harry in the Rozelle school yard that morning in late 1956.

———

Harry remembers the fight with Mackenzie. He can hear the fat boy grunting with effort. He remembers how he felt that he didn't care if Mackenzie hurt him, that he had no fear of pain. He remembers his anger erupting, speeding through him like a tornado, the sudden burst of rage as from a great distance, as though Tubsy wasn't even then clinging to his back, he remembers he was thinking about Judy, her disappearance, the great unending ache inside him, he remembers throwing off the fat boy, watching him hit the ground hard howling with pain.

———

Harry's fight with Mackenzie served another purpose. He began to see the sense in being aggressive. While he'd been brawling with Mackenzie he'd felt a new pleasure, that being angry, being aggressive, using his fists, kept the horrors at bay.

There was one fight that stood out among the others. With Jimmy Leonard. Jimmy was from Balmain and had his own gang of two younger brothers and a half-dozen lesser hangers-on. Jimmy was a thickset youth, with dangerous eyes. He was renowned for his murderous in-fighting. He was very short, with a short reach, but when he got close, the fight was over. No-one had ever survived Jimmy Leonard's fists at close range.

Jimmy challenged Harry. He'd heard of the O'Brien kid.

'They reckon O'Brien's fuckin' tough,' said one of the Leonard gang.

'Yeah, they reckon he never feels pain, so he never gives up.'

'Oh, yeah,' sneered Jimmie., 'I'll make the bastard feel pain.'

Jimmy was a devious youth. He reckoned his best chance of beating Harry was to upset him badly first, set him up for defeat by making him madder'n hell, while he, Jimmy, cool as shit, punched hell out of the big bastard.

'Anyone know who's O'Brien's best mate,' he asked his gang.

'Yeah, a bloke called Gordie Sloan.'

'The Sloan whose old man runs the furniture shop?'

'Yeah, mate, that's him.'

A couple of nights later, the Leonard gang jumped Gordie Sloan, dragged him struggling down to Elkington Park on the edge of Sydney Harbour's Iron Cove, where Jimmy commenced his plan to beat up Gordie and thus goad Harry into fighting him.

Gordie fought well. For a while Jimmy had to bide his time because the slighter built youth kept coming back for more, flailing his arms in front of him so that Jimmy had trouble getting in close and had to be satisfied with picking off Gordie with the odd jab to the nose, or the odd thump behind the ear when Gordie wavered and had to catch his breath and let his arms fall lower so that Jimmy danced in and delivered the blow. Then he moved in close, got his fists going in their deadly rhythm, knocked the breath out of Gordie's body so that Gordie stopped fighting, let his arms drop, stood there defencelessly, struggling for breath.

Jimmy landed a heavy one on Gordie's mouth. Gordie staggered back, tottering but somehow keeping his feet.

'Give up, Sloany,' yelled Jimmy.

'Fuck you,' gasped Gordie through eyes streaming with tears.

Jimmy thumped him on the nose.

Blood spouted. More tears flowed. And Gordie had trouble seeing the whereabouts of his enemy.

Then another blow and Gordie was on the ground without remembering how, and Jimmy was straddling him, and yelling at him to give up, and Gordie still said nothing, but spat blood at Jimmy and tried to knee him in the crotch, but all he achieved was more punishment from the enraged Jimmy who kept thumping him and screaming at him to give up.

'Kill him, Jimmy,' yelled Jimmy's gang.

'Give up, yer stupid bastard,' screamed Jimmy.

'Fuck you,' croaked Gordie who could take no more.

The next day word got around that Harry and Jimmy were going to sort it out once and for all. The biggest grudge fight in the district they said. 'Jimmy'll fuckin' murder O'Brien,' said the Leonard faction. 'Harry'll kick Leonard's teeth out his arsehole,' declared the O'Brien gang. Bets were made. Maybe three dozen kids turned up at the park. But the fight itself turned into an anti-climax. Harry clobbered Jimmy with such unstoppable fury that the Balmain Bull's defence crumbled in seconds and they had to drag the frenzied Harry off the whimpering boy whose busted lip hung flapping, whose front tooth had chipped against Harry's fist, whose nose now bled like a broken hose-pipe and redder and more generously than Gordie's had bled the day before.

That was almost the end of it. Jimmy had had enough. He never admitted he was scared of Harry, but there were no more challenges to fight. He could see there was something different about Harry O'Brien.

'That O'Brien's fuckin' mad,' he said to his gang. 'Fuckin' mad, I'm tellin' yer.'

But Jimmy wasn't quite finished yet.

It was known that Harry took dares.

'Another fuckin' sign he's mad,' said Jimmy.

Harry accepted a dare from the subdued but still seething Jimmy Leonard to swim across Iron Cove to Rodd Island and back. Scornfully, he did this at night even though the dare only specified day time. Successfully. And so his reputation grew. The pebble he'd brought back from the island to prove he'd landed there became a symbol of his power. He finally sold the pebble to one of Jimmy Leonard's underlings for five shillings. Jimmy hated the pebble. At home in Balmain he smashed it with a hammer. Cursing Harry O'Brien, he threw the bits into the Harbour from the Darling Street Wharf.

At high school Harry was different again. In the classroom, he chose the role of muggins; his demotion to the slow-learner stream occurred after his first half-yearly exams. Down there, nothing was expected of him—in 1956 expert opinion had it that little could be done for intellectual dregs such as Harry. Once he was pestered by a zealous young female teacher into putting pen to paper. It was trivial work, more trivial than work he'd completed in primary school years before. In disgust he wrote down some nonsense unconnected with the fifth-grade standard arithmetic. The teacher, scanning Harry's work, decided that further effort on her part would be futile. So he was freed again to sink back into classroom oblivion. 'A typical pick-and-shovel type,' was the conclusion rapidly arrived at by his teachers. 'Oh yes, and a handy footballer,' they granted, one whose strength and size made him formidable enough, 'cunning if not brilliant on the field; a big bugger, yes, and capable of intimidating the opposition; fearless, yes, like all kids with more bone than grey matter between the ears.'

40

At home Harry lived his life independently of Flan O'Brien. He cooked for himself, made no enquiries into Flan's needs nor expected Flan to enquire into his. These days, though barely middle-aged, Flan's energy had sagged and visits from his women were much fewer. Sometimes weeks might pass without the sound of a woman's voice reaching drunkenly from the lounge room to Harry as he lay in bed. At night the bottle was Flan's main comfort. He husbanded his financial resources well enough to sustain his body's demand for drink. He ate nothing solid. Now and again, an old heartthrob, as derelict as himself, might turn up for a night's accommodation and a share of Flan's whiskey. At forty-three, Flan was growing very thin; his features had become gaunt, yet, curiously, as flesh fell from his cheeks and jowls, traces of his handsome face returned; strangely he looked like a younger man, and Harry had the uncanny feeling, especially when he saw his father's face in the shadows, that he might be looking at himself, as though his father's face was his own, peering at him, as though it was himself who wore the haunted look.

About a year after the Rodd Island affair, Flan did talk to Harry. Though he still managed to drag himself to work each day, he was very ill. The disease in his airways, once intermittent, was now permanent.

He still smoked and drank heavily. Tempting Providence, he would simultaneously fight for breath, drink whiskey, and suck smoke. Miraculously he survived.

Harry had been in the kitchen when he heard Flan arrive home from work. As usual, Flan immediately made his way to the lounge room and the couch which he used frequently as his bed. Harry listened. He guessed Flan was lighting a cigarette. Frantic coughing confirmed this guess. The TV came on, hiding the sounds of Flan gulping whiskey. Eventually Flan would drift off into his nightly stupor.

Harry was in serious training. Tonight he was going out for his run. He ran three nights a week, on the other days trained at school with the school football team he now played for. He was about to slip out of the back door when he heard Flan's voice. 'Harry; Harry.' It was a voice gone hoarse from illness. 'Harry; Harry.' Harry paused at the back door, his fingers around the big latch key. 'Harry,' called his father again. Harry went into the lounge room.

Flan was sitting upright, whiskey bottle in one hand, cigarette in the other. The TV flickered in the corner opposite his couch. Raelene's china cabinet, alongside Harry where he stood just inside the door, rested unpolished against the back wall. Mostly the shelves of the cabinet lay empty, for Raelene had long ago removed everything of value; behind the leaded glass, a jam jar with dried-up contents and an opened but now also dried-up can of tomato soup stood shoulder to shoulder with a cheap Toby style jug won years ago at a shooting gallery by the then recently demobilised Able Seaman O'Brien. Various items of clothing, not all Flan's, not all male, were strewn around the room. The combined smell of fresh and stale tobacco smoke hung heavily in the air; a blue haze, hovering above the couch, formed a visible turbulence just above and in front of Flan's head. On the wall above the TV set hung a cheap framed view of Sydney Harbour; the print featured ships masts which rose gallows-like above the buildings surrounding Sydney Cove.

The carpet, now pock-marked with cigarette burns, had been Flan's wedding gift to Raelene. Two easy chairs, inherited from his mother along with the couch, made up the sum of furniture in the room. On one of them lay Flan's bedding, on the other, a pile of newspapers mixed with his dirty washing.

Flan was dressed in trousers and singlet. Sitting on the couch, his body seemed to Harry all of a sudden to be shrunken, his skin grey and lifeless. Only his eyes, which were bloodshot and staring short-sightedly, seemed fully alive. Flan lifted them towards Harry. He seemed about to speak. Instead, he coughed and spat something into his already discoloured handkerchief. 'Bloody cough won't go away,' he wheezed. Defiantly, he sucked hard on his cigarette. The nicotine, apparently numbing the gland in his throat, stilled his cough. Breathing again, Flan took a generous swallow of whiskey.

'We haven't talked for a while.'

'No.'

Flan tried to smile. He proffered Harry his bottle.

'Have a drink?' he said.

Harry looked at the bottle. He'd never drunk whiskey before. Beer he had drunk. Once, down at Elkington Park, down by the cove, he'd drunk some green stuff that one of his mates had sneaked from home, and there'd been enough to make him feel sick and giddy.

'Go on,' urged Flan, 'have a fuckin' drink, son, for Christ's sake.'

Harry stepped forward, took the bottle, and drank from it. The liquor tasted hot and fiery and burned his throat on the way down. He handed the bottle back to Flan, stepped back and leaned back against the wall. He watched Flan greedily consume the whiskey. His father's huge Adam's apple bobbed up and down. Flan paused and smacked his lips.

'And how's school goin' these days?'

It was a bizarre question, and Harry had no answer for it.

Flan said: 'I mean, as well as the football?'

'Football's all I want to do.'

Flan sniffed. 'It don't matter about the other stuff anyhow,' he said. 'Never did me no good.'

'There's one teacher I like,' said Harry.

'He'd be your coach, right?'

'Mr Howard.'

'A good sort of a bloke, is he?'

'Reckons I could make it into the juniors, in a couple of years. Reckons I got the size and the speed.'

'You got to have the wind fer it, too.'

'That's why I go running.'

'So that's where you've bin' goin'?'

'Three times a week.'

'Yer not smokin' cigarettes, are yer?'

'No.' answered Harry truthfully.

'That's good. Here, have another drink,' said Flan.

Harry moved forward. His stomach churned. He felt drunk. Yet he took the bottle and drank while his father watched and grinned, as though pleased at how sociable they were being. But then, suddenly, Flan grabbed the bottle back, examined the contents, frowned then and drank again, deeply, and anxiously, as though the drink were medicine and the dose long overdue. Then he fumbled with his cigarette packet. He couldn't open the packet and Harry opened it for him. Flan took a cigarette and Harry helped him light up. 'Come an' sit down, son,' he wheezed. Harry sat down alongside his father. Flan seemed suddenly very old, he was having trouble focussing his eyes and he nudged his pocket with his elbow. 'My glasses,' he said. Harry leaned forward, removed Flan's glasses from the trouser pocket. He felt the coarse cloth against his fingers, the unhealthy warmth of Flan's body. For a few moments they achieved a kind of intimacy. 'Thanks, son,' said Flan.

Harry felt very strange, sitting so close to his father. There was something very disturbing about it. But he did not move. 'Harry, there's things I want to tell you,' said Flan.

'What kind of things?'

'About us. Me an' you, and yer mum. And about you gettin' older an' all that, an' havin' women.' He paused to suck air, then peered earnestly at Harry through the lenses of his glasses. His eyes glowed red with bloodshot. 'Just don't go doin' what I fuckin' did, son,' he said. 'Never get fuckin' married, see. And never put the bitches up the fuckin' duff. Never do that. That's what they all want, I'm tellin' yer.' He stabbed his foot weakly into the carpet. 'Bought her this,' he said. He looked up, into Harry's eyes. 'I tried to make yer mum happy, son. I worked fuckin' hard. She can't say I never worked hard.' His voice rose to a whine. 'She was nuthin' when I met her. I was a sailor with four years active service. She was nuthin'. Worse than nuthin'. On the street she was. Yeah, she was makin' a quid down Palmer Street, during the war. Met her one night in 1944. She reckoned I was her first customer ever. Ha! Me! Her first customer! Pig's fuckin' arse I was! Paid her two quid, I did. Two fuckin' quid! An' bloody fell for her. Made me promise to take her away from it all, all that stuff she was doin'. An' I did. I fuckin' did. I gave her a chance.'

Flan paused, stared into the space in front of him, swigged whiskey. It seemed to Harry that his father was behaving as though he really was alone, drunk and alone, as he often was, talking to himself, in his own lounge room, 'Jesus,' he said, swigging from his bottle, 'fancy a bloke puttin' a prossie up the duff! An' then marryin' her.' Flan looked earnestly into space. 'We were all as randy as hell,' he said without mirth. 'After bein' at sea.'

Harry takes a deep breath; suddenly sees he's in the Pokie Lounge at Mid-City Leagues. He blinks away the image of the boy Gordie's damaged face, tries to banish the memory of Flan O'Brien wallowing in self-pity.

'Played juniors for Balmain back in the sixties,' he mumbles to the Johnson's. 'The Juniors. Bloody good team we were, too.'

Then he jabs his finger down hard on Thirty-three's five-play button.

41

When Harry left school he received two references. The headmaster, an expert bureaucrat and thus determinedly non-committal, wrote that in general terms his teachers believed that Harry was honest and trustworthy and appeared to be employable in any position which matched his scholastic achievements. Bill Howard, Harry's football coach, was less equivocal.

***

Harry, wrote Howard, *plays football with skill and determination. He was an able captain of the school's 9 stone 7 football team during the 1958 season. In my opinion he is more intelligent than indicated by his school reports. If given adequate training Harry would be a trustworthy employee in the skilled or semi-skilled trades. Harry should be able to work efficiently without close supervision. He has the ability, in my opinion, to play rugby league football at the professional level...*

***

Later, Howard phoned Jim Ross, his next-door neighbour and the manager of an inner-city Pollards Department store, and asked him if he would consider Harry for employment. Ross said yes, interviewed Harry, saw the boy was big and strong and offered him a position as trainee storeman-packer at a starting wage of five pounds ten shillings a week.

'You're making a good decision, Harry,' smiled Ross. 'Keep your wits about you, work hard, and you'll go far with Pollards.' The manager grinned. 'If it's any help to say it, I started off in the storeroom, myself. It's hard work, but a good way of learning the system. Learn the system and you'll get ahead, Harry.'

For a while then, soon after his fifteenth birthday, Harry hovered at the margins. He stopped brawling. He neither smoked nor drank. He was superbly fit, growing tall, building muscle, looking already at fifteen more man than boy. And he sensed he was close to opportunity. Rugby League, certainly. But already a second idea was taking shape. He knew the traineeship could set him up for the future. And he'd decided he would one day have his own business. First, he'd learn about 'the system' as Ross had put it, get some experience, make some business contacts—he already had Mr Ross, and then there was Gordie's dad, Mr Sloan. Mr Sloan had a furniture store in Petersham. Most of all, of course, Harry would have a career as a professional rugby league player. Everything he was planning came second to that. But you had to have a second string. All the football stars had a second string. Usually a shop. Something like a sports outlet, a connection with sporting goods. Yeah, that was it, sporting goods, decided Harry. It was easy to get started in sporting goods if you were a football celebrity. Make a power of money in sporting goods. Yeah, he'd do that. And specialise in footy boots. He'd invent something new, a revolutionary football boot, one that you wouldn't even think was on your feet but made you run like the wind, like one of those big hunting cats, yeah, the ones that run sixty miles an hour, yeah, those cheetahs. He'd call them 'O'Brien Flyers'—there'd be a flying cheetah on the heels, yeah, a winged cheetah. Yeah, that's what he'd do. And sell millions of them, all over the world. Yeah, 'O'Brien Flyers', as worn by Harry O'Brien, captain of Balmain, State and National representative.

Harry tried out for Balmain Juniors. He went well. He was very fit. And very fast. And very strong. He tackled well. And weaved and bobbed with the ball. They just couldn't stop him.

During the trial he slipped on the wet turf and wrenched his knee. It seemed nothing. He got to his feet, tested the knee, found the pain was slight, carried on with the trial.

He was selected. In his first game he scored two tries. In his second game he strapped his left knee and scored three tries. Four games later, his knee very heavily strapped, he collapsed in agony after a vicious tackle. His knee seemed suddenly fragile, hopelessly weak. He hobbled off the field on the arm of the coach. The next week he played his last game, or the first fifteen minutes of it, until the knee gave way.

———

'Played for Balmain Juniors, eh?' Mrs Johnson is saying.

'My very word, I did.?'

'You must have been alright, then?'

'Yeah, I wasn't bad.'

'You ever play firsts?'

'Nah,' Harry hears himself admitting.

'Bet you could have, if you'd wanted?'

'Yeah, I reckon.'

'Why'd you give it up, then?'

'Football?'

'Yes.'

'Things were pretty complicated. Injured my knee. The old man was ill.'

42

Flan entered his final illness when Harry was seventeen. Now, he barely had strength enough to lever himself between couch and bathroom. Crazily, or maybe because he feared death so much, he persisted with his habits. Against doctor's orders, Lettie, his oldest and most loyal flame, smuggled in supplies, including cigars, telling him someone in the bar at the Cricketers Arms claimed that cigar smokers never caught the flu. So he smoked cigars. Lettie had heard, too, that vodka was good for the lungs, that they drank it in Russia to ward off pneumonia and lung cancer. Flan drank vodka. Naturally he continued with his unfiltered cigarettes, his beer, and his daily half-bottle of Australian whiskey. Once a fortnight, he even managed a gentle tumble with Lettie on the couch in the lounge room. Somehow his body insisted on surviving. His survival became a topic of interest to those with gambling instincts. Several old cronies secretly set up a sweep on the estimated date of Flan's demise. When the event finally took place some weeks later, there was thirty-seven quid for the lucky winner in the kitty under the bar at the Cricketers' Arms.

A few months before Flan died, Raelene hired a live-in housekeeper. Marge was sixty-eight, friendly, very strong, and, with few words beyond normal civilities, ideal for the now breathless Flan who, on her arm, was just able to hobble the distance to the bathroom. Sometimes, paused and panting like a blown-out old dog, he would meet Harry and smile weakly and try to speak, but his breath would fail him and the light in his eyes would fade and his skin would become tinged with blue and Marge would have to support his flagged body with both arms and half drag him back to the couch in the lounge room. Father and son never did speak again.

There were lessons in all this for young Harry. Watching Flan, seeing him shrink towards death, knowing his father had once weighed over fourteen stones, that he'd once been the strongest man in the textile factory down Alexandria where he'd ruled his gang of cronies with indisputable authority, that he'd survived six years of war, the consumption of countless gallons of whiskey and beer, truckloads of cigarettes, Harry saw that life, in the end, was capricious, cruel. He saw existence in terms of chance. If chance favoured you, if fortune smiled, you would be alright, you would win. Effort had nothing to do with it. Everything was chance, a gamble. Sometimes the odds were in your favour, sometimes they weren't. Take Flan. Flan ought to be dead. Yet he was still alive. Against all logic, all medical wisdom. The bastard was alive. He'd beaten the odds. Well, almost. Anyhow, he'd had a long run of good luck. Longer than he deserved. On the other hand, take Harry's knee. That was bad luck.

Nowadays Harry's knee had to be permanently strapped. The strapping forced him to accept that his knee was fragile. Sometimes, in order not to be reminded of his fragility he slept with the tight strapping in place. Then he felt free to dream of playing football, of running on the Sydney Cricket Ground with the great champions. Yet, curiously, though Harry craved the opportunity to play football again, he refused to seek medical help. It was as if he needed some perversion of his nature to sustain his illusions. Deep down he knew he could not bear to discover that his knee was permanently damaged. He invented a clever strategy to deal with this fear. He created a new illusion, a kind of dream while he was awake. He convinced himself the knee injury was temporary, that the knee would soon heal, and he would once again take to the football field.

'Yeah, she'll be right. Only a bad sprain,' he would say.

'Maybe you've done in the cartilage, mate?' they would commiserate.

'Nah. Just need to rest it a while.'

'They can be real buggers, knees.'

'Not this one, mate.'

'Well, good luck, anyhow, Harry.'

So it would go.

And he had sympathetic workmates among the women staff at Pollards.

'Shame weren't it,' they said, 'Harry mucking up his knee like that?'

'Yeah, a real shame.'

'They reckoned he would've made first grade.'

'Yeah.'

'He's good looking, but.'

'Poor bloke don't say much, anymore, does he?'

'Not a lot.'

'He's still nice, though.'

'Yeah, real nice.'

What Harry truly felt, he had no intention of disclosing. He would ejaculate inside his young women in a mood of ecstatic self-pity, while they would imagine the glow of sadness in his eye was the light of rapture given him by their young bodies. Deep down he was trapped in despair; no-one guessed that sex was the analgesic for his self-pity. Rather, young women preferred to think of him as a mysterious stranger with the beauty of a matinée idol.

'Reminds me of Robert Taylor.'

'I reckon he's just like Tyrone Power.'

'Looks like him, too.'

'Who? Tyrone Power.'

'Nah, Robert Taylor, o' course.'

Harry used the storeroom at Pollards as his rendezvous. From there, if the circumstances were right, if he had enough time, if he was sure the young woman possessed the minimum of discretion, he would take her to his 'boudoir', more accurately, his boss's, Alf Parson's, cleverly insignificant little office, a perfect love nest, for it was windowless, secure, and set darkly shadowed under the lee of huge storage bins and ceiling-high shelves in the most distant and inaccessible corner of the storeroom. Lunchtimes were the most popular, mainly for the reason that Alf always went out to lunch—a customary liquid lunch of four schooners and a couple of nips—and could always be relied on to slip back through the rear access door ten minutes late at least and thus unaware of the fornication which had concluded just minutes before his glassy eyes and trembling fingers began their struggle to connect key with keyhole.

Occasionally Harry's domestic arrangements would misfire. Then there would be a flurry of excited debate in the store.

'Hey, Nora. You heard the latest?'

'About Freda?'

'Yeah. Weird, isn't it? Won't have a thing to do with her, will he?'

'No. And she's not a bad looking sort, too.'

'A bit on the big side.'

'Yeah, but sort of pretty.'

'Sort of.'

'And well sprung, don't you reckon?'

'The blokes all think so.'

'Nice set of lungs?'

'If you like 'em big.'

'Harry likes 'em big.'

'What! sheilas?'

'No, stupid. Tits!'

'Yeah! now you tell me.'

'Weird though, why Harry hasn't gone for her.'

'Yeah, really weird.'

Then Doreen Wilcox arrived one morning in 1962 to take up duties on the lingerie counter. She was very pretty, small-made, rounded in all the right places.

'Jeez! Look at her, will yer?'

'She'd be married, for sure.'

'Can't see no wedding ring.'

'Reckon she'd be divorced.'

'Stuck-up looking sheila, ain't she?'

'Yeah; and get the way she talks.'

'Nobody talks like that. Nobody real.'

'They do where she comes from.'

'Where's that?'

'Up Pymble, I reckon; or one of them other North Shore suburbs.'

'Why's she workin' here, then?'

'A bloody good question, Cath. Anyway, she won't last.'

'Why's that, Nora?'

'What! Here! Behind a counter? Nah; wouldn't be her style. She'll move on; bet'cha a quid she will.'

———

Harry remembers Doreen.

'She was a good-looking girl,' he says to Mrs Johnson.

'Who's that, love; your wife?'

'No, Doreen...Doreen Wilcox. A girlfriend of mine.'

'Doreen, eh—you don't see that name around much, these days, do you?'

'She worked at Pollards for a while.'

Mrs Johnson chuckles.

'One of your old flames, was she?'

'Yeah, sort of. Until she got married again.'

43

Doreen had been married before. So disastrously that a year before taking the job at Pollards she'd come very close to taking her own life. She'd certainly had that intention. 'Suicidal ideation' as her husband, Sid, who was a specialist in physiological psychology, diagnosed it.

Except that by then Doreen knew Sid was a thorough bastard. Knowing this helped her step back from the cliff edge. Afterwards she survived alone but isolated more than ever from the comfortable North Shore suburb of St Ives where she was born and raised. St Ives had been such a different reality. School, her mother, constant supervision, eternal suspicion; God! the only thing missing was the chastity belt. Oh, she'd had a boyfriend, once, during those days. He'd been her allocated partner at the dance arranged between his all-boys' college and her all-girls' one. He'd been very polite, had asked her all the polite questions, about her schoolwork, about her hobbies, about the sports she played. And she'd felt his arm round her waist, and the warmth in his fingers, and then—O, God!—the strange and slightly alarming stirrings in her breast, the dangerously exciting sense of wetness lower down, as they'd danced in their stiff-legged, inexperienced way. He'd asked if he could take her home, and, as instructed, she'd thanked him and politely declined. Later, surrounded by the other girls in the dorm doing much the same thing, she'd masturbated as quietly as she could to the vivid visual fantasy of Robert's naked body—'the night of the compulsory wank' the girls later christened it.

Like other girlfriends at such a school, Doreen became obsessed by thoughts of sex. Enforced abstinence, the cloistered fortress of a Sydney girls boarding school at the end of the nineteen fifties, the frustration of possessing a young woman's glands and the unquenchable fire they created in what seemed a permanently swollen clitoris, all fuelled the obsession.

At university she went totally insane. Even her old girl friends—who themselves were no slouches when it came to kicking over the traces—thought so. She met Sid Randall. Sid was tall and handsome, five years older, sophisticated, an atheist, a free-thinking liberal.

'He's wonderful,' Doreen told her open-mouthed and still virginal girlfriends, for she was in love with her brilliant tutor in psychology. 'He's got so much poise—oh, and he's doing a Ph.D.,' she informed them. 'In physiological psychology,' she added condescendingly, as she lit up and drew the smoke of a badly rolled joint deeply into her lungs and expertly held it there for a few seconds, in the manner taught her by Sid, before she expelled the smoke into the faces of her gaping friends. 'He works with rats. Laboratory bred rats. Sid does research on rats. (Slight giggle) Sid says they're very much like human beings.'

Sid swept her off her feet, blinded her with his attention, his flattery, his willingness to treat her as a mature woman, worthy of someone like himself, with brains, a researcher, an expert in 'behaviour' as he put it, giving heavy and breathy emphasis to the second syllable so that the sound seemed charged with extra significance to the seventeen year-old Doreen.

She learned to drink, how to carry her liquor with the rest of them. Her first experience of sex with Sid occurred with fatalistic irony as she was sinking into an alcoholic swoon. Even so, her inhibitions tried to assert themselves. In her partial consciousness she fought weakly against Sid's hands, Sid's searching mouth. Vaguely, sensing the nearness of hysteria, she wondered if this really was sex she was experiencing. There were no great chords of heavenly music, no glorious, transporting ecstasies in her loins. As she surrendered to unconsciousness, she was aware of some activity between her legs, some discomfort there, pain deadened by alcohol, the feeling of discharge as Sid—half-stewed himself—finally managed to slip himself partially into her. The second time she was fully conscious. And in love. And sex with Sid was so wonderful, she told herself, feeling grateful to Sid for wanting her so much, yet feeling strangely numb down there as Sid grunted his way towards release and squeezed her buttocks so hard that the dark blue thumb-marks persisted sorely long after she and Sid had parted company.

Doreen's insurance policy matured on her eighteenth birthday. She received five thousand pounds. In August of that year—1958—Doreen secretly married Sid. She agreed to have a new birth date forged onto her birth certificate. She saw this as a kind of prank, a clever ruse to confuse authority, a way of proving to Sid she was as sophisticated, as morally liberated, as he was.

She became pregnant. Sid arranged the abortion. She recovered quickly, suppressed her guilt, saw herself as a woman of the world, was now reading literature alongside her psychology studies, was beginning to understand the transcendent nature of artistic morality, was seeing how much this applied to Sid, an artist himself, an artist creating new, ratomorphic, knowledge in his laboratory.

She contracted gonorrhoea. Having squandered all of Doreen's money, Sid, discovering Doreen's funds truly had dried up, underwent a sort of spontaneous personality change. Suddenly Doreen was married to this terrible monster. He accused her of promiscuity, which she timidly denied, then informed her that her habits of hygiene were the culprit, which for a while she naively believed, until she discovered he was secretly treating himself for the same complaint, and had been doing so for some time, so he scathingly declared on a drunken evening, and thus helped her finally to comprehend the extent of the catastrophe. Even so, she stayed with him, could not stop loving him so she convinced herself. Sid's treatment of her condition, without proper medical supervision and with antibiotics acquired from a friend of his in final year of medicine, seemed successful. Then a second pregnancy was self-aborted. Doreen was left sterile, or so she convinced herself. Then there were the drugs, supplied to her by Sid of course. There were the periods of withdrawal, and Doreen's illnesses, her pneumonia, the weeks of near madness in the Camperdown flat culminating finally in Sid's drug-frenzied attack on her with a kitchen knife which she'd survived by kicking him in the balls—glorious feeling—a split second before the knife was about to slice its way into her neck. There was her frantic exodus from Sid's flat. There was her last ditch (but ultimately failed attempt) to speak to her uncomprehending mother about her two and a half year ordeal and to try to explain to her why she'd withdrawn from her course over a year earlier and why she'd told her nothing of her marriage to Sid Randall, or how she'd totally fucked up her life, her future, her chances of marriage and children with an ordinary middle-class Australian chap, etcetera, etcetera...

Later she phoned her mother a second time to tell her she was moving to New Zealand but hung up before any queries about details could be asked.

Then she changed her name. She loathed her real name, for it reminded her so much of that different and ignorant and undisciplined and really stupid person she'd once been. Her married name she loathed even more.

She called herself Doreen Wilcox.

Now at age twenty-one she abandoned all her old friends, all her old connections. She was determined no one would discover who she really was, had been. She'd discovered the habit of anger, how anger could sustain energy, provide a substitute for hope, provide a substitute for meaning. She was angry with herself, with her mother, with her religion, her schooling.

Most of all she was angry with Sid Randall, with everything he was and stood for, angry with all the men like him in the world, angry with all men. Angry enough to do the unthinkable.

She would save the deposit for a small inner-city house. She would put everything Sid had taught her into practice. She had little self-respect, little need to worry about the niceties of her now abandoned middle-class upbringing. 'Fuck it!' she said out loud to herself, strangely enjoying the sound of her own voice mouthing the obscenity she'd once thought so vulgar. 'Why not? Why the fuck not?' She'd been used, hadn't she? And ruined? So she would become the user. She would use men. She would use her body to use men. She would use her body to make men give her money. She would become rich by using men. She would take money off men by pretending she enjoyed their bodies, by letting them believe they were great lovers fixed to a most beautiful Venus...

That was the Doreen who turned up that morning to work on the lingerie counter at Pollards, the Doreen who needed just that amount of extra income to bridge the gap between the income from her clients and the income she needed to cover the balance of her rent, the payments on her Volkswagen, and her housekeeping expenses.

———

'Bit flighty was she, then?' asks Mrs Johnson, her face aglow with brandy. 'Eh?'

Harry is absently playing Thirty-three. He and the machine are idling along together.

'That Doreen. Yer girlfriend.'

'Oh, her...Nah, she wasn't flighty. Just knew what she wanted, then went for it.'

'Oh, yes, tough sort of person, was she?'

'Yeah, tough. Tough as bloody nails.'

44

Five months before she started work at Pollards Doreen had rented a terrace house on Flower Street, Paddington, just north of Victoria Barracks. She set up the front room in the way she imagined would meet with her clients' approval. She placed her two Scandinavian easy chairs on each side of her antique Afghan rug. Here she would break the ice, set her clients at ease, give them tea in China cups, or coffee brewed in her blue and white Corningware pot. In a corner of the room sat her tiny bureau desk, a gift from her mother when she'd moved to the inner-city before commencing her studies at the university. Then there was the drop side table, the one valuable piece she'd acquired while married to Sid, her books (mostly literary, mostly unread, all of which Doreen was determined to read), her records (which included the symphonies of Mahler, Bruckner, and Beethoven), her portable stereo, a number of art prints—among which several Cézanne landscapes took pride of place, and indoor plants which included a large pot of African violets soon to be put to use in the bay window as a private signal to those admitted into Doreen's confidence.

It was all very antiseptic. The world could be kept at arm's length behind the barred windows and bolted doors. Doreen was very selective with her clients. She picked them up on nearby Oxford Street. Not *any* men, of course, but men she judged had no wish to be seen drifting about under the gaudy lights of King's Cross a few blocks away. She picked up only those men who were not only well dressed but who wore their clothes well. She rejected immediately anyone who showed the slightest signs of aggression, or drunkenness. Shrewdly, for someone still very much the amateur in these affairs, she guessed that among the men wandering the Paddington streets there was a percentage of lonely, frustrated, middle-aged, modestly well-off middle-class individuals, who had no interest in a 'quickie' in some sleazy hotel room, but who craved fresh sheets and a clean woman with a pleasant manner and clean smelling breath.

Even so there was a great deal of danger. On the few occasions she was threatened with violence, she countered by employing her pre-determined plan. She would simply jab her concealed hatpin into the assailant's arm, or leg, depending on availability, then take off like a bat out of hell. Once she did receive a heavy blow to the head, delivered without warning by an impeccably well dressed and well-spoken man who suddenly swung at her the instant she'd agreed to go with him; but, in the main, she was lucky; she was operating outside the designated working zone, at the Woollahra end of Paddington and so it was the middle-aged bank officer, or solicitor, or public servant, pretending to be out for an innocent stroll, who ended up lighting her cigarette and engaging her in the kind of embarrassed small talk which men in such circumstances find themselves suddenly using before it dawns on them how studied and school boyish it must be sounding to this petite, apparently sophisticated, and very gutsy young lady with the wide oval eyes and the pretty mouth with the slightly crossed-over front teeth which made her seem all the more attractive, all the more sexy, chatting to them as though they were old friends, and making them suddenly so very glad they'd decided that night to do what they'd been desperately wanting to do for years.

In the early 1960's Paddington was showing signs of becoming the thriving, trendy inner-city suburb into which it was to mature by the mid-

1970's. All this fitted into Doreen's plan to carry out her business with utmost discretion, for there were respectable agencies of all kinds springing up in Paddington. And so her clients would not be visiting Doreen Wilcox, prostitute; they would, as had been cleverly suggested by a client with legal training, be consulting with 'Wilcox Financial Planning Services' as the nameplate which eventually appeared on her door announced.

However, her circle of clients remained small. And the shortfall in income was the result. For a couple of months she needed a job to supplement her income. Hence the lingerie counter at Pollards.

And her brief love affair with Harry O'Brien.

45

Later Doreen would laugh at the absurdity of it, at the sheer, bloody, misguided, moronic absurdity of falling in love with Harry. Yet she cannot help herself. It is as though all her newfound discipline has gone. She sees Harry as a lover. Not as a client. How strange that she should do so, she thinks.

'I'm Harry O'Brien,' he says.

She sees the eagerness in his eyes, behind the sadness. She holds out her hand, sees how tiny her fingers seem against his, feels his warmth.

'Doreen Wilcox.'

'Nice to meet you, Doreen.'

(What a great voice?)

'Nice to meet you, Harry.'

'I work in the store-room.'

(She's breathing too heavily.)

'Right.'

(Dammit! stop blushing.)

'Just call me when you need new stock.'

(He's breathing heavily, too, isn't he?)

'Right.'

'Office is downstairs, near the back entrance.'

'Right.'

(God! he cannot be more than eighteen or nineteen; God! he's so young.)

Harry is in love, too. Spontaneously. His first glimpse of Doreen sets his heart pounding. She is just like Judy Connell herself so his heightened sensitivities tell him. For a long moment he imagines she *is* Judy Connell. Her size, her shape, her hair, darker than Judy's but still fair, the same v-shaped cleft in her upper front teeth.

'I love you, Doreen,' he says to her only a week later.

(How perfectly adolescent of you, thinks Doreen.)

'Oh, I love you, too, Harry, darling,' she says.

They are in the Paddington terrace. They make love. For once Doreen can feel totally absorbed by the natural pleasure of sex with Harry, totally freed from the commercial demands of her trade, and for a while no other need exists, they merely live to exhaust themselves in each other's arms, sleep, awake, make love, sleep. It is the perfect symbiosis, the mutual satisfaction of desire. Doreen is stunned by the revelation. She feels so at peace with Harry, for the while, for the first week, as they achieve blissful exhaustion again, and sleep, and reawaken, then join, and sleep.

At length they try serious talk.

'Do you read much, Harry?'

(Doreen has found the motivation to resume her interest in literature.)

'No, love, not much.'

(Doreen loves Harry calling her 'love'. It seems so natural; she, his *Connie*, he, her *Mellors*.)

'I read all the time.'

She talks about her books, takes it for granted Harry will want to know about her books, she loves him, he loves her, she is certain he will love everything that she loves.

Harry does own a few books, she manages to find out, boys' books given to him by someone called Mrs Reilly, and a bible given him, he says with a sarcastic giggle, by his Protestant-raised mother—Catholics don't read bibles, only their Sunday Missal, Daily Missal if they're really keen, he says— but there's nothing much else—okay, no problem, she can do something about it.

She tells him about *Riders in the Chariot*, Patrick White's recent novel. Harry has never heard of Patrick White, finds the idea of a Jew being crucified in Australia really silly.

'Nah,' he says, shaking his head, 'nobody'd do that—nah.'

'But it's so full of irony, and so symbolic, you know, of the Crucifixion, Mordecai Himmelfarb was a Jew, like Jesus.'

'Still can't see it happening, Doreen. Not in Australia.'

'Harry, for Christ's sake, there are people in Australia who really hate the Jews.'

'Jews! Nah! Maybe Abos, or wogs. Or poms. Yeah, definitely the poms. But the Jews. Nah. We freed the Jews, didn't we? In the war. Why would we hate them?'

'It's true, Harry. That's why Patrick White's book is so important.'

He tried to be kind.

'Maybe I'll read him sometime.'

'Oh, you should, Harry.'

And, dutifully, he tries. Yet he finds White's novel impenetrable, as though the words are written in a strange language, made all the stranger because he could, individually speaking, read and accurately mouth every single one of them. And yet he senses there is beauty in the words, but he cannot feel it. And yet he does try. He tries to please Doreen. But he fails, even though, on one or two occasions, he finds passages which he thinks he understands, which he tries to convince himself he has enjoyed reading, even though he knows, deep down, he hasn't enjoyed them at all, that he'd only wanted to enjoy them, for Doreen's sake, but had failed, passages like:

———

One evening on a bare hillside, which the wind had treated with silver, he lay down, and it seemed at first as though the earth might open, gently, gently, to receive his body, but his soul would not allow, and dragged him to his feet, and he ran, or stumbled, down a hill, his coat-tail flying...

———

He does not persist. Harry has no urge to understand. He enjoys Doreen's body, her physical image, its memory to him of Judy. He does not even tell Doreen about the passage, about his inchoate sense that there is something important there, buried in the words.

Her music baffles him. He listens to her talking about her music. And makes the effort to show interest in what she tells him. She loves Mahler. Harry has never heard of Mahler. She plays him Mahler, the Fourth Symphony, her favourite, and Bruckner's Eighth, and the Eroica, and Wagner's Siegfried Idyll, and so many other pieces of music none of which he's heard and all of which sound dull and repetitious to his untutored ear.

'I reckon Elvis is pretty good.'

'Yes, he's good; not a serious musician, though.'

'Oh, why not?'

'Well, he's just a pop singer.'

'Rock.'

'What's that, Harry?'

'Rock. He's a rock singer. Elvis.'

'Oh, yes, I know, that, Harry.'

He tries to tell Doreen about his love of football. He hasn't the words. Once he mutters a phrase he'd picked up from a *Daily Tabloid.*

'Poetry in motion's what they are, players like Norm Provan and Reg Gasnier.'

Doreen looks at him in astonishment, then bursts into a giggle.

'Poetry? Christ! that's really funny, Harry.'

Harry becomes confused. Doreen sees this, cannot understand it. Now Harry begins his struggle with the relationship. Soon his pleasure during sexual intercourse seems to be ebbing away.

Naturally Harry says nothing of this to Doreen.

———

'Funny thing,' says Harry as though to himself, but loud enough to turn Mrs Johnson's head, make hubby sniff, 'how you can go head over heels for a sheila you haven't a bloody thing in common with?'

'Yes, love,' answers Mrs Johnson quietly.

'Think she's the right one, and everything. Think you'll get married, all that sort of thing.'

'Know what you mean, Harry,' says Mrs Johnson.

'She was nice, though, Doreen. Real nice. And well educated. Knew about books. And music. Posh music. High falutin' stuff like they play on the ABC.'

'Symphony music?' suggested Mrs Johnson.

'Yeah, Beethoven.'

'Tchaikovsky.'

'Yeah.'

Harry pauses, watches his unmoving reflection remain unmoving in Thirty-three's window; watches the eyes in there watching him.

'We was real close, but,' he says, 'Doreen and me. Real close.'

As though he and Doreen had achieved something together, he suddenly thinks, seeing the eyes in the window open wider. As though despite their inability to understand one another, their failure to truly connect with one another, there was some understanding, some connection.

46

There was the time Harry discovered Doreen's other profession. Harry arrived early one Saturday afternoon. Saturday afternoon was George's appointment time, from 2:00 to 3:30 pm. George was a retired solicitor, sixty-seven years old, a widower, and, while only mildly interested in physical sex, determined to re-discover his wild oats once and for all before he died. George loved the pure thrill, as he experienced it, of spending time with the young, exciting Doreen. He referred to her as his 'secret young lady friend'. George was exactly the kind of client Doreen sought after. His needs were simple. Mostly he was happy to just talk. They would listen to Mozart, drink Earl Grey tea, eat water biscuits and smoked oysters, and, if George's liver seemed up to it, perhaps drink a glass of champagne. Very occasionally, and since George was the most modest of men, they would completely darken the bedroom, and Doreen would perform her skills in silence. George would then insist on dressing in the darkness and would exit the bedroom without comment, kiss Doreen lightly on the cheek in the manner of a doting uncle, then depart until his next appointment four weeks hence.

In fact, it was George who suggested the nameplate, and the kind of information it might convey.

When Harry first saw the nameplate on that Saturday afternoon, his first reaction was one of panic. Maybe Doreen had sold up and left without telling him. He stared at it. Then calmed down. It bore Doreen's surname. But, 'Financial Planning Services'? He frowned heavily as he studied the words. Then the door opened, and a portly old bloke dressed in tweeds, his head down, and his hat, an old trilby, pulled over his brow, hurried past him, heading in the direction of Oxford Street.

Just inside the doorway he saw Doreen.

'Who the hell was that?'

'Come in, Harry,' said Doreen, clearly put out by Harry's early arrival. 'I thought I told you four-o-clock. Why are you so early?'

'Thought I'd surprise you.'

'You surprised me alright.'

Harry closed the front door behind him.

'And who was the old bloke?'

'A client, Harry.'

'A client? What sort of a client?'

Doreen ushered him to her new settee.

'Sit down, Harry, darling,' she said.

Harry sat down; his long legs drawn up nearly to his chin. He stared at Doreen. He saw she was ill at ease.

'That name-plate...'

Doreen interrupted him.

'Harry, there's something I have to tell you.'

Later, when Harry had calmed down, she told him about Sid Randall, about her lost pregnancies, about everything. She spoke slowly, and unemotionally. She was proud of herself for not displaying emotion. She felt a new strength as she told Harry the dismal story of her recent past.

'But you're not still married to the bastard?' asked Harry dully.

'I never was legally married to him.'

She explained about the forged birth certificate.

'You could get the mongrel for that.'

'I wouldn't bother, Harry.'

Suddenly she was very bitter.

'I just wanted to get away from him, Harry,' she said. 'I just wanted to forget I'd ever set eyes on the bastard.'

'But you let him have everything? '

'Yes, I did. Well,' Doreen gestured vaguely, 'nearly everything. Anyway, there wasn't that much left after he'd spent the money. Oh, he lived it up for a whole year. The toast of Sydney he was, my fucking husband.'

She began to weep, and Harry took her in his arms. After a while she fell asleep and Harry stayed with her through the night. Now and then, as she sighed, and her mouth opened, he would see her front teeth, and he would think of Judy, and try to conjure up her image in his mind, but the image seemed dimmer than before, and its features less distinct, and Harry felt a great sadness as he realized that his love affair with Doreen was ending.

For a while they said nothing about their break-up at Pollards. Of course, all the female staff knew that Doreen had changed Harry's life. Harry was eighteen now. He'd never looked more beautiful 'in his manly sort of way, o'course'. And he'd caused universal disappointment among the young women at the store, for he was now totally inaccessible. There were no more lunchtime liaisons, no more jockeyings for his attention, none of the outrageous lies about sexual performance passing from one excited mouth to another. Harry was well and truly spoken for as scuttlebutt would have it.

'A bloody waste, if you ask me.'

'I knew it'd flamin' happen.'

'Thought you were next on his list, did yer, Brenda?'

'Listen, love. I was bloody next!'

'Gawd she's old, but.'

'Thirty if she's a day.'

'Nothing but a flamin' cradle snatcher.'

'And a bloody stuck-up little snob.'

'Told yer she was from the North Shore.'

'Bet'cha her old man threw her out.'

'Yeah,' the girls all agreed.

'Bet'cha she got herself up the duff.'

'And had to have it adopted,'

'Yeah,' they all said.

'Or, you know, had it terminated, like.'

'Ohh,' they said.

'Well, that's what them rich people get up to,' said Brenda.

'I wouldn't let them do that to me,' said Nelly.

47

In the end, Doreen played it safe and married a forty-year-old client named Derek Mulholland. She still felt attracted to Harry. She could still enjoy sex with him, become absorbed in the sheer physical pleasure of his perfect body. But something was wrong. Harry, the persona, was becoming boring she realised suddenly one evening as she lay back after completing her orgasm and waited for Harry to finish, as though, now she herself was expended, like the least of her clients he was no more than expelling himself into a rubber container which was in mere sterile contact with her vaginal passage. She was feeling unfeeling with Harry inside her.

Even so, she made extra efforts to please him. She felt obliged to do so. She felt that Harry was part of her recovery, that her having met Harry, as it were, was providential, part of the redemptive process that had begun that day on the cliff edge when she'd contemplated then rejected suicide. Thus, she sought extra ways of bringing them closer together. She tried out her Italian cooking on him. The smell of the food bothered him. Even after her diplomatic attempts to instruct him, he had difficulty getting the unfamiliar food off his plate. She reverted to giving him the plain fare he preferred. She played Elvis on her stereo. He seemed suspicious of her motives, even queried why she wasn't playing Beethoven. Yet when she played the

Triple Concerto, he sat fidgeting, lighting cigarettes one after the other, unable to relax. She showed him her new books, she was reading Margaret Drabble and Thea Astley. He glanced at the dust covers briefly.

'Would you like to borrow them, Harry?'

'Nah, love, it's okay.'

'Maybe something else?'

'Nah, mate.'

Then she realised how much she hated him calling her, 'mate'.

'Sometimes I find a book very calming,' she said.

But Harry missed the criticism in her voice.

'Yeah?'

'You know,' said Doreen impatiently, 'because Harry, darling, you can fucking lose yourself in the story; imagine you're inside the fucking book.'

Harry saw how her eyes flashed, how they no longer seemed anything like Judy's beautiful eyes.

'Would you like to fuck?' Doreen said coldly, 'At least we can still do that, can't we, Harry, *mate*?'

'Nah, it's alright,' he muttered, looking down.

A few days later she asked him:

'You don't have another girlfriend, do you?'

From the look on Harry's face, Doreen was certain that he had. She wondered who it might be. Someone from the store, no doubt. Maybe the hot little number on the lingerie counter. Yet Harry said:

'No, I don't. Why'd you ask me that?'

He sighed heavily.

'I did have a friend once, years ago, Judy.'

'I suppose you were jilted,' said Doreen.

'Yeah, something like that,' shrugged Harry.

48

A week after breaking up with Doreen, Harry's annual holidays fell due. On the first morning of his two weeks off he awoke early. He lay very still for a while, thinking about Doreen, the Paddington terrace, wondering if the African violets were on display right now, if they were in flower, who of Doreen's twenty-one clients might be about to call on her.

Later, washed and shaved, and dressed for going out, Harry went downstairs. Marge was getting Flan's breakfast. She was putting food on a wooden tray to take to Flan's bedroom. It was a pointless ritual, for Flan never ate solid food.

Harry grabbed some bread and buttered it.

'Would you like me to cook you something, love?' asked Marge.

'No, thanks, I have to go out.'

He had to go out. He needed to walk, to think, be alone. It was a glorious day. The air was dry and crisp. A gentle nor'easter moved across Sydney, purifying the air before it needed to be drawn into the lungs. He breathed in. The air tasted fresh in his mouth. And the light was dazzling so that Harry felt its thrust on his face as he jumped down the couple of wooden steps at the back door and let himself out into the laneway. He set off, munching bread.

He walked down to Balmain. At length he arrived at the Darling Street wharf. He stood near the small crowd awaiting the arrival of the ferry. When the ferry pulled in a couple of minutes later, he decided to take it into the city. He stood at the craft's stern, watching the hiss and bubble of its wake. It was peaceful on the water. The ferry swayed very gently as it moved. He caught a whiff of female scent among the other, more masculine smells on the harbour. He flexed the muscles in his thighs and calves, felt them swell and harden. He smiled at a young woman, the one whose scent he'd smelled. Coyly, she dropped her eyes, but Harry knew he'd been fully appraised and, he guessed, fully approved of. He stepped off the ferry and saw the girl hurrying ahead of him towards the city. She had a pretty figure and she wobbled as she strutted along on her high heels, the calves on her lovely Sydney-sider legs flexing as her beautiful body moved inside its snug-fitting skirt and blouse. The girl reminded him of his ex-girlfriend Rhonda. Rhonda, whom Doreen had replaced on the cosmetics counter at Pollards, had moved to Melbourne. Suddenly Harry decided to go to Melbourne. Yes, spend a few days with Rhonda. He was sure Rhonda would be glad to see him.

He hurried to George street where he caught a tram for Railway Square. At Central Station he bought a return ticket to Melbourne. Yet by the time the train reached Albury, Harry's interest in Rhonda had faded. He got off the train. He paced up and down the platform. The train was about to leave. He hesitated. Slowly the train glided past him. He watched the carriages going by. Soon he was standing alone on the platform.

He wandered round Albury all day. It was very hot. People moved slowly. He couldn't think clearly. He was tired. He was no closer to making plans than he'd been yesterday in Sydney. Then he was back at the station. The train from Melbourne was arriving. Between Albury and Junee, he sat immobile, oblivious of other people in the carriage, of parents chastising a crying child, of people snoring, of an old man breaking wind slackly in his sleep, listening to the silence inside his mind. A few seconds after the train ground to a halt in the Riverina town Joanie Thomas sat down next to him.

49

There was a sense in which because of the Doreen affair Harry had become a different person, for he now surrendered himself completely to the Judy Connell fantasy. The fantasy became his most powerful motivation. Inside himself, caressing Judy's presence there, Harry lived and re-lived his fantasy. He still said nothing to his mates. On the outside he instinctively understood how his mates would react if he opened his soul to them. They'd be embarrassed, of course, wouldn't know what to say to him. Mackenzie would probably start one of his stupid arguments. And so, to his friends he remained unchanged. A few days later, though he felt no need to raise a query about it, Gordie Sloan did wonder that Harry seemed maybe happier than usual for someone who'd just been dumped by his girl-friend, but then it was only a fleeting notion, for Harry still behaved otherwise normally.

'You're pretty chirpy, today, Harry?'

'Yeah, why not, Gordie?'

'Yeah, why not? She wasn't your type, mate.'

'Who wasn't?'

'Doreen!'

'Oh, yeah, Doreen.'

'You've met someone else, then?'

'Yeah,' smiled Harry.

'Oh, right,' said Gordie, hiding his disappointment.

'Met the wife on the train coming up from Albury,' Harry says to the Johnsons. He speaks cheerfully, clearly, as though his drunkenness has gone away.

At that instant Mrs Johnson pulls in four sevens. 'Now there's a bit of good luck,' she sighs, nodding towards the fifth but unaligned seven, 'mixed with a bit o' bad.'

Vincenzio pays the hundred dollars. While Mrs Johnson is signing for the money, he throws Harry a questioning look. 'Everything okay, mate?' he asks.

'Real sweet, Vincenzio,' replies Harry. He's relieved that only four sevens have come up on Thirty-four. He turns to the Johnsons. 'That was a close one,' he said affably. 'But them sevens are comin' up, the five of 'em.'

'Tom and me's takin' a holiday in New Zealand if we win the big one, aren't we, Tom?'

Tom nods.

'Always wanted to see New Zealand,' says Mrs Johnson. 'They reckon it's really beautiful over there, with them hot springs and everything.'

'We've never been out of Australia,' Harry says.

'Us neither.'

'Wouldn't mind taking the wife on a trip,' says Harry, looking over at Joanie. She's still seated next to that Andy bloke, the one with the twisted elbow. He wonders why she's staying there so long. At least he knows where she is, that she's safe. He feels happy she's safe. 'Nothing's too good for Joanie,' he murmurs under his breath.

Then Gordie's at his elbow again. Swaying slightly, he holds two schooners, wears the set expression of a drunken man trying to appear sober.

'Hey, Gordie,' beams Harry accepting the drink. 'How's it goin'?'

Gordie's wispy hair is slightly disarranged. He squints at Harry, taking time to focus. Harry winks broadly at the Johnsons. 'My best mate,' he says. 'Mr Gordon Sloan. Gordie, meet my good friends, the Johnsons.'

Gordie takes Tom Johnson's hand. 'Pleased to meet you,' he says thickly. He turns to Harry. 'I thought you'd have left by now.'

Harry raises his eyebrows.

'Oh, why's that?'

'You said you were meeting Joanie tonight.'

Harry leans close to Gordie. He's smirking.

'Met her already, ' he says. He points. 'Over there, see.'

Gordie follows the direction of Harry's finger.

'Over where?' he says.

'Over there, on the dollar pokie, sitting down next to that short bloke, the one with the bald head. See her?'

Gordie stared for a few seconds.

'See. With the bloke wearin' the thick glasses.'

'That's not Joanie,' says Gordie.

'Course it bloody well is,' says Harry.

Gordie shakes his head worriedly.

'No it isn't, mate.'

Harry looks hard at Joanie. Then back at Gordie.

'Gordie,' he says. 'You're really pissed up tonight, mate? Jen's not goin' to be real thrilled when you get home, is she?'

'Jen's not at home.'

'Jeez, you're lucky, then.'

'She's up the hospital.'

'She's where?'

'Up the hospital. St Vincent's.'

Harry stares at Gordie. His friend's glassy eyes are fixed on him. The scar on Gordie's cheek suddenly seems familiar. He frowns. He knows about Gordie's skin, course he does, fair skin, blotchy like Andy's over there, Andy standing alongside Joanie. Joanie? Where's Joanie? For a moment anxiously he thinks she isn't there, that the woman isn't Joanie. Hospital? No, no, he assures himself, she's not at the hospital. She's here, with him. They're having a night out together, aren't they? Him and Joanie. Like old times. Okay, she's still with Andy Simpson, yeah, the left winger with the twisted elbow. Safe as houses he'd be, the old left winger, har, har har. His eyes flick back to Gordie. Suddenly he remembers something, like lead weights in his guts, the same feeling he'd had back at the flat—the flat? this morning? when he'd woken up? come round? drank that brandy? oh Jesus!—'Gordie,' he whispers. He grabs Gordie's shirt, feels a sudden nausea. Maybe he's drunker than he thinks. 'Gordie,' he says, 'it's Keithy, isn't it? It's Keithy.'

Gordie's now struggling to look Harry in the eye.

Harry grabs his shoulders. His squeeze makes Gordie wince.

'Harry, for Christ's sake!'

'Is Keithy alright?'

Gordie feels very confused. He's very drunk. Drunker than usual. He can't focus his eyes properly. He feels very inadequate, out of his depth. He feels like a coward. He feels angry with Harry. He feels as though he's been swindled by Harry, emotionally swindled. He's felt that way for so long now, so many years, so many painful years, being swindled by Harry. And now Harry's having a breakdown. Oh, he'd seen it coming, so it's no surprise to Gordie. He tightens his lips, now he feels as angry with himself as he does with Harry. Maybe he might have been more help; maybe if he'd tried to see more of Harry these past five years, since Harry and Joanie had separated, since Harry had moved to Bondi Junction.

'As far as I know, he's okay, Harry,' he decides to say.

Harry relaxes his grip on Gordie's shoulders. He looks over to Joanie. Jeez! she's playing the dollar pokie with the Andy bloke. Anyhow this makes him feel reassured. If Joanie's here and playing the pokies, Keithy must be okay.

'That's good, Gordie,' he says, 'real good, mate.'

He turns to the Johnsons. He has a weird glint in his eye. He pulls himself up to his full height. He examines Gordie's stocky figure, swaying gently near him.

'Keithy means everything to me, Gordie.'

Gordie sighs, rolls drunkenly on his heels.

'I know he does, mate.'

Then he takes Harry's arm. Gently he says:

'Listen, he'll be alright, mate. No worries. Keithy'll be alright.'

'Yeah, Harry, yeah.'

Harry's eyes seem to grip Gordie tightly.

'Mate, I love that boy,' he says.

50

Harry does love the boy. He does not easily understand his love. Sometimes his love for the boy is like fear. In his darkest moments he fears the boy *is* Flan O'Brien, as if, in some terrible science fiction, he, Harry O'Brien, has given birth to his own father. Sometimes, if the fear does not fully develop, or something distracts his mind, or if he is drunk, he will, for a while, succeed in pulling himself together and tell himself that of course Keithy is an O'Brien, but then, after time, he will sink back into his fear and he will lie awake at night, seeing the boy's features in his mind, and his agitation will grow, so that despite it still being the early hours he will get out of bed and pad down the hall to Keithy's bedroom, and stare down at the face of the boy, and sometimes the face does become the face of his own father, lying there, and he will have a fluttering sensation in his chest, and his breath will seem difficult to catch, and maybe he will cry a little, and then he will calm down, and feel love, and his love will overwhelm him, and he will lean forward and want to scoop his child up into his arms, and absorb him, make the child into himself, become the child, and then he will lean down closer and his fingers will almost touch the child lying there in the darkness, but then he will pull away, and feel defeated, as though he hasn't the courage to do whatever it was he had thought, momentarily, he had come into the bedroom to do, and then he will feel a strangeness about him, as though he were a gentler, softer person than he knew himself to be, and he will lean forward again, and brush his fingers lightly over the boy's face, and feel the softness of the skin, and feel very warm inside, as though maybe he, Harry O'Brien, could even be the boy's mother as well as the father, and then his mind, as though fragmented, seems everywhere at once, and thoughts tumble around, and he stands shivering in the dark, feeling confused, trying to deal with his mind, his memory, as though there is only a *now*, no *then*, and his life is *here* as well as *there,* as though he *always* has been here before, and his life *is* memories, and he will feel as though the room has no walls and is space, himself surrounded by endless space, as though there is no time, only memories, only dream, the condition of dream, like a world of dream, of a boy cowering breathlessly under a woman's fat thighs, a boy gaping through the keyhole at his father taking sexual pleasure, then him, Harry, suddenly grown, and wanting to be a good husband, to do things right, be loyal, leave other women alone, use his virtue to wipe out the crimes of his father, yet he fails, he's imperfect, finds that wrong is the easier to commit, is the more attractive, the more addictive, that he is as he is, controlled, determined, which is why he is what he is, as though that is his fate, like his injured knee is his fate, and he will return to his own bed, and his mind will continue seething as it continues to review his life, the trivial as well as the significant, as though now it is all dreamlike. And, as though it is programmed into his brain, the dream of his father, of Flan O'Brien, grandson of old Rory, will creep up on him, stealthily, as though he is its prey, and it is his turn to be hunted, to be caught, to be devoured, and he will awake in fear and lie quite still, listening, and then he will try to shift his mind to other thoughts, thoughts of his other women, of Tanya, scrawny little Tanya, and Kate Stilwell, Kate...

51

Harry had slipped up there, over the new manageress at Pollards, the hard-eyed Miss Kate Stilwell who'd turned up after that sex scandal between Jim Ross and fat Freda on confectionery; Kate, his new boss, who'd slunk up on him without warning, wanted to improve the efficiency of the storeroom she said, breathing peppermint fumes and cigarette smoke all over him, 'shift more stock', 'up the quotas'; he was lucky he'd escaped that little lot, as he drifts into sleep, tries to avoid dream, is dreaming, is awake, feels Joanie stirring alongside, feels her warmth, dreams of Keithy, cold floorboards under his toes, the baby not an O'Brien, stupid how he's afraid of a little kid like that, but he loves him, thinks again how lucky he'd been to escape the Kate Stilwell thing, she'd had the advantage, being his boss, not like with Doreen, it was so uncomplicated with Doreen, before Joanie, before Keithy, and he was missing Beethoven, well maybe not Beethoven, he was missing Doreen's mangey street cat, the ugliest cat he'd ever seen, no fucking whiskers, bits of ginger fur missing from all that scrapping and screwing in the Paddington lanes, it was good with Doreen, no strings attached, a good set-up, maybe he should have read those books, married Doreen, must get some sleep, he really missed the Paddington terrace, he loved Joanie, he wanted to be married to Joanie, Col Maguire died; why'd he have to die? best mate he'd ever had, old Maggoty and his worm farm, 'feed 'em well an' they won't let you down,' but there'd be no Keithy if old Col hadn't died on the carpet with brown tea spilling from his mouth, didn't use the diaphragm that night, clever of Joanie to trick him like that, but he'd loved the old bugger like a father, mutters, 'like a father', Joanie stirs, old Col older than Alf Parsons, Alf, friendly old coot, no teeth, never understood a word he said except his swearing, knew his way around that storeroom though, like an old tom cat, stuffed up his kidneys with powders, always complaining about his kidneys, the old so-and-so should have retired years ago, gave the wrong age when they hired him, seventy-five if he was a day, World War I vet and all, might even have known Alice Reilly's husband, poor bugger only had half a lung, good worker though, drank plonk for morning tea just like the old derro in Belmore Park, and those headache powders, two fucking packets a day would you believe, no wonder his kidneys collapsed, washing the powders down with sweet sherry all those years, says a lot about the human body, the punishment it can take, funny that old Alf never did die from the grog, just shows you, doesn't it, what a load of old rubbish they talk about how drink can kill you, it didn't kill Alf, bloody powders killed him, drink didn't kill Flan O'Brien, did it? the bugger was still putting away plenty when they carted him off to hospital, his lungs were shot though, that's what killed old Flan—'Respiratory failure' they'd written on the death certificate 'secondary to emphysema and infective pneumonia'— looked like a concentration camp inmate when he died, skin the exact colour of his nicotine stains, stretched over his bones, like dried cowhide, he'd even felt compassion for him, a weird kind of compassion, compassion mixed with disgust, he'd even wanted to forgive the old bastard (he wasn't that old), hated the bastard, hatred and forgiveness, and compassion, and disgust, and love? he didn't know what he felt, forgiveness? he'd forced himself to believe he was forgiving Flan O'Brien, what was it like? to feel forgiving, how do you feel forgiving to this body on a hospital bed, this excuse for a body, lying on the bed, like a corpse but alive, making those obscene noises, these bones that are all that is left of his life?

Flan's fingers had clutched at Harry. He'd tried but had been unable to speak and could only look at Harry with longing in his eyes as he struggled to breathe behind the oxygen mask. Then he must have died, because he stopped making all those crackling and gurgling sounds, and his fingers gave up their feeble hold, and he seemed to sink back and become strangely flattened as though his body was just a piece of embroidery on the bed clothes, but with the eyes still glistening above the silent mouth, eyes which still stared at Harry as they shed Flan's tears even after he'd drawn his last breath, and all you could hear now was the hiss of oxygen wasting itself inside the mask.

52

And Harry depresses the five-play button, and the lights in the club seem to be hurting his eyes, and he thinks he's forgiven his father as he scores three bells.

Three bells. He stares at the three gold coloured icons lined up in the pokie window. He remembers three bells. A cluster of three brass bells. On the desk in Kate Stilwell's office at Pollards city store. She used them to call Ivy, her secretary. It gave Kate pleasure to make Ivy jump to her feet and watch her rush into the office every time she gave the bells a tinkle. A sharp, hard sounding tinkle, he remembered, like Kate's voice, brassy, like her personality.

Kate would have rung her bells a couple of minutes before Ivy told Harry the new manageress wanted to see him.

'Tell Harry O'Brien to come up straight away.'

A week after it had become evident that Harry's boss, Alf Parsons, was very ill and would not be returning to work Kate offered Harry the position of acting head storeman-packer.

'It'll be for three months.'

'Thanks, Miss Stilwell,' said Harry, looking down on the tiny woman seated at her desk. She had powerful eyes and a peremptory manner of speech

'I suppose you'll be able to handle the job?'

'I reckon,' he said.

'You're sure?'

'Yes.'

She eyed him like she might have been judging a prize animal.

'Do the job well, and you'll be fine,' she said.

Almost everything she said carried a veiled threat.

'I need a shipshape store, Harry. Efficient and effective at all times. I hope that's clear?'

'It's clear.'

She was playing with the bells, stroking the polished metal surface with the back of her finger.

'I understand you're married?'

'Yes.'

'Happily.'

'Yes.'

But he'd hesitated for the tiniest fraction of a second.

'I see.'

She lifted her eyes. They were very pale, their colour unclear, maybe blue, maybe grey. She looked up at Harry, suddenly smiling.

'And you're ambitious?'

'Yes.'

'It'll take real effort, Harry.'

She saw his quizzical look.

'To become a manager. That's what you'd like, isn't it?'

'Yes, I suppose so.'

'And your wife would like it, wouldn't she?'

'Yes.'

Her eyes bored into him. He could feel them. Then she smiled her clever smile. It required little effort, just a slight uplift of her cheeks and an almost imperceptible gathering of the crow's feet in the corners of her eyes.

'Right. Good. Thank you, Harry. That'll be all.'

Harry turned to go. Kate rang the bells. Ivy rushed in.

'Harry will be head storeman-packer from now on. Make out the necessary changes to his salary details, will you?

Harry was at the door.

'Oh, yes, Harry,' Kate called out. 'You can expect me in the storeroom sometime today. I need to be familiarised with your, er...' (she smiled) '*modus operandi*.'

So, there *was* another agenda, thought Harry as he walked back to the storeroom. Briefly he considered his options. She was a feisty little sheila. A hellcat. Like Tanya, he reckoned. Yet, as the store manageress, he was certain she'd be the soul of discretion. He reached the office and sat down at his desk. He twirled a pencil between his fingers. Yeah, he thought, brushing aside feelings of guilt, why not? Anyhow, it would all be for Joanie and the kid's benefit, later, when he became a manager himself.

It was ridiculously easy for them. Unlike the counter staff, Kate could come and go as she pleased, vary the hour and duration of her visits to the store room, and, as she believed, deceive the staff into thinking she was merely performing her normal managerial supervision by checking on the work going on downstairs in the storeroom. And, like the aggressive, unscrupulous, and amazingly successful (for the nineteen sixties) female executive that she was, she took it for granted that Harry's body was part of the deal, and she would expect him to drop whatever he was doing, and then, in the style of an examining physician, she would pause to gaze, as though diagnostically, at his body, at his thighs, then she would move very close to him, and trail her fingers across his stomach, and move them lower, until they reached his groin, then she would loosen his trousers, and wait as he sprouted into stiffness, whereupon she would smile her mirthless smile and, in her peremptory fashion, raise her skirts, gasp a little, then insert him in her like a fork into meat and thrust at him savagely, mechanically, so that he would have the strangest sensation that she was emptying herself into him, and he would feel her strong fingers gripping his thighs, and feel the sharp, convulsive contractions in her vagina, and hear her congratulating him in her crisp and only slightly breathless voice as though he had just passed an exam for promotion.

Afterwards she would let him make her coffee, and she would discuss details of storeroom practice with him. She would sit very upright on her chair, her hair and clothes neatly rearranged, and they would talk together as tutor and tyro, as though their coupling might not have taken place, and it was a strange experience for Harry, this intense discipline of the emotions, possessed by Kate, a single-minded attention to the physical details of sex, without the messy baggage of relationship.

For once in his life, he blushed. On just the one occasion, after they'd had sex, she said: 'I like the way you fuck, Harry.' She said this as though she might be congratulating him on his choice of tie colour. Yet, there was something strangely exciting about Kate's directness; she talks like a bloke, thought Harry, yeah, just like a bloke. 'Thanks,' he'd replied sheepishly. 'Remember, you're on my executive team, now, Harry,' Kate had said. 'We have our own little set of rules, don't we?' She stared at him. His face was still flushed from his efforts. He nodded. Kate continued: 'It's a very strict code, Harry.' The iciness was back in her voice. 'We never let the side down, do we?' 'No,' said Harry. 'And we never breathe a word about what happens in the privacy of our offices?' 'Definitely not,' said Harry with enough fervour to raise the smile again on Kate's features. 'Very good, Harry,' she said, allowing him to light her cigarette.

For a few weeks this became their routine. Harry, as it were, doing his duty in the store room office; Kate taking her pleasure quickly and efficiently, and expecting to do so at least every second day; the management system improving under Kate's driving energy, the staff throwing Harry suspicious looks when he appeared on the sales floor, the girls beginning to suspect he and the manageress might have become secret lovers, Kate, keeping her usual emotional distance from the staff, giving them not a sliver of evidence in support of their suspicions, Harry, giving devoted attention to his new position of responsibility, now avoiding all unnecessary contact with the women on the staff.

Despite their careful attention to secrecy, rumours began to surface on the sales floor. Brenda Williams, the redhead on cosmetics, the one who'd once claimed Harry had proposed to her, was the worst offender.

'I bet you he's givin' it to that Miss Stilwell,' she grizzled to Nora.

'But she's the boss.'

'And a true bitch, if ever I saw one.'

'Funny that Harry's never said nuthin' about it.'

'He wouldn't, would he? Now he's one of them.'

'What d'you mean?'

'Part of the bloody executive, of course, stupid!'

Yet there was nothing any of the staff could discover which substantiated such rumours. And so Brenda, waited, and watched, and seethed with jealous anger every time she saw Kate emerge from the storeroom with her clothing perfectly in place and every hair on her head, every skerrick of her make-up, undisturbed.

'She's too bloody perfect,' grumbled Brenda. 'Look at her. Jeez! Look how she's got her hair. It weren't that neat when she went down there, that's for sure.'

At home, Joanie could not bring herself to suspect Harry. She was not yet ready to accept the possibility—there might have been occasions when she contemplated it—that her own relationship with Harry was less than perfect. She did not question Harry when he came home smelling slightly of the peppermints Kate Stilwell ate to subdue the smell on her breath of the Turkish cigarettes she chain-smoked.

'Busy day at work, Harry?'

'Yes, love.'

'Must be hard, getting used to being in charge of the storeroom.'

'I'm taking special training.'

'Oh?'

Harry threw Joanie an enormous grin.

'With the manageress.'

Joanie's face remained unchanged.

'That's good, Harry, love,' she said.

Then there was a phone call, during the day, when Harry was at work.

'Is that Mrs O'Brien?' asked a woman's voice.

'Yes, who's this?' answered Joanie.

'That don't matter. Let's just say I'm one of your husband's workmates.'

'Oh, yes,' said Joanie uncertainly.

'Listen, love, I'm ringin' to tell you what's goin' on down the store.'

'What do you mean?'

'It's about Harry, your husband.'

'What about him?'

'Well, he's havin' it off with the manageress.'

Then the woman hung up. And Joanie was staring at the handset. She was cradling Keithy in her other arm. She put the phone down, tickled Keithy's cheeks. 'How's my big boy, then,' she clucked. Keithy grinned up at her. 'How's my great big young fella doing, then?' she said.

Later, as she was breast-feeding the baby, she told Harry.

Harry was incredulous.

'With Kate Stilwell!'

'Yes; ridiculous isn't it?' said Joanie.

'Bloody ridiculous,' he said as indignantly as he could, and thinking immediately of Brenda Williams.

'I suppose they're jealous of you, Harry,' said Joanie, 'down at the store. Now you've been promoted, I mean?'

Harry lit a cigarette. He was watching Joanie. Her nipple stood out from her blouse. It was bright pink, it reminded him suddenly of Doreen's nipples, not Kate's, he'd never seen Kate's nipples.

'About my promotion? Nah, not about that,' he said.

'Oh; then what?'

'Of you, love. I reckon they're jealous of you, you know, because you're such a good-looking sort.'

Joanie smiled, hitched Keithy up higher, watched the baby's mouth already making urgent sucking movements as it approached the nipple.

'That woman, Harry,' she said. 'Accusing you like that. I'd like to scratch her eyes out.'

'She's just some silly old crank, Joanie.'

An hour later, they made love. As far as Harry could tell, Joanie took her usual pleasure with him. Yet he took much longer than usual, and, for the first time in his marriage, he found himself forced to pretend his climax had been as intense as usual. But he was truly thankful he had the kind of stiffness Joanie expected of her husband after nearly a week without sex (as it was supposed to be), and then, as though he was being simultaneously mocked and rescued by the Creator to whom he was about to appeal for assistance, Joanie was coming a second time, and this had happened only once before, when they'd arrived home from the New Year's Eve ball that first summer after they were married.

(They'd crept in at five in the morning, trying not to disturb old Col, and had made love for the next couple of hours. They'd taken so long over it because, though both of them were feeling very randy, both were very drunk, and they'd had all kinds of trouble trying to stop themselves from giggling as they'd struggled to take off each other's clothes, then they giggled a whole lot more at the sight of Harry's stubby little cock, which seemed 'dead from the neck up' as Harry, though for once embarrassed, had joked, but then as they began to concentrate on creating the mood within which performance might be encouraged to match desire, he'd begun to respond, and, under Joanie's gentle urging had sprouted as extravagantly as he had on that famous afternoon with Tanya.)

In the morning he awoke still tired. He wandered around the kitchen, bleary-eyed and uncommunicative, cranky with Joanie—who'd slept very well and still wore the bloom of sexual satisfaction on her face—uncaring that he'd given his wife even greater pleasure last night than he'd given her during all the scant few months when he'd been totally faithful to her, which just goes to show that there is something deeply humorous in creation after all.

He was also impatient with Keithy, to whom he normally paid little attention, and Keithy began grizzling as he reacted to Harry's bad temper and thus dominated Joanie's attention so that Harry had to get his own breakfast and burnt the toast, and there was a minor disaster in the kitchen as he scorched a tea towel trying to put out the toaster fire, and almost electrocuted himself because he forgot to unplug the toaster and instead, because the same providence was watching over him, blew the power fuses which he replaced and ended up nearly being late for work.

When he arrived at the store, he sought out Brenda Williams. Brenda was busy setting up her cash register.

'G'day, Harry,' said Brenda affably. She was a self-assured nineteen-year-old.

Unwisely, Harry, his burnt fingers still smarting, came straight to the point.

'Why'd you phone Joanie last night, Brenda?'

'Me? Phone your wife, Harry?'

'Yeah, and tell her all those lies about me and Kate Stilwell?'

'Kate Stilwell, Harry? I thought she was Miss Stilwell, to all us ordinary employees?'

'Why'd you tell her that stuff, Brenda?'

Brenda paused from her work of emptying packets of coins into her cash drawer. She knew she was about to wreck her chances with him forever. But Harry or no Harry, she had her pride. She looked up, fixed her eyes on Harry. Here goes, she thought, realising she was about to close off her opportunity for ever. 'Harry,' she said evenly, 'I didn't tell her nuthin'. Now, fuck off, okay!'

The rumours increased, began to spread round the store. Someone was gunning for Kate Stilwell. Harry was sure it was Brenda. Of course Brenda, like everyone else, admitted nothing. But there was a heavy atmosphere in the store. Staff spoke in subdued tones, as though they were all waiting for something to happen.

'Betcha Harry's still givin' it to that Stilwell woman.'

'Yeah, an' him married an' all.'

'Yeah, I heard his wife's a bit on the—you know—a bit stupid.'

'Yeah, stupid enough to have married that arsehole, O'Brien,' growled Brenda.

One evening, several days after Harry's incident with Brenda, Kate received a phone call.

'Is that Kate Stilwell?' said a woman's voice.

'Yes, who is this?'

'Never you mind, bitch!' the voice snapped out. 'O'Brien givin' you a good time, is he, sweetheart? Well, he won't be for much longer! And, bitch,' went on the voice, 'start lookin' for another job. You're goin' to need it when I tell the big bosses on you down Pitt Street.'

The next morning Kate called Harry into her office.

Harry saw immediately that he was in trouble. Kate's fingers were tapping the brass bells.

'Pitt Street just called,' she said, mentioning the location of head office.

Harry's eyes narrowed.

'They did,' he said stupidly.

'You're fired, Harry,' said Kate.

Harry tried to speak.

Kate got in first.

'You just couldn't keep your bloody mouth closed, could you?'

'But, what about—'

Her eyes flashed dangerously.

'I thought you were smart enough to understand the rules.'

'I am smart...'

'You're fucking stupid, Harry.'

'I did everything you told me.'

'It's over, Harry.'

'I—I thought—'

'No discussion,' she snapped. 'It never happened. Just go.'

And that was that. Harry was on his way, holding his final pay envelope which Kate had already made up for him, moving past the dropped expressions on the faces of the women staff, past the sneering faces of the male staff, feeling stunned, amazed how easy it had seemed for Kate to dismiss him, discard him, as though he was nothing. As he passed cosmetics he looked straight ahead. He couldn't risk turning his head in case Brenda was watching him.

Then he was on the busy Oxford Street pavement, surrounded by movement and noise. He set off, his mind now curiously blank, allowing himself to move with the flow of people, across the intersection at Oxford and Elizabeth Streets, past the low stone wall bordering Hyde Park, heading north. It was ten minutes past nine.

Soon he was at Circular Quay. He passed beneath the elevated railway, hearing the heavy rumble of electric trains above him on the city circle route. He was at the water's edge, standing by the safety railing, near the Manly Ferry wharf. The water below his feet was becoming disturbed by the great bulk of the *South Steyne* heading towards him. He heard the deep roar of engines, watched the steamer shudder to a halt, saw foam boiling angrily around its waterline then wash against the thick wooden pylon buffers a few yards out from where he stood. For a long while he gazed at the turbulence in the water, waiting for it to subside.

At half-past ten he rang Gordie Sloan. They agreed to meet that afternoon at St George Leagues Club.

Harry bought the first schooner. When he returned to their table with the drinks, he pulled three twenties and a ten from his pay packet.

'What I owe you, mate,' he said.

Gordie was reluctant to take the money.

'I'm not pushed for it, Harry.'

'Take it, Gordie,' said Harry.

He shoved the money into Gordie's shirt pocket. They drank more schooners.

A few friends arrived, started drinking, smoking, chatting.

'...givin' the commies what they bloody deserve...'

'...hear about Jimmy?'

'...yeah, poor bastard.'

'...flew his mother to Saigon.'

'...Yeah, I heard.'

'...Waited till she arrived, they reckon.'

'...Yeah.'

'...Balmain...in with a chance...'

'...You're jokin'...'

'...Gaznier's out...'

'...Yeah, bugger it!'

'...Hey; d'you hear Newcombe lost in America...'

'...Poms have one of them nuclear subs...'

'...Yanks still have that spacecraft goin' round the moon...'

'...Soon have blokes runnin' round up there...'

'...Yeah, that's what we need. A trip to the bloody moon.'

After a while Gordie asked:

'How'd it happen, Harry?'

Harry shrugged his shoulders.

'Someone obviously had it in for me.'

'That girl—'

'Yeah, Brenda; the one on cosmetics.'

'How about Stilwell?'

'Her too, I reckon.'

'Don't suppose she gave you a reference?'

'Not bloody likely.'

'You told Joanie, yet?'

'No.'

'She won't be real happy.'

'It's no big deal, Gordie. I'll get another job.'

Gordie studied his glass.

'Why not come and work for me?' he said.

'In the furniture store?'

'Yeah.'

'What would I do?'

'Well, deliveries mainly. And stock control. You know, the sort of thing you were doing at Pollards.'

'You really want me to work for you?'

'Yeah, Harry. You could be my assistant manager.'

'Seriously?'

'Seriously.'

Harry looked at his friend. Gordie's eyes were still down, his fingers still toying with his glass.

'Thanks Gordie,' he said quietly.

Gordie looked away, embarrassed.

'Anyhow, you've got a kid to think of, right?'

'Yeah, that's right.'

Later on, he asked:

'Keithy walking yet, Harry?'

'No, not yet, mate.'

53

As though his life is spinning by him faster than these speeding pokie icons, so much happening, could he really have done all these things, could he really have been fucking Kate Stillwell like that in the store room office—as though Harry is imagining himself inside his conscience, as though he isn't a moral cretin after all (a Doreen expression, whatever it means, oh, yes, Harry, he fucking knows what *it* means), as though he's seeing himself for the first time, seeing the burden of himself and his life and the way he's shrugged off that burden, so lightly, so casually, smelling of Kate Stillwell as he makes love to poor little Joanie, Joanie, Joanie, Judy, Judy, O Christ! what the fuck's happening, I'm in the club, he tells himself, as though he's part of the club, part of its structure, as though he's part of the wall there, the dome there, the dance floor, giggles, I can feel the feet of the dancers sliding over me, he thinks, I'm pissed out of my mind, he thinks, watching the pokie icons whizzing past, giddy, giddy, Gordie, Gordie, Joannie, Joanie, Judy, Judy, Keithy, Keithy, O Christ, Keithy, Keithy, a voice screams inside Harry's skull as he calmly presses Thirty-three's play button and she takes off at full belt, her barrels spinning fast, throwing up, yeah, spew 'em up you bitch, yeah, three sevens, Jesus! only three of the bastards, Jesus! gimme five sevens, you cunt of a machine, gimme five sevens why don'tcher, fer fuck's sake! he screams inside himself as thoughts tumble around like dirty washing inside his head, thoughts he can't control, subdue, destroy, kill, kill, thoughts poor old Harry can't kill, a little kid, no more'n a babe, on his feet, wobbling, wobbling, on his feet though, wobbling on his feet...

———

Keithy took his first unaided steps when he was thirteen months old. Joanie was busy in the kitchen. Harry was in the lounge room keeping an eye on Keithy. His newspaper lay unread on his lap and his beer stubby, untouched, hung slackly in his fingers. The TV chattered emptily over in the corner. Though he had no idea what programme was showing, he made no effort to turn the set off for the TV's babble and flicker seemed strangely soothing. He sat still, only his eyes moved, as Keithy pulled himself along the edges of a chair. The boy worked hard. He was panting. He used his limbs cleverly, one foot moving while the other waited, both feet firmly planted as the hands sought a new grip on the chair. Then he paused, as though listening, as though thinking. Then he lifted his hands. The movement caught Harry's eye. Keithy was standing unaided. Harry watched more fully. The child wobbled, seemed about to plop down on his nappy-clad backside, instead, remained standing, his eyes fixed on Harry, who watched in silence, unaware his mouth was open, that he was holding his breath.

'Joanie,' he whispered, 'Joanie, come in here.'

Joanie appeared in the doorway.

'Look.'

Keithy held his hands out from his body, wobbling still, but staying erect, like a nappied tightrope walker.

Then he took his first step.

'Come on, mate, come on,' urged Harry, holding his arms outstretched towards Keithy.

'Go to daddy,' said Joanie.

Keithy fell over. Joanie bent down, picked him up, held him as he wobbled and then found his feet.

'Come on, mate,' said Harry.

Keithy stood there wobbling.

'Come on, Keithy.'

Keithy stepped forward: one step, two steps, three steps, paused, wobbled, fell.

Harry scooped him up in his arms.

'He walked, Joanie,' said Harry, hugging Keith, 'the little bugger walked!'

That night Harry dreamed. It was such an uncontaminated dream. Everything seemed just right. A happy dream. He was holding the baby under the armpits, holding him high, laughing at the boy, seeing the boy laughing at him. Then, in the magic of his dream, Keithy's face is the face of a teen-age boy, and he's standing in front of Harry, he's as tall as Harry, and he's smiling, and then they're running together, he and Keithy, on a football field, there's a crowd, cheering, they're in the city, at the Sydney Cricket Ground, a Grand Final's about to start, Harry can see the referee putting his whistle to his mouth, there's a pause, the crowd, the players, the flags flying at the mast heads, all are suddenly still, and quiet, sharing a synergy of stillness and quietness, as everything in the world waits for Keithy. Then, Keithy comes up close to Harry, gives Harry a broad wink, and they're shaking hands, Harry can feel Keithy's firm handshake, palpable, in his dream, which isn't a dream, as though he's fully awake, and there's a sublime sense of perfection in that handshake with his son, as though he and the boy have become one person for those few moments... Then Keithy trots back to the centre of the field. The crowd roars, the game starts, Keithy's running, diving, scoring, being a champion.

Harry awoke early. He showered. His head cleared rapidly. The memory of his dream persisted. He hummed as he shaved. He saw himself in the mirror. He saw his freshly shaved skin, his eyes looking out at him. He paused, examining his eyes. He smiled.

Now, in Mid-City Leagues, he remembers the dream, feels the shape of same smile on his face. The dream seems so fresh, so recent, he cannot believe that he dreamed the dream so very long ago. He does not, for the moment, thus attend to Gordie standing next to him, or be aware of the Johnsons and their compassionate eyes, or Waddling Thighs over there throwing him sneering glances, or Vincenzio, hovering a few machines away, frowning, or Trish, collecting empty glasses, also worrying about the big man, or the woman he thinks is Joanie, or Andy, or, or...

'It can't have been that bloody long ago.'

'What can't, Harry?' says Gordie uncertainly.

'Keithy can't be that old.'

'Harry—' begins Gordie, falls silent.

Harry is perplexed. 'Keithy, eighteen?' he asks in disbelief. He turns to Gordie. 'Keithy isn't eighteen, is he, Gordie?'

Gordie shrugged his shoulders, smiles weakly.

Harry says: 'He's alright? Keithy's alright?'

––––––

Even as Harry remembers. Vividly. What a wonderful dream it had been. So wonderful. Such a fulfilling dream. As though he and Keithy really had been a single person, totally one, how was that possible? It had seemed so real. He tried to recall the feeling, of being Keithy, as though he truly had become Keithy inside his dream, as though Keithy had been him, how strange, how could that be, how could two people become one, it wasn't possible, was it? Yet it had happened. It was no dream. Too vivid, too real, to be a dream. That's what Harry recalls now. That it was no dream, no ordinary dream, a vision maybe, yes, some kind of vision, beyond the normal, beyond flesh and blood experience, yes, that's it, that was it... Then why? Why? Why is he feeling the way he is feeling? Why does he feel so empty? As though his guts are gone. The way they seemed gone this morning. This morning?

Was it this morning? He cannot believe it was only this morning. Unlike his remembered dream, it seems so long ago. He remembers the book in the linen cupboard. The book with the bloke on the cover. Holding the teddy bear. He remembers pulling down the book, dusting it off, wondering about the story, whether he ought to read it. Maybe he did read that book Doreen had given him? *'These memories, which are my life...'*

'He's alright? Keithy's alright?'

'Yes mate, as far as I know.'

'Thank God,' he whispers and punches the five-play button. Gordie watches, uncertain about what he should do. He places Harry's glass on Thirty-three's side shelf.

'There's your drink, Harry,' he says softly.

'Thanks,' says Harry. His voice is very flat. As though he is very far away. He does not turn his head.

Gordie turns at the Johnsons. 'Listen,' he whispers to them very softly. 'My mate's had a hell of a shock.' He lowers his voice still further. 'Very messy. Serious problems in the family. Blames himself for it all.' Then he points towards the Members' Bar. 'I'm over there, in the corner, with a few of my mates. Give me a yell, will you? You know, if he seems like he's not real good.'

'Yeah, sure, love,' whispers Mrs Johnson.

Harry is grateful to Gordie. He knows he can trust his friend, that Gordie is the most trustworthy person he knows. He punches Thirty-three. The barrels spin. He watches but does not register the result, for in his mind he is at Arncliffe Park, on wet turf now, with his son. Keithy is three years old, dressed in home-made shorts and footy shirt. The shirt is white and has a wide red V-neck stitched to it from an old frock of Joanie's. On his stocky legs he wears footy socks knitted in red and white bands. On his feet he wears kids' sandshoes because they couldn't find boots for a three-year-old's feet.

And Harry wears shorts and his old Balmain guernsey, and black and yellow socks fallen round his ankles. He runs in his old black footy boots with the old-fashioned leather studs and the wide white laces criss-crossing ankle and instep, and the off-white elastic bandage gripping his left leg four inches above and below the knee.

They run together, Keithy flat out, always flat out, there is no other speed, Harry trotting alongside, not limping, moving his legs easily, they are still very young, very strong legs, moving them from the hips, long, muscular legs, with plenty of power in reserve, like he's always had, his knee holding up beautifully, as though uninjured, it isn't injured in Harry's mind, as he runs with Keithy, as he runs now, without effort, his body, like Keithy's body, a perfect unity,

They run without weariness, Harry and Keithy. Sometimes Harry gives Keithy his head. 'Go, Keithy, go,' he yells. Keithy accelerates, runs like mad, his legs stout pistons pumping effortlessly, his face uplifted as he reaches high speed, the tiny kids'-sized football clutched under his arm as Harry has taught him, puffing breath like an engine as he speeds towards the line that Harry has marked with their pullovers.

'Go Keithy, Go...'

'Dive, Keithy, dive...'

And Keithy dives, and skids his little body the last few yards, and crosses the line, and plunges the ball down, and lies there spreadeagled on the wet turf, and lifts his head as Harry arrives.

'Did I score? Did I score?' he cries.

And Harry scoops up the boy in one great sweeping movement of his arms, and holds the boy out from him, and stares into his eyes.

'Too right, you did, matey. Too right, you did.'

And the boy smiles and his smile becomes a great, laughing grin, and Harry hugs him to his chest, and now he can feel the boy's lungs still heaving from effort, and feel the trembling in his son's arms as they encircle his neck, and Keithy's hot breath on his cheek.

'He's as good as Reg Gasnier, ' says Harry suddenly. Mrs Johnson looks at Harry. It is ten-o-clock. More people swirl around them. In the pokie lounge, business is picking up.

'He is?' says Mrs Johnson.

'There's nobody can stop him,' says Harry.

He is thinking about Keithy at five and a half. A quick-witted boy. Bright-eyed. And tall and strong for his age. And with this great smile, as though he was smiling it just for you, especially just for you. That was Keithy. The kid who controlled you with his smile, made you want to do anything for him. And his laugh. He had this terrific laugh, like his laugh was something you could see, and feel, not just hear, as though his mouth was alive with laughter, and his laugh was made up of all these sparkling colours, the colours you see bouncing off soap bubbles in bright sunlight.

Harry froze, his hand fixed in the air above Thirty-three. Like Judy. Yeah, Keithy's laugh was just like Judy's. Just like Judy's. Keithy's laugh. Just like Judy used to laugh. As though Judy had come back to him. In Keithy's laugh. He remembered the night Judy had disappeared, how he'd had to stay calm in case Judy came home. He wanted to be calm when she came home. He wouldn't have wanted to upset her. Yet he knew something had happened. Almost expected it. As though his preparations for their meal that night merely provided activity, a diversion, while he waited, waited, hearing the 'plop', 'plop' of water dripping into the overflow tray of Raelene's ice chest.

Then the police had come. And Flan had been asleep. And Harry had answered their questions. Calmly. Very calmly. Like a grown-up. '...Yes, I'm expecting her...' (Which he truly was, desperately.) Spoken very calmly. '...Yes, I'm expecting her...' Very calmly. As though she really would come home. Home? As she had come home. In the park. After the rain. On the wet turf of Arncliffe Park. In Keithy's eyes. His smile. He searched the boy's eyes.

They were shining. His own eyes shone. He could feel their shine. As though they possessed fire. Keithy was grinning up at him, puffing noisily, standing with his strong legs apart, holding the football in front of him, easily, professionally thinks Harry, casually, in the upturned palms of his hands.

Suddenly the boy darted at Harry.

'Get me, dad,' he yelled. 'Get me.'

He swerved just in front of Harry, threw a dummy pass, then side-stepped so that Harry was fooled and lunged one way while Keithy lunged the other. And then Keithy was off, flying towards goal posts marked with their pullovers, and Harry was after him, galloping after him, and this time Harry caught the boy, grabbed his shirt, yanked him off his feet, and Keithy was yelling angrily and struggling to free himself so that he could dive forward the last few yards to score a try.

'Dad, aw, dad! Don't be a mongrel, dad!'

Then they were both on the grass, struggling, Harry clinging to Keithy's wriggling body, the ball, spilled from Keithy's hands, lying a few yards away, Keithy stretching towards it, fingers grasping, trying to pull himself away from Harry's bulk. And Harry saw that Keithy was just like Judy, yes, like Judy; as though the boy staring at him now as he lay on the ground breathing heavily was not only himself, but was Judy, Judy mixed into himself, as a boy, Judy's face, Harry was sure of it, Judy's face staring up at him from the wet turf, in Keithy's eyes, on Keithy's face, flushed, yes, flushed; as it might have been if they'd just made love, he and Judy, Harry suddenly thought, and felt suddenly shamed by his thought, and he rolled off the boy who quickly jumped to his feet and grabbed the ball and dived over the try-line while Harry felt stunned inside his mind, as he contemplated his discovery.

'Dad, dad: I scored a try. I scored a try.'

It was very strange. The way Keithy reminded him of Judy. Very strange. He remembered what had happened that evening as he was saying goodnight to Keithy. The boy was lying on his back, he was looking up at Harry, his eyes were shining. He smiled. 'I scored a try, dad.' Then Harry leaned down and kissed the boy, and he'd closed his eyes, and stayed with his lips on Keithy's cheek for a long moment, and felt himself enjoying the kiss, and thinking of Judy, and the turmoil in his mind, images of Kate, of Doreen, of Judy again, her teeth, of Joanie, of himself, of Judy, strongly of Judy, as though she was real again, not in his mind, he was kissing her, because the boy had lain there passively, and very still, not moving, while Harry kissed him, and felt himself kissing Judy, as though somehow it was Judy he was kissing, and knew that the boy trusted him, which was why he was lying there quietly, passively, while Harry used the boy, absorbed him into himself, as though he was kissing a part of himself, he *was* kissing a part of himself, wasn't he, why shouldn't he kiss a part of himself, give himself pleasure, make the pain go away, because Joanie could never take the place of his friend Judy Connell, yet he loved Joanie, wanted to love her, he loved the idea that he loved Joanie, as though it was his way of justifying his marriage to her, a way of excusing the deceit he'd practised in marrying her, how he'd cheated her into marriage, poor Joanie, thinking he was some kind of shining knight—but the boy *was*, wasn't he, wasn't he like Judy returned to him, a kind of miracle, like a reincarnation, yes, that was it, a reincarnation, Keithy was a reincarnation of Judy he told himself, convinced himself, that was it, that was why he was doing this now, kissing the boy, Judy, kissing her the way he'd wanted to kiss her when she was alive, she was alive now, here, in the bedroom, 'I scored a try, didn't I dad. I scored a try.' Of course she would come back to him this way. Now he was married to Joanie. Of course she wouldn't want to destroy his marriage, his family. How clever of her that she would choose to come back as his son. How clever. How thoughtful of Judy. 'Dad, dad: I scored a try. I scored a try.'

———

'We do everything together,' Harry explains to the Johnsons. 'We do it all together, me and Keithy..'

———

And Joanie. She'd watched in a kind of silent shock. Becoming aware, yet not aware, yet fearful she was becoming aware, yet suppressing her awareness, which is the way we all defend ourselves when threatened with destruction, and we thus seek escape, as Joanie was seeking, yet not fully aware she was seeking escape, as she began to think about herself, and wondered how she could deal with such a depth of ignorance as she possessed, for it seemed like a possession, like a deep tumour, part of her substance, yet inaccessible, gorging itself on her, as Harry gorged himself on Keithy.

She knew she had been deceived in so many ways.

'Harry...' she began to say once.

Harry lifted his head, glanced at her. He did not smile. He did not show any expression.

'Oh, it doesn't matter.'

He turned back to the TV. She watched him through the corner of her eye. She could see the gentle rise and fall of his chest as he breathed. She could smell the familiar workaday smell of him before it was washed away by his nightly shower. She suppressed a deep sigh, returned to her knitting. She worked furiously but quietly. She'd become very deft at knitting.

54

Thus, while Joanie knitted, cleverly, without warning, as though mimicking the fading of Joanie's illusions about herself, about her marriage, about her son, the years began slipping away. They slipped away quietly, stealthily, as though not slipping away at all, as though life had found a means of suspending itself in timelessness. And so, there was a kind of pause, as Joanie saw it, a period of remission in her family life, a suspension of ordinary family affairs, a period of waiting, a period of hoping that something would happen, as though the hoping of it would be its cause, and yet, in another sense, secretly, invasively, like a cure that the body, sometimes the mind, designs for itself, the hope was being realised in Joanie, as though hope truly was a motive force, capable of action, of itself, by itself, if only someone possesses it, as Joanie, still young, possessed it, and had caused, at another level of her being, a great spasm of activity, and so she was changing, she was beginning to change, as though invoking her own metamorphosis, even as the girl child was still strong inside her, the girl child who'd survived the isolation of her mother's madness, as though madness had itself been fearful of competing with Una Thomas, and had left Joanie alone, allowed her to remain untouched, sequestered in her dreams, her childhood fantasies, and yet, to her astonishment, she had borne her own child, she had performed the miracle of the body, felt the strengthening of her spirit, of her sense of independence, of a mother giving birth, had behaved truly like a woman, and so her sense of separation had grown strong, her sense that the child and the woman, like the mother and her baby, had reached the point where they must become independent creatures, that her life was changing, that she could feel the thinning of the shell of her childhood chrysalis, that her mind, hammering at the shell, hearing the cracking of it, seeing it fall away, was now more completely elaborated by experience, so that her childhood constructions were no longer even remotely able to cover the territory of her expanding life.

In another sense, as though in the end life were merely a joke, and all the insight in the world nothing more than whimsy, Joanie was suffering from the boredom of a marriage gone sour.

'Sometimes I feel like I'm two people,' she confided to Jen Sloan.

Jen is also very bored. With marriage, with childlessness, with her husband.

'Sometimes I feel like chucking a brick through Grace Brothers' window,' she replies.

'Sometimes I wonder what it's all about,' says Joanie.

'Sometimes I think it's all a great big fucking meaningless joke,' says Jen.

Joanie is seeing a great deal of Jen Sloan. Jen seems so alive, thinks Joanie. It is the way Jen's presence touches her, this aliveness. And Joanie is becoming aware of the new path down which she has begun to travel. It is as though she must be accompanied by Jen Sloan, as though Jen and she are somehow connected. She had begun to understand this one evening in the winter of 1971. It was dark outside. She and Jen were waiting for the menfolk to get back from a late delivery. They were drinking wine. Jen was in one of her sullen moods, drinking too much and too quickly.

'I bet'cha those two bastards are up the club,' said Jen.

'Yes, I suppose so,' murmured Joanie. She was deep in thought.

'They're always up the club,' growled Jen.

'It's not as though I think Harry's playing up with other women, or anything,' said Joanie suddenly. She sighed, glanced towards the lounge room and Keithy who was in there, watching TV. 'It's just that he seems more distant, these days,' she said, looking earnestly at Jen. 'You know; he— well, we don't talk much.'

Jen raised her eyebrows. She had auburn eyebrows.

'What! You're not admitting the honeymoon's finally over?'

'Oh, we still have regular sex.'

'Yeah, what a drag, isn't it? Gordie and me have regular sex, too.'

'It's just that Harry never seems to have time for me anymore,' said Joanie. 'He's always out with Keithy, when he's not at work, or up the club.'

'At least he's got a kid to take out,' said Jen.

'And he won't even discuss having another baby.'

Jen said nothing, drained her glass.

'And Keithy's nearly six years old,' said Joanie looking over at the boy.

Jen followed her eyes.

'Yeah, he's getting to be a big feller.'

Jen sat up straight, ruffled her close-cropped hair. It was rich and silky and dark red.

'I think I'll grow my hair long, really long, and straight, straight down to my waist.'

'To your waist?'

'Yeah, real hippie style; what do you reckon?'

'It'd be alright, I suppose.'

Jen giggled. 'Maybe that'll turn him on.'

'Turn who on?' said Joanie, absent mindedly.

'Why, Gordie, for Christ's sake.'

'Oh,' said Joanie.

'Why, who'd you think I meant?'

Joanie looked puzzled.

'Jen, I...'

'You don't think I've got a boyfriend?'

'No, of course not, Jen, love.'

Jen pouted her lips. She had lips which made Joanie think of red cherries.

'Or a girlfriend?' she said

The two women's eyes met. Joanie blushed, said nothing. Jen dangled her empty glass on her finger. It was such a characteristic gesture thought Joanie.

'You got any more of this?' said Jen.

Joanie glanced at the nearby wine bottle. It was empty. Her own glass, still holding her first drink, she'd hardly touched.

'Finish mine off, if you like,' she said.

Jen shrugged her shoulders.

'Whatever you say, sweetie.'

She drank the wine. Joanie watched her closely. She thought Jen looked so carefree, knocking back her wine like that. Jen was grinning at her, maybe mocking her, maybe even tempting her—tempting her? How could she be tempting her?

'You got any more?'

Joanie hesitated a fraction. Jen's green eyes flashed. They were pretty eyes. Prettier when they flashed.

'Joanie, I need a drink, okay. Just give me another drink will you, sweetie?'

Joanie frowned.

'Christ! you're not out of booze?' said Jen.

'There's some sherry.'

'That'll do.'

Joanie fetched the sherry. Jen poured herself a generous drink, brandished her glass.

'Here's to men,' she said loudly. 'To hell with the lot of them.'

She emptied her glass, refilled it quickly, drank deeply, then, with a sudden shaking of her shoulders, fell into a brooding silence.

For a moment Joanie watched her friend. Jen's eyes were downcast. She seemed to have retreated deep inside herself.

'Are you alright, Jen?' she asked.

Jen did not answer.

Joanie stood up, made to reach forward, to touch her friend, caught herself before she could follow through with the movement, then slowly drew back.

'I'll just put Keithy to bed,' she said.

As she tucked the boy in, he said:

'What's wrong with Aunty Jen, mum?'

'Oh, it's nothing.'

'Is she drunk?'

'No, no, 'course she isn't.'

Joanie leaned down and kissed Keithy's forehead.

'Now, come on, settle down and go to sleep, love.'

The boy looked beyond her, towards the open bedroom door.

'Will dad take me out footy training tomorrow?'

'Oh, yes,' said Joanie, 'he'll take you out footy training, don't you worry about that.'

'I like footy training,' said Keithy.

'Yes, love.'

'How long will Dad be?'

'Not long.'

'Will he come in and kiss me goodnight?'

'Yes, he will.'

'Footy training's real good,' murmured the boy sleepily.

'Goodnight, Keithy,' said Joanie. She heard the cool, abrupt tone of her voice. She couldn't help it. She resented the self-satisfaction in Keithy's voice whenever he mentioned his father or football. She felt a sense of being separated from the boy, from Harry.

Back in the kitchen she poured herself a small sherry. At first, she sipped the wine. Then she drank it down in a single gulp. The wine felt warm inside her. She poured another one, lifted it to her lips, then caught herself watching Jen through the corner of her eye. The top buttons of Jen's blouse had come undone. Joanie's eyes dropped until she found herself staring at Jen's breasts; they swelled out almost to the nipples. She caught her breath, felt her cheeks becoming hot. How strange, she thought; how strange that I am enjoying the sight of Jen's breasts, felt herself catching her breath again, yes, enjoying the idea of touching Jen's breasts. She looked at Jen's face. It was a nice face, with nice features, she thought. Jen suddenly lifted her head, caught Joanie's eyes, watching her. For a second neither spoke, then Jen shrugged her shoulders and said:

'It's men who're the bitches.'

'Yes,' said Joanie.

'Especially Australian men.'

'Yes.'

'Especially husbands.'

'Hmm.'

'Oh, you don't agree?'

'Oh, yes, Jen, yes, I do.'

'Good.' Jen looked solemnly at Joanie. 'Women aren't bitches,' she said.

'No.'

'But damn bloody superior, though.'

'Yes.'

'That's why men are scared of us.'

'Scared of us?'

'Absolutely!' said Jen. 'We threaten them. That's why they treat us the way they do, you know, as though we're foreigners, aliens, bloody parasites from Mars, that's what we are—here on a secret bloody mission to take over the world.' She giggled. 'Mission Impossible, I'd say, wouldn't you, my sweetie.' Joanie blushed. 'Don't usually get this drunk,' said Jen, eyeing her glass. 'Only on really special occasions.' Carefully she stood up. 'I think I'll go' up the North Coast, sweetie. Yeah, that's what I'll do.' She giggled again, stood upright on her wobbly feet, drained her glass then smacked her lips. Her lips looked sexy, thought Joanie, they were wet with wine. Jen put down her glass, walked over to Joanie. She missed her step, fell forward into Joanie's arms. 'whoops, wheee,' she yelled. 'Wheeee... Wheeeee... Men are bitches... Wheeee.' She threw her arm round Joanie's neck, looked into Joanie's eyes. 'I'm goin' up the North Coast, I am. An' my little Joanie's comin' with me, right, sweetie?' (Suddenly the smell of wine on Jen's breath was wonderfully intoxicating.) 'Gonna grow our hair real long, aren't we Joanie, love,' said Jen. 'Then we're goin' up to join a commune. That's what we're goin' to do; join a commune, an' take off all our clothes.' She giggled, 'An' wander around in our birthday suits, show 'em our bare beautiful arses, okay, sweetie?' She raised her hand, held it in front of her face for a moment, then uncurled her finger and began shaking it at Joanie. 'An' we're leaving the men behind, right, sweetie? Jus' me an' you'll go, okay, darlin'?' She giggled again and leaned heavily against Joanie. Their eyes met. Suddenly Jen leaned down and kissed Joanie on the mouth. Joanie pulled away, briefly felt revulsion, quickly discarded the feeling, felt herself relaxing, surrendering, casting off things, ideas, girlish fancies, fairy tales, tales she'd actually believed were true, then felt herself leaning forward, shrugging off fear, embarrassment, allowing the kiss to resume, enjoying the softness of Jen's lips, the taste of wine mixed with the taste of Jen's mouth, wanting the kiss to go on, and on. Then Jen pulled away and spoke in a kind of husky, drunken voice. 'We're goin' back to nature, love; like Adam and Eve.' She moved back a few more inches, thinking, staring into Joanie's eyes. 'Nah,' she said, shaking her head, 'not Adam. Fuck Adam. We don't need him, do we, Joanie, sweetie?'

Later that night, while Harry is in the lounge room, drowsing in front of TV, Joanie lies in bed, thinking about Harry's girlfriends, about his deceits, his unfaithfulness, her own blind trust of him, her own stupidity in making it so easy for him, her own childish belief that Harry is different from other men. Then, her anger with Harry suddenly abating, she allows herself a new luxury, she allows herself to think about Jen Sloan, but in a very new kind of way, about the smell of her friend's body, her perfume, the faint musky under-arm smell she'd smelled as Jen had embraced her. And feels new feelings inside herself, about herself, feelings brought on by Jen's nearness, by Jen's kiss.

Later still she dwells on the preposterous idea that she is in love with Jen. Yet is it so preposterous? Why can't two women love each other?

It is such a revelation, such a departure for her, as though the doors to her cultural prison have been opened, it seems very strange, this knowledge, yet she has known it for some time, and Harry? She feels love for Harry, strange, how she still feels love for Harry, but it is a diluted kind of love, not the rushing, soaring, innocent, all-trusting, passion of the girl on the Albury train, not that kind of desperate, overwhelming, never to be threatened, kind of love, for she now sees Harry truly for what he is, that he is a very ordinary, very flawed human being, that though she loves him, her love is cool, and paper thin, and so that is why life is becoming too stressful to be in love only with Harry, there is no emotional anchorage left in her love affair with Harry; and he has girlfriends now, this minute, maybe several girlfriends out there, waiting for him, preparing their beds for him, why pretend, she argues with herself, of course he has lied to her, through their seven years of marriage, of course he has, and she has known it, known it all along, known it even as he was making love to her, known he was cheating on her even as they were joined to one another, how clever of him, as though she now admires him for this discovery, for his skill, how clever of him to be so deceitful, what a wonderful actor he must be, maybe he despises her for being so stupid, no she is not stupid, just trusting, blindingly loyal, which she used to be.

As usual she was knitting football socks for Keithy.

'Don't you ever get tired of doing that?' said Jen.

Joanie paused, studied the knitting. The activity in itself was useful, the result pointless, Keithy already had more football socks in his drawer than he could ever wear out.

She put down the knitting, sat still, wondering what to do with her fingers.

She poured herself a glass of wine. It was alive with froth and bubbles.

Together they sipped wine. Joanie could feel Jen's presence. She could feel something radiating from her, an energy. Then Jen sighed, pulled herself to her feet.

'I think I'll go home,' she said.

Joanie tried to sound casual.

'Oh, do you have to?'

Jen finished her drink, put down the glass, stretched her shoulders. Joanie saw her breasts stretching tightly against her blouse.

'Jen, you're not wearing a bra,' she managed to say.

Jen looked down at herself. Joanie thought: How unselfconscious she is.

'Eh? Oh, no; no, I'm not,' said Jen lightly.

Joanie stood up, drew a deep breath.

'Can I get you another drink?'

Jen pursed her lips, examined her empty glass.

'Oh, better not, Joanie. I seem to be drinking too much of this stuff, these days.'

Then she picked up her bag.

'Don't go,' said Joanie.

'Joanie, I've got some shopping to do.'

But there was something in the way she said this which encouraged Joanie.

'Let it wait a while.'

Jen smiled. and caught Joanie's eye, saw the blush forming on Joanie's cheeks, smiled her sly, catlike smile, the one Joanie liked so much.

'What—you've got something better in mind?'

Joanie was feeling very excited. Pinpoints of colour shone on her cheeks. She was taking the initiative, being very outgoing, enjoying the thrill of it. She was finally getting rid of the silly, simple-minded little girl inside her.

'I'd like you to stay for a while,' she said confidently.

Jen looked at Joanie, then down at her glass. She picked up the glass, held it towards Joanie.

'What the hell; Gordie won't be home for hours.'

'And Harry and Keithy are up at the park,' said Joanie softly.

Jen smiled. 'Then we've got some time, haven't we?'

They drank sherry together.

55

Two young women making love with their eyes, and drinking wine, clumsily, spillingly, because they are unwilling to move their eyes, unwilling to break the spell of this looking, for it possesses a special sweetness, this looking, as though, by this gazing, by sharing this ecstasy of vision, they have discovered a way of absorbing themselves fully into each other

Joanie feels very calm inside her excitement, as though calmness is part of her excitement. It is as though she has finally understood, accepted, the futility of all her hopes and dreams, her notions of love, of marriage, of men, of motherhood; how ingenuous they were, how childish, her means of escape, fantasy, unreality, not like this, this wonderful reality, this wonderful sense of being a woman, this wonderful way of being a woman, how liberating, how easy it is to discard her childish fantasies, how silly she has been, imagining herself so feeble and submissive, how unnatural all that seems, how really stupid.

...finishing their wine, sitting very still, continuing to make love with their eyes. Their hands begin to move, they hear each other's breath, bathe themselves in the sound of it, and then their fingers touch.

She wonders if it would have been like this for her mother. She wonders if Una Thomas would have enjoyed another woman's body, if her mother's waiting for her husband merely denied her the discovery of another kind of love.

...moving closer, sensing the nearness of each other, feeling the closeness of the life in each other, feeling movement, of limbs, of mouths, of mouths breathing warm breath, breath smelling of sweet wine, breathing in each other's sweet breath, mouths near, touching, lips touching, kissing.

Joanie feels so sorry for her mother, her waiting mother, waiting like she, herself, had waited. How empty, thinks Joanie, all that waiting, all that time waiting to discover Harry's unfaithfulness, after all she had given him, all the trust she had placed in him, all the love, all her unbounded love, everything she was, had ever been, given to him, freely. Fuck Harry, she hears herself thinking, fuck him.

As they touch and feel, and know the other is awakening and wanting, as they stand together, without speaking, as they caress, as they embrace, as they kiss, and touch, and draw each other away, to where they can lie together, make love.

And Jen Sloan. Jen, too, is very sure about what she is doing. Oh, how much better than Gordie's feeble embrace, she thinks. So much nicer than his beery breath, than the chore of sex with Gordie, the discomfort, the weight of him on her, her anger as he comes off inside her, the terrible drabness of him coming off in her, feebly, barrenly, as though it is Gordie who is barren, before she is hardly aware he is inside her, as he shrinks rapidly and mumbles goodnight and snores, as she cleans herself up and sees the unabated anger in those unfulfilled eyes staring at her in the bathroom mirror.

And as they make love, they are aware they have fallen in love, that their menfolk can be forgotten, that Harry's infatuation with Keithy does not exist, that the pain of Keithy's casual indifference to Joanie no longer exists, that the sexual deadness in Gordie's body does not matter, that Jen's guilt at being childless can be ignored. Yet they do not speak during their lovemaking, not as their bodies come together. It is as though the discipline of silence gives legitimacy to their lovemaking, gives their actions a moral correctness. And so, neither feels guilt; instead, each feels an overwhelming sense of freedom as she abandons herself to the other. For the time being both exist outside their own histories.

———

'Fuck Harry,' Joanie is murmuring, feeling the sensuous hardness of the words, words enhancing the ecstasy exploding inside her, 'Fuck Harry,' she says as Jen stretches her body against her murmuring, too, 'Yeah, fuck Harry; fuck Gordie; fuck 'em all.'

Two young women existing outside their own histories.

For as long as they can.

56

Harry is drinking his eighth or ninth schooner. Or maybe it is his tenth. 'You know,' he says, watching the barrels spin on Thirty-three. 'I never ever met a dinky-di lesbian.'

Tom's eyelids flicker.

'A what?' asks Mrs Johnson.

'A lezzo. One of them that does it only with other women.' A cigarette dangles from Harry's lips. Smoke trickles out of his mouth, drifts upwards into his eyes so that he wears a permanent squint. 'You know, women only, never with blokes.'

'Yes, love,' says Mrs Johnson softly. She is pleasantly drunk and feels sadness for the big man with so many unresolved problems.

'My wife had a girlfriend once who was a sort of lezzo.'

'You mean she was a bit of both, then?'

'Yeah, a bit of both.'

He remembers Joanie had suddenly started calling Jen, 'Jen, darling.'

'Jen, darling, get the milk from the fridge, will you?'

'Oh, Jen, darling, it's you,' (as she answered the phone).

'Jen, darling, come over for tea.'

And so on.

At first Harry thought it was merely quaint.

'So, what's this 'darling' talk, then, all of a sudden?' he asked.

'Oh, nothing,' said Joanie lightly.

'You got something going with Jen Sloan?' joked Harry.

Joanie threw him a smile. 'Oh, Harry, don't be ridiculous.'

Keithy raced into the room. He was togged-up for football practice. His boots hung round his neck.

'I'm ready dad,' he announced.

'We're off, then,' said Harry.

And they were heading for the door.

'Will you be your usual time?' Joanie called out.

'Yeah, I reckon.'

'About an hour and a half?'

'About that.'

Then Joanie would phone Jen and learn that Gordie was tied up at the furniture store for at least another hour.

'Come over.'

'Joanie, I'm coming in the morning,' Jen would tease her.

'Come now.'

'There's only an hour, love.'

Joanie knew Jen was just teasing, yet she said:

'Don't you want to see me?'

'Of course I do, darling?'

'You're sure?'

'Bloody certain, Joanie.'

'Then come now.'

'Joanie, I'm about to start cooking the tea.'

'Can't you put it off for a while?'

'Joanie...'

'Please Jen, please.'

'Oh, alright.'

'And be quick.'

'Yes.'

'Oh, Jen...'

'Yes.'

'It's alright? Everything's alright, isn't it?'

'Yes, of course everything's alright.'

'Jen, I love you.'

'I love you, too, Joanie.'

Sometimes, as though she hadn't said it a hundred times before, Jen would ask:

'Harry doesn't know anything?'

'Of course not.'

'You're sure, Joanie?'

'Yes.'

'He's never said anything?'

'No.'

'But you still make love to him?'

'Yes.'

'I suppose you have to.'

'Yes.'

'Do you enjoy it?'

'No, not really.'

'Honestly?'

'Honestly.'

Then it would be Joanie's turn.

'What about Gordie?'

'Oh, he's never said anything. Anyhow, he wouldn't, would he?'

'Do you still have sex?'

'Oh, yes. We still have the standard five minutes of bliss, once a week.'

Then Jen would sigh, and Joanie would embrace her and for a few moments, as though both had tacitly agreed to play a different game.

'It's so good to be with you,' one of them would murmur.

'Yes.'

'It's different, isn't it? Than with men?'

'Yes.'

'Better.'

'Oh, yes. Much better.'

'Strange.'

'What's strange?'

'That it's better.'

'Maybe we did it this way on Mars.'

'Right; before we discovered men.'

'Bloody shame we were stupid enough to discover them.'

'Right.'

Then they would laugh, and drink wine, and wind their legs around each other.

'We could go away together.'

'Yes.'

Then they would kiss. Be intoxicated by each other's smell, and taste, and feel. And sigh. And make love again, and again, as though they were born to do so, as though nothing other than making love could possibly matter in the world, and the sensation of their joining bodies, and the ecstasies of their climax, first one, then the other, both of them, sometimes together, which didn't matter, for there was no anxiety, none at all, for they knew it would happen, that there would be no rapid detumescence, that there would only be one caring for the other, wanting for all time, for the other. And then there would be a kind of dream for a while. Then Joanie, finished, aware that Jen was finished, that they were themselves again, would hear herself say:

'I don't think I could leave Harry.'

'No,' Jen would reply.

They would lie still, clasped in each other, and think about this for a while.

'Sometimes I wish I could leave him,' Joanie would say.

A sad look would come into Jen's eyes.

'Yes,' she would say, 'I know.'

In the end Joanie found herself able to say:

'I suppose Harry's been doing it ever since we were married,'

'With other women, you mean?'

'Yes.'

'Of course, he has.'

'You know, Jen, I don't care anymore. I just don't bloody care.'

57

Naturally it wasn't long before Harry noticed something was different. First of all, it was the smell in the bedroom, a fragrance, something new, though not entirely new, he'd smelled it before, somewhere. Where? At the club? At the store? Yes, at the store, when Jen was around; it was Jen Sloan he could smell; Gordie Sloan's sexy little wife Jen Sloan; on the sheets in his bedroom. What did it mean? Maybe Joanie was using the same perfume. Maybe Joanie had borrowed Jen's perfume. That was probably it. Joanie seemed to smell like that perfume.

Harry struggles with his drunkenness. He lights a cigarette from the stub of the old one, then pulls money from his pocket. He still has the two twenties plus some coins. He scans the credit meter; it registers five hundred. 'My shout,' he says, then sets off, heading unsteadily for the Long Bar, unaware that Vincenzio's eyes are on him and that Gordie and Mackenzie and young Les the touch-footballer nursing a glass of orange juice are watching him, or that Trish is aware he is approaching, that the woman at the dollar pokie with the smouldering eyes is glaring at him, thinking how much pleasure it would give her to scratch his eyes out.

'Schooner, middy, and a double brandy, love,' he says when he reaches the bar.

He totters back to the pokie lounge; he is still watched by many eyes; Gordie is half-risen from his seat as he watches; Mackenzie scowls through eyes lazy from drink. Harry sees nothing, is concentrating on maintaining his pretence of sobriety, he hands the Johnsons their drinks, drinks from his own glass, nudges the vertical edge of the poker machine with his drinking elbow, spills beer on his shirt, stares stupidly at the spreading wetness of the beer stain, starts talking, as though to himself, in disconnected phrases: '... never really liked the pokies much in them days; she was a lezzo, alright, though; never drank that much, neither; needed to stay fit, for the kid, so's I could run with him; Jeez, could the little bugger run! We used to run up at Arncliffe Park. Yeah, a lezzo, a lezzy. One of them. A dyke; nowadays they all do it; nobody gives a shit; lezzos, gays, straight blokes, straight sheilas— Keithy, my kid, was a quiet little bloke; do anything for you, you know, never complain, never give you any lip, not like other kids; and real popular; had this smile; got you in, his smile; and his laugh; melt your bloody heart it would; reminded me of—of...' Harry's voice tailed off. Drunk or not he couldn't admit publicly how much Keithy reminded him of Judy Connell, how he knew in his heart of hearts Keithy *was* his Judy.

58

Harry was so busy with Keithy's football career he had to come to an arrangement with Gordie.

'Mate, I've got to be at Keithy's school on sport afternoons. Don't worry. I'll work back. I'll put the hours in, okay? Oh, and Gordie, I need to get off early on Tuesdays, to get to the kid's practice.'

'Not a problem,' said Gordie just as Harry knew he would.

Harry spent Thursday afternoons on the touchline. At half-time he hovered impatiently around the team, trying not to take over from Keithy's teacher-coach; usually, to control his eagerness, he would peel oranges, distribute them to the players, yet, so enthused was he that he could not stop himself from passing on a tip here, a tip there, nothing too obvious, not enough to upset the coach who tolerated Harry because he was Keithy's dad. Later, at the club, flushed and excited, Harry would announce to his mates:

'The champ kicked four out of four, this afternoon.'

'Terrific, Harry,' they would reply with enthusiasm but without surprise—everyone took it for granted Keithy was headed for a big career.

'And scored three tries.'

'Real good, Harry.'

Once, at the club, a well-known ex-first grader sought out Harry.

'Saw your boy playing last week, Harry,' said the Great Man.

'Saw yours, too,' replied Harry diplomatically.

'Reckon young Keithy's got a great future, Harry?'

'Yours too, mate,' said Harry generously.

At home, Harry talked football to Keithy. 'Listen, mate. I want you to watch every move Kenny Irvine makes. Every move, okay?'

'Okay, dad,' said Keithy wide-eyed. He was eight years old. He loved talking football with Harry.

'Kenny's got a few tricks I want you to learn.'

'Yes, dad.'

'Watch his swerve. And his anticipation.'

'What's that, dad?'

And then Harry's eyes would light up, and he would lean forward and grip the boy's shoulders.

'Okay, right. Now listen to what I'm telling you. Watch how Kenny always gets himself in position when the team's moving the ball, as though he's three moves ahead of everyone else. Watch him real close, Keithy; watch how he moves as though he's controlling the game—which he is, and they know it, and they can't do a damn thing about it—watch how the ball always gets to him in the end, like he's a kind of magnet, and the ball hasn't any option but to finish up in Kenny's hands, and then he's off, because he'll have a gap that he's made—'

'And he scores a try, right, dad?'

'Right. And it'll be exactly the way Kenny's planned it.'

'And he'll score again?'

'Yeah, he'll score again, from another angle, or he'll just dodge and weave his way through 'em, make 'em all look real stupid, you know, like they've all got lead sinkers in their boots.'

Then there was the occasion when Keithy arrived home from school because of a wildcat teachers' strike, and found Aunty Jen 'having a nap in bed with mum,' as Joanie explained it to him, which might have been enough explanation for an eight year-old going on nine except that mum and Aunty Jen had all their clothes off and Keithy caught a glimpse of his mum stroking Aunty Jen's breasts as he burst into the bedroom.

He let it slip to Harry.

'Why do women have really big breasts, dad?' he asked as they made their way up to Arncliffe Park. The boy was breaking into a trot, getting ahead, then slowing down, waiting for Harry to catch up, twirling the football in his fingers.

'That's the way nature made them,' said Harry.

'Why, dad?'

'So's they can feed their babies, you know that.'

'Aunty Jen doesn't have any babies.'

'What's Aunty Jen got to do with it?'

'She's got real big ones,' said the boy artlessly.

'Oh, how would you know?'

'I've seen them, dad. When she was having a lie-down with mum.'

They'd just arrived at the park. Harry kicked the ball hard. It soared away from him, a powerful torpedo kick. He set off after it, galloping in his cockeyed way, aware of his knee, enjoying the sharp pain he gave himself every time he jabbed his left foot down hard into the turf. He reached the ball, picked it up, lashed it into the air with his boot, watched it rocket skywards.

'Jeez! that's a beauty, dad,' he heard Keithy yelling.

For half an hour he thrashed the ball all over the park, and then, as though that was enough, as though his rage had been merely reflex, unable to be justified, he calmed down, sat on a park bench watching Keithy racing around the park, ducking and weaving, wanting to please Harry, running over to him from time to time, expecting and getting the praise he deserved, needed, making Harry have strange thoughts about everything, about himself, about Joanie, about Keithy....

He said nothing to Joanie. What could he have said that would make any difference? She was no more hypocrite than he. At least Harry admitted that to himself. He was seeing someone himself, a tidy little blond woman with a 'really fabulous set of lungs' as Harry, ever on the lookout, noted as she wandered into the store one afternoon when he was working the sales floor. Handily, he learned, her husband was an inter-state truck driver. Yet dallying with Fay was no deception, he reasoned, merely a harmless diversion. He only needed diversion. Men were like that. Harry found this age-old argument convincing enough. Especially since he was no longer enjoying his sex life with Joanie. Anyway, these affairs weren't personal. Purely physical. No one needed to suffer. Anyhow, Joanie was having sex with Jen. And even though, at first, Harry for all his pretended knowledge of these things—he'd once pooh-poohed Mackenzie's sneering claim that 'lezzies use plastic cocks, har, har! front and rear, mate'—naively believed that two women could hardly have proper sex with one another, the evidence of his own experience suggested so strongly how much more skilled his wife had become in bed than she'd ever been before the Jen thing started. Maybe Mackenzie was right. Maybe something more was going on than the girlish hugging and cuddling with their clothes off that Harry had first imagined was all they were doing together. Then, the beer doing its work, he would sink into unconsciousness in front of television, Joanie would go quietly to bed, and he would awake in the early hours, lying on Col Maguire's couch, thinking. Then he would stumble his way out to the backyard, and relieve himself under the stars, and wonder for a while why he was there, standing alone, urinating into one of Annie Maguire's ancient hydrangeas, under the stars, alone, like a dot, an invisible dot, wondering if all his efforts were worth anything, wondering if he and Keithy would remain friends all their lives, feeling a kind of dread as he wondered this, wondering why he felt like this. Then, with the feeling of dread growing stronger, he would hurry back indoors and tip-toe into Keithy's room, and stand very still, and listen for the sound of his son's breathing, and feel such a soaring of joy when he heard the breath moving in his son's body, and he would lean forward and try to see his son's face in the gloom, and finally Keithy would stir, as though a silent message had passed between the boy and the father, and then Harry would whisper: 'Are you awake, son?' And Keithy would murmur: 'Yes, dad.' Then Harry would pad over to Keithy's bed, and lean over the boy and kiss his cheek, and ruffle his hair, and feel comforted, and say, 'Good on you, mate?' as though everything between them was simple and straight-forward, as though everything was alright. Sometimes he would crawl into bed with his son, lie next to him through the night, listening to him breathe.

———————

Harry starts, shakes his head, blinks rapidly under the bright lights above the Pokie Lounge, then turns because Tom Johnson is having a coughing fit, and watches Mrs Johnson patting him firmly on the back. Tom coughs up something into his handkerchief. Harry senses the old man is very ill.

'Come on, now, old son,' encourages Mrs Johnson with worried eyes. 'Come on, mate.'.

The coughing fit subsides. Tom breathes rapidly. His eyes have watered. But he says nothing. He does lean on the edge of the poker machine while labouring to catch his breath.

Mrs Johnson turns to Harry.

'He'll be alright,' she says.

Tom opens his mouth, shows his gums. He sneezes, then blows his nose with a heavy, snorting sound. This seems to help him, his mouth closes, he resumes his deadpan expression, almost as though the coughing and sneezing hadn't happened.

'Tom lost all his front teeth playing cricket,' says Mrs Johnson, patting the old man's arm affectionately. 'Didn't you, love; when you was only a boy?'

Tom sniffs.

'Copped a fast ball in the mouth, didn't you, you poor old thing.'

Tom's lips move a little.

'His false teeth hurt him; don't they love?' She pats Tom's arm again.

Tom grimaces.

'So he doesn't wear 'em these days.'

Tom tightens his lips.

'Doesn't like me talkin' about it,' explains Mrs Johnson unnecessarily. She empties her brandy, examines the glass, gives out a raspy little giggle, catches Tom's eye.

'Go on, love,' she says to him. 'Let's have one more before we go home.'

Tom moves his cheeks a little as though in agreement and he sets off for the bar. Mrs Johnson turns to Harry.

'You ever play cricket, Harry?'

'Nah.'

'How about your boy? Is he a cricketer?'

The barrels spin and Harry scores a fifty pay.

'The kid's a natural,' he hears himself saying. 'Another Bradman, they reckoned.'

The kid *was* a natural. One in a million. The trouble started in 1977, the year Keithy went to high school.

'I told him it'd be no good.'

'How do you mean?'

'That it'd mess up his football career.' says Harry, staring into Thirty-three's window, seeing his reflection, like his memory, as though raw, and exposed, trying for consolation

behind the glittering icons.

59

Harry knows it isn't just the cricket. Cricket is only the symptom. The disease has a different cause. And it's all of Harry's making. The idea just slips out. Harry is astounded. All of his making. Jesus! It's true, isn't it? The disease *is* all of his making.

But what disease?

'What disease?' he whispers to himself, squinting under the lights inside Mid-City Leagues. What disease?'

'You say something, Harry?'

It is Mrs Johnson, speaking absent-mindedly, eyeing the almost jackpot sitting in Thirty-four's window.

Then he says:

'It was the cricket bat.'

It sounds so damned stupid in his ears. Yet he says it again, as though weirdly, insanely, just the saying of it has finally created deep insight.

'It was the cricket bat.'

Mrs Johnson looks at him, frowns.

'Cricket bat,' mumbles Harry, feeling hopelessly sorry for the face staring back at him shadow like from the pokie window; oh, how sorry he feels for that face, so much sorrow, so much suffering, the face that only wanted the best for the boy, only wanted to give the boy everything he'd ever wanted for himself, oh, how he suddenly feels such anguish on behalf of that face, over the depth of its own sorrow, over the bottomless depth of its self-pity.

The disease. He remembers he'd felt like he'd had some sort of disease himself.

'You wouldn't think getting a cricket bat in his hands would've made all that much difference, would you?'

'No, love,' says Mrs Johnson softly.

———

The feel of a cricket bat in Keithy's hands is the most natural, the most perfect, feeling he has ever experienced. To the adolescent boy it is like the feel of a finely made weapon. The feeling could not be improved if the bat truly was an edged weapon, glittering in the sun, waiting to be used in glorious battle, for the feeling is archetypal, masculine; and power flows into his body as he grasps the bat by its rubber sheathed handle, wields it in front of him like a two-handed sword. The power Keithy feels is amplified by his knowledge that he is doing this independently of Harry, in defiance of Harry's will; that it is something therefore that he desperately needs to do, must do.

It is a clean feeling.

———

Harry turns and looks at Mrs Johnson. His face looks yellow under the lights.

'He defied me,' he mutters. 'I did everything I could for him, and he defied me.'

———

Keithy is a fine-looking youth of thirteen. Like his father he is very handsome. He is, in all physical respects, a replica of his father. Emotionally, he is very close to his late grandfather, the melancholy Denis O'Brien. The melancholy aspect is becoming more dominant as Keithy reaches into manhood; his laughing smile appears very infrequently these days; his eyes now reflect the interior sadness which seems to characterise all O'Brien men; his skin, paler than Harry's, his hair, lighter than Harry's, his eyes, more intelligent than Harry's, his growing hunger to escape the dominance of Harry's personality in his life, and his growing fear that he will never be free from the influence of the man he once imagined he adored, all contribute to give him an air of brooding despair which, today, for the first time in more than five years, seems, through the miracle of the cricket bat in his hands, to be fading away.

It had all begun when the cricket coach at Bayside High School, Allan Cameron, cajoled him into taking strike in the school's cricket nets during a lunchtime break.

'It won't bite you, son.'

'I'm not interested in cricket, sir.'

But Cameron instinctively knew the boy was lying.

'Just take hold of the bat.'

'I don't want to, sir.'

'Now listen to me, son—'

Still, Keithy hesitated.

'Take the bat, when I tell you!' said the teacher firmly, thrusting the bat at Keithy, and, as Keithy still hesitated, shouted, 'For crying out loud, O'Brien, take the bloody thing!'

And that had been the end of it. The teacher's pushiness; the feel of a hundred watching eyes on him; Keithy's overwhelming need to find emotional escape from Harry—And then the bat is in his hands, and its feel entices him; 'Hey, O'Brien, take strike, will yer?' someone is yelling, and he does so, feels the bat handle fit snugly in his fingers, yes, it is the most natural feeling in the world—steady—watch for it, the bowler roars in, fires one down at him—use the bat, defy Harry—whack! the glorious feel of bat on ball, cleanly, effortlessly, him cracking the ball easily to what would have been the long-on boundary...

They could not bowl him out. He hit them everywhere. They tried everything. He dealt with everything. He was the most natural batsman Allen Cameron had ever seen.

It was a different story at home.

'Dad, it won't interfere with football.,' Keithy said reasonably.

Joanie was in the bedroom, reading. She heard the voices down the hall in the kitchen. She frowned, got to her feet, closed the door, refilled her glass. She'd long since abandoned her role as mediator between father and son.

'Keithy, I've told you before, son. I don't want you playing cricket.'

He spoke very calmly, very firmly. And, like all the other times, he expected that would be the end of it.

'That's not fair, dad.'

Harry felt the hair bristling on his neck. He lifted his eyes up from the paper he'd been reading. Keithy was standing a few feet away. In the corner, the TV was cackling away. A game show assistant was beaming at him from the middle of the picture tube. Off camera, the audience screamed advice to the contestant. The assistant smiled directly at Harry from the tube. She was tall and was one of those women whose face seems all lip and front teeth. Harry imagined sex would be very good with her.

'What the hell did you say, son?'

'I said it's not fair.'

He picked up his beer bottle, examined it for a moment.

'It's that bloody schoolteacher, isn't it?'

'No, dad.'

310

'He's making you play, isn't he?'

'No, he isn't.'

Carefully he placed the stubby down.

'Then what's the bloody problem, Keithy?'

Keithy stood there facing Harry. He wasn't frowning or smiling. Harry knew his son was exercising constraint. He could feel it. He could imagine Judy would behave that way. Oddly, though he sensed danger was close, he admired the boy, admired his qualities.

He put down his paper and stood up. Keithy was still much shorter than he was, maybe a good six inches. But he was stocky, he had muscles, and he was fast, as fast as Harry had been at that age, reflected Harry gratefully. Suddenly he realised how much he loved his son. He'd do anything for Keithy, anything. Slowly he moved over to the TV set, paused, and watched the compère's assistant flashing her teeth at a successful contestant, sighed, switched off the set. He turned. Keithy was looking straight at him.

'I just want to play cricket, dad,' said Keithy.

Harry wasn't aroused. He and Keithy understood one another. As thick as thieves he and his son. Sometimes Harry made chips in the kitchen. Harry loved making chips for Keithy. And lamb chops. Yes, grilled lamb chops. Short loin. Best quality. He smiled at Keithy.

'Listen, son, football's your game. That's what you do best. Stick to what you do best.'

'I'm sick of football,' Keithy said.

They were standing, facing one another.

'Ah, come on, Keithy, you don't mean that.'

'I've told them I'm not playing next season.'

The soft side of Harry ebbed away.

'You bloody well haven't!'

'I have.'

Suddenly, there's this stranger that's himself screaming at the boy.

'You're playing football next season. And you're bloody well not playing cricket now or ever.'

'I'm already in the cricket team,' says Keithy. 'I'm the vice-captain.'

'You're no such fucking thing, matey.'

'Yes, I am, dad, I fucking well am,' yells Keithy.

Harry feels the surprise as the hand strikes the boy. His hand. Striking the boy. Weirdly. Like a dream. A nightmare. Him, Harry, striking Keithy. Whack! He feels the hand collide with the side of Keithy's head. He feels the weight of the blow transmitting through his own body, into the hand, into Keithy's head. There is a moment of silence. Keithy stands his ground. Their eyes meet. Then Harry strikes again. He feels the weight again, hand against cheek bone, whack! feels the head snap back again, then forward, gun-like.

———

Harry is fumbling in his pocket for money. He pulls out notes and change. He counts the change, it amounts to three dollars; he stares at the coins and crumpled notes; twenty-eight dollars; he remembers something else; he takes out his wallet; secreted in the zippered compartment he finds a five-dollar bill which he keeps for taxi fare; sometimes he even uses it for that purpose, when he hasn't blown it on the pokies with the rest of his money.

Tonight, Harry pulls out the five-dollar bill, adds it to his other money. He is convinced he will need every penny he can scrape together tonight.

He counts his money again.

Thirty-three dollars. Thirty-three. He stares at the glittering face of Thirty-three. It mocks him. Above its window, on the left corner of the casing, the machine's number mocks him too.

Then, silently, he begins to cry.

Soon he is talking to himself again. Sometimes the talk is all in his mind; sometimes real words form behind his lips, dribble from his mouth. When he speaks audibly the sound is a low and distant drone, it seems projected elsewhere than in front of his mouth, as though he is throwing his voice, ventriloquially, to a point somewhere behind Thirty-three's metal casing. Sometimes his fingers pause in mid-air, hovering above Thirty-three's play buttons. They hover long enough for Waddling Thighs, standing nearby, watching as she slowly thumbs an unlinked machine, to hope he is about to cash in for the night. Sometimes his fingers lower themselves until they rest on but do not disturb the play buttons. Then, as though in response to an inner memory, the fingers will press down slowly until they finally trigger the machine. As the barrels spin, as the coloured icons make their frenzied passage past Harry's eyes, he will seem to be watching, as though his interest in the game is not yet extinguished. Sometimes, it will seem as though Harry is surrounded by a small knot of people. They will stand watching, eyes fixed on Harry as though he might be a curiosity, an attraction put on display by the club. Then the knot of people will slowly disperse, and Harry will be alone again, playing Thirty-three as though nothing has happened, as though today is just an ordinary day.

He has remembered words he once read in a newsletter from Keithy's school. He'd picked up the newsletter carelessly left in the Marsden Street kitchen by Keithy. He read the first few articles without serious interest, then flicked to the back page where he read the article by Allen Cameron in which the teacher had extolled the skills of the 'greatest cricketing sensation the school has ever seen'. He murmurs the words 'greatest cricketing sensation'. They sound in his ears, he repeats the words, as though repetition might invalidate their meaning, make them meaningless, as though the words if separated from their meaning might lose their power. 'How easy it was,' he says, 'to destroy each other. So bloody easy. And so bloody stupid. Over the kid playing fucking cricket.'

He re-lives his actions on the day of Keithy's cricket match. He is in his car heading for Barton Park on the Cook's River. It is a fine November morning. The sun is already high and glittering on the windscreen. He turns east into Wickham Street, then south on to West Botany Road, finds a parking spot on a reserve abutting the expanse of Barton Park. He sits motionless in the car, his moist palms gripping the steering wheel. He gets out of the car, walks on to the park, sees the cricket match in progress. He approaches the boundary line. A cluster of people watch the game. Cameron is at the wicket, umpiring. Another teacher, Cameron's assistant, writes notes on a clipboard pad. The match is a trial game between two teams of potential A-grade players. A bowler is running in to bowl. It is the long run of a quick bowler, a tall, lanky youth with a shock of dark hair washing over his forehead, a set expression on his face as he hurls the ball down. Harry sees the batsman facing up. It is Keithy. Then, with the ball on its way, Keithy lifts his head, turns. He sees Harry. Their eyes meet. And then the ball strikes Keithy's temple, and the boy is down, flat on the earth, spreadeagled, stationary, and people are suddenly running, and Harry is running, and screaming out his son's name.

'Keithy! Keithy! Oh, Jesus Christ, Keithy, son!'

He looks so pale, his face is so white, so white—but he's breathing; someone says he's breathing—pulse—he has a pulse—a weak pulse—keep his airways clear—someone says to keep his airways clear—so he can breathe—he *is* breathing—concussion—maybe he's got concussion—the boy's coming round—his eyes are opening—O Christ! he's so white—and the lump on his head—O Christ, look at that lump on Keithy's head!—a towel, some bastard get a towel, wipe up that blood, hold something over his head, get that bloody sun out of his eyes, for God's sake!—look, O Jesus! his eyes are closing, Christ! don't close your eyes Keithy—.it's me, mate—it's dad—I'm here, son—...you're alright—you'll be alright—his eyes are opening—he's looking at me—Oh, Jesus, Keithy, I'm sorry mate, I'm sorry son....

As the tune of *My Bonny lies over the Ocean* blares out of Thirty-three.

He's won a hundred dollars. Vincenzio pays him the money. 'You're having a good night, Harry,' he says.

'He was alright,' mutters Harry, 'just concussion, that was all, nothing serious.'

'Harry...' begins Vincenzio.

'He was only in for two days,' blurts Harry. He turns to Vincenzio. 'Concussion; only a touch of concussion. Urgently he grabs Vincenzio's arm. 'Only concussion,' he says. 'Jesus! it was only a mild concussion.'

And now Mrs Johnson's hand lies on Harry's shoulder. She gives him a handkerchief, guides it into his fingers, guides his fingers holding the handkerchief to the wetness on his face. Slowly Harry wipes his eyes.

She feels Tom's hand on her arm. She turns. Her husband gestures with his glass. Very soberly she says: 'Yes, Tom, get me a cold drink of something, will you, love, something soft?' Casually, she adds, 'And get yourself and Harry a beer?'

'It was just a knock on the head,' says Harry. 'He was only out of it for a couple of seconds. They kept him under observation for two days.' He lifts his head, nods in the direction of the woman at the dollar poker machine. 'Me and the wife stayed there, the whole time.' Harry's finger triggers Thirty-three's five-play button. The barrels spin, come to rest, the icons cleverly arranging themselves in losing mode.

'Jeez! he was playing cricket again a week later.'

'And get me another twenty of tens,' Mrs Johnson says to her husband as he heads away, handing him her last fifty-dollar bill.

'What the hell,' she says to Harry, 'it's only money, isn't it, love?'

60

Fred Donaldson has finally gone home. On the stage the members of the downstairs band are packing up their gear. The lead singer—not so many years ago he'd attracted as much as two thousand dollars a gig—wears an expression of studied resignation as he lowers his aging Rickenbacker carefully into its felt-lined case. A few diners, sprawled at their tables in the 'Flavours of Peking', still finger coffee cups, languidly tap cigarette ash into glass ashtrays. Upstairs the disco, raging on, collaborates with the muzak now playing downstairs so that curious discords echo throughout the Mixed lounge. Over behind the Long Bar, Trish and her mates doggedly stand and wait for custom; one, an older woman with children at home, glances at her watch, sighs and drags breathily on a cigarette; another, fat and sweaty, scratches at her bra; Trish, the youngest, just finished her chore of stacking washed glasses, stands back and brushes her fingers across her hair. At the rear of the Pokie Lounge, Shirl, behind the metal bars of her change booth, bundles up thick wads of notes, readying them for Vincencio who will deposit them in the club's night safe. Waddling Thighs, heavy-limbed and red-faced, lumbers over for yet another stake, slaps down her last fifty-dollar bill angrily in front of Shirl's deadpan eyes. Poised above the dance floor, the chandelier hangs loosely, casting its immobile shadows on the empty parquetry below. Across the way, in the closed cafeteria, fluorescent light reflects coolly off the empty stainless-steel servers which, with the banks of tables, wait quietly for tomorrow's clients. In the Members' Bar, Gordie, grim-faced and anxious, sits with Mackenzie and the whippet-faced Nev. The others have gone home. Over in the Pokie Lounge the regulars are at work, the machines drone on, the bustling figure of Vincenzio re-sets a machine here, pays out a jackpot there, keeps a weather eye on Harry O'Brien.

'O'Brien's unreal,' Mackenzie mutters. He is breathing heavily, like an old bull. Massively distended, his beer belly slops over his thighs, flows into his crotch.

'He's trying to hang on,' says Gordie thickly.

'Yeah,' answers Mackenzie, shifting heavily in his chair, 'I reckon the poor bugger's hanging on, alright.'

'He doesn't know how to handle it,' frowns Gordie.

'Reckon he's had it coming to him,' growls Mackenzie.

'He's been a good mate to you,' chastises Gordie.

'Yeah, yeah, alright,' says Mackenzie.

But even as Mackenzie falls silent, Gordie knows he secretly agrees with the fat man. Harry has had it coming to him, and for a very long time. He frowns, fingers his schooner of beer. Because he is drunk, he is especially careful as he lifts his glass to his mouth and drinks. He has his eye on Harry's tall figure over in the Pokie Lounge, he watches his friend punching at Thirty-three. To some extent, and he is not proud about it, Harry's problems have left Gordie with a feeling of gratification, provided him with a sense of power, and he enjoys it, for his admiration for Harry has never exceeded his envy. Yet even now he feels his anger rising, weirdly, for it seems confused with the compassion he feels for Harry, he wonders if he still loves his old friend, if his secret love still survives, if his feelings possess at least a remnant of love.

As a youth he'd been infatuated by Harry, had idolised him. Often, in the secret of his darkened bedroom, he'd fantasised about Harry, yeah, actually agonised over the bastard, hated him for being so unattainable, so...so fucking good looking. Later on, after all those years, after all those years of self-control, of marriage, of pretending to Jen he was as straight as any of them, as straight as Harry, he'd finally summoned the courage to make his move, and been rejected—'for fuck's sake, Gordie'— Harry's scathing words still ring in his ears—'for fuck's sake! Yer not fuckin' serious, are yer!' Gordie shivers, attracts Mackenzie's attention.

'You alright, Sloanie?'

'Yeah, I'm fine.'

Mackenzie slumps as deeply as he can into his chair. His stomach, wobbling like an ocean swell, comes slowly to rest.

'Marriage never suited O'Brien,' he says.

'Marriage never suited anyone,' says Gordie.

'Some blokes do alright,' pipes up Nev.

'For Christ's sake, Nev!' snarls Mackenzie.

Nev looks at Mackenzie with his unhappy, lap-dog eyes. Gordie wonders if 'Stringybark Nev' ('the bugger'd be invisible if he didn't wear clothes') really has a thing for the barrel of fat sitting across from him.

'You blokes ready for another beer?' Nev asks, trying to sound cheerful.

'Your shout, is it?' asks Mackenzie.

Nev cringes.

'Yours, I think, Mac,' he mutters

Mackenzie glares at him.

'You sure?' he says.

'Yes, mate,' says Nev defensively, 'mine next.'

With great difficulty Mackenzie finds his pocket, pulls out a note. He gives it to Nev who scuttles off to the Long Bar.

Gordie watches this through half-closed eyes. It is at that most desultory of times in the club, the time just before he decides to go home.

He sighs, raises his eyes, sees Nev at the bar, feels a sudden contempt for the skinny man, for the shameless way he fawns over Mackenzie. At the instant he thinks this, he starts forward in his chair. Just like the role he plays for Harry. As though he'd never truly understood this before tonight. As though his friendship with Harry was, after all, as everyone else except himself knew, had known, since they were kids in Rozelle together, one-sided, as though he, Gordie, had made all the moves, made all the allowances, all the sacrifices, taken all the crap. He sits upright, and his eyes take on an angry glint. Harry's lapdog. That's what he is. Harry's lapdog. And his keeper as well. Harry's little lapdog, and Harry's little keeper. Always there to bail out his mate. Just like he was supposed to, thinks Gordie, just like they all said—'O'Brien's bloody lucky to have a mate like Gordie Sloan. Do anything for O'Brien, Sloanie would,' they said, imagining Gordie wasn't listening, that he was totally absorbed by Harry's conversation, and Gordie's eyes become more slitted as he remembers his second and even feebler attempt to seduce Harry that evening at the store, after they'd arrived back from a late delivery, 'Harry—' he'd said in a voice husky because he was overwhelmed by Harry's nearness, for once in his life summoning the guts to tell Harry how he felt about him... 'Harry, I—Harry, listen—sometimes a bloke feels—Jesus Christ! Harry—Don't you know what I'm trying to say—'

'For fuck's sake, Gordie!'

'Harry, listen to me, listen to me, Harry.'

'Jesus Christ!'

'Harry—Harry just give me a minute or two—please, Harry.'

'Fuckin' hell, Gordie!'

'Harry, I—I can't fucking bear it any longer, mate.'

'Gordie,' Harry had said, 'You're just fuckin' well going to have to, aren't yer, mate!'

And then Harry had pushed him away, pushed him with his big hands. Even that amount of touching had made Gordie grateful.

Mackenzie breaks into his thoughts.

'O'Brien must be having a good run on Thirty-three, tonight.'

Gordie squares his shoulders, sighs, tries to be civil to the fat man.

'Yeah.'

'The bugger hasn't touched you for a loan yet—right?'

'No.'

'Must be a bloody first.'

'Listen, Mac ...' begins Gordie.

'Okay, okay—Didn't mean nuthin.''

'He's paid back every penny he owes me.'

'Yeah, yeah.'

Gordie subsides into his chair, broodily, his eyes red-rimmed and sore, the scar on his cheek suddenly giving out uncomfortable heat. Then Nev is back, handing him his beer.

'Thanks,' he mutters.

'Nice pair of lungs on that new barmaid,' announces Nev conversationally.

'You'll never get your hands on 'em, mate,' sneers Mackenzie.

'Nah, but you can always look, can't you,' says Nev sullenly.

Gordie's eyes close. He feels quite strange. As though everything tonight is all very unreal. Maybe Nev's straight after all. Maybe he sucks up to Tubs because the poor bastard's lonely, because Tubsy gives him a lot of attention, makes him feel wanted even as he verbally kicks the shit out of him. Maybe that's a kind of sexual thing, thinks Gordie. Maybe that's how men relate to each other sexually, the kind of men he knocks around with, anyway.

'Wonder what O'Brien'll do if things go bad?' says Mackenzie.

'Maybe they'll go alright,' says Nev.

'I fuckin' well hope so,' says Gordie.

'Wonder if that Joanie O'Brien'd ever remarry?' asks Nev. 'You know, if they get divorced.'

Gordie gives out a thin laugh.

'Why would she?' he says.

'Whadda you mean?' asks Nev.

'Don't be fuckin' stupid,' says Mackenzie.

Nev looks injured, and mystified.

'Joanie O'Brien's a lezzo,' says Gordie flatly.

'No kiddin',' says Nev.

'Used to be, anyhow,' says Gordie, looking towards Harry in the pokie lounge.

'Well, bugger me,' says Nev artlessly, as Mackenzie sniggers.

They fall silent. The members of the band leave the dance floor. The three friends watch.

'I remember them coming here the year I joined the club,' observes Nev.

'Reckon he still fuckin' thinks he's John Lennon,' says Mackenzie, referring to the lead singer.

'Yeah,' agrees Nev.

Gordie glances at Mackenzie. He pushes aside the terrible erotic thought of what Mackenzie's naked body might look like. He shivers again, drinks his beer.

'See old Fred Donaldson was in tonight,' says Nev, throwing a hopeful glance at Mackenzie.

'Yeah, the dirty old bastard,' grins Mackenzie.

'Lives in the club since his wife died,' says Nev.

'And still racin' off all his old pupils.'

'Yeah, half his luck,' squeaks Nev.

'Dirty old bastard,' repeats the fat man.

Gordie watches as Nev offers Mackenzie a light for his cigarette. He sees the look in Nev's eye. He sees the sucking in of Mackenzie's fat lips as he draws flame into his cigarette.

He swallows the whiskey he's had sitting in front of him for the past half-hour. Then he drains his beer glass. Suddenly he wants to smash Harry's face in. But it is too late. You don't smash a man's face in when he's already down for the count, not if you're Gordie Sloan. He allows his eyes to move over to where Harry plays Thirty-three. The big man's head hangs low, yet it is visible above the top of the machine. Gordie sighs heavily, wonders what the old bastard's thinking about.

61

Harry is thinking about many things.

About Gordie.

'Look, Harry,' Gordie had whined. (There was something very wrong about Gordie whining.) 'Christ! mate, I don't know what it's all about. Jesus! I tried to sort things out when I was a kid. I married Jen, didn't I? What more could I do?'

Okay, so he'd failed Gordie.

He could see that now.

He could see he'd hurt the poor bastard.

'Get a fuckin' grip on yerself, Gordie,' he'd said as Gordie had come up close, touched him. On that boat. On the way up the coast. The boat was corkscrewing through the gentle Pacific swell. Richie from the boat hire was at the wheel. The boys were passed out or sleeping. Harry wished he hadn't said those things to Gordie. He wished he hadn't hurt his mate.

An emptiness.

As he thinks.

And there's Gordie over there.

Good old Gordie.

Watching out for him.

He's always watched out for him. Best mate a bloke ever had. The old Gordie.

And Doreen.

'Oh, Harry, you're so vigorous, darling, Oh, Harree, Harreee...'

And his wife and son.

They're walking along a promenade. The sea rolls gently in on the beach. And great pine trees rise upwards, like sentinels, and it is Sunday he remembers, wondering why it has to be Sunday, as though the day ought to have been significant, which it doesn't seem to be, yet he remembers it is a Sunday, before the Monday, suddenly remembers, yes, the Monday when he'd struck Keithy on the face, mentally he reels back, feels the sting of the blow, almost cries out—yes, the day before the Monday, while they were still pretending to each other, as though nothing was wrong, before he'd struck his son—thinks, O Christ! maybe when he'd struck him like that, he'd started something, weakened something, inside his son's head—O Christ! suppresses the thought—as though they were a family, having family outings, like now, on the promenade at Manly, eating fish and chips under the pines, and it is a warm day, and the sea breeze wafts gently across their faces, and day-trippers—parents, and kids in swimming costumes with towels round their waists, and young couples holding hands—stroll by, and there are black dots in the water, the heads of swimmers drifting on the placid ocean, as they look out to sea, and the ocean stretches out forever, like it had stretched out forever for old Rory, on his way out from England per favour of the Crown, Rory, the son of Mary O'Brien of Dingle Bay, and Harry wonders what it is like over there, where he has never been, across the ocean, looking towards America, imagining America, as though it was a coloured map, like one he has seen in a school atlas, and then another vast ocean, and then Ireland, where he may still have family, and then there is a white sail, rising and falling on the slight swell, about a mile off shore, and then he sees the boat itself, the dark hull, clean cut, cutting cleanly through blue water, all dead now, his rellies, old Rory, the convict, stole his employer's silver they said, lucky the dirty thievin' rascal hadn't been strung up said Great Aunty Leah, Grandma Meg from down the Rocks—a five bob whore said Leah—and Uncle Paddy, Denis's brother, and Paddy being a good-for-nothing beer swilling soft-in-the-head poor bugger they said, never held down a proper job in his life, and cousin Kevin, the family larrikin, swearing in church and making the priest suck at his brown teeth as he marries Harry and Joanie, and, Flan O'Brien's fingers, and, and... and Harry and Keithy running together at Arncliffe Park, and the old man who watched them all the time from his seat on the park bench under the big tree telling Harry he had a real champion in that kid... and the sail boat is just beyond the line of breakers and the steersman is ducking his head as he swings on the rudder bar, and the boat heels gently in the light wind, and the big boom swings across the crouching steersman, and the tidy little craft hesitates for a few seconds as its mainsail gathers new wind... He remembers it was a Sunday, a couple of weeks before Joanie's mother had died.

'Missed her step,' he says.

'Who did, love?' says Mrs Johnson.

'My old mother-in-law, Mrs Thomas. Joanie's mum. Missed her step on a busy road.'

'Then she...'

'Killed her outright. A bloody great cement truck.'

'Oh, dear, dear.'

'Left us the house, though. Brought fourteen thousand dollars.'

(Una had been walking home to Lilyfield. She'd reached Parramatta Road, paused near traffic lights, watched traffic streaming by.)

'Reckon she did it on purpose.'

'Oh...?'

'Found out she had cancer.'

(She could see Corporal Thomas' image. She reached outwards, clutched at the space to her front. The image grew brighter, dazzlingly bright. 'Keith,' she sobbed, 'Oh, Keith, Keith. Please let it be Keith.' Now the traffic was stopped, yet still she did not move. 'Keith, Keith,' she cried. 'Oh. Keith, where are you, my darling?' And then he was there, and he was wearing his uniform, and smiling, and looking so handsome, just the way she remembered him, just the way she had always wanted it to be, no more staring at the photo on the bedside table, no more anguish, or fear, no more pain, no more pain clawing at her belly... and the traffic surges forward, and she stretches forward, feels like a young girl again, being courted, being envied, being made love to, and her Keith holding his arms out to her as she steps on to the highway.)

'In 1970, it was. We did up the house with the money; paid off a few bills.'

Yeah, thinks Harry, he'd paid Gordie the thousand he owed him in crisp new bills, which Gordie hadn't wanted to take, and his friend had smiled that funny smile of his, and said those strange things to him which Harry hadn't fully comprehended at the time, and he'd tried to stuff the notes back into Harry's pocket, and Harry had resisted, and Gordie had begun to cry, yeah, the tough old bugger had cried...

Yeah, thinks Harry, remembering how he'd drummed up business for Gordie. When he worked the floor. On his delivery rounds. Women. Yeah, women. Jeez! they'd flocked after him to the shop. Like that schoolteacher who'd bought that antiqued desk, hadn't even opened the drawers, didn't know if they were stapled or dove tailed. And what about Fay, the truckie's wife? Jeez! she'd nearly refurnished her entire home unit out of the store after she'd met him. And that Hilary, the one he met in the fish and chip shop out Bankstown. She'd bought a lounge suite worth six hundred—and the nest of coffee tables which should have been on special, but the woman was so rapt in him he'd sold them to her full price.

Which was the way he drifted along after Keithy's accident, wasn't it? The way he'd spent the next five-odd years, womanising, having women casually, on the whim, like they were flavoured milkshakes, Debbie the strawberry blonde, Hilary with the caramel lips that stuck to you like glue so you nearly fucking suffocated, Belinda who smelled of chocolate and ate the stuff like an addict but was really thin and everyone said she must have a giant worm in there—someone in the club (Which club?) once said she knew a girl down Balmain with twenty feet of worm inside her that never did her any great harm—and, and, all the rest of them he'd had, just so he could get through his life, as though women were pills, prescriptions, which had to be filled regularly, so his supply of them wouldn't run out, so he could pretend everything was normal with Harry O'Brien, so he could deal with the face of his adolescent son, who had grown very tall, had a wonderful athletic body, almost never spoke to him anymore, just like he and Flan, years ago, in the house at Rozelle, not speaking, choosing silence, because of the hurt they both felt, could not subdue, and so used silence, like a shield—Keithy's the spitting image of Harry they all said, including the resident expert, and such a talented batsman they all agreed, congratulating Harry for producing a son who looked like he might open for Australia someday.

And Joanie and her affair with Jen. Give him some credit. He'd accepted that. Hadn't interfered. Understood why they were doing it. Knew it was all the rage in San Francisco. Jesus! Sydney was heading that way, too. Gays and lezzos and straights, all in together now—And wife-swapping. All the rage in the sixties and seventies. He'd heard of judges who'd swapped their wives, and blokes on communes up the far north coast with their own harems, and dozens of kids they said all reading Shakespeare and singing folk music, real tribes they were, back to nature, roughing it in the wilderness of Northern New South Wales in their hand-built houses, with running water and petrol engines generating electricity and Beethoven's Ninth playing in the living room. Gave him scope, of course, the affair between Joanie and Jen. He ought to have been grateful. He bloody well was grateful. Got him off the hook. Gave him what he wanted, unlimited time with the ladies, unlimited time with Keithy—and, as a married man with a son to raise, the excuse, when he needed it, to break things off with this girlfriend or that, with Yvonne, the blond from Tempe, who'd tried to get pregnant so she could have Harry, and nearly killed herself that night when Harry told her it was over and he'd had to wrestle with her so she wouldn't do something stupid with the meat knife which he didn't believe for a second that she would do because she was too much in love with herself, that bloody Yvonne.

He punches the five-play button.

Yvonne.

Sounded real French, he reminded himself. Yeah, real French.

Over in the Members' Bar Gordie sips his beer. There's a new sort of silence around the table. Mackenzie stares sullenly into his glass. Nev puffs nervously on a hand-rolled cigarette. Most of the tables in the Members' Bar are empty. A single game is being played in the snooker area. Gordie smiles to himself. A woman sitting some distance away is looking at him. He returns the look. The woman sits with two men who are engaged in intense debate. The woman, as though alone, smokes and sips a glass of wine. And flirts, so she thinks, with Gordie Sloan. If the woman had been a man, then... If he'd had Harry; and Joanie had had Jen... Permanently... For ever... Angrily he drains his glass, swears under his breath, mutters:

'Bloody fucked up world we live in.'

Mackenzie grunts. Nev looks sharply at Gordie. The woman sitting nearby smiles at Gordie. He sniffs heavily, glares at the woman, she looks away.

'A fuckin' massive screw up, that's what it is, a fuckin' massive screw up,' he mumbles.

62

By 1983 a deep lethargy had settled on the two married couples so that infidelity on either side seemed hardly to matter anymore; Gordie, for example, though he hadn't encouraged Jen's love affair with Joanie, had actually shown an unbelievable degree of tolerance.

'Jen, I understand, love,' he'd said.

Jen had been ready for a monumental row.

'But, Gordie, for Christ's sake!'

She'd had great trouble accepting his sincerity, his refusal to judge.

'Jen, it's alright, I said,' repeated Gordie.

Jen had stood there open-mouthed. Gordie had looked at her with kindness in his eyes. She felt like an unmitigated bitch. She'd even found herself getting angry with Gordie for being so fucking decent about everything.

'Gordie—don't you—don't you want to—well—bloody do something about it?'

'Jen, I understand,' he said again.

Jen thought she understood.

'Oh, I see; because you're gay, yourself, you think I'm fucking gay, too, do you?'

Gordie just stood quietly. His expression hadn't changed. There was no malice, no sign of affront, just that crinkling around his eyes, on the poor bugger's delicate skin, just that look of kindness.

'It doesn't matter if you're gay, or not,' he said quietly.

'Well, I'm not!' said Jen, hating the petulant ring of her own voice.

'Jen, you have to do what you think is right for you.'

Then he turned away, spoke to the wall.

'What I should have done in the first place.'

And so, in that instant, Jen truly did understand. But she was too angry with herself, too ashamed of her cruelty, to do anything other than stalk out of the room.

Later that night Gordie made love to her. Jen remained very still, made no effort to respond, was amazed at his stiffness inside her, made her laugh in dismay that her gay husband was probably fantasising over Harry O'Brien, doing what she had done so often, before she and Joanie began their *affaire*, but was now beginning to do again, bless Harry's sweet little arse, as she and Joanie O'Brien were making love. Jesus! what an amazing fucked-up life she was living, thought Jen; what a monumental, fucked-up existence; why the fuck hadn't she been born a man, or in nineteen-fucking-sixty-four instead of nineteen-fucking-forty-six, she admonished herself, as poor old Gordie, poor old dutiful, gay old Gordie, jerked inside her, gasped in his gentle, apologetic way, then was finished and mumbling something under his breath which sounded like 'sorry', but of course might very well have been 'Harry'.

———

The fact was Jen was tiring of her *affaire* with Joanie. After all those years something was happening. Maybe their lovemaking had become routine; maybe love itself had never truly developed; maybe both of them, now no longer expressing themselves sexually with their husbands, sought each other out more in sexual frustration than in the genuine pursuit of love.

Yet they had once proclaimed such abiding love for each other. And this had at first given them new anchorages in their lives.

'Could you love a man just as much as you love me?' Jen had asked.

It was towards the end of their *affaire*.

'No,' lied Joanie, 'of course not.'

'I could,' said Jen flatly.

'But—but you love me,'

'Yes, I do.'

'Then?'

The question remained hanging there, and Jen had risen from the bed where they were lying together, poured herself a glass of wine. She drank deeply, then turned, looking down at Joanie.

'I suppose I'm still in love with Gordie,' she said, 'and I suspect you're still in love with Harry.'

'Jen...' began Joanie.

'Look, Joanie, so what? So bloody what if we're still in love with our husbands. Okay, Harry's a creep. We both know that. And Gordie's gay, and so I'm married to him. Hell, there must be thousands of women married to gay men.' She finished her wine. 'Look, it's all a matter of being bored out of our minds, right? That's what it's all about, you know, you and me getting together, bloody boredom.'

'Yes, boredom, I suppose,' muttered Joanie. 'And—and loneliness.'

'Yeah, that, too,' agreed Jen, suddenly subdued.

Jen poured more wine for them. Tacitly they decided to get drunk together.

'You're damn right,' Jen said with feeling. 'I was fucking lonely.'

'Yes,' said Joanie, understanding.

'I used to enjoy sex with Gordie—at first,' said Jen.

'I used to enjoy sex with Harry,' said Joanie.

'When I was sixteen my Uncle John jumped me in the bathroom,' said Jen.

'I never used to think you could have sex with another woman,' said Joanie, feeling drunk.

'My dad took off when I was five,' said Jen.

'My dad was killed in the war,' said Joanie.

'My mother left a year later,' said Jen.

'My mother was mad,' said Joanie 'She used to talk to my dead dad all the time.'

'I went to live with my Uncle John and his second wife,' said Jen.

'I used to sit in my bedroom listening through the wall to my mum talking to herself,' said Joanie.

'Uncle John hated his second wife. That's why he jumped me. Out of spite. Just to spite his old woman,' said Jen.

'My mum should've been put in a home,' said Joanie.

'Give Uncle John credit,' said Jen. 'He was nice to me, though. Bought me things, you know, presents, chocolates.'

Joanie sighed, looked at Jen. 'What was that?' she said vaguely.

Jen repeated everything.

'I guess he was a lonely man.' said Joanie, drinking wine.

'Yes, lonely,' said Jen. She giggled. 'And fuckin' randy as hell, the bastard.'

'Did you enjoy it?'

'What? Sex with Uncle John?'

'Yes, with—well, your own relative.'

Jenny swigged wine, threw Joanie her slyest look.

'Fuckin' oath, I did, sweetie. Great technique, he had, my Uncle John. Until he died, that is. Stroke it was. Dropped dead in the toilet.' She let out a hollow laugh. 'The bastard hadn't had time to wipe his arse. I was eighteen. Six months afterwards, I married Gordie.'

'On the rebound, I suppose,' said Joanie.

'Out of spite, more's the truth,' growled Jen. She sighed, thought for a moment. 'No, I take that back; that's unfair. I felt safe with Gordie. I still feel safe with him—in spite of—well, of everything.'

'I used to feel safe with Harry,' said Joanie. 'Now—well, it's over, isn't it?' She looked tearful. 'I guess I'm just one of the mob, now.'

'One of the mob?' said Jen.

'One of his hundreds of ex-girlfriends,' said Joanie.

Jen laughed drunkenly. 'Yeah,' she said. 'I see what you mean. One of the mob.'

For a while they drank wine, kept to their own thoughts.

'I used to enjoy sex with Harry,' said Joanie for the second time.

'Yeah, 'course you did, sweetheart,' said Jen, ''course you did.' Jen giggled, burped. 'Whoops, excuse me!' she squealed. 'Anyhow, so would've I enjoyed it, if I'd have been you.' She saw Joanie's eyebrows raise, laughed. 'Oh, don't worry, Joanie, darling. I never slept with your husband; not like half the fucking female population of Sydney.'

That was how it had become between them when they were drunk, careless; they were becoming careless with the words they spoke to one another.

'You know, we're bloody strange creatures, aren't we?' continued Jen. 'I mean, I like men, I really do. I like their little arses.' She giggled a little. 'Jesus! I like the way their little dicks spring up like they do. And yet I married a gay bloke.'

'Gordie's a really nice person,' said Joanie.

'Yeah, he is,' frowned Jen. They had lain down together, and Jen turned, leaning on her elbow as she peered at Joanie. 'Really weird, isn't it, how things turn out. I mean, despite everything, us, everything, I still need Gordie. He's good, and honest, and he doesn't interfere with my life. Okay, so he's a much better person than me. I can live with that.' She paused, and a frown chased itself around her pretty mouth. 'Anyhow, we don't pretend any more that we enjoy each other's body. He's gay. Okay, so what! He doesn't flaunt it. He's just not the type to come out. And he's too strait-laced to even think of leaving me. He's just a fucking good man, that's all. Hard to bloody find, eh, Joanie?'

'Then it really is Gordie you love?'

Jen tightened her lips. 'Yep, I guess it is. In a sort of sexless sort of way if that's possible. But then I love you, too.' She reached for her glass. 'Anyhow, there's nothing wrong with loving the both of you at the same time, now, is there, Joanie?'

'No,' said Joanie, feeling suddenly tired, wanting to sleep, realising how empty the word 'love' sounded these days.

For there was a heavy weariness in their relationship. And it showed. They no longer jumped excitedly into bed together when opportunity arose. Now, they preferred to drink a bottle or two of wine, sometimes three, maybe lie close, but not touching, for an hour or two, drowsing, or sleeping, often without sexual contact, often without conversation, as though they'd fallen into an almost silent marriage, were merely a pair of drinking mates, sleeping it off alongside one another, conveniently, on the same bed.

Joanie suffered most. Emotionally she persisted with her *affaire* with Jen beyond the point where Jen herself cared for it to continue. For a long while Jen was simply too lazy to call it a day. She needed sexual release. She could achieve that with Joanie. Joanie needed more, felt her life at home truly was beyond rescue, thus made greater efforts to maintain her relationship with Jen, gave Jen everything she needed, even agreed to some of the more bizarre sexual practices she'd once refused to perform, and, for a month or two, the love affair seemed to revive. Yet, by the beginning of 1983, it was clearly over. There was simply nothing there. No love. No arousal. Joanie finally gave up, admitted at last that she felt emotionally dead inside her relationship with Jen. She was thirty-eight. She ought to have made more effort to do something about her life. She ought to have left Harry, ought to have found a job, ought to have given herself a chance at a better life. But she stayed at home, pretended to herself that that was where she was needed, that despite her enfeebled relationship with Keithy he would suffer greatly if she stopped being there for him. And then, as though it was her last chance, she aroused herself sufficiently to confront Harry. She was tired of being in the same house with him. She was tired of the way his presence now seemed so invasive, of his habits, of all the trivia of his behaviour, of the way he left the TV on then snored the night away on the couch. Vaguely she imagined she might divorce him, find another man, someone like Gordie Sloan, without the gayness.

'Maybe you should go away, Harry,' she said.

Harry was slumped in his chair. He'd drunk a few beers, he was tired. Nowadays, when home, he remained more or less permanently silent, the newspapers, television, and his growing love affair with the bottle, his only household companions.

'You want me to go?'

'Yes, Harry, I want you to go.'

He shifted his big frame so that he could look directly at Joanie. Strangely he did not feel surprised. He knew it had been coming. They were already separated in their minds, in their hearts. He looked at Joanie. These days she was reminding him more and more of Una Thomas. She was developing the same thickening in her upper arms, around her backside.

'Why'd you want me to go?'

The words sounded stupid, the kinds of words he might have once expected from a drunken Flan O'Brien.

'It's the only way I think we can both survive, Harry?' said Joanie.

He gestured vaguely with his stubby and made a few drops of beer spill onto the carpet. He rubbed at them with the toe of his shoe, persisted with his stupid words.

'You mean—like it's all over; marriage; all that.'

'Yes, Harry.'

'What about Keithy?'

Joanie took a very deep breath.

'I've already spoken to him about it. He agrees.'

Harry wasn't surprised to hear this either, yet he said:

'Oh, he agrees, does he?'

'Yes, Harry, he knows what he wants.'

'What's that?'

'He wants a fresh start, Harry. Your son wants a fresh start.'

Harry already knew this. As though they'd said these things before. He felt emotionally empty. He felt he did not care. He suspected he might care later, when he'd actually left Marsden Street, when there was no longer even the awareness that his son was under the same roof, when his wife, despite their estrangement, no longer prepared his meals, ironed his shirts. He had a brief sense that he must have really disappointed Judy, that she would truly be pissed off with him for all his failures. So he just said:

'Playing cricket, I suppose you mean.'

'Harry, he'll play cricket if he wants to.'

Harry even smiled, as though at last he was beginning to understand at least the more rudimentary aspects of the joke played on him.

'And what about you and Jen? Is *that* over, too?'

'Yes, it's over,' she said evenly.

'You sure?' he said, as though it might have mattered to him.

'It's finished, Harry.'

'But you'll still be friends?'

'Oh, yes, I suppose so.'

'Well, that's something,' he conceded.

He could not help feeling as though he *was* Flan O'Brien. Literally. And the idea made him think someone (God? Flan himself—in between piss-ups in Hell, of course?) was playing a joke on him, had been playing a joke on him, all his life, for right now there was a sense of Flan's presence, his eyes, his face, the way he, as did Harry these days, pinched the flesh on his jaw when thinking. He and Flan O'Brien, growing into one another. More pieces of the joke. There, in the Rozelle terrace. And now here, in Marsden Street, as he saw it, the same cloud of indifference over everything.

He checked himself. Everything? Everything? What everything was that? There'd been no everything. Only the monumental stuff up of his marriage; the monumental stuff up of his relationship with Keithy. That was all. Yet Harry then had a sudden fear that there would be no future for him if he left Marsden Street, that there was hope while he still lived there, some chance left that they might all suddenly burst out laughing, might all suddenly see the full text of the joke, might all realise how they'd been sucked in by this fucking wonderful, fucking hilarious joke. 'Hey, everyone,' he could hear himself shouting, 'hey, what's the bloody fuss about; come on, let's all have a few fucking beers.' Instead, he heard his own flat-sounding voice say:

'Okay, if that's what you want, I'll go.'

He left the next morning. Without seeing Keithy since his son was already on his way to school. He paused on the veranda, remembered their first arrival there so many years ago, the thin figure of Col Maguire squinting at them in the sunlight. He tried hard to look Joanie in the eye. Though she'd come out on the veranda, and the sun lit up her hair, she seemed already sealed off, a stranger, already so much older than even the night before.

'I'm sorry, Joanie,' he said. 'I'm sorry for being such a useless bastard.' Then he was gone

———

As he remembers and stares into Thirty-three's window, towards the stationary icons, and the three lined up queens grinning cheekily at him, he can barely stand the sight of them.

'Maybe you ought to go home, son.'

Slowly Harry turns. Tom Johnson is looking at him. The voice is gummy, crackly, thin. As though the old man has no spittle.

'Whassat?' he says, confused, the light suddenly hurting his eyes.

'Harry,' says Mrs Johnson. 'You need a good rest, love,' then adds quietly, 'Why don't you go home now.'

Harry looks over for Joanie.

Christ! she's not there. The machine she was at is vacant. Then he sees her. She's walking towards the exit with the old bloke. Why would she be leaving with *him*?

'Joanie!' he shouts.

But she ignores him.

'Joanie! Joanie!'

He slams his hand on Thirty-three's collect button. His three hundred-odd coins clatter into the tray. He scoops them up, stuffs them into his pockets. The weight of the metal feels uncomfortable against his thighs. Then he's off, wild-eyed, unaware that Waddling Thighs has come up behind him, that like a jackal sniffing out carrion she will wait until the reserve light has stopped flashing, then pounce...

And now he's in the foyer, limping heavily, pushing through a knot of people who await the club's courtesy bus, pushing through the big entrance doors. 'Goodnight, Harry,' says Reg as normal as anything—seen it all, has Reg, seen Harry dragging himself home empty-pocketed often enough, sees Harry now, sees the few coins cascading from Harry's trouser pocket, calls out, 'Harry... Harry...' but Harry has disappeared into the carpark, and the darkness has claimed him it seems to Reg as he squints into the gloom but sees nothing, cannot even hear the uneven sound of Harry's footsteps against the squall which passes over the club, dumping more rain.

63

He's outside. Lurching around in the carpark. It is very dark, the new squall swirls in the blackness overhead. Gusts of wind smack him hard, fresh rain cuts across his path, stings his face.

He feels his body shivering inside his shirt, wishes he'd remembered to grab his jacket.

But he desperately wants to find Joanie. There are things to talk about. Imperative things. Even if she is running off with the man with the twisted elbow.

He pauses, begins to invent sentences, the sorts of things he imagines he will say to Joanie. But there is only a jumble of words, a mess of them racing around inside his head.

'Joanie, Joanie,' is all that comes out, but the wind whips the words away before he can hear them.

And then headlights suddenly switch on. They're very close, blinding him. It's the Hi-Ace. He stretches out his arms, reaching for the light.

He lunges towards the van. It swerves, heels over, misses him, just barely.

'Stop, stop!'

He thinks he's caught a glimpse of the driver's face, the glasses on the bridge of the nose, the bald head, and Joanie's figure next to him, stiff, formal.

As though she insists on ignoring him.

'Joanie, Joanie!'

He yells again as the van turns and disappears, and he is alone in the darkness.

Surrounded by motionless shapes. Metal and glistening. As though watching him.

He keeps moving.

He arrives on the street, but there is no van, no sound of it, no traffic at all.

Only a single streetlight, its pole humming in the high wind, its shivering lamp making shadowy phantoms dance crazily back and forth over the road.

Harry pauses: he watches the shadows. They criss-cross his body as he leans on the lamp pole. The pole's vibrations resonate with a frequency which reaches deep inside him.

Like energy.

He takes a deep breath. There is still some determination in him. He wonders how this is possible. He stumbles forward. He is like a foot soldier who must make one last advance.

Up the slope. Towards Oxford Street.

Epilogue-
winter ending

Even on Oxford Street hardly any people are on foot, only an old schizo, who reels along, mumbling to his voices, pleading with them to forgive him (forgive *him*!), and a couple of girls, in short skirts, tight round their bums, and wearing high, stiletto heels, and leather wind jackets; 'You lookin' for sex, mate?' one of them says; 'Fuck off,' says Harry; 'Fuck you,' they reply then saunter off, arm in arm.

He heads towards Taylor Square.

'Joanie, Joanie, where are you, Joanie?' he mumbles.

A Kingswood comes up from behind, pulls up, startles him, skids a little on the wet road; he hops away, scared, recovers, then sees the two prossies talking through the car window, sees them get into the car; the stink of exhaust envelops him as the car takes off; he remembers his own first time, down Palmer Street, near where he is now, how he shot his bolt straight away but still had to pay, the prossie who's face he couldn't remember, just a faceless blank where the face was supposed to be, himself, a kid with a smirk on his face, making a mug of himself. He presses forward, breathes damp air.

'Must hurry. Must find Joanie.'

He passes the spill of light at a doorway, turns, his eyes brush against glistening leather, it is 1988 and the sound of 1940's music licks his ears;

he crosses Victoria Street, avoids turning his head and so does not allow his eyes to pick out the hospital building down there; he limps past the dark shadow of the Sacred Heart church, pauses, thinks, holds his watch to the light; it is after eleven; he frowns heavily, makes as if to retrace his steps, pauses, thinks, examines his watch again, as if in a trance he moves forward; he crosses Taylor Square, alone, no young girls this time, just traffic, a few derro's in the little island of park, a couple embracing, a couple of men.

'Joanie.... Joanie....'

———

He reaches Palmer Street, his face reddens with memory; he smiles a little, pushes on; there are few pedestrians now and he's glad of the solitude of empty stretches of footpath; then he's at Crown Street and waiting for the walk sign; traffic is busy here, rolling towards Woolloomooloo and the Harbour Bridge; he feels calmer; the walking has calmed him, yes, the walking, and moving traffic, he remembers, like earlier that day, after he'd been in the park, Centennial Park—then sees the figure on the other side of the crossing, sees that it is a man; he cannot make out the face only the feathery hair floating round the man's ears; he guesses he is old, from the clothes he's wearing that he's a Sydney derro.... The lights change and he crosses; the man hasn't moved; Harry sees he's gripping the light pole with both fists. 'Jesus, mate,' says the old man as Harry reaches him; the voice is feeble, barely a croak; Harry sees that he's very thin under his clothes, that his teeth are chattering with cold, that his face looks weird, that the skin is a blue, a strange transparent blue. 'Mate, I can't breathe,' he wheezes. 'Can't get me breath.' Suddenly, the old man's fingers come loose from the light pole and he collapses into Harry's arms; Harry lunges away from the curb, carrying the old man's body cradled in his arms like a child's; he heads back up Oxford Street; he is only a few hundred yards from the hospital—surely the old man will last until he gets there—he limps forward; now and then, as though to lighten his burden, a silver coin works its way through the hole

343

in his trouser pocket, the sound as it strikes the footpath lost in the noise of traffic; occasionally it will roll into the gutter, disappear down the storm water drain—

Then he's fifty yards from Taylor Square.

'Must get to St Vincent's.'

Suddenly the old man's body slumps in his arms; he stops, looks into the old man's face, sees the eyes are closed, sees the blue lips, the strange blueness of the face, cannot tell if there is breathing; 'Christ! You okay, mate?' He lays the old man on the footpath, unbuttons the shirt, reels back at the smell of the old man's unwashed body, then bravely leans forward, presses his ear against the old man's chest, hears nothing; 'Jesus! don't croak on me, now.' Ah, haa—he thinks he can feel the beating of the heart; he lifts the head, looks at the blue face; the lips are darker blue, nearly black; there is very little sign that the old man breathes, only the faintest whistling sound which Harry can just make out against the noise of traffic. Gently he lays the head back on to the pavement; he raises his eyes, stares at the traffic; it sits there, in long, stationary rows, its engines growling, ignoring the dying man; Harry suddenly feels rage—What the fuck's the matter with the people in those cars! Why the fuck don't they get out and help! The traffic begins to flow; 'STOP, YOU BASTARDS, STOP,' he shouts; 'THERE'S A FUCKIN' OLD MAN FUCKIN' DYIN' DOWN HERE! He sobs in anger, lifts the old man's head, cradles it in his hands, is about to shout again, but the words freeze on his lips, and he speaks softly, is suddenly gentle; 'You okay, mate?' The old man's eyes flicker but do not open, yet Harry is sure a smile is trying to form around the old man's lips; the smile seems very strange to Harry, a blue smile, but the old man hasn't enough energy to let the smile fill up his face so it sits around his lips, makes the lips seem to glow with light; very strange, thinks Harry; old Col's face looked like that when he was lying in his coffin; yeah, with a smile on his lips; not as blue though as this old cove; maybe it was blue under the make-up; for a moment he imagines it is old Col lying in his arms; he blinks away the moisture in his eyes, strokes the old man's forehead; 'Thanks mate,' the old man whispers; the old man's eyes are open; not wide open, just tiny slits; but there's life in them, Harry can see; 'Real good of you, mate,' says the old man somehow; the smile seems to have moved towards the eyes, thinks Harry; carefully he lays the old man's head on the ground, pulls himself to his feet; an ambulance, siren blaring, races by on its way to St Vincent's; Harry sighs deeply, then bends down and picks up the old man; he sets off, heading in the same direction as the ambulance; then something urges him to run and despite his knee and the burden of the old man in his arms, he runs in his lopsided gallop, and his knee throbs, but he runs even faster, as if trying to match the speed of the ambulance up there. Ha! he sees that the ambulance is stopped, honking at solid traffic, it's siren screaming; Harry runs faster still, faster, faster, gasps, gulps air, the ambulance moves—'Wait... wait... For Christ's sake wait!' The ambulance punches its way through traffic, Harry sobs, watches the ambulance disappear into Victoria Street and he lunges forward, runs even faster still, like it is his own life racing away with him, from him, as though years are passing by at great speed, which they are passing, because there is no change, no variation, as though time becomes timeless, suspends him inside itself, a face in the mirror of the Marsden Street bathroom, staring at him, as he scrapes away its whiskers, watches the face transform, sees fifteen, twenty years, pass him by, 1964, 1974, 1984, timelessly, sees the face of himself, of Keithy, of Flan, as he carries the old man towards St Vincent's, as though to do so is the most ordinary strangest logical thing in the world, Harry and the Blue Man going to St Vincent's, as though working at Pollards, working at Gordie's, as though whoring, drinking, drinking and whoring, whiling away his life in front of a poker machine, are really all that is his life, as though life is a crazy game he has to play, Christ! his knee's a mongrel, hurting like a mongrel, and the old man is bobbing up and down in his arms, and little gasps of wind come out of the old man's mouth as he bobs in Harry's arms, and he makes these little groaning sounds as he jostles against Harry's ribs, so he must be alive, maybe he'll make it to the hospital alive, maybe the old bugger'll survive, he runs even faster, as though now he's got second wind, his chest fills easily, with cool air, at least the bloody rain's stopped, he runs, hears the old man's whimperings, 'Oh, oh, oooh.' 'Hang on, mate, hang on,' gasps Harry, he can smell the smell from inside the old man's body, as though it is the smell of his own life, the way his own life smelled, as he flies down Victoria Street, maybe he'll score a try, as though he's on the Tigers' ground, crowd cheering, his knee good, nothing left between him and the posts, he flies, knows he should have been here a long time ago, that Joanie is waiting for him, that he should have met her hours ago, that when he was needed in the hospital he'd been playing the pokies, one pokie anyhow—'Jesus! the biggie', what if he's missed the biggie? Waddling Thighs, God, maybe she'll pick up the biggie, Jesus! this old bugger stinks; and he's getting fuckin' heavy; wonder if he's still alive, 'You still alive, mate? Christ! what you bin' eatin'? Jeez! when'd you last have a bath?' Poor Joanie, hadn't given her much of a chance, no wonder she'd gone for Jen Sloan all those years ago; haven't seen her much in all that time, never speak any more, just like all the blokes, none of 'em talk to their wives, no point, nuthin' to talk about, anyhow that's all over now, his marriage, finished, never really started, yeah, well, most marriages fail, right? And Jen? She never did divorce poor old Gordie, weird though, how he, good old straight-as-a-die Harry O'Brien couldn't save his own marriage, Hell!, anyhow, he was used to living alone, in the flat at Bondi Junction, yeah, in the flat, it was okay, he could manage, had managed, 'course he had, and Keithy, well it was a moral they'd never get on, a different sort of person, Keithy, like a stranger really, strange how things turn out, nothing like him, Harry, or Flan, after all those bad dreams, all that fear, he wasn't anything like an O'Brien, or even a Thomas; joke! it's all a big bloody cosmic joke—Keithy gets on real well with his mum, though, now he's grown up; all that crap about him not loving his mum—and him playing bloody cricket, doing well at school getting into Sydney University, Jeez! Sydney University for Christ's sake, his son, with all them private school

346

kids, half his luck, just like Doreen, passed his first year and all—Harry is crying now—Keithy just said he was feeling funny, looked at him when he'd come to visit Harry in the flat, they'd just had a beer, first time in their lives they'd had a proper drink together, 'Cheers, son,' it had sounded real good, 'Cheers, son,' it was real nice, drinking beer with his son, a real nice feeling—hard having a conversation with him though, lot of bad stuff in the way, lot of hurt, got to forgive this time, not like Flan, that was different, the old bastard got everything he deserved—Keithy using all that high-falutin talk, just like Doreen and her books, and Mahler, Mawler, the Malabar Mawler, then, then, O fucking hell! O Christ!—Keithy just fell on his face, while he was going on about how great it was studying at uni, fell on his face just like old Col on the lounge room carpet in front of TV, that accident at Barton Park did it, must have weakened an artery in his brain said the young medico in intensive care, Jeez! he looked young, that doctor, only a kid, spoke well, made you feel confident though, not a massive bleed he thought, there was a chance, a chance, wonder how the operation's gone, 'whack! Harry winces, feels the blow on Keithy's head as he strikes, Jesus Christ Almighty! 'Whack! And Keithy's head snapping back like that. Jesus! But the boy never complained, never said a word, never had a headache, or a dizzy spell, Jesus! you can't get a stroke just from a fuckin' smack on the head! 'Course you bloody well can't. Jesus! that's where he was going, to the hospital, he should be with Joanie, didn't matter they'd been separated for years, never really worked, his marriage, wasn't the marrying kind, Joanie reminded him of Judy Connell, that was all, weren't nobody's fault; weren't poor little Joanie's fault she reminded him of Judy; Hell, though! Keithy needed both of 'em, forget all the crap, yeah, that's all it is, crap, all the other stuff doesn't matter, Joanie's no lesbian, what if she is; Gordie's gay, Mackenzie's probably gay; always knew the old Tubsy was funny; and poor fucking stringybark Nev's gay; everybody's fucking gay, a fuckin' gay old world we live in, right, old man, 'Don't fuckin' croak on me, you ol' bastard', feels real sorry for Gordie, though, must try and make it up to Gordie, poor bugger doesn't know if he's

Arthur or Martha, giggles, wishes he had a stubby or two, breathes hard, downhill now, can make it now, must have a proper talk with Gordie, tell him he understands, that it's okay, not to worry, who cares if he's the fucking queen of the gays?—that's the way things were nowadays, it's all different, not like when they were young fellers, poofter-bashing youngsters—Jesus! he's still Gordie, still his best mate—fuck! this old man's heavy. Why's he so heavy? nothing to him, just a bag of bones, wonder if he's still alive, he isn't whinging anymore, 'Gawd! what a stink. Hey, old man, you still alive?' maybe his eyes are flickering, still got that weird blue colour, maybe it isn't too late, maybe they'd have a chance, maybe they'd have *another* chance, yeah, all of them, yeah, that's what it's all about, another chance, yeah, he'd do that, he would, hell! he's been doing it all his life, yeah, starting off again, having another go, yeah, he'd do that, Good Christ! he would, yeah, yeah, come on, come on, yeah, that's what all this was about, all this madness, all this stuff he was going through, like a stage actor, as though he was watching himself, what he had been all of his life, as though he was becoming someone new— yeah, he told the old man, someone new, 'Come on old man, open your eyes, damn you, you stupid bastard, open them! open your fucking eyes...' nearly there, 'Soon have you fixed, give him air, Jesus! does the old bugger stink! give him air, let him still be alive, is he still alive, Is Keithy still alive?' he screams at the old man, he desperately wants the old man to be alive, he needs the old man to be alive, to have the power of life, of senses, senses through which life is confirmed, exalted, proven to be, and so he screams out the words, into the old man's dimming consciousness—'Is he alive?' 'Is Keithy alive? O Christ let Keithy be alive—'

Material quoted in the text

'*One evening on a bare hillside, which the wind had treated with silver, he lay down, and it seemed at first as though the earth might open, gently, gently, to receive his body, but his soul would not allow, and dragged him to his feet, and he ran, or stumbled, down the hill, his coat-tail flying...*'

Patrick White, *Riders in the Chariot*, Penguin, 1964,

'*These memories, which are my life...*'

Evelyn Waugh, *Brideshead Revisited*, Penguin, 1967